THREE BY LAUMER

ALSO BY KEITH LAUMER

IMPERIUM

Worlds of the Imperium (1962)
The Other Side of Time (1965)
Assignment in Nowhere (1968)
Zone Yellow (1990)

RETIEF

Envoy to New Worlds (1963)
Galactic Diplomat (1965)
Retief's War (1965)
Retief and the Warlords (1968)
Retief: Ambassador to Space (1969)
Retief of the CDT (1971)
Retief's Ransom (1972) (aka Retief and the Pangalactic Pageant of Pulchritude)
Retief: Emissary to the Stars (1975)
Retief at Large (1978)
Retief Unbound (1979)
Diplomat at Arms (1982)
Retief to the Rescue (1983)
The Return of Retief (1984)
Retief in the Ruins (1986)
Reward for Retief (1989)
Retief and the Rascals (1993)
Retief! (2001)
Gambler's World (2009)
The Yillian Way (2009)

LAFAYETTE O'LEARY

The Time Bender (1966)
The World Shuffler (1970)
The Shape Changer (1973)
The Galaxy Builder (1984)

TIME TRAP

Time Trap (1970)
Back to the Time Trap (1992)

BOLO

Bolo! (2005) (with David Weber)
Rogue Bolo (1986)
The Compleat Bolo (1990)
Bolo Brigade (1997) (with William H. Keith)
Bolo Rising (1998) (with William H. Keith)
Bolo Strike (2001) (with William H. Keith)
Annals of the Dinochrome Brigade (1976)
Bolos: Their Finest Hour (2010)

OTHER NOVELS

A Trace of Memory (1963)
The Great Time Machine Hoax (1964)
A Plague of Demons (1965)
Catastrophe Planet (1966)
Earthblood (1966) (with Rosel George Brown)
The Monitors (1966)
Galactic Odyssey (1967) (aka Spaceman!)
The Day Before Forever (1969)
The Long Twilight (1969)
The Seeds of Gonyl (1969)
The House in November (1970)
Fat Chance (1971) (aka Deadfall)
The Star Treasure (1971)
Dinosaur Beach (1971)
Night of Decisions (1972)
The Infinite Cage (1972)
Night Of Delusions (1972)
The Glory Game (1973)
The Ultimax Man (1978)
The Breaking Earth (1981)
Star Colony (1981)
End as a Hero (1985)
The Stars Must Wait (1990)
Judson's Eden (1991)

THREE BY LAUMER

WORLDS OF THE IMPERIUM

RETIEF: ENVOY TO NEW WORLDS

BOLO

KEITH LAUMER

First published in Great Britain in 2017 by Gollancz
an imprint of the Orion Publishing Group Ltd
Carmelite House, 50 Victoria Embankment
London EC4Y 0DZ

An Hachette UK Company

1 3 5 7 9 10 8 6 4 2

A CIP catalogue record for this book
is available from the British Library.

ISBN 978 1 473 21599 3

Typeset by Deltatype Ltd, Birkenhead, Merseyside

Printed and bound by CPI Group (UK) Ltd, Croydon, CR0 4YY

www.orionbooks.co.uk
www.gollancz.co.uk
www.sfgateway.com

CONTENTS

WORLDS OF THE IMPERIUM

CHAPTER 1

I stopped in front of a shop with a small wooden sign which hung from a wrought-iron spear projecting from the weathered stone wall. On it the word *Antikvariat* was lettered in spidery gold against dull black. The sign creaked as it swung in the night wind. Below it a metal grating covered a dusty window with a display of yellowed etchings, woodcuts, and lithographs, and a faded mezzotint. Some of the buildings in the pictures looked familiar, but here they stood in open fields, or perched on hills overlooking a harbor crowded with sails. The ladies in the pictures wore great bell-like skirts and bonnets with ribbons, and carried tiny parasols, while dainty-footed horses pranced before carriages in the background.

It wasn't the prints that interested me though, or even the heavy gilt frame embracing a tarnished mirror at one side; it was the man whose reflection I studied in the yellowed glass, a dark man wearing a tightly-belted grey trench coat that was six inches too long. He stood with his hands thrust deep in his pockets and stared into a darkened window fifty feet from me.

He had been following me all day.

At first I thought it was coincidence when I noticed the man on the bus from Bromma, then studying theatre announcements in the hotel lobby while I registered, and half an hour later sitting three tables away sipping coffee while I ate a hearty dinner.

I had discarded the coincidence theory a long time ago. Five hours had passed and he was still with me as I walked through the Old Town, medieval Stockholm still preserved on an island in the middle of the city. I had walked past shabby windows crammed with copper pots, ornate silver, dueling pistols, and worn cavalry sabers; they were all very quaint in the afternoon sun, but grim reminders of a ruder day of violence after midnight. Over the echo of my footsteps in the silent narrow streets the other steps came quietly behind, hurrying when I hurried, stopping when I stopped. Now the man stared into the dark window and waited. The next move was up to me.

I was lost. Twenty years is a long time to remember the tortuous turnings of the streets of the Old Town. I took my guide book from my pocket and turned to the map in the back. My fingers were clumsy.

I craned my neck up at the stone tablet set in the corner of the building; it was barely legible: *Master Samuelsgatan*. I found the name on the folding map and saw that it ran for three short blocks, ending at *Gamla Storgatan*; a dead end. In the dim light it was difficult to see the fine detail on the map. I twisted the book around and got a clearer view; there appeared to be another tiny street, marked with crosslines, and labeled *Guldsmedstrappan*.

I tried to remember my Swedish; *trappan* meant stair. The Goldsmith's Stairs, running from *Master Samuelsgatan* to *Hundgatan*, another tiny street. It seemed to lead to the lighted area near the palace; it looked like my only route out. I dropped the book back into my pocket and moved off casually toward the stairs of the Goldsmith. I hoped there was no gate across the entrance.

My shadow waited a moment, then followed. As I was

ambling, I slowly gained a little on him. He seemed in no hurry at all. I passed more tiny shops, with ironbound doors and worn stone sills, and then saw that the next doorway was an open arch with littered granite steps ascending abruptly. I paused idly, then turned in. Once past the portal, I bounded up the steps at top speed. Six leaps, eight, and I was at the top, darting to the left toward a deep doorway. There was just a chance I'd cleared the top of the stair before the dark man had reached the bottom. I stood and listened. I heard the scrape of shoes, then heavy breathing from the direction of the stairs a few feet away. I waited, breathing with my mouth wide open, trying not to pant audibly. After a moment the steps moved away. The proper move for my silent companion would be to cast about quickly for my hiding place, on the assumption that I had concealed myself close by. He would be back this way soon.

I risked a glance. He was moving quickly along, looking sharply about, with his back to me. I pulled off my shoes and without taking time to think about it, stepped out. I made it to the stairs in three paces, and faded out of sight as the man stopped to turn back. I leaped down three steps at a time; I was halfway down when my foot hit a loose stone, and I flew the rest of the way.

I hit the cobblestones shoulder first, and followed up with my head. I rolled over and scrambled to my feet, my head ringing. I clung to the wall by the foot of the steps as the pain started. Now I was getting mad. I heard the soft-shod feet coming down the stairs, and gathered myself to jump him as he came out. The footsteps hesitated just before the arch, then the dark round head with the uncut hair peeped out. I swung a haymaker—and missed.

He darted into the street and turned, fumbling in his

overcoat. I assumed he was trying to get a gun, and aimed a kick at his mid-section. I had better luck this time; I connected solidly, and had the satisfaction of hearing him gasp in agony. I hoped he hurt as badly as I did. Whatever he was fumbling for came free then, and he backed away, holding the thing in his mouth.

"One-oh-nine, where in bloody blazes are you?" he said in a harsh voice, glaring at me. He had an odd accent. I realized the thing was some sort of microphone. "Come in, one-oh-nine, this job's going to pieces ..." He backed away, talking, eyes on me. I leaned against the wall; I was hurt too badly to be very aggressive. There was no one else in sight. His soft shoes made whispering sounds on the paving stones. Mine lay in the middle of the street where I had dropped them when I fell.

Then there was a sound behind me. I whirled, and saw the narrow street almost blocked by a huge van. I let my breath out with a sigh of relief. Here was help.

Two men jumped down from the van, and without hesitation stepped up to me, took my arms and escorted me toward the rear of the van. They wore tight white uniforms, and said nothing.

"I'm all right," I said. "Grab that man." About that time I realized he was following along, talking excitedly to the man in white, and that the grip on my arms was more of a restraint than a support. I dug in my heels and tried to pull away. I remembered suddenly that the Stockholm police don't wear white uniforms.

I might as well not have bothered. One of them unclipped a thing like a tiny aerosol bomb from his belt and sprayed it into my face. I felt myself go limp.

CHAPTER 2

There was a scratching sound which irritated me. I tried unsuccessfully to weave it into a couple of dreams before my subconscious gave up. I was lying on my back, eyes closed. I couldn't think where I was. I remembered a frightening dream about being followed, and then as I became aware of pain in my shoulder and head, my eyes snapped open. I was lying on a cot at the side of a small office; the scratching came from the desk where a dapper man in a white uniform sat writing. There was a humming sound and a feeling of motion.

I sat up. At once the man behind the desk looked up, rose, and walked over to me. He drew up a chair and sat down.

"Please don't be alarmed," he said in a clipped British accent. "I'm Chief Captain Winter. You need merely to assist in giving me some routine information, after which you will be assigned comfortable quarters." He said all this in a smooth lifeless way, as though he'd been through it before. Then he looked directly at me for the first time.

"I must apologize for the callousness with which you were handled; it was not my intention. However," his tone changed, "you must excuse the operative; he was uninformed."

Chief Captain Winter opened a notebook and lolled back in his chair with pencil poised. "Where were you born, Mr. Bayard?"

They must have been through my pockets, I thought; they know my name.

"Who the hell are you?" I said.

The chief captain raised an eyebrow. His uniform was immaculate, and brilliantly jeweled decorations sparkled on his chest.

"Of course you are confused at this moment, Mr. Bayard, but everything will be explained to you carefully in due course. I am an Imperial officer, duly authorized to interrogate subjects under detention." He smiled soothingly. "Now please state your birthplace."

I said nothing. I didn't feel like answering any questions; I had too many of my own to ask first. I couldn't place the fellow's accent. He was an Englishman all right, but I couldn't have said from what part of England. I glanced at the medals. Most of them were strange but I recognized the scarlet ribbon of the Victoria Cross, with three palms, ornamented with gems. There was something extremely phony about Chief Captain Winter.

"Come along now, old chap," Winter said sharply. "Kindly co-operate. It will save a great deal of unpleasantness."

I looked at him grimly. "I find being chased, grabbed, gassed, stuffed in a cell, and quizzed about my personal life pretty damned unpleasant already, so don't bother trying to keep it all on a high plane. I'm not answering any questions." I reached in my pocket for my passport; it wasn't there.

"Since you've already stolen my passport, you know by now that I'm an American diplomat, and enjoy diplomatic immunity to any form of arrest, detention, interrogation and what have you. So I'm leaving as soon as you return my property, including my shoes."

Winter's face had stiffened up. I could see my act hadn't much impression on him. He signaled, and two fellows I hadn't seen before moved around into view. They were bigger than he was.

"Mr. Bayard, you must answer my questions, under duress, if necessary. Kindly begin by stating your birthplace."

"You'll find it in my passport," I said. I was looking at the two reinforcements; they were as easy to ignore as a couple of bulldozers in the living room. I decided on a change of tactics. I'd play along in the hope they'd relax a bit, and then make a break for it.

One of the men, at a signal, handed Winter my passport from his desk. He glanced through it, made a number of notes, and passed the booklet back to me.

"Thank you, Mr. Bayard," he said pleasantly. "Now let's get on to particulars. Where did you attend school?"

I tried hard now to give the impression of one eager to please. I regretted my earlier truculence; it made my present pose of co-operativeness a little less plausible. Winter must have been accustomed to the job though, and to subjects who were abject. After a few minutes he waved an arm at the two bouncers, who left the room silently.

Winter had gotten on to the subject of international relations and geopolitics now, and seemed to be fascinated by my commonplace replies. I attempted once or twice to ask why it was necessary to quiz me closely on matters of general information, but was firmly guided back to the answering of the questions.

He covered geography and recent history thoroughly with emphasis on the period 1879–1910, and then started in on a biographic list; all I knew about one name after another. Most of them I'd never heard of, a few were minor public figures. He quizzed me in detail on two Italians, Cocini and Maxoni. He could hardly believe I'd never heard of them. He seemed fascinated by many of my replies.

"Niven an actor?" he said incredulously. "Never heard

of Crane Talbot?" and when I described Churchill's role in recent affairs, he laughed uproariously.

After forty minutes of this one-sided discussion, a buzzer sounded faintly, and another uniformed man entered, placed a good-sized box on the corner of the desk, and left. Winter ignored the interruption.

Another twenty minutes of questions went by. Who was the present monarch of Anglo-Germany? Winter asked. What was the composition of the royal family, the ages of the children? I exhausted my knowledge of the subject. What was the status of the Viceroyalty of India? Explain the working of the Dominion arrangements of Australia, Northern America, Cabotsland …? I was appalled at the questions; the author of them must have been insane. It was almost impossible to link the garbled reference to non-existent political sub-divisions and institutions to reality. I answered as matter-of-factly as possible. At least Winter did not seem to be much disturbed by my revision of his distorted version of affairs.

At last Winter rose, moved over to his desk, and motioned me to a chair beside it. As I pulled the chair out, I glanced into the box on the desk. I saw magazines, folded cloth, coins—and the butt of a small automatic protruding from under a copy of the World Almanac. Winter had turned away, reaching into a small cabinet behind the desk. My hand darted out, scooped up the pistol, and dropped it into my pocket as I seated myself.

Winter turned back with a blue glass bottle. "Now let's have a drop and I'll attempt to clear up some of your justifiable confusion, Mr. Bayard," he said genially. "What would you like to know?" I ignored the bottle.

"Where am I?" I said.

"In the city of Stockholm, Sweden."

"We seem to be moving; what is this, a moving van with an office in it?"

"This is a vehicle, though not a moving van."

"Why did you pick me up?"

"I'm sorry that I can tell you no more than that you were brought in under specific orders from a very high-ranking officer of the Imperial Service." He looked at me speculatively. "This was most unusual," he added.

"I take it kidnapping inoffensive persons is not in itself unusual."

Winter frowned. "You are the subject of an official operation of Imperial Intelligence. Please rest assured you are not being persecuted."

"What is Imperial Intelligence?"

"Mr. Bayard," Winters said earnestly, leaning forward, "it will be necessary for you to face a number of realizations; the first is that the governments which you are accustomed to regard as supreme sovereign powers must in fact be considered tributary to the Imperium, the Paramount Government in whose service I am an officer."

"You're a fake," I said.

Winter bristled. "I hold an Imperial Commission as Chief Captain of Intelligence."

"What do you call this vehicle we're in?"

"This is an armed TNL scout based at Stockholm Zero Zero."

"That tells me a lot; what is it, a boat, car, airplane . . . ?"

"None of those, Mr. Bayard."

"All right, I'll be specific; what does it travel on, water, air . . . ?"

Winter hesitated. "Frankly, I don't know."

I saw it was time to try a new angle of attack. "Where are we going?"

"We are presently operating along coordinates zero-zero, zero, zero-six, zero-ninety-two."

"What is our destination? What place?"

"Stockholm Zero Zero, after which you'll probably be transferred to London Zero Zero for further processing."

"What is the Zero Business? Do you mean London, England?"

"The London you refer to is London B-1 Three."

"What's the difference?"

"London Zero Zero is the capital of the Imperium, comprising the major portion of the civilized world—North Europe, West Hemisphere, and Australia."

I changed the subject. "Why did you kidnap me?"

"A routine interrogational arrest, insofar as I know."

"Do you intend to release me?"

"Yes."

"At home?"

"No."

"Where?"

"I can't say; at one of several concentration points."

"One more question," I said, easing the automatic from my pocket and pointing it at the third medal from the left. "Do you know what this is?

"Keep your hands in sight; better get up and stand over there."

Winter rose and moved over to the spot indicated. I'd never aimed a pistol at a man point-blank before, but I felt no hesitation now.

"Tell me all about it," I said.

"I've answered every question," Winter said nervously.

"And told me nothing." Winter stood staring at me.

I slipped the safety off with a click. "You'll have five seconds to start," I said. "One ... two ..."

"Very well," Winter said. "No need for all this; I'll try." He hesitated. "You were selected from higher up. We went to a great deal of trouble to get you in particular. As I've explained, that's rather irregular. However," Winter seemed to be warming to his subject, "all sampling in this region has been extremely restricted in the past; you see, your continuum occupies an island, one of a very few isolated lines in a vast blighted region. The entire configuration is abnormal, and an extremely dangerous area in which to maneuver. We lost many good men in early years before we learned how to handle the problems involved."

"I suppose you know this is all nonsense to me," I said. "What do you mean by sampling?"

"Do you mind if I smoke?" Winter said. I took a long brown cigarette from a box on the desk, lit it, and handed it to him. "Sampling refers to the collection of individuals or artifacts from representative B-I lines," he said, blowing out smoke. "We in Intelligence are engaged now in mapping operations. It's fascinating work, old boy, picking up the trend lines, coordinating findings with theoretical work, developing accurate calibrating devices, instruments, and so on. We're just beginning to discover the potentialities of working the Net. In order to gather maximum information in a short time, we've found it expedient to collect individuals for interrogation. In this way we quickly gain a general picture of the configuration of the Net in various directions. In your case, I was directed under sealed orders to enter the Blight, proceed to Blight-Insular Three, and take over custody of Mr. Brion Bayard, a diplomat representing, of all things, an American republic." Winter spoke enthusiastically now. As he relaxed, he seemed younger.

"It was quite a feather in my cap, old chap, to be selected to conduct an operation in the Blight, and I've found it fascinating. Always in the past, of course, I've operated at such a distance from the Imperium that little or no analogy existed. But B-I Three! Why it's practically the Imperium, with just enough variation to stir the imagination. Close as the two lines are, there's a desert of Blight around and between them that indicates how frightfully close to the rim we've trodden in times past."

"All right, Winter. I've heard enough," I said. "You're just a harmless nut, maybe. But I'll be going now."

"That's quite impossible," Winter said. "We're in the midst of the Blight."

"What's the Blight?" I asked, making conversation as I looked around the room, trying to pick out the best door to leave by. There were three. I decided on the one no one had come through yet. I moved towards it.

"The Blight is a region of utter desolation, radiation, and chaos," Winter was saying. "There are whole ranges of A-lines where the very planet no longer exists, where automatic cameras have recorded nothing but a vast ring of debris in orbit; then there are the cinder-worlds, and here and there dismal groups of cancerous jungles, alive with radiation-poisoned mutations. It's frightful, old chap. You can wave the pistol at me all night, but it will get you nothing. In a few hours we'll arrive at Zero Zero; you may as well relax until then."

I tried the door, it was locked. "Where's the key?" I said.

"There's no key. It will open automatically at the base."

I went to one of the other doors, the one the man with the box had entered through. I pulled it open and glanced out. The humming sound was louder and down a short and narrow corridor I saw what appeared to be a pilot's compartment. A man's back was visible.

"Come on, Winter," I said. "Go ahead of me."

"Don't be a complete ass, old boy," Winter said, looking irritated. He turned toward his desk. I raised the pistol. The shot boomed inside the walls of the room, and Winter leaped back from the desk holding a ripped hand. He whirled on me, for the first time looking really scared. "You're insane," he shouted. "I've told you we're in the midst of the Blight."

I was keeping one eye on the man up front, who was looking over his shoulder while frantically doing something with his other hand.

"You're leaking all over that nice rug," I said. "I'm going to kill you with the next one. Stop this machine."

Winter was pale; he swallowed convulsively. "I swear, Mr. Bayard, that's utterly impossible. I'd rather you shoot me. You have no conception of what you're suggesting."

I saw now that I was in the hands of a dangerous lunatic. I believed Winter when he said he'd rather die than stop this bus—or whatever it was. In spite of my threat, I couldn't shoot him in cold blood. I turned and took three steps up the passage and poked the automatic into the small of the back that showed there.

"Cut the switch," I said. The man, who was one of the two who had been standing by when I awoke in the office, continued to twist frantically at a knob on the panel before him. He glanced at me, but kept on twiddling. I raised the pistol and fired a shot into the instrument panel. The man jumped convulsively, and threw himself forward, protecting the panel with his body.

"Stop, you bloody fool," he shouted. "Let us explain!"

"I tried that," I said. "It didn't work. Get out of my way. I'm bringing this wagon to a halt one way or another."

I stood so that I could see both men. Winter half crouched

in the doorway, face white. "Are we all right, Doyle?" he called in a strained voice. Doyle eased away from the panel, turned his back to me, and glanced over the instruments. He flipped a toggle, cursed, and turned over to face Winter.

"Communicator dead," he said. "But we're still in operation."

I hesitated now. These two were genuinely terrified of the idea of stopping; they had paid as little attention to me and my noisy gun as one would to a kid with a water pistol. Compared to stopping, a bullet was apparently a trifling irritation.

It was also obvious that this was no moving van. The pilot's compartment had more instruments than an airliner, and no windows. Elaborate ideas began to run through my mind. Space ship? Time machine? What the devil had I gotten into?

"All right, Winter," I said. "Let's call a truce. I'll give you five minutes to give me a satisfactory explanation, prove you're not an escapee from the violent ward, and tell me how you're going to go about setting me down right back where you found me. If you can't or won't cooperate, I'll fill that panel full of holes—including anybody who happens to be standing in front of it."

"Yes," Winter said. "I swear I'll do all I can. Just come away from the control compartment."

"I'll stay right here," I said. "I won't jump the gun unless you give me a reason, like holding your mouth wrong."

Winter was sweating. "This is a scouting machine, operating in the Net. By the Net, I mean the complex of Alternative lines which constitute the matrix of all simultaneous reality. Our drive is the Maxoni-Cocini field generator, which creates a force operating at what one might call a perpendicular to normal entropy. Actually, I know little about the physics of the mechanism; I am not a technician."

I looked at my watch. Winter got the idea. "The Imperium

is the government of the Zero Zero A-line in which this discovery was made. The device is an extremely complex one, and there are a thousand ways in which it can cause disaster to its operators if a mistake is made. Judging from the fact that every A-line within thousands of parameters of Zero Zero is a scene of the most fearful carnage, we surmise that our line alone was successful in controlling the force. We conduct our operations in all of that column of A-space lying outside the Blight, as we term this area of destruction. The Blight itself we ordinarily avoid completely."

Winter wrapped a handkerchief around his bleeding hand as he talked.

"Your line, known as Blight-Insular Three, or B-I Three, is one of two exceptions we know to the general destruction. These two lines lie at some distance from Zero Zero, yours a bit closer than B-I Two, B-I Three was discovered only a month or so ago, and just recently confirmed as a safe line. All this exploratory work in the Blight was done by drone scouts unmanned.

"Why I was directed to pick you up, I don't know. But believe me when I say that if you succeed in crippling this scout, you'll precipitate us into identity with an A-line which might be nothing more than a ring of radioactive dust around the sun, or a great mass of mutated fungus. We cannot stop now for any reason until we reach a safe area."

I looked at my watch again. "Four minutes," I said. "Prove what you've been telling me."

Winter licked his lips. "Doyle, get to the recon photos of this sector, the ones we made on the way in."

Doyle reached across to a compartment under the panel and brought out a large red envelope. He handed it to me. I passed it to Winter.

"Open it," I said. "Let's see what you've got."

Winter fumbled a moment, then slipped a stack of glossy prints out. He handed me the first one. "All these photos were made from precisely the same spatial and temporal coordinates as those occupied by the scout. The only differences are the Web coordinates."

The print showed an array of ragged fragments of rock hanging against a backdrop of foggy grey, with a few bright points gleaming through. I don't know what it was intended to represent.

He handed me another; it was similar. So was the third, with the added detail that one rock fragment had a smooth side, with tiny lines across it. Winter spoke up. "The scale is not what it appears; that odd bit is a portion of the earth's crust, about twenty miles from the camera; the lines are roads." I stared, fascinated. Beyond the strangely scribed fragment, other jagged pieces ranged away to the limit of sight, and beyond. My imagination reeled at the idea that perhaps Winter was telling me the literal truth.

Winter passed over another shot. This one showed a lumpy black expanse, visible only by the murky gleam of light reflected by the irregularities in the surface in the direction of the moon, which showed as a brilliant disc in the black sky.

The next was half-obscured by a mass which loomed across the lens, too close for focus. Beyond, a huge sprawling bulk, shapeless, gross, immense, lay half-buried in tangled vines. I stared horrified at the tiny cowlike head which lolled uselessly on the slope of the mountainous creature. Some distance away a distended leglike appendage projected, the hoof dangling.

"Yes," Winter said. "It's a cow. A mutated cow which no longer has any limitation on its growth. It's a vast tissue culture, absorbing nourishment direct from the vines. They grow all through the mass of flesh. The rudimentary head and occasional limbs are quite useless." I pushed the pictures back at him. I was sick. "I've seen enough," I said. "You've sold me. Let's get out of this." I pushed the pistol into my pocket. I thought of the bullet hole in the panel and shuddered.

Back in the office, I sat down at the desk. Winter spoke up again. "It's a very unnerving thing, old chap, to have it shown to you all at once that way."

Winter went on talking while I tried to assemble his fragmentary information into a coherent picture. A vast spider web of lines, each one a complete universe, each minutely different from all the others; somewhere, a line, or world, in which a device had been developed that enabled a man to move across the lines. Well, why not, I thought. With all those lines to work with, everything was bound to happen in one of them; or was it?

"How about all the other A-lines, Winter," I said at the thought, "where this same discovery must have been made, where there was only some unimportant difference. Why aren't you swarming all over each other, bumping into yourself?"

"That's been a big question to our scientists, old chap, and they haven't yet come up with any definite answers. However, there are a few established points. First, the thing is a fantastically delicate device, as I've explained. The tiniest slip in the initial experimentation, and we'd have ended like some of those other lines you've seen photos of. Apparently the odds were quite fantastically against our escaping the consequences of the discovery; still, we did, and now we know how to control it.

"As to the very close lines, theory now seems to indicate that there is no actual physical separation between lines; those microscopically close to one another actually merge or blend. It's difficult to explain. One actually wanders from one to another, at random, you know. In fact, such is the number of infinitely close lines we're constantly shifting about in. Usually this makes no difference; we don't notice it, any more than we're aware of hopping along from one temporal point to the next as normal entropy progresses."

At my puzzled frown he added, "The lines run both ways, you know, in an infinite number of directions. If we could run straight back along the normal E-line, we'd be travelling into the past. This won't work, for practical reasons involving two bodies occupying the same space, and all that sort of thing. The Maxoni principle enables us to move in a manner which we think of as being at right angles to the normal drift. With it, we can operate through 360 degrees, but always at the same E-level at which we start. Thus, we will arrive at Stockholm Zero Zero at the same moment we departed from B-I Three." Winter laughed. "This detail caused no end of misunderstanding and counter-accusation on the first trials."

"So we're all shifting from one universe to another all the time without knowing it," I said skeptically.

"Not necessarily all of us, not all the time," Winter said. "But emotional stress seems to have the effect of displacing one. Of course with the relative positions of two grains of sand, or even of two atoms within a grain of sand being the only difference between two adjacent lines, you'd not be likely to notice. But at times greater slips occur with most individuals. Perhaps you yourself have noticed some tiny discrepancy at one time or another; some article apparently moved or lost; some sudden change in the character of someone you know; false recollections of past events. The universe isn't all as rigid as one might like to believe."

"You're being awfully plausible, Winter," I said. "Let's pretend I accept your story. Now tell me about this vehicle."

"Just a small mobile MC station, mounted on an auto-propelled chassis. It can move about on level ground or paved areas, and also in calm water. It enables us to do most of our spatial maneuvering on our own ground, so to speak, and avoid the hazards of attempting to conduct ground operations in strange areas."

"Where are the rest of the men in your party?" I asked. "There are at least three more of you."

"They're all at their assigned posts," Winter said. "There's another small room containing the drive mechanism forward of the control compartment."

"What's this stuff for?" I indicated the box on the desk from which I'd gotten the gun.

Winter looked at it, then said ruefully, "So that's where you acquired the weapon. I knew you'd been searched. Damned careless of Doyle—bloody souvenir hunter! I told him to submit everything to me for approval before we returned, so I suppose it's my fault." He touched his aching hand tenderly.

"Don't feel too bad about it. I'm just a clever guy," I said. "However, I'm not very brave. As a matter of fact, I'm scared to death of what's in store for me when we arrive at our destination."

"You'll be well treated, Mr. Bayard," Winter assured me. I let that one pass. Maybe when we arrived, I could come out shooting, making an escape. That line of thought didn't seem very encouraging either. What would I do next, loose in this Imperium of Winter's? What I needed was a return ticket home. I found myself thinking of it as B-I Three, and realized I was beginning to accept Winter's story. I took a drink from the blue bottle.

"Why don't we explode when we pass through one of those empty-space lines, or burn in the hot ones?" I asked suddenly. "Suppose we found ourselves peeking out from inside one of those hunks of rock you were photographing?"

"We don't linger about long enough, old boy," Winter said. "We remain in any one line for no finite length of time, therefore there's no time for us to react physically to our surroundings."

"How can you take pictures and use communicators?"

"The camera remains inside the field. The photo is actually a composite exposure of all the lines we cross during the instant of the exposure. The lines differ hardly at all, of course, and the prints are quite clear. Light, of course, is a condition, not an event. Our communicators employ a sort of grating which spreads the transmission."

"Winter," I said, "this is all extremely interesting, but I get the impression that you have small regard for a man's comfort. I think you might be planning to use me in some sort of colorful experiment, and then throw me away—toss me out into one of those cosmic junk heaps you showed me. And that stuff in the blue bottle isn't quite soothing enough to drive the idea out of my mind."

"Great heavens, old boy!" Winter sat bolt upright. "Nothing of that sort, I can assure you. Why, we're not blasted barbarians! Since you are an object of official interest of the Imperium, you can be assured of humane and honorable treatment."

"I didn't like what you said about concentration points a while back. That sounds like jail to me."

"Not at all," Winter expostulated. "There are a vast number of very pleasant A-lines well outside the Blight which are either completely uninhabited, or are occupied by backward or underdeveloped peoples. One can well nigh select the technological and cultural level in which one would like to live. All interrogation subjects are most scrupulously provided for; they're supplied with everything necessary to live in comfort for the remainder of their normal lives."

"Marooned on a desert island, or parked in a native village? That doesn't sound too jolly to me," I said. "I'd rather be at home."

Winter smiled speculatively. "What would you say to being set up with a fortune in gold, and placed in a society closely resembling that of, say, England in the seventeenth century with the added advantage that you'd have electricity, plenty of modern literature, supplies for a lifetime, whatever you wished. You must remember that we have all the resources of the universe to draw upon."

"I'd like it better if I had a little more choice," I said.

"Suppose we keep right on going, once we're clear of the Blight," I said. "That reception committee wouldn't be waiting then. You could run this buggy back to B-I Three. I could force you."

"See here, Bayard," Winter said impatiently. "You have a gun. Very well, shoot me; shoot all of us. What would that gain you? The operation of this machine requires a very high technical skill. The controls are set for automatic return to the starting point. It is absolutely against Imperium policy to return a subject to the line from which he was taken. The only thing for you to do is cooperate with us, and you have my assurance as an Imperial officer that you will be treated honorably."

I looked at the gun. "According to the movies," I said, "the fellow with the rod always gets his own way. But you don't seem to care whether I shoot you or not."

Winter smiled. "Aside from the fact that you've had quite a

few draughts from my brandy flask and probably couldn't hit the wall with that weapon you're holding, I assure ..."

"You're always assuring me," I said. I tossed the pistol onto the desk. I put my feet up on the polished top, and leaned back in the chair. "Wake me up when we get there. I'll want to fix my face."

Winter laughed. "Now you're being reasonable, old boy. It would be damned embarrassing for me to have to warn the personnel at base that you were waving a pistol about."

CHAPTER 3

I woke up with a start. My neck ached abominably; so did the rest of me, as soon as I moved. I groaned, dragged my feet down off the desk, and sat up. There was something wrong. Winter was gone and the humming had stopped. I jumped up.

"Winter," I shouted. I had a vivid picture of myself marooned in one of those hell-worlds. At that moment I realized I wasn't half as afraid of arriving at Zero Zero as I was of not getting there.

Winter pushed the door open and glanced in. "I'll be with you in a moment, Mr. Bayard," he said. "We've arrived on schedule."

I was nervous. The gun was gone. I told myself it was no worse than going to one of the ambassador's receptions. My best bet was to walk in as though I'd thought of it myself.

The two bouncers came in, followed by Winter. One of the two men pushed the door open, and stood at attention beside it. Beyond the opening I could see muted sunshine on a level paved surface, and a group of men in white uniforms, looking in our direction.

I stepped down through the door and looked around. We were in a large shed, looking something like a railroad station. A group of men in white uniforms were waiting.

One of them stepped forward. "By Jove, Winter," he said.

"You've brought it off. Congratulations, old man." The others came up, gathered around Winter, asking questions, turning to stare at me. None of them said anything to me. To hell with them, I thought. I turned and started strolling toward the front of the shed. There was one door with a sentry box arrangement beside it. I gave the man on duty a glance and started past.

"You'd better memorize this face," I said coolly. "You'll be seeing a great deal of it from now on. I'm your new commander." I looked him up and down. "Your uniform is in need of attention." I turned and went on.

Winter appeared at that point, putting an end to what would have been a very neat escape. But where the hell would I have gone?

"Here, old man," he said. "Don't go wandering about. I'm to take you directly to Royal Intelligence, where you'll doubtless find out a bit more about the reasons for your, ah—" Winter cleared his throat, "visit."

"I thought it was Imperial Intelligence," I said. "And for the high level operation this is supposed to be, this is a remarkably modest reception. I thought there would be a band, or at least a couple of cops with handcuffs."

"Royal Swedish Intelligence," Winter explained briskly. "Sweden will bring tributary to the Emperor, of course. Imperial Intelligence chaps will be on hand. As for your reception, we don't believe in making much fuss, you know." Winter waved me into a boxy black staff car which waited at the curb. It swung out at once into light traffic which pulled out of our way as we rode down the center of the broad avenue.

"I thought your scout just travelled cross-ways," I said, "and stayed in the same spot on the map. This doesn't look like the hilly area of the Old Town."

"You have a suspicious mind and an eye for detail," Winter said. "We maneuvered the scout through the streets to the position of the ramps before going into drive. We're on the north side of the city now."

Our giant car roared across a bridge, and swirled into a long gravel drive leading to a wrought-iron gate before a massive grey granite building. The people I saw looked perfectly ordinary, with the exception of a few oddities of dress and an unusually large number of gaudy uniforms. The guard at the iron gate was wearing a cherry-colored tunic, white trousers, and a black steel helmet surmounted by a gold spike and a deep purple plume. He presented arms—a short and wicked looking nickel-plated machine gun—and as the gate swung wide we eased past him and stopped before broad doors of polished ironbound oak. A brass plate beside the entrance said *Kungliga Svenska Spionage.*

I said nothing as we walked down a spotless white marble-floored hall, entered a spacious elevator, and rode up to the top floor. We walked along another hall, this one paved with red granite, and paused before a large door at the end. There was no one else around.

"Just relax, Mr. Bayard. Answer all questions fully, and use the same forms of address as I do."

"I'll try not to fall down," I said. Winter looked as nervous as I felt as he opened the door after a polite tap.

The room was an office, large and handsomely furnished. Across a wide expanse of grey rug three men sat around a broad desk, behind which sat a fourth. Winter closed the door, walked across the room with me trailing behind him, and came to a rigid position of attention ten feet from the desk. His arm swung up in a real elbow-buster of a salute and held it.

"Sir, Chief Captain Winter reports as ordered," he said in a strained voice.

"Very good, Winter," said the man behind the desk, sketching a salute casually. Winter brought his arm down with a snap. He rotated rigidly toward the others.

"*Kaiserliche Hochheit,*" he said, bowing stiffly from the waist at one of the seated figures. "Chief Inspector," he greeted the second, while the third, a rather paunchy fellow with a jolly expression and a somehow familiar face, rated just "Sir."

"'*Hochwelgeboren*' will do," murmured the lean aristocratic-looking one whom Winter had addressed first. Apparently instead of an imperial highness he was only a high-well-born. Winter turned bright pink. "I beg your Excellency's pardon," he said in a choked voice. The round-faced man grinned broadly.

The man behind the desk had been studying me intently during this exchange. "Please be seated, Mr. Bayard," he said pleasantly, indicating an empty chair directly in front of the desk. Winter was still standing rigidly. The man glanced at him. "Stand at ease, Chief Captain," he said in a dry tone, turning back to me.

"I hope that your being brought here has not prejudiced you against us unduly, Mr. Bayard," he said. He had a long gaunt face with a heavy jaw.

"I am General Bernadotte," he went on. "These gentlemen are the Friherr von Richthofen, Chief Inspector Bale, and Mr. Goering." I nodded at them. Bale was a thin broad-shouldered man with a small bald head. He wore an expression of disapproval.

Bernadotte went on. "I would like first to assure you that our decision to bring you here was not made lightly. I know that you have many questions, and all will be answered fully.

For the present, I shall tell you frankly that we have called you here to ask for your help."

I hadn't been prepared for this. I don't know what I expected, but to have this panel of high-powered brass asking for my puny assistance left me opening and closing my mouth without managing to say anything.

"It's remarkable," commented the paunchy civilian. I looked at him. Winter had called him Mr. Goering. I thought of pictures of Hitler's gross Air Chief.

"Not Hermann Goering?" I said.

The fat man looked surprised, and a smile spread across his face.

"Yes, my name is Hermann," he said. "How did you know this?" He had a fairly heavy German accent.

I found it hard to explain. This was something I hadn't thought of—actual double or analogs of figures in my own world. Now I knew beyond a doubt that Winter had not been lying to me.

"Back where I came from, everyone knows your name," I said. "Reichmarshall Goering …"

"Reichmarshall!" Goering repeated. "What an intriguing title!" He looked around at the others. "Is this not a most interesting and magnificent information?" He beamed. "I, poor fat Hermann, a Reichmarshall, and known to all." He was delighted.

"Multi-phased reality is, of course, rather a shocking thing to encounter suddenly," the general said, "after a lifetime of living in one's own narrow world. To those of us who have grown up with it, it seems only natural and in keeping with the principles of multiplicity and continuum. The idea of a monolinear causal sequence is seen to be an artificially restrictive conception, an oversimplification of reality growing out of human egotism."

The other four men listened as attentively as I. It was very quiet, with only the occasional faint sounds of traffic from the street below.

"Insofar as we have been able to determine thus far from our studies of the B-I Three line, from which you come, our two lines share a common history up to about the year 1790. They remain parallel in many ways for about another century; thereafter they diverge rather sharply.

"Here in our world, two Italian scientists, Giulio Maxoni and Carlo Cocini, in the year 1893, made a basic discovery, which, after several years of study, they embodied in a device which enabled them to move about at will through a wide range of what we now term Alternative lines, or A-lines.

"Cocini lost his life in an early exploratory test, and Maxoni determined to offer the machine to the Italian government. He was rudely rebuffed.

"After several years of harassment by the Italian press, which ridiculed him unmercifully, Maxoni went to England, and offered his invention to the British government. There was a long and very cautious period of negotiation, but eventually a bargain was struck. Maxoni received a title, estates, and one million pounds in gold. He died a year later.

"The British government now had sole control of the most important basic human discovery since the wheel. The wheel gave man the power to move easily across the surface of his world; the Maxoni principle gave him all the worlds to move about in."

Leather creaked faintly as I moved in my chair. The general leaned back and drew a deep breath. He smiled.

"I hope that I am not overwhelming you with an excess of historical detail, Mr. Bayard."

"Not at all," I replied. "I'm very much interested."

He went on. "At that time the British government was negotiating with the Imperial Germanic government in an effort to establish workable trade agreements, and avoid a fratricidal war, which then appeared to be inevitable if appropriate spheres of influence were not agreed upon.

"The acquisition of the Maxoni papers placed a different complexion on the situation. Rightfully feeling that they now had a considerably more favorable position from which to negotiate, the British suggested an amalgamation of the two empires into the present Anglo-Germanic Imperium, with the House of Hanover-Windsor occupying the Imperial throne. Sweden signed the Concord shortly thereafter, and after the resolution of a number of differences in detail, the Imperium came into being on January 1, 1900."

I had the feeling the general was over-simplifying things. I wondered how many people had been killed in the process of resolving the minor details. I kept the thought to myself.

"Since its inception," the general continued, "the Imperium has conducted a program of exploration, charting, and study of the A-continuum. It was quickly determined that for a vast distance on all sides of the home line, utter desolation existed; outside that blighted region, however, were the infinite resources of countless lines. Those lines lying just outside the Blight seem uniformly to represent a divergence point at about 400 years in the past; that is to say, our common histories differentiate about the year 1550. As one travels further out, the divergence date recedes. At the limits of our explorations to date the CH dated is about 1,000,000 B.C."

I didn't know what to say, so I said nothing. This seemed to be all right with Bernadotte.

"Then, in 1947, examination of photos made by automatic camera scouts revealed an anomaly; an apparently normal, inhabited world, lying well within the Blight. It took weeks of careful searching to pinpoint the line. For the first time, we were visiting a world closely analogous to our own, in which many of the institutions of our own world should be duplicated.

"We had hopes of a fruitful liaison between the two worlds, but in this we were bitterly disappointed."

The general turned to the bald man whom he had introduced as Chief Inspector Bale.

"Chief Inspector," he said, "will you take up the account at this point?"

Bale sat up in his chair, folded his hands, and began.

"In September 1948 two senior agents of Imperial Intelligence were dispatched with temporary rank of Career Minister and full diplomatic accreditation, to negotiate an agreement with the leaders of the National People's State. This political unit actually embraces most of the inhabitable world of the B-1 Two line. A series of frightful wars, employing some sort of radioactive explosives, had destroyed the better part of civilization.

"Europe was a shambles. We found that the NPS headquarters was in North Africa, and had as its nucleus the former French colonial government there. The top man was a ruthless ex-soldier who had established himself as uncontested dictator of what remained of things. His army was made up of units of all the previous combatants, held together by the promise of free looting and top position in a new society based on raw force.

"Our agents approached a military sub-chief, calling himself Colonel-General Yang, in charge of a ragtag mob of ruffians in motley uniforms, and asked to be conducted to the headquarters of the dictator. Yang had them clapped into a cell and beaten insensible in spite of their presentation of diplomatic passports and identity cards.

"He did however send them along to the dictator to have an interview. During the talk, the fellow drew a pistol and shot one of my two chaps through the head, killing him instantly. When this failed to make the other volunteer anything further than that he was an accredited envoy of the Imperial government requesting an *exequatur* and appropriate treatment, prior to negotiating an international agreement, he was turned over to experienced torturers.

"Under torture, the agent gave out just enough to convince his interrogators that he was insane; he was released to starve or die of wounds. We managed to spot him and pick him up in time to get the story before he died."

I still had no comment to make. It didn't sound pretty, but then I wasn't too enthusiastic about the methods employed by the Imperium either. The general resumed the story.

"We resolved to make no attempt at punitive action, but simply to leave this unfortunate line in isolation.

"About a year ago, an event occurred which rendered this policy no longer tenable." Bernadotte turned to the lean-faced man.

"Manfred, I will ask you to cover this part of the briefing."

"Units of our Net Surveillance Service detected activity at a point of some distance within the area called Sector 92," Richthofen began. "This was a contingency against which we had been on guard from the first. A heavily armed MC unit of unknown origin had dropped into identity with one of our most prized industrial lines, one of a group with which we conduct a multi-billion pound trade. The intruder materialized in a population center, and released virulent poisonous gases, killing hundreds. Masked troops then emerged, only a platoon or two of them, and proceeded to strip bodies, loot shops—an orgy of wanton destruction. Our NSS scout arrived some hours after the attackers had departed. The scout, in turn, was subjected to a heavy attack by the justifiably aroused inhabitants of the area before it was able to properly identify itself as an Imperium vessel."

Richthofen had a disdainful frown on his face. "I personally conducted the rescue and salvage operation; over four hundred innocent civilians dead, valuable manufacturing facilities destroyed by fire, production lines disrupted, the population entirely demoralized. A bitter spectacle for us."

"You see, Mr. Bayard," Bernadotte said, "we are well nigh helpless to protect our friends against such forays. Although we have developed extremely effective MC field detection devices, the difficulty of reaching the scene of an attack in time is practically insurmountable. The actual transit takes no time, but locating the precise line among numerous others is an extremely delicate operation. Our homing devices make it possible, but only after we have made a very close approximation manually."

"In quick succession thereafter," Richthofen continued, "we suffered seven similar raids. Then the pattern changed. The raiders began appearing in numbers, with large cargo-carrying units. They also set about rounding up all the young women at each raid, and taking them along into captivity. It became obvious that a major threat to the Imperium had come into existence.

"At last we had the good fortune to detect a raider's field in the close vicinity of one of our armed scouts. It quickly dropped in on a converging course, and located the pirate about twenty minutes after it had launched its attack. The commander of the scout quite properly opened up at once with high explosive cannon and blew the enemy to rubble. Its crew, although demoralized by the loss of their vessel, nevertheless resisted capture almost to the last man. We were able to secure only two prisoners for interrogation."

I wondered how the Imperium's methods of interrogation compared with those of the dictator of B-I Two, but I didn't ask. I might find out soon enough.

"We learned a great deal more than we expected from our prisoners. They were the talkative, boastful type. The effectiveness of the raiding parties depended on their striking unexpectedly and departing quickly. The number of pirate vessels was placed at no more than four, each manned by about fifty men. They boasted of a great weapon held in reserve, and which would be used to avenge them. It was apparent from the remarks of the prisoners that they had not had the MC drive long, and that they knew nothing of the configuration of the Net, or of the endless ramifications of simultaneous reality.

"They seemed to think their fellows would find our base and destroy it with ease. They also had only a vague idea of the extent and the nature of the Blight. They mentioned that several of their ships had disappeared, doubtless into that region. It appears also, happily for us, that they have only the most elementary detection devices and that their controls are erratic in the extreme. But the information of real importance was the identity of the raiders."

Richthofen paused for dramatic effect. "It was our unhappy sister world, B-I Two."

"Somehow," Bernadotte took up the story, "in spite of their condition of chaotic social disorder and their destructive wars, they had succeeded in harnessing the MC principle. Their apparatus is even more primitive than that with which we began almost sixty years ago; yet they have escaped disaster.

"The next move came with startling suddenness. Whether by virtue of an astonishingly rapid scientific development, or by sheer persistence and blind luck, one of their scouts succeeded, last month, in locating the Zero Zero line of the Imperium itself. The vessel dropped into identity with our continuum on the outskirts of the city of Berlin, one of the royal capitals.

"The crew had apparently been prepared for their visit. They planted a strange device atop a flimsy tower in a field, and embarked instantly. Within a matter of three minutes, as well as we have been able to determine, the device detonated with unbelievable force. Over a square mile was absolutely desolated; casualties ran into the thousands. And the entire area still remains poisoned with some form of radiation-producing debris which renders the region uninhabitable."

I nodded. "I think I understand," I said.

"Yes," the general said, "you have something of this sort in your B-I Three world also, do you not?"

I assumed the question was rhetorical and said nothing.

Bernadotte continued. "Crude though their methods are, they have succeeded already in flaunting the Imperium. It is only a matter of time, we feel, before they develop adequate controls and detection devices. We will then be faced with the prospect of hordes of ragged but efficient soldiers, armed with the frightful radium bombs with which they destroyed their own culture, descending on the mother world of the Imperium.

"This eventuality is one for which it has been necessary to make preparation. There seemed to be two possibilities, both equally undesirable. We could await further attack, meanwhile readying our defenses, of doubtful value against the fantastic explosives of the enemy; or we could ourselves mount an offensive, launching a massive invasion force against B-I Two. The logistics problems involved in either plan would be unbelievably complex."

I was learning a few things about the Imperium. In the first place, they did not have the atomic bomb, and had no conception of its power. Their consideration of war against an organized military force armed with atomics was proof of that. Also, not having had the harsh lessons of two major wars to assist them, they were naive, almost backward, in some ways. They thought more like Europeans of the nineteenth century than modern westerners.

"About one month ago, Mr. Bayard," Bale took over, "a new factor was introduced, giving us a third possibility. In the heart of the Blight, at only a very little distance from B-I Two, and even closer to us than it, we found a second surviving line. That line was of course your home world, designated Blight-Insular Three.

"Within seventy-two hours one hundred and fifty special agents had been placed at carefully scouted positions in B-I Three. We were determined to make no blunders; too much was at stake. As the information flowed in from our men, all of whom, being top agents, had succeeded in establishing their cover identities without difficulty, it was immediately passed to the General Staff and to the Imperial Emergency Cabinet for study. The two bodies remained in constant session for over a week without developing any adequate scheme for handling the new factor.

"One committee of the Emergency Cabinet was assigned the important task of determining as closely as possible the precise CH relationship of B-I Three with both B-I Two and the Imperium. This is an extremely tricky chore as it is quite possible for an amazing parallelism to exist in one phase of an

A-line while the most fantastic variants crop up in another.

"One week ago today the committee reported findings they considered to be ninety-eight per cent reliable. Your B-I Three line shared history of the B-I Two until the date 1911, probably early in the year. At that point, my colleague, Mr. Goering, of German Intelligence, who had been sitting in on the meeting, made a brilliant contribution. His suggestion was immediately adopted. All agents were alerted at once to drop all other lines of inquiry and concentrate on picking up a trace of—" Bale looked at me.

"Mr. Brion Bayard."

They knew I was on the verge of exploding from pure curiosity, so I just sat and looked back at Bale. He pursed his lips. He sure as hell didn't like me.

"We picked you up from records at your university—" Bale frowned at me. "Something like aluminum alloy ..."

Bale must be an Oxford man, I thought.

"Illinois," I said.

"At any rate," Bale went on, "it was a relatively simple matter to follow you up then through your military service and into your Diplomatic Service. Our man just missed you at your Legation at Viat-Kai."

"Consulate General," I corrected.

It annoyed Bale. I was glad; I didn't like him much either.

"You had left the post the preceding day and were proceeding to your headquarters via Stockholm. We had a man on the spot; he kept tabs on you until the shuttle could arrive. The rest you know."

There was a lengthening silence. I shifted in my chair, looking from one expressionless face to another.

"All right," I said. "It seems I'm supposed to ask, so I'll oblige, just to speed things along. Why me?"

Almost hesitantly General Bernadotte opened a drawer of the desk and drew out a flat object wrapped in brown paper. He removed the paper very deliberately as he spoke.

"I have here an official portrait of the dictator of the world of Blight-Insular Two," he said. "One of the two artifacts we have been able to bring along from that unhappy region. Copies of this picture are posted everywhere there."

He passed it over to me. It was a crude lithograph in color, showing a man in uniform, the chest as far down as the picture extended covered with medals. Beneath the portrait was the legend: His Martial Excellency, Duke of Algiers, Warlord of the Combined Forces, Marshal General of the State, Brion The First Bayard, Dictator."

The picture was of me.

CHAPTER 4

I stared at the garish portrait for a long time. It wasn't registering; I had a feeling of disorientation. There was too much to absorb.

"Now you will understand, Mr. Bayard, why we have brought you here," the general said, as I silently handed the picture back to him. "You represent our hidden ace. But only if you consent to help us of your own free will." He turned to Richthofen again.

"Manfred, you will outline our plan to Mr. Bayard?"

Richthofen cleared his throat. "Quite possibly," he said, "we could succeed in disposing of the Dictator Bayard by bombing his headquarters. This, however, would merely create a temporary diversion until a new leader emerged. The organization of the enemy seems to be such that no more than a very brief respite would be gained, if any at all, before the attacks would be resumed; and we are not prepared to sustain such onslaughts as these.

"No, it is far better for our purpose that Bayard remain the leader of the National People's State—and that we control him." Here he looked intently at me.

"A specially equipped TNL scout, operated by our best pilot technician, could plant a man within the private apartment which occupies the top floor of the dictator's palace at Algiers. We believe that a resolute man introduced into the palace in this manner, armed with the most effective hand weapons at our disposal, could succeed in locating and entering the dictator's sleeping chamber, assassinating him, and disposing of the body.

"If that man were you, Mr. Bayard, fortified by ten days' intensive briefing and carrying a small net-communicator, we believe that you could assume the identity of the dead man and rule as absolute dictator over Bayard's twenty million fighting men."

"Do I have another double here," I said, "in your Imperium?"

Bernadotte shook his head. "No, you have remote cousins here, nothing closer."

They all watched me. I could see that all three of them expected me to act solemn and modest at the honor, and set out to do or die for the fatherland. They were overlooking a few things, though. This wasn't my fatherland; I'd been kidnapped and brought here. And oddly enough, I could not see myself murdering anybody—especially, I had the grotesque thought—myself. I didn't even like the idea of being dropped down in the midst of a pack of torturers.

I was ready to tell them so in very definite terms, when my eye fell on Bale. He was wearing a supercilious half-smile, and I could see that this is what he expected. His contempt for me was plain. I sensed that he thought of me as the man who had killed his best agent in cold blood, a cowardly blackguard. My mouth was open to speak; but under that sneering expression, different words came out—temporizing words. I wouldn't give Bale the satisfaction of being right.

"And after I'm in charge of B-I Two, what then?" I said.

"You will be in constant touch with Imperial Intelligence via communicator," Richthofen said eagerly. "You'll receive detailed instructions as to each move to make. We should be able to immobilize B-I Two within six months. You'll then be returned here."

"I won't be returned home?"

"Mr. Bayard," Bernadotte said seriously, "you will never be able to return to B-I Three. The Imperium will offer you any reward you wish to name, except that. The consequences of revealing the existence of the Imperium in your line at this time are far too serious to permit consideration of the idea. However—"

All eyes were on Bernadotte. He looked as though what he was about to say was important.

"I have been authorized by the Emergency Cabinet," he said with gravity, "to offer you an Imperial commission in the rank of Major General, Mr. Bayard. If you accept this commission, your first assignment will be as we have outlined." Bernadotte handed a heavy piece of parchment across the table to me. "You should know, Mr. Bayard, that the Imperium does not award commissions, particularly that of General Officer, lightly."

"It will be most unusual rank," Goering said, smiling. "Normally there is no such rank in the Imperium Service; Lieutenant General, Colonel General, Major General. You will be unique."

"We adopted the rank from your own armed forces, as a special mark of esteem, Mr. Bayard," Bernadotte said. "It is not less authentic for being unusual."

It was a fancy sheet of paper. The Imperium was prepared to pay off well for this job they needed done—anything I wanted. And doubtless, they thought the strange look on my face was greed at the thought of a general's two stars. Well, let them think it. I didn't want to give them any more information which might be used against me.

"I'll think about it," I said. Bale looked disconcerted now.

After expecting me to back out, he had apparently then expected me to be dazzled by the reward I was being offered. I'd let him worry about it. Suddenly Bale bored me.

Bernadotte hesitated. "I'm going to take an unprecedented step, Mr. Bayard," he said. "For the present, on my personal initiative as head of State, I'm confirming you as Colonel in the Royal Army of Sweden without condition. I do this to show my personal confidence in you, as well as for more practical reasons." He rose and smiled ruefully, as though unsure of my reaction. "Congratulations, Colonel," he said, holding out his hand.

I stood up too. I noticed everyone had.

"You must have twenty-four hours to consider your decision, Colonel," he said. "I'll leave you in the excellent care of Graf von Richthofen and Mr. Goering until then."

Richthofen turned to Winter, standing silently by, "Won't you join us, Chief Captain," he said.

"Delighted," Winter said.

"Congratulations, old boy, er, Sir," Winter said as soon as we were in the hall. "You made quite a hit with the general." He seemed quite his jaunty self again.

I eyed him. "You mean King Gustav?" I said.

Winter blinked. "But how did you know?" he said. "I mean dash it, how the devil did you know?"

"But it must be," Goering said with enthusiasm, "that also he in your home world is known, not so?"

"That's right, Mr. Goering," I said, "now you've dispelled my aura of mystery."

Goering chuckled. "Please, Mr. Bayard, you must call me Hermann." He gripped my arm in friendly fashion as we moved down the hall. "Now you must tell us more about this intriguing world of yours."

Richthofen spoke up. "I suggest we go along to my summer villa at Drottningholm and enjoy a dinner and a couple of good vintages while we hear all about your home, Mr. Bayard; and we shall tell you of ours."

CHAPTER 5

I stood before a long mirror and eyed myself, not without approval. Two tailors had been buzzing around me like bees for half an hour, putting the finishing touches on their handiwork. I had to admit they had done all right.

I now wore narrow-cut riding breeches of fine grey whipcord, short black boots of meticulously stitched and polished black leather, a white linen shirt without collar or cuffs beneath a mess jacket of royal blue, buttoned to the chin. A gold bordered blue stripe ran down the side of the trousers and heavy loops of gold braid ringed the sleeves from wrist to elbow. A black leather belt with a large square buckle bearing the Royal Swedish crest supported a jeweled scabbard containing a slender rapier with an ornate hilt.

In the proper position on the left side of the chest were, to my astonishment, a perfectly accurate set of my World War II Service medals and the Silver Star. On the shoulder straps, the bright silver eagles of a U.S. Colonel gleamed. I was wearing the full dress uniform of my new position in the Imperium society.

I was glad now I hadn't let myself deteriorate into the flabby ill-health of the average Foreign Service Officer, soft and pale from long hours in offices and late hours of heavy drinking at the interminable diplomatic functions. My shoulders were reasonably broad, my back reasonably straight, no paunch marred the lines of my new finery. This outfit made a man look like a man. How the devil had we gotten into the habit of draping ourselves in shapeless double-breasted suits, in mousy colors, of identical cut?

Goering was sitting in a brocaded armchair in the luxurious suite to which Richthofen had shown me in his villa.

"You cut a martial figure, Brion," he said. "It is plain to see you have, for this new job, a natural aptitude."

"I wouldn't count on it, Hermann," I said. His comment had reminded me of the other side of the coin; the deadly plans the Imperium had in mind for me. Well, I could settle that later. Tonight I was going to enjoy myself.

Over a dinner of pheasant served on a sunny terrace in the longer Swedish summer evening, Richthofen had explained to me that, in Swedish society, to be without a title was an extremely awkward social encumbrance. It was not that one needed an exalted position, he assured me; merely that there must be something for others to call one—Herr Doctor, Herr Professor, Ingenjor, Redaktor. My military status would ease my entry into the world of the Imperium.

Winter came in then, carrying what looked like a crystal ball.

"Your topper, sir," he said with a flourish. What he had was a chrome-plated steel helmet, with a rib running along the top, and a gold-dyed plume growing out of it.

"Good God," I said. "Isn't that overdoing it a little?" I took the helmet; it was feather light, I discovered. The tailor took over, placed the helmet just so, handed me a pair of white leather gloves, and faded out.

"You have to have it, old boy," Winter said. "Dragoons, you know."

"You are complete," Hermann said. "A masterpiece."

He was wearing a dark grey uniform with black trim and white insignia. He had a respectable but not excessive display of ribbons and orders.

"Hermann," I said expansively, "you should have seen yourself when you were all rigged out in your medals back home. They came down to here." I indicated my knees. He laughed.

Together we left the suite and went down to the study on the ground floor. Winter, I noted, had changed from his whites to a pale yellow mess jacket with heavy silver braid and a nickel-plated Luger.

Richthofen showed up moments later; his outfit consisted of what looked like a set of tails, circa 1880, with silver buttons and a white beret.

"We're a cool bunch of cats," I said. I was feeling swell. I caught another glimpse of myself in a mirror. "Sharp, daddy-o," I murmured.

A liveried butler swung the glass door open for us and we descended the steps to a waiting car. This one was a yellow phaeton, with the top down. We slid into our places on the smooth yellow leather seats and it eased off down the drive.

It was a magnificent night, with high clouds and a brilliant moon. In the distance, the lights of the city glittered. We rolled smoothly along, the engine so silent that the sound of the wind in the tall trees along the way was clearly audible.

Goering had thought to bring along a small flask, and by the time we had each tapped it twice we were passing through the iron gates of the summer palace. Colored flood-lights bathed the gardens and people already filled the terrace on the south and west sides of the building. The car dropped us before the gigantic entry and moved off. We made our way through the crowd, and into the reception hall.

*

Light from massive crystal chandeliers glittered on gowns and uniforms, polished boots and jewels, silks, brocades and velvets. A straight-backed man in rose-pink bowed over the hand of a lovely blonde in white. A slender black-clad fellow with a gold and white sash escorted a lady in green-gold toward the ballroom. The din of laughter and conversation almost drowned out the strains of the waltz in the background.

"All right, boys," I said. "Where's the punch bowl?"

I don't often set out to get stewed, but when I do, I don't believe in half measures. I was feeling great, and wanted to keep it that way. At the moment, I couldn't feel the bruises from my fall, my indignation over being grabbed was forgotten, and as for tomorrow, I couldn't care less. I was having a wonderful time. I hoped I wouldn't see Bale's sour face.

Everybody talked, asked me eager questions, made introductions. I found myself talking to someone I finally recognized as Douglas Fairbanks, Sr. He was a tough-looking old fellow in a naval uniform. I met counts, dukes, officers of a dozen ranks I'd never heard of, several princes, and finally a short broad-shouldered man with a heavy sun tan and a go-to-hell smile whom I finally realized was the son of the Emperor.

I was still walking and talking like a million dollars, but somewhere along the line I'd lost what little tact I normally had.

"Well, Prince William," I said, weaving just a little, "I understood the House of Hanover-Windsor was the ruling line here. Where I come from the Hanovers and the Windsors are all tall, skinny and glum-looking."

The Prince smiled. "Here, Colonel," he said, "a policy was established which put an end to that unfortunate situation. The Constitution requires that the male heir marry a commoner. This not only makes life more pleasant for the heir, with so many beautiful commoners to choose from, but maintains the vigor of the line. And it incidentally produces short men with happy faces occasionally."

I moved on, meeting people, eating little sandwiches, drinking everything from aquavit to beer, and dancing with one heavenly-looking girl after another. For the first time in my life my ten years of Embassy elbow-bending were standing me in good stead. From the grim experience gained through seven evenings a week of holding a drink in my hand from sundown till midnight while pumping other members of the Diplomatic Corps who thought they were pumping me, I had emerged with a skill; I could hold my liquor.

Somewhere along the line I felt the need for a breath of fresh air and stepped out through the tall French doors onto a dark balustraded gallery overlooking the gardens. I leaned on the heavy stone rail, looked up at the stars visible through tall tree-tops, and waited for the buzzing in my head to die down a little.

The night air moved in a cool torrent over the dark lawn, carrying the scent of flowers. Behind me the orchestra played a tune that was almost, but not quite, a Strauss waltz.

I pulled off the white gloves that Richthofen had told me I should keep on when I left my helmet at the checkroom. I unbuttoned the top button of the tight-fitting jacket.

I'm getting old, I thought, or maybe just tired.

"And why are you tired, Colonel?" a cool feminine voice inquired from behind me.

I turned around. "Ah, there you are," I said. "I'm glad. I'd rather be guilty of talking out loud than of imagining voices."

I worked on focusing my eyes a little better. She had red hair, and wore a pale pink gown that started low and stayed with the subject.

"I'm very glad, as a matter of fact," I added. "I like beautiful redheads who appear out of nowhere."

"Not out of nowhere, Colonel," she said. "From in there, where it is so warm and crowded."

She spoke excellent English in a low voice, with just enough Swedish accent to render her tritest speech charming.

"Precisely," I said. "All those people were making me just a little bit drunk, so I came out here to recover." I was wearing a silly smile, and having a thoroughly good time being so eloquent and clever with this delightful young lady.

"My father has told me that you are not born to the Imperium, Colonel," she said. "And that you come from a world where all is the same, yet different. It should be so interesting to hear about it."

"Why talk about that place?" I said. "We've forgotten how to have fun back there. We take ourselves very seriously, and we figure out the most elaborate excuses for doing the rottenest things to each other ..."

I shook my head. I didn't like that train of thought. "See," I said, "I always talk like that with my gloves off." I pulled them on again. "And now," I said grandly, "may I have the pleasure of this dance?"

It was half an hour before we went back inside to visit the punchbowl. The orchestra had just begun a waltz when a shattering blast rocked the floor, and the tall glass doors along the east side of the ballroom blew in. Through the cloud of dust which followed up the explosion, a swarm of men in motley remnants of uniforms leaped into the room. The leader, a black-bearded giant wearing a faded and patched U.S. Army-type battle jacket and baggy Wehrmacht trousers, jacked the lever on the side of a short drum-fed machine gun, and squeezed a long burst into the thick of the crowd.

Men and women alike fell under the murdering attack, but every man who remained on his feet rushed the nearest attacker without hesitation. Standing in the rubble, a bristle-faced redhead wearing an undersized British sergeant's blouse pumped eight shots from the hip, knocking down an on-coming officer of the Imperium with every shot; when he stepped back to jam a new clip into the M-1, the ninth man ran him through the throat with a jewel-encrusted rapier.

I still stood frozen, holding my girl's hand. I whirled, started to shout to her to get back, to run; but the calm look I saw in her eyes stopped me. She'd rather be decently dead than flee this rabble.

I jerked my toy sword from its scabbard, dashed to the wall, and moved along it to the edge of the gaping opening. As the next man pushed through the cloud of dust and smoke, peering ahead, gripping a shotgun, I jammed the point of sword into his neck, hard, and jerked it back before it was wrenched from my hands. He stumbled on, choking, shotgun falling with a clatter. I reached out, raked it in, as another man appeared. He carried a Colt .45 in his left hand, and he saw me as I saw him. He swiveled to fire, and as he did I brought the poised blade down on his arm. The shot went into the floor and the pistol bounced out of the loose hand. He fell back into the trampling crowd.

Another fellow lunged out of the dust, cutting across the room, and saw me. He levelled a heavy rifle on its side across his left forearm. He moved slowly and clumsily. I saw that his left hand was hanging by a thread. I grabbed up the shotgun and blew his face off. It had been about two minutes since the explosion.

I waited a moment, but no more came through the blasted window. I saw a wiry ruffian with long yellow hair falling back toward me as he pushed another magazine into a Browning automatic rifle. I jumped two steps, set the point of the sword just about where the kidneys should be, and rammed with both hands. No very elegant style, I thought, but I'm just a beginner.

I saw Goering then, arms around a tall fellow who cursed and struggled to raise his battered sub-machine gun. A gun roared in my ear and the back of my neck burned. I realize my jump had literally saved my neck. I ran around to the side of the grappling pair, and shoved the blade into the man's ribs. It grated and stuck, but he wilted. I'm not much of a sport, I thought, but I guess guns against pig-stickers makes it even.

Hermann stepped back, spat disgustedly, and leaped on the nearest bandit. I wrenched at my sword, but it was wedged tight. I left it and grabbed up the tommy gun. A long-legged villain was just closing the chamber of his revolver as I pumped a burst into his stomach. I saw dust fly from the shabby cloth of his coat as the slugs smacked home.

I glanced around. Several of the men of the Imperium were firing captured guns now, and the remnant of the invading mob had fallen back toward the shattered wall. Bullets cut them down as they stood at bay, still pouring out a ragged fire. None of them tried to flee.

I ran forward, sensing something wrong. I raised my gun and cut down a bloody-faced man as he stood firing two .45 automatics. My last round nicked a heavy-set carbine man, and the drum was empty. I picked up another weapon from the floor, as one lone thug standing pounded the bolt of his rifle with his palm.

"Take him alive," someone shouted. The firing stopped and a dozen men seized the struggling man. The crowd milled, women bending over those who lay on the floor, men staggering from their exertions. I ran toward the billowing drapes.

"Come on," I shouted. "Outside ..." I didn't have time or breath to say more, or to see if anyone came. I leaped across the rubble, out onto the blasted terrace, leaped the rail, and landed in the garden, sprawled a little, but still moving. In the light of the colored floods a grey-painted van, ponderously bulky, sat askew across flower beds. Beside it, three tattered crewmen struggled with a bulky load. A small tripod stood on the lawn, awaiting the momentary mental vision of what a fission bomb would do to the summer palace and its occupants, before I dashed at them with a yell. I fired the pistol I had grabbed, as fast as I could pull the trigger, and the three men hesitated, pulled against each other, cursed, and started back toward the open door of their van with the bomb. One of them fell, and I realized someone behind me was firing accurately. Another of the men yelped and ran off a few yards to crumple on the grass. The third jumped for the open door, and a moment later a rush of air threw dust against my face as the van flicked out of existence. The sound was like a pool of gasoline igniting.

The bulky package lay on the ground now, ominous. I felt sure it was not yet armed. I turned to the others. "Don't touch this thing," I called. "I'm sure it's some kind of atomic bomb."

"Nice work, old boy," a familiar voice said. It was Winter, blood spattered on the pale yellow of his tunic. "Might have known those chaps were fighting a delaying action for a reason. Are you all right?"

"Yeah," I said, breathless. "Let's go back inside. They'll need tourniquets and men to twist them."

We picked our way through the broken glass, fragments of flagstones, and splinters of framing, past the flapping drapes, into the brightly lit dust-rolled ballroom.

Dead and wounded lay in rough semicircle around the broken wall. I recognized a pretty brunette in a blue dress whom I had danced with earlier, lying on the floor, face waxen. Everyone was splattered with crimson. I looked around frantically for my redhead, and saw her kneeling beside a wounded man, binding his head.

There was a shout. Winter and I whirled. One of the wounded intruders moved, threw something, then collapsed as shots struck him. I heard the thump and the rattle as the object fell, and as in a dream I watched the grenade roll over and over, clattering, stop ten feet away and spin and turn. I stood frozen. Finished, I thought. And I never even learned her name.

From behind me I heard a gasp as Winter leaped past me and threw himself forward. He landed spread-eagled over the grenade as it exploded with a muffled thump, throwing Winter two feet into the air.

I staggered, and turned away, dizzy. Poor Winter. Poor damned Winter.

I felt myself passing out, and went to my knees. The floor was tilting.

She was bending over me, face pale, but still steady.

I reached up and touched her hand. "What's your name?" I said.

"My name?" she said. "Barbro Lundane. I thought you knew my name." She seemed a bit dazed.

I sat up. "Better lend a hand to someone who's worse off than I am, Barbro," I said. "I just have a weak constitution."

"No," she said. "You've bled much."

Richthofen appeared, looking grim. He helped me up. My neck and head ached. "Thank God you are alive," he said.

"Thank Winter I'm alive," I replied. "I don't suppose there's a chance . . . ?"

“Killed instantly,” Richthofen said. “He knew his duty.”

“Poor guy,” I said. “It should have been me.”

“We’re fortunate it wasn’t you,” Richthofen said. “It was close. As it is, you’ve lost considerable blood. You must come along and rest now.”

“I want to stay here,” I said. “Maybe I can do something useful.”

Goering had appeared from somewhere, and he laid an arm across my shoulders, leading me away.

“Calmly, now, my friend,” he said. “There is no need to feel it so strongly; he died in performance of his duty, as he would have wished.”

Hermann knew what was bothering me. I could have blanked out that grenade as easily as Winter, but the thought hadn’t even occurred to me. If I hadn’t been paralyzed, I’d have run.

I didn’t struggle; I felt washed out, suddenly suffering a premature hangover. Manfred joined us at the car, and we drove home in near silence. I asked about the bomb and Goering said that Bale’s men had taken it over. “Tell them to dump it at sea,” I said.

At the villa, someone waited on the steps as we drove up. I recognized Bale’s rangy figure with the undersized head. I ignored him as he collared Hermann.

I went into the dining room, poured a stiff drink at the sideboard, sat down.

The others came behind me, talking. I wondered where Bale had been all evening.

Bale sat down, eyeing me. He wanted to hear all about the attack. He seemed to take news calmly but sourly.

He looked at me, pursing his lips. “Mr. Goering has told me that you conducted yourself quite well, Mr. Bayard, during the fight. Perhaps I was hasty in my judgment of you."

"Who the hell cares what you think, Bale?" I said. "Where were you when the lead was flying? Under the rug?"

Bale turned white, stood up glaring and stalked out of the room. Goering cleared his throat and Manfred cast an odd look at me as he rose to perform his hostly duty of conducting a guest to the door.

"Inspector Bale is not a man easy to associate with," Hermann said. "I understand your feeling." He rose and came around the table.

"I feel you should know," he went on, "that he is among the most skillful with sabre and epee. Make no hasty decision now—"

"What decision?" I asked.

"Already you have a painful wound," he said. "We must not allow you to be laid up at this critical time. Are you sure of your skill with a pistol?"

"What wound?" I said. "You mean my neck?" I put my hand up to touch it. I winced; there was a deep gouge, caked with blood. Suddenly I was aware that the back of my jacket was soggy. That near-miss was a little nearer than I had thought.

"I hope you will accord Manfred and myself the honor of seconding you," Hermann continued, "and perhaps of advising you ..."

"What's this all about, Hermann?" I said. "What do you mean—seconding me?"

"Why," he seemed confused, "we wish to stand with you in your meeting with Bale."

"Meeting with Bale?" I repeated. I knew I didn't sound very bright. I was beginning to realize how lousy I felt.

Goering stopped and looked at me. "Inspector Bale is a man most sensitive of personal dignity," he said. "You have given him a tongue-lashing before witnesses, and a well deserved one it was; however, it remains a certainty that he will demand satisfaction." He saw that I was still groping. "Bale will challenge you, Brion," he said. "You must fight him."

CHAPTER 6

I was cold, chilled to the bone. I was still half asleep, and I carried my head tilted forward and a little to the side in a hopeless attempt to minimize the vast throbbing ache from the furrow across the back of my neck.

Richthofen, Goering and I stood together under spreading linden trees at the lower end of the Royal Game Park. It was a few minutes before dawn and I was wondering how a slug in the kneecap would feel.

There was the faint sound of an engine approaching, and a long car loomed up in the gloom on the road above, lights gleaming through morning mist.

The sound of doors opening and slamming was muffled and indistinct. Three figures were dimly visible, approaching down the gentle slope. My seconds moved away to meet them. One of the three detached itself from the group and stood alone, as I did. That would be Bale.

Another car pulled in behind the first. The doctor, I thought. In the dim glow from the second car's small square cowl lights I saw another figure emerge. I watched; it looked like a woman.

I heard a murmur of voices, a low chuckle. They were very palsy, I thought. Everything on a very high plane.

I thought over what Goering had told me on the way to the field of honor, as he called it.

Bale had offered his challenge under the Toth convention. This meant that the duelists must not try to kill each other; the object of the game was to inflict painful wounds, to humiliate one's opponent.

This could be a pretty tricky business. In the excitement of the fight, it wasn't easy to inflict wounds that were thoroughly humiliating but definitely not fatal.

Richthofen had lent me a pair of black trousers and a white shirt for the performance, and a light overcoat against the pre-dawn chill. I wished it had been a heavy one. The only warm part of me was my neck, swathed in bandages.

The little group broke up now. My two backers approached, smiled encouragingly, and in low voices invited me to come along. Goering took my coat. I missed it.

Bale and his men were walking toward a spot in the clear, where the early light was slightly better. We moved up to join them.

"I think we have light enough now, eh, Baron?" said Hallendorf.

I could see better now; the light was increasing rapidly. Long pink streamers flew in the east; the trees were still dark in silhouettes.

Hallendorf stepped up to me, and offered the pistol box. I picked one of the pistols, without looking at it. Bale took the other, methodically worked the action, snapped the trigger, examined the rifling. Richthofen handed each of us a magazine.

"Five rounds," he said. I had no comment.

Bale stepped over to the place indicated by Hallendorf and turned his back. I could see the cars outlined against the sky now. The big one looked like a '30 Packard, I thought. At Goering's gesture, I took my post, back to Bale.

"At the signal, gentlemen," Hallendorf said, "step forward ten paces and pause; at the command turn and fire. Gentlemen, in the name of the Emperor and of honor!"

The white handkerchief in his hand fluttered to the ground. I started walking. One, two, three ...

There was someone standing by the smaller car. I wondered who it was ... eight, nine, ten. I stopped, waiting. Hallendorf's voice was calm. "Turn and fire."

I turned, holding the pistol at my side. Bale pumped a cartridge into the chamber, set his feet apart, body sideways to me, left arm behind his back, and raised his pistol. We were seventy feet apart across the wet field.

I started walking toward him. Nobody had said I had to stay in one spot. Bale lowered his pistol slightly and I saw his pale face, eyes staring. The pistol came up again, and almost instantly jumped as a flat crack rang out. The spent cartridge popped up over Bale's head and dropped on the wet grass, catching the light. A miss.

I walked on. I had no intention of standing in the half dark, firing wildly at a half-seen target. I didn't intend to be forced into killing a man by accident, even if it was his idea. And I didn't intend to be pushed into solemnly playing Bale's game with him.

Bale held the automatic at arm's length, following me as I approached. He could have killed me easily, but that was against the code. The weapon wavered; he couldn't decide on a target. My moving was bothering him.

The pistol steadied and jumped again, the shot sounding faint on the foggy air. I realized he was trying for the legs; I was close enough now to see the depressed angle of the barrel.

He stepped back a pace, set himself again, and raised the Mauser higher. He was going to try to break a rib, I guessed.

A tricky shot, easy to miss—either way. My stomach muscles tensed with anticipation.

I didn't hear the next one; the sensation was exactly like a baseball bat slammed against my side. I felt that I was stumbling, air knocked from my lungs, but I kept my feet. A great warm ache spread from just above the hip. Only twenty feet away now. I fought a draw of breath.

Bale's expression was visible, a stiff shocked look, mouth squeezed shut. He aimed at my feet and fired in rapid succession; I think by error. One shot went through my boot between the toes of my right foot, the other in the dirt. I walked up to him. I sucked air in painfully. I wanted to say something, but I couldn't. It was all I could do to keep from gasping. Abruptly, Bale backed a step, aimed the pistol at my chest and pulled the trigger; it clicked. He looked down at the gun.

I dropped the Mauser at his feet, doubled my fist, and hit him hard on the jaw. He reeled back as I turned away.

I walked over to Goering and Richthofen as the doctor hurried up. They came forward to meet me.

"Lieber Gott," Hermann breathed as he seized my hand and pumped it. "This story they will never believe."

"If your object was to make a fool of Inspector Bale," Richthofen said with a gleam in his eye, "you have scored an unqualified success. I think you have taught him respect."

The doctor pressed forward. "Gentlemen, I must take a look at the wound." A stool was produced, and I gratefully sank down on it.

I stuck my foot out. "Better take a look at this too," I said, "it feels a little tender."

The doctor muttered and exclaimed as he began snipping at the cloth and leather. He was enjoying every minute of it. The doc, I saw, was a romantic.

A thought was trying to form itself in my mind. I opened my eyes. Barbro was coming toward me across the grass, dawn light gleaming in her red hair. I realized what it was I had to say.

"Hermann," I said. "Manfred. I need a long nap, but before I start I think I ought to tell you; I've had so much fun tonight that I've decided to take the job."

"Easy, Brion," Manfred said. "There's no need to think of it now."

"No trouble at all," I said.

Barbro bent over. "Brion," she said. "You are not badly hurt?" She looked worried.

I smiled at her and reached for her hand. "I'll bet you think I'm accident prone; but actually I sometimes go for days at a time without so much as a bad fall."

She took my hand in both of hers as she knelt down. "You must be suffering great pain, Brion, to talk so foolishly," she said. "I thought he would lose his head and kill you." She turned to the doctor. "Help him, Dr. Blum."

"You are fortunate, Colonel," the doctor said, sticking a finger into the furrow on my side. "The rib is not fractured. In a few days you will have only a little scar and a big bruise to remind you."

I squeezed Barbro's hand. "Help me up, Barbro," I said.

Goering gave me his shoulder to lean on. "For you now, a long nap," he said. I was ready for it.

CHAPTER 7

I tried to relax in my chair in the cramped shuttle. Just in front of me the operator sat tensed over a tiny illuminated board, peering at instrument faces and tapping the keys of what looked like a miniature calculating machine. A soundless hum filled the air, penetrating my bones.

I twisted, seeking a more comfortable position. My half-healed neck and side were stiffening up again. Bits and fragments of the last ten days' incessant briefing ran through my mind. Imperial Intelligence hadn't been able to gather as much material as they wanted on Marshal of the State Bayard, but it was more than I was able to assimilate consciously. I hoped the hypnotic sessions I had had every night for a week in place of real sleep had taken at a level where the data would pop up when I needed it.

Bayard was a man of mystery, even to his own people. He was rarely seen, except via what the puzzled Intelligence men said seemed to be a sort of electric picture apparatus. I had tried to explain that TV was commonplace in my world, but they never really understood it.

They had given me a good night's sleep the last three nights, and a tough hour of cleverly planned calisthenics every day. My wounds had healed well, so that now I was physically ready for the adventure; mentally, however, I was fagged. The result was an eagerness to get on with the thing and find out the worst of what I was faced with. I had enough of words; now I wanted the relief of action.

I checked over my equipment. I wore a military tunic duplicating that shown in the official portrait of Bayard. Since there was no information on what he wore below the chest, I had suggested olive drab trousers, matching what I recognized as the French regulation jacket.

At my advice, we'd skipped the ribbons and orders shown in the photo; I didn't think he would wear them around his private apartment in an informal situation. For the same reason, my collar was unbuttoned and my tie loosened.

They had kept me on a diet of lean beefsteak, to try to thin my face a bit. A hair specialist had given me vigorous scalp massages every morning and evening, and insisted that I not wash my head. This was intended to stimulate rapid growth and achieve the unclipped continental look of the dictator's picture.

Snapped to my belt was a small web pouch containing my communication transmitter. We had decided to let it show rather than seek with doubtful success to conceal it. The microphone was woven into the heavy braid on my lapels. I had a thick stack of NPS currency in my wallet.

I moved my right hand carefully, feeling for the pressure of the release spring that would throw the palm-sized slug-gun into my hand with the proper flexing of the wrist.

The little weapon was a marvel of compact deadliness. In shape it resembled a water-washed stone, grey and smooth. It could lie unnoticed on the ground, a feature which might be of great importance to me in an emergency.

Inside the gun a hair-sized channel spiraled down into the grip. A compressed gas, filling the tiny hole, served as both propellant and projectile. At a pressure on the right spot, unmarked, a minute globule of the liquefied gas was fired with tremendous velocity. Once free of the confining walls of the tough alloy barrel, the bead expanded explosively to a volume of a cubic foot. The result was an almost soundless blow, capable of shattering one-quarter inch armor, instantly fatal within a range of ten feet.

It was the kind of weapon I needed—inconspicuous, quiet, and deadly at short range. The spring arrangement made it almost a part of the hand, if the hand were expert.

I had practiced the motion for hours, while listening to lectures, eating, even lying in bed. I was very conscientious about that piece of training; it was my insurance. I tried not to think about my other insurance, set in the hollowed-out bridge replacing a back tooth.

Each evening, after the day's hard routine, I had relaxed with new friends, exploring the Imperial Ballet, theatres, opera and a lively variety show. With Barbro, I had dined sumptuously at half a dozen fabulous restaurants and afterwards walked in moonlit gardens, sipped coffee as the sun rose, and talked. When the day came to leave, I had more than a casual desire to return. The sooner I got started, the quicker I would get back.

The operator turned. "Colonel," he said, "brace yourself, sir. There's something here I don't understand."

I tensed, but said nothing. I figured he would tell me more as soon as he knew more. I moved my hand tentatively against the slug-gun release. I already had the habit.

"I've detected a moving body in the Net," he said. "It seems to be trying to match our course. My spatial fix on it indicates it's very near."

The Imperium was decades behind my world in nuclear physics, television, aerodynamics, etc., but when it came to the instrumentation of these Maxoni devices, they were fantastic. After all, they had devoted their best scientific efforts to the task for almost sixty years.

Now the operator hovered over his panel controls like a nervous organist.

"I get a mass of about fifteen hundred kilos," he said. "That's about right for a light scout, but it can't be one of ours ..."

There was a tense silence for several minutes.

"He's pacing us, Colonel," the operator said. "Either they've got better instrumentation than we thought, or this chap has had a stroke of blind luck. He was lying in wait."

Both of us were assuming the stranger could be nothing but a B-I Two vessel.

The operator tensed up suddenly, hands frozen. "He's coming in on us, Colonel," he said. "He's going to ram. We'll blow sky-high if he crosses our fix."

My thoughts ran like lightning over my slug-gun—the hollow tooth; I wondered what would happen when he hit. Somehow, I hadn't expected it to end here. The impossible tension lasted only a few seconds. The operator relaxed.

"Missed," he said. "Apparently his spatial maneuvering isn't as good as his Net mobility. But he'll be back; he's after blood."

I had a thought. "Our maximum rate is controlled by the energy of normal entropy, isn't it?" I asked.

He nodded.

"What about going slower?" I said. "Maybe he'll overshoot."

I could see the sweat start on the back of his neck from here.

"A bit risky in the Blight, sir," he said, "but we'll have a go at it."

I knew how hard that was for an operator to say. This young fellow had had six years of intensive training, and not a day of it had passed without a warning against any unnecessary control changes in the Blight.

The sound of the generators changed, the pitch of the whine descending into the audible range, dropping lower.

"He's still with us, Colonel," the operator said.

The pitch fell lower. I didn't know what critical point would be reached when we would lose our artificial orientation and rotate into normal entropy. We sat rigid, waiting. The sound dropped down, almost baritone now. The operator tapped again and again at a key, glancing at a dial.

The drive hum was a harsh droning now; we couldn't expect to go much further without disaster. But then neither could the enemy.

"He's right with us, Colonel, only—" Suddenly the operator shouted.

"We lost him, Colonel! His controls aren't as good as ours in that line, anyway; he dropped into identity."

I sank back, as the whine of our MC generator built up again. My palms were wet. I wondered into which of the hells of the Blight they had gone. But I had another problem to face in a few minutes. This was not the time for shaken nerves.

"Good work, operator," I said at last. "How much longer?"

"About—good God—ten minutes, sir," he answered. "That little business took longer than I thought."

I started a last minute check. My mouth was dry. Everything seemed to be in place. I pressed the button on my communicator.

"Hello, Talisman," I said, "here is Wolfhound Red. How do you hear me? Over."

"Wolfhound Red, Talisman here, you're coming in right and bright, over." The tiny voice spoke almost in my ear from the speaker in a button on my shoulder strap.

I liked the instant response; I felt a little less lonesome.

I looked at the trip mechanism for the escape door. I was to wait for the operator to say, "Crash out," and hit the lever. I had exactly two seconds then to pull my arm back and kick the slug-gun into my palm before the seat would automatically dump me, standing, out the exit. The shuttle would be gone before my feet hit the floor.

I had been so wrapped up in the business at hand for the past ten days that I had not really thought about the moment of my arrival in the B-I Two world. The smoothly professional handling of my hasty training had given the job an air of practicality and realism. Now, about to be propelled into the innermost midst of the enemy, I began to realize the suicidal aspects of the mission. But it was too late now for second thoughts—and in a way I was glad. I was involved now in this world of the Imperium; it was a part of my life worth risking something for.

I was a card the Imperium held, and it was my turn to be played. I was valuable property, but that value could only be realized by putting me into the scene in just this way, and the sooner the better. I had no assurance that the dictator was in residence at the palace now; I might find myself hiding in his quarters awaiting his return, for God knows how long—and maybe lucky at that, to get that far. I hoped our placement of the suite was correct, based on information gotten from the captive taken at the ballroom, under deep narcohypnosis. Otherwise, I might find myself treading air, 150 feet up.

There was a slamming of switches, and the operator twisted in his chair.

"Crash out, Wolfhound," he cried, "and good hunting."

Reach out and slam the lever; arm at the side, snap the gun into place in my hand; with a metallic whack and a rush of air the exit popped and a giant hand palmed me out into dimness. One awful instant of vertigo, of a step missed in the dark, and then my feet slammed against carpeted floor. Air whipped about my face, and the echoes of the departing boom of the shuttle still hung in the corridor.

I remembered my instructions. I stood still, turning casually to check behind me. There was no one in sight. The hall was dark except for the faint light from a ceiling fixture at the next intersection. I had arrived.

I slipped the gun back into its latch under my cuff. No point in standing here; I started off at a leisurely pace toward the light. The doors lining the hall were identical, unmarked. I paused and tried one. Locked. So was the next. The third one opened, and I looked cautiously into a sitting room. I went on. What I wanted was the sleeping room of the dictator, if possible. If he were in, I knew what to do; if not, presumably he would return if I waited long enough. Meanwhile, I wanted very much not to meet anyone.

There was the sound of an elevator door opening, just around the corner ahead. I stopped. I eased back to the last door I had checked, opened it and stepped inside, closing it almost all the way behind me. My heart was thudding painfully. I didn't feel daring; I felt like a sneak thief. Faintly, I heard steps coming my way.

I silently closed the door, taking care not to let the latch click. I stood behind it for a moment before deciding it would be better to conceal myself, just in case. I glanced around, moving into the center of the room. I could barely make out outlines in the gloom. There was a tall shape against the wall—a wardrobe, I thought. I hurried across to it, opened the door, and stepped in among hanging clothes.

I stood for a moment, feeling foolish, then froze as the

door to the hall opened and closed again softly. There were no footsteps, and then a light went on. My closet door was open just enough to catch a glimpse of a man's back as he turned away from the lamp. I heard the soft sound of a chair being pulled out, and then the tiny jingle of keys. There were faint metallic sounds, a pause, more faint metallic sounds. The man was apparently trying keys in the lock of a table or desk.

I stood absolutely rigid. I breathed shallowly, tried not to think about a sudden itch on my cheek. I could see the shoulder of the coat hanging to my left. I turned my eyes to it. It was almost identical with the one I was wearing. The lapels were adorned with heavy braid. I had a small moment of relief; I had found the right apartment, at least. But my victim must be the man in the room; and I had never felt less like killing anyone in my life.

The little sounds went on. I could hear the man's heavy breathing. All at once I wondered what he would look like, this double of mine. Would he really resemble me, or more to the point, did I look enough like him to take his place?

I wondered why he took so long finding the right key; then another thought struck me. Didn't this sound a little more like someone trying to open someone else's desk? I moved my head a fraction of an inch. The clothes moved silently, and I edged a little farther. Now I could see him. He sat hunched in the chair, working impatiently on the lock. He was short and had thin hair, and resembled me not in the least. It was not the dictator.

This was a new factor for me to think over, and in a hurry. The dictator was obviously not around, or this fellow would not be here attempting to rifle his desk. And the dictator had people around him who were not above prying. That fact might be useful to me.

It took him five minutes to find a key that fit. I stood with muscles aching from the awkward pose, trying not to think of the lint that might cause a sneeze. I could hear the shuffling of papers and faint muttering as the man looked over his finds. At length there was the sound of the drawer closing, the click of the lock. Now the man was on his feet, the chair pushed back, and then silence for a few moments. Steps came toward me. I froze, my wrist twitching, ready to cover him and fire if necessary the instant he pulled the door open. I wasn't ready to start my imposture just yet, skulking in a closet.

I let out a soundless sigh as he passed the opening and disappeared. More sounds as he ran through the drawers of a bureau or chest.

Suddenly the hall door opened again, and another set of steps entered the room. I heard my man freeze. Then he spoke, in guttural French.

"Oh, it's you, is it, Maurice."

There was a pause. Maurice's tone was insinuating.

"Yes, I thought I saw a light in the chief's study. I thought that was a bit odd, what with him away tonight."

The first man sauntered back toward the center of the room. "I just thought I'd have a look to see that everything was OK here."

Maurice tittered. "Don't try to rob a thief, Georges; I know why you came here—for the same reason as I."

"What are you up to?" the first man hissed. "What do you want?"

"Sit down, Flic. Oh, don't get excited; they call you that." Maurice was enjoying himself. I listened carefully for half an hour while he goaded and cajoled, and pressured the other. The first man, I learned, was Georges Pinay, the chief of the dictator's security force. The other man was a civilian military adviser to the Bureau of Propaganda and Education. Pinay, it seemed, had been less clever than he thought in planning a *coup* that was to unseat Bayard. Maurice knew all about it, and had bided his time; and now he was taking over. Pinay didn't like it, but he accepted it after Maurice mentioned a few things nobody was supposed to know about a hidden airplane and a deposit of gold coins buried a few miles outside the city.

I listened carefully, without moving, and after a while even the itch went away. Pinay had been looking for lists of names, he admitted; he planned to enlist a few more supporters by showing them their names in the dictator's own hand on the purge schedule. He hadn't planned to mention that he himself had nominated them for the list.

I made the mistake of over-confidence; I was just waiting for them to finish up when a sudden silence fell. I didn't know what I had done wrong, but I knew at once what was coming. The steps were very quiet and there was just a moment's pause before the door was flung open. I hoped my make-up was on straight.

I stepped out, casting a cool glance at Pinay.

"Well, Georges," I said, "it's nice to know you keep yourself occupied when I'm away." I used the same French dialect they had used, and my wrist was against the little lever.

"The devil," Maurice burst out. He stared at me with wide eyes. For a moment I thought I was going to get away with it. Then Pinay lunged at me. I whirled, side-stepped; and the slug-gun slapped my palm.

"Hold it," I barked.

Pinay ignored the order and charged again. I squeezed the tiny weapon, bracing myself against the recoil. There was a solid thump and Pinay bounced aside, landed on his back, loose-limbed, and lay still. Then Maurice hit me from the side.

I stumbled across the room, tripped and fell, and he was on top of me. I still had my gun, and tried to bring it into play, but I was dazed, and Maurice was fast and strong as a bull. He flipped me and held me in a one-handed judo hold that pinned both arms behind me. He was astride me, breathing heavily.

"Who are you?" he hissed.

"I thought you'd know me, Maurice," I said. With infinite care I groped, tucked the slug-gun into my cuff. I heard it click home and I relaxed.

"So you thought that, eh?" Maurice laughed. His face was pink and moist. He pulled a heavy blackjack from his pocket as he slid off me.

"Get up," he said. He looked me over.

"My God," he said. "Fantastic. Who sent you?"

I didn't answer. It seemed I wasn't fooling him for a minute. I wondered what was wrong. Still, he seemed to find my appearance interesting. He stepped forward and slammed the sap against my neck, with a controlled motion. He could have broken my neck with it, but what he did was more painful. I felt the blood start from my half-healed neck wound. He saw it, and looked puzzled for a moment. Then his face cleared.

"Excuse me," he said grinning. "I'll try for a fresh spot next time. And answer when spoken to." There was a viciousness in his voice that reminded me of the attack at the palace. These men had seen hell on earth and they were no longer fully human.

He looked at me appraisingly, slapping his palm with the blackjack. "I think we'll have a little talk downstairs," he said. "Keep the hands in sight." His eyes darted about, apparently looking for my gun. He was very sure of himself; he didn't let it worry him when he didn't see it. He didn't want to take his eyes off me long enough to really make a search.

"Stay close, Baby," he said. "Just like that, come along now, nice and easy."

I kept my hands away from my sides, and followed him over to the phone. He wasn't as good as he thought; I could have taken him any time. I had a hunch, though, that it might be better to string along a little, to find out something more.

Maurice picked up the phone, spoke softly into it and dropped it back in the cradle. His eyes stayed on me.

"How long before they get here?" I asked.

Maurice narrowed his eyes, not answering.

"Maybe we have just time enough to make a deal," I said.

His mouth curved in what might have been a smile. "We'll make a deal all right, Baby," he said. "You sing loud and clear, and maybe I'll tell the boys to make it a fast finish."

"You've got an ace up your sleeve here, Maurice," I urged. "Don't let that rabble in on it."

He slapped his palm again. "What have you got in mind, Baby?"

"I'm on my own," I said. I was thinking fast. "I'll bet you never knew Brion had a twin brother. He cut me out, though, so I thought I'd cut myself in."

Maurice was interested. "The devil," he said. "You haven't seen your loving twin in a long time, I see." He grinned. I wondered what the joke was.

"Let's get out of here," I said. "Let's keep it between us two."

Maurice glanced at Pinay.

"Forget him," I said. "He's dead."

"You'd like that, wouldn't you, Baby?" Maurice said. "Just the two of us, and maybe then a chance to narrow it back down to one." His sardonic expression turned suddenly to a snarl, with nostrils flaring. "By God," he said, "you, you'd plan to kill me, you little man of straw—" He was leaning toward me now, arm loosening for a swing. I realized he was insane, ready to kill in an instantaneous fury.

"You'll see who is the killer between us," he said. His eyes gleamed as he swung the blackjack loosely in his hand.

I couldn't wait any longer. The gun popped into my hand, aimed at Maurice. I felt myself beginning to respond to his murder lust. I hated everything he stood for.

"You're stupid, Maurice," I said. "Stupid and slow, and in just a minute, dead. But first you're going to tell me how you knew I wasn't Bayard."

It was a nice try, but wasted.

Maurice leaped and the slug-gun slapped him aside. He hit and lay limp. My arm ached from the recoil. Handling the tiny weapon was tricky. It was good for about fifty shots on a charge; at this rate it wouldn't last a day.

I had to get out fast now. I reached up and smashed the ceiling light, then the table lamp. That might slow them up for a few moments. I eased out into the hall and started for the dark end. Behind me I heard the elevator opening. They were here already. I pushed at the glass door, and it swung open quietly. I didn't wait around to see what their reaction would be when they found Maurice and Georges. I went down the stairs two at a time, as softly as I could. I thought of my communicator and decided against it. I didn't have anything good to report.

I passed three landings before I emerged into a hall. This would be the old roof level. I tried to remember where the stair had come out in the analogous spot at Zero Zero. I spotted a small door in an alcove; it seemed to be in about the right place.

A man came out of a room across the hall and glanced toward me. I rubbed my mouth thoughtfully, while heading for the little door. The resemblance was more of a hindrance than a help now. He went on, and I tried the door. It was locked, but it didn't look very strong. I put my hip against it and pushed. It gave way with no more than a mild splintering sound. The stairs were there, and I headed down.

I had no plan other than to get in the clear. It was obvious that the impersonation was a complete flop. All I could do was get to a safe place and ask for further instructions. I had gone down two flights when I heard the alarm bell start.

I stopped dead. I had to get rid of the fancy uniform. I pulled off the jacket, then settled for tearing the braid off the wrists, and removing the shoulder tabs. I couldn't ditch the lapel braid; my microphone was woven into it. I couldn't do much else about my appearance.

This unused stair was probably as good a way out as any. I kept going. I checked the door at each floor. They were all locked. That was a good sign, I thought. The stair ended in a cul-de-sac filled with barrels and mildewed paper cartons. I went back up to the next landing and listened. Beyond the door there were loud voices and the clatter of feet. I remembered that the entry to the stair was near the main entrance to the old mansion. It looked like I was trapped.

I went down again, pulled one of the barrels aside. I peered behind it at the wall. The edge of a door frame was visible. I maneuvered another barrel out of place and found the knob. It was frozen. I wondered how much noise I could make without being heard. Not much, I decided.

I needed something to pry with. The paper cartons looked like a possibility; I tore the flaps loose on one and looked in. It was filled with musty ledger books; no help.

The next was better. Old silverware, pots and pans. I dug out a heavy cleaver and slipped it into the crack. The thing was as solid as a bank vault. I tried again; it couldn't be that strong, but it didn't budge.

I stepped back. Maybe the only thing to do was forget caution and chop through the middle. I leaned over to pick the best spot to swing at—then jumped back flat against the wall, slug-gun in my hand. The door knob was turning.

CHAPTER 8

I was close to panic; being cornered had that effect on me. I didn't know what to do. I had plenty of instructions on how to handle the job of taking over after I had succeeded in killing the dictator, but none to cover retreat after failure.

There was a creak, and dust sifted down from the top of the door. I stood as far back as I could get, waiting. I had an impulse to start shooting, but restrained it. Wait and see.

The door edged open a crack. I really didn't like this; I was being looked over, and could see nothing myself. At least I had the appearance of being unarmed; the tiny gun was concealed in my hand. Or was that an advantage? I couldn't decide.

I didn't like suspense. "All right," I said. "You're making a draft. In or out." I spoke in the gutter Parisian I had heard upstairs.

The door opened farther, and a grimy-faced fellow was visible beyond it. He blinked in the dim light, peered up the stairs. He gestured.

"This way, come on," he said in a hoarse whisper. I didn't see any reason to refuse under the circumstances. I stepped past the barrels and ducked through the low doorway. As the man closed the door, I slipped the gun back into its clip. I was standing in a damp stone-lined tunnel, lit by an electric lantern sitting on the floor. I stood with my back to it. I didn't want him to see my face yet, not in a good light.

"Who are you?" I asked.

The fellow pushed past me and picked up his lantern. He hardly glanced at me.

"I'm just a dumb guy," he said. "I don't ask no questions, I don't answer none. Come on."

I couldn't afford to argue that point so I followed him. We made our way along the hand-hewn corridor, then down a twisting flight of steps, to emerge into a dark windowless chamber. Two men and a dark-haired girl sat around a battered table where a candle spluttered.

"Call them in, Miche," my guide said. "Here's the pigeon."

Miche lolled back in his chair and motioned me toward him. He picked up what looked like a letter-knife from the table and probed between two back teeth while he squinted at me. I made a point not to get too close.

"One of the kennel dogs, by the uniform," he said. "What's the matter, you bit the hand that fed you?" He laughed humorously.

I said nothing. I thought I'd give him a chance to tell me something first if he felt like it.

"A ranker, too, by the braid," he said. "Well, they'll wonder where you got to." His tone changed. "Let's have the story," he said. "Why are you on the run?"

"Don't let the suit bother you," I said. "I borrowed it. But it seemed like the people up there disliked me on sight."

"Come on over here," the other man said. "Into the light."

I couldn't put it off forever. I moved forward, right up to the table. Just to be sure they got the idea, I picked up the candle and held it by my face.

Miche froze, knife point in his teeth. The girl started violently and crossed herself. The other man stared, fascinated. I'd gone over pretty big. I put the candle back on the table and sat down casually in the empty chair.

"Maybe you can tell me," I said, "why they didn't buy it."

The second man spoke. "You just walked in like that, sprung it on them?"

I nodded.

He and Miche looked at each other.

"You've got a very valuable property here, my friend," the man said. "But you need a little help. Chica, bring wine for our new friend here."

The girl, still wide-eyed, scuttled to a dingy cupboard and fumbled for a bottle, looking at me over her shoulder.

"Look at him sitting there, Gros," Miche said. "Now that's something."

"You're right that's something," Gros said. "If it isn't already loused up." He leaned across the table. "Now just what happened upstairs?" he said. "How long have you been in the palace? How many have seen you?"

I gave them a brief outline, leaving out my mode of arrival. They seemed satisfied.

"Only two seen his face, Gros," Miche said, "and they're out of the picture." He turned to me. "That was a nice bit of work, mister, knocking off Souvet; and nobody ain't going to miss Pinay neither. By the way, where's the gun? Better let me have it." He held out his hand.

"I had to leave it," I said. "Tripped and dropped it in the dark."

Miche grunted.

"The Boss will be interested in this," Gros said. "He'll want to see him."

Someone else panted up the stairs into the room. "Say, Chief," he began, "we make it trouble in the tower—" He stopped dead as he caught sight of me, and dropped into a crouch, utter astonishment on his face. His hand clawed for a gun at his hip, found none, as his eyes darted from face to face.

"What—what—"

Gros and Miche burst into raucous laughter, slapping the table and howling. "At ease, Spider," Miche managed. "Bayard's throwed in with us." At this even Chica snickered.

Spider still crouched. "OK, what's the deal?" he gasped. "I don't get it." He glared around the room, face white. He was scared stiff. Miche wiped his face, whooped a last time, hawked and spat on the floor.

"OK, Spider, as you were," he said. "This here's a ringer. Now you better go bring in the boys. Beat it."

Spider scuttled away. I was puzzled. Why did some of them take one startled look and relax, while this fellow was apparently completely taken in? I had to find out. There was something I was doing wrong.

"Do you mind telling me," I said, "what's wrong with the get-up?" Miche and Gros exchanged glances again.

"Well, my friend," Gros said, "it's nothing we can't take care of. Just take it easy, and we'll set you right. You wanted to step in and take out the Old Man, and sit in for him, right? Well, with the Organization behind you you're as good as in."

"What's the Organization?" I asked.

Miche broke in. "For now we'll ask the questions," he said. "What's your name? What's your play here?"

I looked from Miche to Gros. I wondered which one was the boss. "My name's Bayard," I said.

Miche narrowed his eyes as he rose and walked around the table. He was a big fellow with small eyes.

"I asked you what's your name, mister?" he said. "I don't usually ask twice."

"Hold it, Miche," Gros said. "He's right. He's got to stay

in this part, if he's going to be good; and he better be plenty good. Let's leave it at that; he's Bayard."

Miche looked at me. "Yeah," he said, "you got a point." I had a feeling Miche and I weren't going to get along.

"Who's backing you, uh, Bayard?" Gros said.

"I play a lone hand," I said. "Up to now, anyway. But it seems I missed something. If your Organization can get me in, I'll go along."

"We'll get you in, all right," Miche said.

I didn't like the looks of this pair of hoodlums, but I could hardly expect high-toned company here. As far as I could guess, the Organization was an underground anti-Bayard party. The room seemed to be hollowed out of the walls of the palace. Apparently they ran a spying operation all through the building, using hidden passages.

More men entered the room now, some via the stair, others through a door in the far corner. Apparently the word had gone out. They gathered around, staring curiously, commenting to each other, but not surprised.

"These are the boys," Gros said, looking around at them. "The rats in the walls."

I looked them over, about a dozen piratical-looking toughs; Gros had described them well. I looked back at him. "All right," I said. "Where do we start?" These weren't the kind of companions I would have chosen, but if they could fill in the gaps in my disguise for me, and help me take over in Bayard's place, I could only be grateful for my good luck.

"Not so fast," Miche said. "This thing is going to take time. We got to get you to a layout we got out of town. We got a lot of work ahead of us."

"I'm here now," I said. "Why not go ahead today? Why leave here?"

"We got a little work to do on your disguise," Gros said, "and there's plans to make. How do we get the most out of this break and how do we make sure there's no wires on this?"

"And no double-cross," Miche added.

A hairy lout listening in the crowd spoke up.

"I don't like the looks of this stool, Miche. I don't like funny stuff. I say under the floor with him." He wore a worn commando knife in a sheath fixed horizontally to his belt buckle. I was pretty sure he was eager to use it.

Miche looked at me. "Not for now, Gaston," he said.

Gros rubbed his chin. "Don't get worried about Mr. Bayard, boys," he said. "We'll have our eyes on him." He glanced up at Gaston. "You might make a special effort along those lines, Gaston; but don't get ahead of yourself. Let's say if he has any kind of accident, you'll have a worse one."

The feel of the spring under my wrist was comforting. I felt that Gaston wasn't the only one in this crew who didn't like strangers.

"I figure time is important," I said. "Let's get moving."

Miche stepped over to me. He prodded my leg with his boot. "You've got a flappy mouth, mister," he said. "Gros and me gives the orders around here."

"OK," Gros said. "Our friend has got a lot to learn, but he's right about the time. Bayard's due back here sometime tomorrow, so that means we get out today, if we don't want the Ducals all over the place on top of the regulars. Miche, get the boys moving. I want things folded fast and quiet, and good men on the stand-by crew."

He turned to me as Miche bawled orders to the men.

"Maybe you better have a little food now," he said. "It's going to be a long day."

I was startled. I had been thinking of it as night. I looked at my watch. It had been one hour and ten minutes since I had entered the palace. Doesn't time go fast, I thought to myself, when everyone's having fun.

Chica brought over a loaf of bread and a wedge of brown cheese from the cupboard, and placed them on the table with a knife. I was cautious.

"OK if I pick up the knife?" I asked.

"Sure," Gros said. "Go ahead." He reached under the table and laid a short-nosed revolver before him.

Miche came back to the table as I chewed on a slice of tough bread. It was good bread. I tried the wine. It wasn't bad. The cheese was good, too.

"You eat well," I said. "This is good."

Chica threw me a grateful smile. "We do all right," Gros said.

"Better get Mouth here out of that fancy suit," Miche said, jerking his head at me. "Somebody might just take a shot at that without thinking. The boys have got kind of nervous about them kind of suits."

Gros looked at me. "That's right," he said. "Miche will give you some other clothes. That uniform doesn't go over so big here."

I didn't like this development at all. My communicator was built into the scrambled eggs on my lapels. I had to say no and make it stick.

"Sorry," I said. "I keep this outfit. It's part of the act. I'll put a coat over it if necessary."

Miche put his foot against my chair and shoved; I saw it coming and managed to scramble to my feet instead of going over with the chair. Miche faced me.

"Strip, mister," he said. "You heard the man."

The men still in the room fell silent, watching. I looked at

Miche. I hoped Gros would speak up. I couldn't see anything to be gained by this.

Nobody spoke. I glanced over at Gros. He was just looking at us.

Miche reached behind, brought out a knife. The blade snickered out. "Or do I have to cut it off you," he growled.

"Put the knife away, Miche," Gros said mildly. "You don't want to cut up our secret weapon here; and we want the uniform off all in one piece."

"Yeah," Miche said. "You got a point." He dropped the knife on the table and moved in on me. From his practiced crouch and easy shuffling step, I saw that he had been a professional.

I decided not to wait for him. I threw myself forward with my weight behind a straight left to the jaw. It caught Miche by surprise, slammed against his chin and rocked him back. I tried to follow up, catch him again while he was still off balance, but he was a veteran of too many fights. He covered up, back-pedaled, shook his head, and then flicked out with a right that exploded against my temple. I was almost out, staggering. He hit me again, square on the nose. Blood flowed.

I wouldn't last long against this bruiser. The crowd was still bunched at the far end of the room, moving this way, now, watching delightedly, calling encouragement to Miche. Gros still sat, and Chica stared from her place by the wall.

I moved back, dazed, dodging blows. I had only one chance and I needed a dark corner to try it. Miche was right after me. He was mad; he didn't like that smack on the jaw in front of the boys. That helped me. He forgot boxing and threw one haymaker after another. He wanted to floor me with one punch to retrieve his dignity. I dodged and retreated.

I moved back toward the deep shadows at the end of the

room, beyond Chica's pantry. I had to get there quickly, before the watching crowd closed up the space.

Miche swung again, left, right. I heard the air whistle as his hamlike fist grazed me. I backed another step; almost far enough. Now to get between him and the rest of the room. I jumped in behind a wild swing, popped a stinging right off his ear, and kept going. I whirled, snapped the slug-gun into my hand, and as Miche lunged, I shot him in the stomach, faked a wild swinging attack as he bounced off the wall and fell full length at my feet. I slipped the gun back into my cuff and turned.

"I can't see," a man shouted. "Get some light down here." The mob pushed forward, forming a wide ring. They stopped as they saw that only I was on my feet.

"Miche is down," a man called. "The new guy took him."

Gros pushed his way through, hesitated, then walked over to the sprawled body of Miche. He squatted, beckoned to the man with the candle.

He pulled Miche over on his back, then looked closer, feeling for the heartbeat. He looked up abruptly, got to his feet.

"He's dead," he said. "Miche is dead." He looked at me with a strange expression. "It's quite a punch you got, mister," he said.

"I tried not to use it," I said. "But I'll use it again if I have to."

"Search him, boys," Gros said. They prodded and slapped, everywhere but my wrist. "He's clean, Gros," a man said. Gros looked the body over carefully, searching for signs of a wound. Men crowded around him.

"No marks," he said at last. "Broken ribs, and it feels like something funny inside; all messed up." He looked at me. "He did it barehanded."

I hoped they would go on believing that. It was my best insurance against a repetition. I wanted them scared of me, and the ethics of it didn't bother me at all.

"All right," Gros called to the men. "Back on the job. Miche asked for it. He called our new man 'Mouth.' I'm naming him 'Hammer-hand.'"

I thought this was as good a time as any to push a little farther.

"You'd better tell them I'm taking over Miche's spot, here, Gros," I said. "We'll work together, fifty-fifty."

Gros squinted at me. "Yeah, that figures," he said. I had a feeling he had mental reservations.

"And by the way," I added, "I keep the uniform."

"Yeah," Gros said. "He keeps the uniform." He turned back to the men. "We pull out of here in thirty minutes. Get moving."

There was a ragged streak of light showing at the end of the dark tunnel. Gros signaled a halt. The men bunched up, filling the cramped passage.

"Most of you never came this way before," he said. "So listen. We push out of here into the Street of the Olive Trees; it's a little side street under the palace wall. There's a dummy stall in front; ignore the old dame in it.

"Ease out one at a time, and move off east; that's to the right. You all got good papers. If the guy on the gate asks for them, show them. Don't get eager and volunteer. If there's any excitement behind, just keep going. We rendezvous at the Thieves' Market. OK—and duck the hardware."

He motioned the first man out, blinking in the glare as the ragged tarpaulin was pushed aside. After half a minute, the second followed. I moved close to Gros.

"Why bring this whole mob along?" I asked in a low voice. "Wouldn't it be a lot easier for just a few of us?"

Gros shook his head. "I want to keep my eye on these slobs," he said. "I don't know what ideas they might get if I left them alone a few days; and I can't afford to have this set-up poisoned. And I'm going to need them out at the country place. There's nothing they can do here while I'm not around to tell them."

It sounded fishy to me, but I let it drop. All the men passed by us and disappeared. There was no alarm.

"OK," Gros said. "Stay with me." He slipped under the moldy hanging and I followed as he stepped past a broken-down table laden with pottery. An old crone huddled on a stool ignored us. Gros glanced out into the narrow dusty street, then pushed off into the crowd. We threaded our way through loud-talking, gesticulating customers, petty merchants crouched over fly-covered displays of food or dog-eared magazines, tottering beggars, grimy urchins. The dirt street was littered with refuse; starving dogs wandered listlessly through the crowd. No one paid the least attention to us. It appeared we'd get through without trouble.

Under a heavy cloak Gros had given me, I was sweating. Flies buzzed about my swollen face. A whining beggar thrust a gaunt hand at me. Gros ducked between two fat men engaged in an argument. As they moved, I had to sidestep and push past them. Gros was almost out of sight in the mob.

I saw a uniform suddenly, a hard-faced fellow in yellowish khaki pushing roughly through the press ahead. A chicken fluttered up, squawking in my face. There was a shout; people began milling, thrusting against me. I caught a glimpse of Gros, face turned toward the soldier, eyes wide in a pale face. He started to run. In two jumps the uniformed man had him by the shoulder, spun him around, shouting. A dog yelped, banged against my legs, scuttled away. The soldier's arm rose and fell, clubbing at Gros with a heavy riot stick.

Far ahead I heard a shot, and almost instantly another, close. Gros was free and running, blood on his head, as the soldier fell among the crowd. I darted along the wall, trying to overtake Gros, or at least keep him in sight. The crowd was opening, making way as he ran, pistol in hand. He fired again, the shot a faint pop in the mob noise.

Another uniform jumped in front of me, club raised; I shied, threw up an arm, as the man jumped back, saluted.

I caught the words, "Pardon, sir," as I went past him at a run. He must have caught a glimpse of the uniform I wore.

Ahead, Gros fell in the dust, scrambled to his knees, head down. A soldier stepped out of an alley, aimed, and shot him through the head. Gros lurched, collapsed, rolled on his back. The dust caked in the blood on his face. The crowd closed in. From the moment they spotted him, he didn't have a chance.

I stopped. I was trying to remember what Gros had told the men. I had made the bad mistake of assuming too much, thinking I would have Gros to lead me out of this. There was something about a gate; everyone had papers, Gros said. All but me. That was why they had had to come out in daylight, I realized suddenly. The gate probably closed at sundown.

I moved on, not wanting to attract attention by standing still. I tried to keep the cloak around me to conceal the uniform. I didn't want any more soldiers noticing it; the next one might not be in such a hurry.

Gros had told the men to rendezvous at the Thieves' Market. I tried to remember Algiers from a three-day visit years before; all I could recall was the Casbah and the well-lit streets of the European shopping section.

I passed the spot where a jostling throng craned to see the body of the soldier, kept going. Another ring surrounded the spot where Gros lay dead. Now there were soldiers everywhere, swinging their sticks carelessly, breaking up the mob. I shuffled, head down, dodged a backhanded swipe, found myself in the open. The street sloped up, curving to the left. There were still a few cobbles on this part, fewer shops and stalls. Wash hung from railings around tiny balconies above the street.

I saw the gate ahead. A press of people packed against it, while a soldier examined papers. Three more uniformed men stood by, looking toward the scene of the excitement.

I went on toward the gate. I couldn't turn back now. There was a new wooden watch tower scabbed onto the side of the ancient brick wall where the sewer drained under it. A carbon arc searchlight and a man with a burp gun slung over his shoulder were on top of it. I thought I saw one of the Organization men ahead in the crowd at the gate.

One of the soldiers was staring at me. He straightened, glanced at the man next to him. The other soldier was looking, too, now. I decided a bold front was the only chance. I beckoned to one of the men, allowing the cloak to uncover the front of the uniform briefly. He moved toward me, still in doubt. I hoped my battered face didn't look familiar.

"Snap it up, soldier," I said in my best *Ecole Militaire* tone; he halted before me, saluted. I didn't give him a chance to take the initiative.

"The best part of the catch made it through the gate before you fools closed the net," I snapped. "Get me through there fast, and don't call any more attention to me. I'm not wearing this flea-circus for fun." I flipped the cloak.

He turned and pushed through the gate, and said a word to

the other soldier, gestured toward me. The other man, wearing sergeant's stripes, looked at me.

I glared at him as I approached. "Ignore me," I hissed. "You foul this up and I'll see you shot."

I brushed past him, thrust through the gate as the first soldier opened it. I walked on, listening for a sound of a round snapping into the chamber of that burp gun on the tower. A goat darted out of an alley, stared at me. Sweat rolled down my cheek. There was a tree ahead, with a black shadow under it. I wondered if I'd ever get that far.

I made it, and breathed a little easier.

I still had problems, plenty of them. Right now I had to find the Thieves' Market. I had a vague memory of such a thing from the past, but I had no idea where it was. I moved along the road, past a weathered stuccoed building with a slatternly tavern downstairs and sagging rooms above, bombed out at the far end. The gate was out of sight now.

Ahead were more bomb-scarred tenements, ruins, and beyond open fields. There was a river in sight to the right. A few people were in view, moving listlessly in the morning heat. They seemed to ignore the hubbub within the walled town. I couldn't risk asking any of them for the place I sought; I didn't know who might be a police informer, or a cop, for that matter. They had been ready for us, I realized.

Gros wasn't as well-hidden as he had thought. Probably a police could have cleared his outfit from the palace at any time; I suspected they had tolerated them against such a time as now. The ambush had been neat. I wondered if any of the boys had made it through the gate.

Apparently word had not gone out to be on the alert for a man impersonating an officer; I didn't know how much Maurice had said when he telephoned for his men, but my bluff at the gate indicated no one had been warned of my disguise.

I paused. Maybe my best bet would be to try the tavern, order a drink, try to pick up something. I saw nothing ahead that looked encouraging.

I walked back fifty feet to the doorless entrance to the bistro. There was no one in sight. I walked in, barely able to make out the positions of the tables and chairs in the gloom. The glassless windows were shuttered. I blinked, made out the shape of the bar. Outside the door, the dusty road glared white.

A hoarse-breathing fellow loomed up behind the bar. He didn't say anything.

"Red wine," I said.

He put a water glass on the bar and filled it from a tin dipper. I tasted it. It was horrible. I had a feeling good manners would be out of place here, so I turned and spat it on the floor.

I pushed the glass across the bar. "I want wine," I said. "Not what you wring out of the bar rag." I dropped a worn thousand franc note on the bar.

He muttered as he turned away, and was still muttering when he shuffled back with a sealed bottle and a wine glass. He drew the cork, poured my glass half full, and put the thousand francs in his pocket. He didn't offer me any change.

I tried it; it wasn't too bad. I stood sipping, and waited for my eyes to get used to the dim light. The bartender moved away and began pulling a pile of boxes, grunting hard.

I didn't have a clear idea of what to do if I did find the survivors of the Organization. At best I might find out what was wrong with the disguise, and use their channels to get back into the palace. I could always call for help on my communicator, and have myself set back inside via shuttle, but I didn't like the idea of risking that again. I had almost been caught arriving last time. The scheme couldn't possibly work if any suspicion was aroused.

A man appeared in the doorway, silhouetted against the light. He stepped in and came over to the bar. The bartender ignored him.

Two more came through the door, walked past me and leaned on the bar below me. The bartender continued to shuffle boxes, paying no attention to his customers. I started to wonder why.

The man nearer me moved closer. "Hey, you," he said. He jerked his head toward the gate. "You hear the shooting back there?"

That was a leading question. I wondered if the sound of the shots had been audible outside the walls of the fortified town. I grunted.

"Who they after?" he said.

I tried to see his face, but it was shadowed. He was a thin broad fellow, leaning on one elbow. Here we go again, I thought.

"How would I know?" I said.

"Kind of warm for that burnoose, ain't it?" he said. He stretched out a hand as if to touch the tattered cape. I stepped back, and two pairs of arms wrapped around me in a double bear-hug from behind.

The man facing me twitched the cape open. He looked at me.

"Lousy Ducal," he said, and hit me across the mouth with the back of his hand. I tasted blood.

"Hold on to them arms," another man said, coming around from behind me. This was one I hadn't seen. I wondered how many more men were in the room. The new man took the old military cape in his hands and ripped it off me.

"Look at that," he said. "We got us a lousy general." He dug his finger under the top of the braided lapel of my blouse and yanked. The lapel tore but stayed put. I started to struggle then; that was my communicator they were about to loot for the gold wire on it. I didn't have much hope of getting loose that way, but maybe it would distract them if I kicked a little. I swung a boot and caught the rangy one under the kneecap. He yelped and jumped back, then swung at my face. I twisted away, and the blow grazed my cheek. I threw myself backward, jerking hard, trying to throw someone off balance.

"Hold him," a man hissed. They were trying not to make too much noise. The thin man moved in close, watched his chance and slammed a fist into my stomach. The pain was agonizing; I crammed up, retching.

The men holding me dragged me to a wall, flung me upright against it, arms outspread. The fellow who wanted the braid stepped up with a knife in his hand. I was trying to breathe, wheezing and twisting. He grabbed my hair, and for a moment I thought he was going to slit my throat. Instead, he sawed away at lapels, cursing as the blade scraped wire.

"Get the buttons, too, Beau Joe," a husky voice suggested.

The pain was fading a little now, but I sagged, acting weaker than I actually was. The communicator was gone, at least the sending end. All I could try to salvage now was my life.

The buttons took only a moment. The man with the knife stepped back, slipping it into a sheath at his hip. He favored the leg I had kicked. I could see his face now. He had straight fine features.

"OK, let him go," he said. I slumped to the floor. For the first time my hands were free. Now maybe I had a chance; I still had the gun. I got shakily to hands and knees, watching him. He aimed a kick at my ribs.

"On your feet, General," he said. "I'll teach you to kick your betters."

The others laughed, called out advice, shuffled around us in a circle. There was an odor of dust and sour wine.

"That General's a real fighter, ain't he" somebody called. "Fights sittin' down." That went over big. Lots of happy laughter.

I grabbed the foot as it came to me, twisted it hard, and threw the man to the floor. He swore loudly, lunged at me, but was up again, backing away. The ring opened and somebody pushed me. I let myself stumble and gained a few more feet toward the shadowed corner. I could see better now, enough to see pistols and knives in every belt. If they had any idea I was armed, they'd use them. I had to wait.

Beau Joe was after me again, throwing a roundhouse left. I ducked it, then caught a couple of short ones. I stepped back two paces, glanced at the audience; they were as far away as I'd get them. It was time to make my play. The man shielded me as the slug-gun popped into my hand, but at that instant he swung a savage kick. It was just luck; he hadn't seen the tiny weapon, but the gun spun into a dark corner. Now I wasn't acting any more.

I went after him, slammed a hard left to his face, followed with a right to the stomach, then straightened him out with another left. He was a lousy boxer.

The others didn't like it; they closed in and grabbed me. Knuckles bounced off my jaw as a fist rammed into my back. Two of them ran me backwards and sent me crashing against the wall. My head rang; I was stunned. I fell down and they let me lie. I needed the rest.

To hell with secrecy, I thought. I got to my knees and started crawling toward the corner. The men laughed and shouted, forgetting about being quiet now.

"Crawl, General," one shouted. "Crawl, you lousy spy."

"Hup, two, soldier," another sallied. "By the numbers, crawl."

That was a good one; they roared, slapped each other. Where the hell was that guy?

He grabbed my jacket, hauled me to my feet as I groped for him. My head spun; I must have a concussion, I thought. He jabbed at me, but I leaned on him, and he couldn't get a good swing. The others laughed at him, now, enjoying the farce.

"Watch him, Beau Joe," someone called. "He's liable to wake up, with you shakin' him that way."

Beau Joe stepped back, and aimed a straight right at my chin, but I dropped and headed for the corner again; that was where the gun went. He kicked me again, sent me sprawling into the wall—and my hand fell on the gun.

I rolled over, and Beau Joe yanked me up, spun me around, and stepped back. I stood, slumped in the corner, watching him. He was enjoying it now. He mouthed words silently, grinning in spite of his bleeding mouth. He intended to keep me propped there in the corner and beat me to death. As he came to me, I raised the gun and shot him in the face.

I wished I hadn't; he did a back-flip, landed head first, but not before I caught a glimpse of the smashed face. Joe was not beau any more.

I held my hand loosely at my side, waiting for the next comer. The same fellow who had grabbed me before rushed up. He jumped the body and twisted to deliver a skull-crusher. I raised the gun a few inches as he leaped and I fired at his belly. The shot made a hollow whop, as the man's feet left the floor. He smashed into the wall as I side-stepped.

The other three fanned out. It was too dark to see clearly here, and they didn't yet realize what had happened. They thought I had downed the two men with my fists. They were going to jump me together and finish it off.

"Freeze, bunnies!" a voice said from the door. We all looked. A hulking brute stood outlined there, and the gun in his hand was visible.

"I can see you rats," he said. "I'm used to the dark. Don't try nothing." He beckoned a man behind him forward. One of the three in the room edged toward the rear, and the gun coughed, firing through a silencer. The man slammed sideways, and sprawled.

"Come on, Hammer-hand," the big man said. "Let's get out of here." He spat into the room. "These pigeons don't want to play no more."

I recognized the voice of Gaston, the big fellow who had wanted to bury me under the floor. Gros had appointed him my bodyguard, but he was a little late. I had taken a terrible beating. I tucked the gun away clumsily and lurched forward.

"Cripes, Hammer-hand," Gaston said, stepping forward to steady me. "I didn't know them bunnies had got to you; I thought you were stringing them. I was wondering when you was going to make music with that punch."

He paused to stare at Beau Joe.

"You pushed his mush right in," he said admiringly. "Hey, Touhey, get Hammer-hand's wraparound, and let's move." He glanced once more around the room.

"So long, bunnies," he said. The two men didn't answer.

CHAPTER 9

I don't remember much about my trip to the Organization's hide-out in the country. I recall walking endlessly, and later being carried over Gaston's shoulder. I remember terrific heat, and agonizing pain from my battered face, my half-healed gunshot wounds, and innumerable bruises. And I remember at last a cool room, and a soft bed.

I awoke slowly, dreams blending with memories, none of them pleasant. I lay on my back, propped up on enormous fluffy feather bolsters, with a late afternoon sun lighting the room through partly-drawn drapes over a wide dormer window. For a while I struggled to decide where I was. Gradually, I recalled my last conscious thought.

This was the place in the country Gros had been headed for. Gaston had taken his charge seriously, in spite of his own suggestion that I be disposed of and although Miche and Gros were dead.

I moved tentatively, and caught my breath. That hurt, too. My chest, ribs and stomach were one great ache. I pushed the quilt down and tried to examine the damage. Under the edges of a broad tape wrapping, purple bruises showed all around my right side.

Bending my neck had been a mistake; now the bullet wound that Maurice had re-opened with the blackjack began to throb. I was a mess. I didn't risk moving my face; I knew what it must look like.

As a secret-service type, I was a complete bust, I thought. My carefully prepared disguise had fooled no one, except maybe Spider. I had been subjected to more kicks, blows, and threats of death in the few hours I had been in the dictator's realm than in all my previous 42 years, and I had accomplished exactly nothing. I had lost my communicator, and now my slug-gun too; the comforting pressure under my wrist had gone. It wouldn't have helped me much anyway; I was dizzy from the little effort I had just expended.

Maybe I had made some progress, though, in a negative way. I knew that walking in and striking a pose wasn't good enough to get by as the Dictator Bayard, in spite of the face. And I had also learned that the dictator's regime was riddled with subversives and malcontents. Perhaps we could somehow use the latter to our advantage.

If, I thought, I can get back with the information. I thought that over. How would I get back? I had no way of communicating. I was completely on my own now.

Always before I had had the knowledge that in the end I could send out a call of help, and count on rescue within an hour. Richthofen had arranged for a 24-hour monitoring of my communications band, alert for my call. Now that was out. If I was to return to the Imperium, I would have to stall one of the crude shuttles of this world, or better, commandeer one as dictator. I had to get back into the palace, with a correct disguise, or end my days in this nightmare world.

I heard voices approaching outside the room. I closed my eyes as the door opened. I might learn a little by playing possum, if I could get away with it.

The voices were lower now, and I sensed several people coming over to stand by the bed.

“How long has he been asleep?” a new voice asked. Or was it new? It seemed familiar somehow, but I connected it with some other place.

“Doc gave him some shots,” someone answered. “We brought him this time yesterday.”

There was a pause. Then the half-familiar voice again. “I don’t like his being alive. However—perhaps we can make use of him.”

“Gros wanted him alive,” another voice said. I recognized Gaston. He sounded sullen. “He had big plans for him.”

The other voice grunted. There was a silence for a few moments.

“He’s no good to us until the face is healed. Keep him here until I send along further instructions.”

I hadn’t liked what I heard, but for the present I had no choice but to lie here and try to regain my strength. At least, I was comfortably set up in this huge bed. I drifted off to sleep again.

I awoke with Gaston sitting by the bed, smoking. He sat up when I opened my eyes, crushed out his cigarette in an ash tray on the table, and leaned forward.

“How are you feeling, Hammer-hand?” he said.

“Rested,” I said. My voice came out in a faint whisper. I was surprised at its weakness.

“Yeah, them pigeons give you a pretty rough time, Hammer-hand. I don’t know why you didn’t lay the punch on them sooner.

“I got some chow here for you,” Gaston said. He put a tray from the bedside table on his lap and offered me a spoonful of soup. I was hungry; I opened my mouth for it. I never expected to have a gorilla for a nursemaid, I thought.

Gaston was good at his work, though. For the next three days he fed me regularly, changed my bedding, and performed all the duties of a trained nurse with skill, if not with grace. I steadily gained strength, but I was careful to conceal the extent of my progress from Gaston and the others who occasionally came in. I didn't know what might be coming up and I wanted something in reserve.

Gaston told me a lot about the Organization during the next few days. I learned that the group led by Gros and Miche was only one of several such cells; there were hundreds of members, in half a dozen scattered locations in Algeria, each keeping surveillance over some vital installation of the regime. Their ultimate objective was the overthrow of Bayard's rule, enabling them to get a share in the loot.

Each group had two leaders, all of whom reported to the Big Boss, a stranger about whom Gaston knew little. He appeared irregularly, and no one knew his name or where he had his headquarters. I sensed that Gaston didn't like him.

On the third day I asked Gaston to help me get up and walk a bit. I faked extreme weakness, but was pleased to discover that I was feeling better than I had hoped. After Gaston helped me back into bed and left the room, I got up again, and practiced walking. It made me dizzy and nauseous but I leaned on the bed post and waited for my stomach to settle down, and went on. I stayed on my feet for fifteen minutes, and slept soundly afterwards. Thereafter, whenever I awoke, day or night, I rose and walked, jumping back into bed when I heard footsteps approaching.

When Gaston insisted on walking me after that, I continued to feign all the symptoms I had felt the first time. The doctor was called back once, but he assured me that my reactions were quite normal, and that I could not expect to show much improvement for another week, considering the amount of blood I had lost. This suited me perfectly. I needed time to learn more.

I tried to pump Gaston about my disguise, subtly; I didn't want to put him on his guard, or give him any inkling of what I had in mind. But I was too subtle; Gaston avoided the subject.

I searched for my clothes, but the closet was locked and I couldn't risk forcing the door.

A week after my arrival, I allowed myself enough improvement to permit a walk through the house, and down into a pleasant garden behind it. The layout of the house was simple. From the garden I had seen no signs of guards. It looked as though I could walk out any time, but I restrained the impulse.

By the time ten days had passed, I was getting very restless. I couldn't fake my role of invalid much longer without arousing suspicion. The inactivity was getting on my nerves; I had spent the night lying awake, thinking, and getting up occasionally to walk up and down the room. By dawn, I had succeeded in fatiguing myself, but I hadn't slept at all.

I had to be doing something. I got out my canes, and reconnoitered the house after Gaston had taken away my breakfast tray. From the upstairs windows I had a wide view of the surrounding country. The front of the house faced a paved highway, in good repair. I assumed it was a main route into Algiers. Behind the house, tilled fields stretched a quarter of a mile to a row of trees. Perhaps there was a river there. There were no other houses near.

I thought about leaving. It looked to me as though my best bet would be to go over the wall after dark and head for the cover of the trees. I had the impression that the line of trees and the road converged to the west, so perhaps I could regain the road at a distance from the house, and follow it into the city. I went back to my room to wait.

It was almost dinner time when I heard someone approaching my door. I was lying down, so I stayed where I was and waited. Gaston entered with the doctor. The doctor was pale, and perspiring heavily. He avoided my eyes as he drew out a chair, sat down and started his examination. He said nothing to me, ignoring the questions I asked him. I gave up and lay silently while he prodded and poked. After a while he rose suddenly, packed up his kit, and walked out.

"What's the matter with doc, Gaston?" I asked.

"He's got something on his mind," Gaston said. Even Gaston seemed subdued. Something was up; something that worried me.

"Come on, Gaston," I said. "What's going on?"

At first I thought he wasn't going to answer me.

"They're going to do like you wanted," he said. "They're getting ready to put you in for Bayard."

"That's fine," I said. That was why I had come here for. This way was as good as any. But there was something about it.

"Why all the secrecy?" I asked. "Why doesn't the Big Boss show himself? I'd like to talk to him."

Gaston hesitated. I had the feeling he wanted to say more, but couldn't.

"They got a few details to fix yet," he said. He didn't look at me. I let it go at that.

After Gaston left the room, I went out into the hall. Through the open back windows I heard the sound of conversation. I moved over to eavesdrop.

There were three men, strolling out into the garden with their backs to me. One was the doctor; I didn't recognize the other two. I wished I could see their faces.

"It was not for this I was trained," the doctor was saying. He waved his hands in an agitated way. "I'm not a butcher, to cut up a side of mutton for you."

I couldn't make out the reply.

I went down to the landing and listened. All was quiet. I descended to the hall on the ground floor, listened again. Somewhere a clock was ticking.

I went into the main dining room; the table was set for three, but no food was in sight. I tried the other dining room; nothing. I went across and eased the parlor door open. There was no one there; it looked as unused as ever.

I passed the door I had found locked once before and noticed light under it. I stepped back and tried it. It was probably a broom closet, I thought as I turned the knob. It opened.

I stood staring. There was a padded white table in the center of the room. At one end stood two floodlamps on tall tripods. Glittering instruments were laid out on a small table. On a stand beside the operating table lay scalpels, sutures, heavy curved needles. There was a finely made saw, like a big hacksaw, and heavy snippers. On the floor beneath the table was a large galvanized steel wash tub.

I didn't understand this; I turned to the door—and heard footsteps approaching.

I looked around, saw a door, jumped to it and jerked it open. When the two men entered the room, I was standing rigid in the darkness of the storeroom, with the door open half an inch.

The floodlights flicked on, then off again. There was a rattle of metal against metal.

"Lay off that," a nasal voice said. "This is all set. I checked it over myself."

"They're nuts," Nasal-voice said. "Why don't they wait

until morning, when they got plenty sunlight for this? No, they gotta work under the lights."

"I don't get this deal," a thin voice said. "I didn't get what was supposed to be wrong with this guy's legs, they got to take them off. How come if he's—"

"You ain't clued in, are you, Mac?" Nasal-voice said harshly. "This is a big deal; they're going to ring this mug in when they knock off the Old Man."

"Yeah, that's what I mean," Thin-voice cut in. "So what's the idea they take off the legs?"

"You don't know much, do you, small-timer?" Nasal-voice said. "Well, listen; I got news for you." There was a pause.

"Bayard's got no pins, from the knees down." Nasal spoke in a hushed tone. "You didn't know that, did you? That's why you never seen him walking around on the video; he's always sitting back of a desk.

"There ain't very many people know about that," he added. "Keep it to yourself."

"Cripes," Thin-voice said. His voice was thinner than ever. "Got no legs?"

"That's right. I was with him a year before the landing. I was in his outfit when he got it. Machine gun slug, through both knees. Now forget about it. But maybe now you get the set-up."

"Cripes," Thin-voice said. "Where did they get a guy crazy enough to go into a deal like this?"

"How do I know?" the other said. He sounded as though he regretted having told the secret. "These revolutionist types is all nuts anyway."

I stood there feeling sick. My legs tingled. I knew now why nobody mistook me for the dictator, as I walked into the room; and why Spider had been taken in, when he saw me sitting.

I was leaving now. Not tomorrow, not tonight; now. I had no gun, no papers, no map, no plans, but I was leaving.

It was almost dark; I went to the back of the house. Through a window I could see the men in the garden standing under a small cherry tree in the gloom, still talking. I found a door, and examined it in the failing light. It was the type that opens in two sections. The upper one was locked, but the lower half swung silently open—below the line of vision of the men outside. I bent over and stepped through.

A short path led off to the drive beside the house; I ignored it and crept along beside the wall, through weed-grown flower beds.

I turned to start out across the plowed field and a dark form rose up before me. I recoiled, my wrist twitching in a gesture that had become automatic; but no slug-gun snapped into my hand. I was unarmed, weak, and shaken, and the man loomed over me, hulking.

"Let's go, Hammer-hand," he whispered. It was Gaston.

"I'm leaving, Gaston," I said. "Just don't try to stop me." Vague ideas of a bluff were in my mind. After all, he called me Hammer-hand.

He came after me. "Hold it down to a roar," he said. "I wondered when you was going to make your break. You been getting pretty restless these last few days."

"Yeah," I said. "Who wouldn't?" I was just stalling; I had no plan.

"You got more nerve than me, Hammer-hand," Gaston said. "I would of took off a week ago. You must of wanted to get a look at the Big Boss real bad to stick as long as you did."

"I saw enough today," I said. "I don't want to see any more."

"Do you make him?" Gaston asked. He sounded interested.

"No," I said. "I didn't see his face. But I've lost my curiosity."

Gaston laughed. "OK, chief," he said. He handed me a soiled card, with something scribbled on it. "Maybe this will do you some good. It's the Big Boss's address out of town. I swiped it; it was all I could find. Now let's blow out of here."

I stuck the card in my pocket. I was a little confused.

"Wait a minute, Gaston; you mean you're helping me get away?"

"Gros said I was supposed to keep an eye on you, look out you didn't have no accident," Gaston said. "I always done all right doing what my brother told me; I don't see no reason to stop now just because they killed him."

"Your brother," I said.

"Gros was my brother," Gaston said. "I ain't smart like Gros, but he always took care of me. I always done what he said. He told me to look out for you, Hammer-hand."

"What about them?" I asked, nodding toward the house. "They won't like it when they find us both missing."

Gaston spat. "To hell with them monkeys," he said. "They gimme the willies."

I was beginning to feel jolly all of a sudden, by reaction.

"Listen, Gaston; can you go back in there and get the clothes I had on when I got here?"

Gaston fumbled in the dark at a sack slung over his shoulder. "I thought you might want that suit, Hammer-hand," he said. "You was real particular about that with Miche." He handed me a bundle. I knew the feel of it. It was the uniform.

"Gaston," I said. "You're a wonder. I don't suppose you brought along the little gimmick I had on my wrist?"

"I think I stuck it in the pocket," he said. "Somebody swiped the fancy gloves you had in the belt, though. I'm sorry about the gloves."

I fumbled over the blouse, and felt the lump in the pocket.

With that slug-gun in my hand I was ready to lick the world.

"That's OK about the gloves, Gaston," I said. I strapped the clip to my wrist and tucked the gun away. I pulled off the old coat I wore and slipped the blouse on. This was more like it.

I looked at the house. All was peaceful. It was dark enough now that we wouldn't be seen crossing the field. It was time to go.

"Come on," I said. I took a sight on a bright star and struck out across the soft ground.

In fifty steps the house was completely lost to view. The wall and high foliage obscured the lights on the first floor; upstairs the house was in darkness. I kept the star before me and stumbled on. I never knew how hard it was to walk in a plowed field in the dark.

It was fifteen minutes before I made out a deeper darkness against the faintly lighter sky ahead. That would, be the line of trees along the river; I was still assuming there was a river.

Then we were among the trees, feeling our way slowly. The ground sloped and the next moment I was sliding down a muddy bank into shallow water.

"Yes," I said, "it's a river all right." I scrambled out, and stood peering toward the west. I could see nothing. If we had to pick our way through trees all night, without a moon, we wouldn't be a mile away by dawn.

"Which way does this river flow, Gaston?" I asked.

"That way," he said. "To Algiers—into the city."

"Can you swim?" I asked.

"Sure," Gaston replied. "I can swim good."

"OK," I said, "strip and make a bundle of your clothes. Put whatever you don't want to get wet in the middle; strap the bundle to your shoulders with your belt."

We grunted and fumbled in the darkness.

I finished my packing and stepped down into the water. It was warm weather; that was a break. I still had the slug-gun on my wrist. I wanted it close to me.

I stepped out into the stream, pushed off as the bottom shelved. I paddled a few strokes to get clear of the reeds growing near the shore. All around was inky blackness, with only the brilliant stars overhead to relieve the emptiness.

"OK, Gaston?" I called.

I heard him splashing quietly.

"Sure," he said.

"Let's go out a little farther and then take it easy," I said. "Let the river do the work."

CHAPTER 10

The current was gentle. Far across the river I saw a tiny light now. We drifted slowly past it. I moved my hands just enough to keep my nose above the water. The surface was calm. I yawned; I could have slept tonight, I thought, remembering the sleepless hours of the night before. But it would be a long time between beds for me.

I saw a glinting reflection on a ripple ahead, and glanced back. There were lights on in the second story of the house we had left.

I called to Gaston, pointing out the lights.

"Yeah," he said. "I been watching them. I don't think we got nothing to worry about."

They could follow our trail to the water's edge easily enough, I knew, with nothing more than a flashlight. As if in response to my thought, a tiny gleam appeared at ground level, wavering, blinking as the trees passed between us. It moved, bobbing toward the river. I watched until it emerged from the trees. I saw the yellow gleam dancing across the water where we had started. Other lights were following now, two, three.

The whole household must have joined the chase. They must be expecting to find me huddled on the ground nearby, exhausted, ready for the table they had prepared for me in the presence of my enemies.

The lights fanned out, moving along the shore. I saw that we were safely ahead of them.

"Gaston," I said, "have they got a boat back there?"

"Nah," he replied. "We're in the clear."

The little lights were pitiful, bobbing along the shore, falling behind.

We floated along then in silence for an hour or more. It was still, almost restful. Only a gentle fluttering of the hands was required to keep our heads above water.

Suddenly lights flashed ahead, over the river.

"Cripes," Gaston hissed, backing water. "I forgot about the Salan bridge. Them bunnies is on there waitin' for us."

I could see the bridge, now, as the lights flashed across the pilings. It was about a hundred yards ahead.

"Head for the far shore, Gaston," I said. "Fast and quiet."

I couldn't risk the splash of a crawl stroke, so I dog-paddled frantically, my hands under the surface. They would have had us neatly, if they hadn't shown the lights when they did, I thought. They wouldn't see us without them, though, so it was just a chance they had to take. They must have estimated the speed of the river's flow, and tried to pin-point us. They didn't miss by much; in fact, they might not have missed at all. I concentrated on putting every ounce of energy into my strokes. My knees hit mud, and reeds brushed my face. I rolled over and sat up, breathing hard. Gaston floundered a few feet away.

"Here," I hissed. "Keep it quiet."

The light on the bridge blinked out suddenly. I wondered what they'd do next. If they headed along the banks, flashing lights, we'd have to take to the water again; and if one man stayed on the bridge, and flashed his light down just about the right moment—

"Let's get going," I said.

I started up the slope, crouching low. The lights appeared again, down at the water's edge now, flashing on the tall grass and cattails. Another appeared on the opposite bank. I stopped to listen. Feet made sloshing sounds in the mud, a hundred feet away. Good; that would cover our noise. My wet shoes dangled by the strings, thumping in my chest.

The ground was firmer now, the grass not so tall. I stopped again, Gaston right behind me, looking back. They'd find our tracks any minute. We had no time to waste. The bundle of clothing was a nuisance, but we couldn't stop to dress now.

"Come on," I whispered, and broke into a run.

Fifty feet from the top we dropped and started crawling. I didn't want to be seen in silhouette against the sky as we topped the rise.

We pulled ourselves along, puffing and grunting. Crawling is hard work for a grown man. Just over the top we paused to look over the situation. The road leading to the bridge wound away toward a distant glow in the sky.

"That's an army supply depot out that way," Gaston said. "No town."

I raised up to look back toward the river. Two lights bobbed together, then started slowly away from the water's edge. I heard a faint shout.

"They've spotted the trail," I said. I jumped up and ran down the slope, trying to breathe deep in for four strides, out for four. A man could run for a long time if he didn't get winded. Stones bruised my bare feet.

I angled over toward the highway, with some idea of making better time. Gaston was beside me.

"Nix," he said, puffing hard. "Them bunnies got a machine."

For a moment I didn't know what he meant; then I heard the sound of an engine starting up, and headlights lanced into the darkness, beams aimed at the distant treetops as the car headed up the slope of the approach to the bridge from the other side. We had only a few seconds before the car would slant down on this side, and illuminate the road and a wide strip on either side; we'd be spotlighted.

Ahead, I saw a fence, just a glint from a wire. That finished it; we were stopped. I slid to a halt. Then I saw that the fence lined a cross road, joining the road we were paralleling twenty feet away. Maybe a culvert … I dived for shelter.

A corrugated steel pipe eighteen inches in diameter ran beside the main road where the other joined it. I scrambled over pebbles and twigs and into the mouth. The sounds I made echoed hollowly inside. I kept going to the far end, Gaston wheezing behind me. I stopped and looked over my shoulder. Gaston had backed in and lay a few feet inside his end. The glow of the headlights gave me a glimpse of a heavy automatic in his hand.

"Good boy," I hissed. "Don't shoot unless you have to."

The lights of the car flickered over trees, highlighting rocks. Through the open end of the pipe I saw a rabbit sitting up in the glare, a few feet away. He turned and bounded off.

The car came slowly along, passed, moved on down the road. I breathed a little easier.

I was on the point of turning to say something to Gaston when a small stone rolled down into the ditch before me. I stiffened. A faint scuff of shoes on gravel, another stone dislodged—and then a flashlight beam darted across the gulley, played on the grass opposite, came to rest on the open end of the drain pipe. I held my breath. Then the steps came nearer, and the light probed, found my shoulder. There was a frozen instant of silence, then the sharp slap of the slug-gun hitting my palm. I caught a glimpse of the car a hundred feet away now, still edging along, heard a sharp intake of breath as the man with the light readied a shout. I pointed the gun to the right of the flash and the recoil slammed my arm back. The flashlight skidded across the rocky ground and went out as the man's body crashed heavily and lay still. I groped for the man's feet, hauled him back toward the pipe.

"Gaston," I whispered. The sound was hollow in the dark tunnel. "Give me a hand." I pulled at the feet. I was glad it wasn't the doctor; he wouldn't have fitted.

I crawled out of the pipe and Gaston came up beside me.

"After the car," I said. I had what I hoped was an idea. I was tired of being chased; the hunted would become the hunter.

I headed up the ditch at a trot, head down, Gaston at my heels. The car had stopped a hundred yards away. I counted three flashlights moving in the edge of the field.

"Close enough," I hissed. "Let's split up now. I'll cross the road and come up the other side. There's only one man over there. You get up in the tall grass and sneak in as close to the car as you can. Watch me and take your cue."

I darted across the road, a grotesque figure, naked, my bundle dangling by its strap from my shoulder. The car's headlights were still on. No one could see us from beyond them, looking into the glare. I dropped down into the ditch, wincing as sharp sticks jabbed my bare feet. The man on my side was casting about in wide circles, fifty feet from the road. A cricket sawed away insistently.

The car started backing, swung to one side of the road, then went forward; the driver was in the car, all right, he was turning around. They must have come up the road to cut us off, planning to move back to the river, searching foot by foot until they flushed us. No one seemed to have missed the man who now lay quietly in the steel pipe.

The car swung around and moved along at a snail's pace, headlights flooding the road I had just crossed. I dropped down to the bottom of the ditch as the lights passed over me. The car came on, and stopped just above me. I could see the driver, staring out through the windshield. He leaned forward, peering. I wondered if he was looking for the man who had been coming along on foot, checking the ditch; he'd be a long time seeing him from here.

He opened the door, stepped out, one foot on the running board. The car was long and top-heavy with flaring fenders. Dust roiled and gnats danced in the beams from the great bowl-shaped headlights.

I picked up a heavy stone, rose silently to hands and knees, and crept up out of the ditch. The chauffeur stood with a hand on the top of the door, looking over it. I came up behind him and hit him as hard as I could on the top of the head. He folded into the seat. I shoved him over, jumped in, and closed the door. It was hard to get the coat off him in the dark, while trying to stay down behind the door, but I managed it. I put it on and sat up. There was no alarm. The three flashlights continued to bob around in the fields. The engine was running quietly.

I looked over the controls. The steering wheel was in the center, and there were three pedals on the floor. I let the center pedal in; the car moved off slowly. I steered to the right side of the road, crept along the edge. Gaston must be about here, I thought. I stared out into the darkness; I could see practically nothing.

I eased to a stop. The flashlight nearest me swung back and forth, moving toward the bridge. I reached out to the dash, and pushed in a lever that projected from it. The headlights died.

I could see better now. The flashlights to my right stopped moving, turned toward me. I waved cheerfully. I didn't think they could make out my face in the dim beam at that distance. One of the lights seemed satisfied, resumed its search; the other hesitated, flashing over the car.

There was a shout then, and I saw Gaston up and running toward me. The flashlights converged on him as he leaped across the ditch ahead, coming into the road. The lights came bounding toward him and someone was yelling. Gaston stopped, whirled toward the nearest light, aiming the pistol. There was a sharp sound. Both lights on his side dropped. Not a bad shooting for a .45, I thought. Behind there was a faint shout from the remaining man on the other side of the road, and the crack of a gun. The slug made a solid thunk as it hit the heavy steel of the car. I floorboarded the center and left pedals; the car jumped ahead, then coasted. Another slug starred the glass beside me, scattering glass chips in my hair. I let my foot off, tried again. The car surged forward. I flipped the lights on. The car shifted up, tires squealing. Ahead, a figure stumbled down into the ditch, scrambled up the other side into the road, waving its arms. I saw the open mouth in the taut white face for an instant in the flare of the lights before it was slammed down out of sight, with a shock that bounced us in our seats.

The bridge loomed ahead, narrow and highly arched. We took it wide open, crushed down in the seat as we mounted the slope, floating as we dropped on the other side. The road curved off to the left, tall trees lining it. The tires howled as we rounded the turn and hit the straightaway.

"This is great, Hammer-hand," Gaston shouted. "I never rode in one of these here machines before."

"Neither did I," I yelled back.

CHAPTER 11

The night was black, with no moon. The next problem was to get into the walled town. The road led along the river's edge into the heart of the city, according to Gaston. The dictator's stronghold lay at the edge of the city north of the highway we were on. He had fortified the area, enclosing shops and houses within an encircling wall like a medieval town, creating a self-sufficient community to support the castle and its occupants, easily patrolled and policed. It was no defense against an army, but practical as a safeguard against assassins and rioters.

"That's us," I said aloud. "Assassins and rioters."

"Sure, chief," Gaston said.

Twenty minutes of driving brought us to the bombed-out edge of the city. The rubble stretched ahead, with here and there a shack or a tiny patch of garden. To the right the mass of the castle loomed up, faintly visible in the glow from the streets below it, unseen behind the wall. To the original massive old country house, Bayard had added rambling outbuildings, great mismatched wings, and the squat tower.

I pulled over, cut the headlights. Gaston and I looked silently at the lights in the tower. He lit a cigarette.

"How are we going to get in there, Gaston?" I said. "How do we get over the wall?"

Gaston stared at the walls, thinking. "Listen, Hammer-hand," he said. "You wait here, while I check around a little. I'm pretty good at casing a layout, and I know this one from the inside; I'll find a spot if there is one. Keep an eye peeled for the street gangs."

I sat and waited. I rolled up the windows and locked the doors. I couldn't see any signs of life about the broken walls around me. Somewhere a cat yowled.

I checked my clothes over. Both lapels were missing; the tiny set was still clipped to my belt, but without speaker or mike, it was useless. I ran my tongue over the tooth with the cyanide sealed in it. I might need it yet.

The door rattled. I had dozed off. Gaston's face pressed against the glass. I unlocked it and he slid in beside me.

"OK, Hammer-hand," he said. "I think I got us a spot. We go along the edge of the drainage ditch over there to where it goes under the wall. Then we got to get down inside it and ease under the guard tower. It comes out in the clear on the other side."

I got out and followed Gaston over broken stones to the ditch. It was almost a creek, and the smell of it was terrible.

Gaston led me along its edge for a hundred yards, until the wall hung over us just beyond the circle of light from the guard tower. I could see a fellow with a burp gun leaning against a post on top of the tower, looking down onto the street inside the wall. There were two large floodlights beside him, unlit.

Gaston leaned close to my ear. "It kind of stinks," he said, "but the wall is pretty rough, so I think we can make it OK."

He slid over the edge, found a foothold, and disappeared. I slid down after him, groping with my foot for a ledge. The wall was crudely laid, with plenty of cracks and projecting stones, but slimy with moss. I groped along, one precarious foot at a time. We passed the place where the light gleamed on the black water below, hugging the shadow. Then we were under the wall, which arched massively over us. The sound of trickling water was louder here.

I tried to see what was going on ahead. Gaston had stopped and was descending. I could barely make out his figure, knee-deep in the malodorous stream. I moved closer. Then I saw the grating. It was made of iron bars, and completely blocked the passage.

I climbed over to the grating, leaned against the rusty iron to ease my arms. The defense system didn't have quite the hole in it we thought it had. Gaston moved around below me, reaching under the surface to try to find a bottom edge. Maybe we could duck under the barrier.

Suddenly I felt myself slipping.

Below me, Gaston hissed a curse, scrabbled upward. My grip was firm, I realized in an instant; it was the grating that was slipping. It dropped another eight inches with a muffled scraping and clank, then stopped. The rusty metal had given under our weight. The corroded ends of the bars had broken off at the left side. There wasn't room to pass, but maybe we could force it a little further.

Gaston braced himself against the wall and heaved. I got into position behind him and added my weight. The frame shifted a little, then stuck.

"Gaston," I said. "Maybe I can get under it now, and heave from the other side." Gaston moved back, and I let myself down into the reeking water. I worked an arm through, then dropped down waist deep, chest deep, pushing. The rough metal scraped my face, caught at my clothing; but I was through.

I crawled back up, dripping, and rested. From the darkness behind Gaston I heard a meshing of oiled metal parts and then the cavern echoed with the thunder of machine gun fire. In the flashing light I saw Gaston stiffen against the grating and fall. He hung by one hand, caught in the grating. There were shouts, and men dropped onto the stone coping at the culvert mouth. Gaston jerked, fumbled his pistol from his blouse.

"Gaston," I said. "Quick, under the bars ..." I was helpless. I knew he was too big.

A man appeared, clinging to the coping with one hand, climbing down to enter the dark opening. He flashed a light at us and Gaston, still dangling by the left hand, fired. The man fell over into the stream with a tremendous splash.

Gaston gasped. "That's ... all ..." The gun fell from his hand into the black water.

I moved fast now, from one hand-hold to the next, slipping and clutching, but not quite falling somehow. I managed to get a look back as I reached the open air. Two men were tugging at the body wedged in the opening. Even in death, Gaston guarded my retreat.

I came up over the side, flattened against the wall, slug-gun in my hand; the street was empty. They must have thought they had us trapped; this side was deserted. I was directly under the tower, I eased out a few feet, and craned my neck; a shadow moved at the top of the tower. There was still one man on duty there. He must have heard the grating fall and called for reinforcements.

I looked down the street ahead. I recognized the Street of the Olive Trees, the same one I had come through on my way out with Gros, ten days earlier. It slanted down, curving to the right. That was where I had to go, into the naked street, under the guns. I liked it here in the shadow of the tower, but I couldn't stay. I leaped forward, running for my life. The searchlight snapped on, swung, found me, burning my leaping shadow against the dusty walls and the loose-cobbled street.

Instinct told me to leap aside. As I did, the gun clattered and slugs whined off the stones to my left. I was out of the light now, and dashing for the protection of the curving wall ahead. The light was still groping as I rounded the turn. No lights came on above me; I ran in utter silence. The dwellers in these scarred tenements had learned to sit silent behind barred windows when guns talked in the narrow streets.

I passed the spot where Gros had died, dashed on. In the distance a whistle blew again and again. A shot rang out, kicking up dust ahead. I kept going.

I heard running feet behind me now. I scanned the shabby stalls ahead, empty and dark, trying to find the one we had used the day we left the palace, where the old woman huddled over her table of clay ware. It had been tiny, with a ragged gray awning sagging over the front and broken pots scattered before it.

I almost passed it, caught myself, skidded, and dived for the back. I fought the stiff tarpaulin, found the opening and squeezed through.

I panted in complete darkness now. Outside, I heard voices as the men shouted to each other, searching. I had a moment's respite; they didn't know this entry.

I looked at my watch. Things happened fast in this war world; it was not yet half past nine. I had left the house at seven. I had killed three men in those two hours, and a man had died for me. I thought how easily a man slips back to his ancient role as nature's most deadly hunter.

I felt the fatigue suddenly. I yawned, sat on the floor. I had an impulse to lie back and go to sleep, but instead I got up and began feeling my way toward the passage. I wasn't finished yet; I was in the palace, unwounded, armed. I had all I had any right to hope for—a fighting chance.

I was no longer the eager neophyte, ignorant of the realities; I came now, steeled by necessity, a hardened fighter, a practical killer. I was armed and I was desperate, and I bore the scars of combat. I did not intend to fail.

Half an hour later, I eased a door open and looked down the length of the same hall into which the shuttle had pitched me headlong two weeks before. It hadn't changed. I stepped into the hall, tried the first door. It opened, and I saw that it was a bedroom. I went in, and by the faint light shining through the curtains from below, looked over a wide bed, a large desk against the far wall, a closet door, an easy chair, and through a partly open door, a roomy bathroom to the right. I closed the door behind me, and crossed to the windows. There were steel shutters, painted light green to match the walls, folded back behind the draperies. I closed them, and went to the desk and flipped on the lamp. I had had enough of groping through the dark for one night.

The room was very handsome, spacious, with a deep pile grey-green rug and a pair of bold water-colors on the wall. Suddenly I was aware of my own neck. The clothes seemed to crawl on my back. I had lain in mud, waded a sewer, crept through the ancient dust. Without considering further, I pulled the encrusted tunic off, tossed my clothes in a heap by the door, and headed for the bath.

I took half an hour soaping myself, and then climbed out and got my uniform. I had nothing else to put on, and I wouldn't wear it as it was. I soaped it up, rinsed it out, and draped it over the side of the tub. There was a vast white bathrobe behind the door, and I wrapped myself in it and went back into the bedroom.

The thought penetrated to my dulled mind that I was

behaving dangerously. I tried again to shake myself alert. But alarm wouldn't come. I felt perfectly safe, secure, comfortable. This won't do, I thought; I'm going to go to sleep on my feet. I yawned again.

I sat down in the chair opposite the door, and prepared to wait it out. I got up, as an afterthought, and turned the light out. I don't remember sitting down again.

CHAPTER 12

I dreamt. I was at the seashore, and the sun reflected from the glassy water. It flashed in my eyes, and I turned away. I twisted in the chair, opened my eyes. My head was thick.

I stared at the pale green walls of the room, across the grey-green rug. It was silent in the room and I didn't move. The door stood open.

I remembered turning the light off, nothing more. Someone had turned it on; someone had opened the door. I had come as a killer in the night; and someone had found me here sleeping, betrayed by my own exhaustion.

I sat up, and in that instant realized I was not alone. I turned my head, and looked at the man who sat quietly in the chair on my left, leaning back with his legs thrust out stiffly before him, his hands lightly gripping the arms of a rosewood chair upholstered in black leather. He smiled, and leaned forward. It was like looking into a mirror.

I didn't move. I stared at him. His face was thinner than mine, more lined. The skin was burned dark, the hair bleached lighter by the African sun; but it was me I looked at. Not a twin, not a double, not a clever actor; it was myself sitting in a chair, looking at me.

"You have been sleeping soundly," he said. I thought of hearing my voice on a tape recorder, except this voice spoke in flawless French.

I moved my hand slightly; my gun was still there, and the man I had come to kill sat not ten feet away, alone, unprotected. But I didn't move. I wasn't ready, not yet. Maybe not ever.

"Are you rested enough," he said, "or will you sleep longer before we talk?"

"I'm rested," I said.

"I do not know how you came here," he said, "but that you are here is enough. I did not know what gift the tide of fortune would bring me, but there could be no finer thing than this—a brother."

I didn't know what I had expected the Dictator Bayard to be—a sullen ruffian, a wild-eyed megalomaniac, a sly-eyed schemer. But I had not expected a breathing image of myself, with a warm smile, and a poetic manner of speech, a man who called me brother.

He looked at me with an expression of intense interest.

"You speak excellent French, but with an English accent," he said. "Or is it perhaps American?" He smiled. "You must forgive my curiosity. Linguistics, accents, they are a hobby of mine and, in your case, I am doubly intrigued."

"American," I said.

"Amazing," he said. "I might have been born an American myself… but that is a long dull tale to tell another time."

No need, I thought. My father told it to me often, when I was a boy.

He went on, his voice intense, but gentle, friendly. "They told me, when I returned to Algiers ten days ago, that a man resembling myself had been seen here in the apartment. There were two men found in my study, quite dead. There was a great deal of excitement, a garbled report. But I was struck by the talk of a man who looked like me. I wanted to see him, talk to him; I have been so very much alone here. It was a thing that caught my imagination. Of course, I did not know what brought this man here; they even talked of danger …" He spread his hands in a Gallic gesture.

"But when I came into this room and found you here, sleeping, I knew at once that you could not have come but in friendship. I was touched, my friend, to see that you came here on your own, entrusting yourself to my hands."

I couldn't say anything. I didn't try.

"When I lit the lamp and saw your face, I knew at once that this was more than some shallow impersonation; I saw my own, face there, not so worn by war as my own, the lines not so deeply etched. But there was the call of blood to blood; I know you for my brother."

I licked my lips, swallowed. He leaned forward, placed his hand over mine, gripped it hard, then leaned back in his chair with a sigh.

"Forgive me again, brother. I fall easily into oratory, I fear; a habit I should do well to break. There is time enough for plans later. But now, will you tell me of yourself? I know you have in you the blood of the Bayards."

"Yes, my name is Bayard."

"You must have wanted very much to come to me, to have made your way here alone and unarmed. No one has ever passed the wall before, without an escort and many papers."

I couldn't sit here silent, but neither could I tell this man anything of my real purpose in coming. I reminded myself of the treatment the Imperial ambassadors had received at his hands, of all that Bale had told me that first morning in the meeting with Bernadotte. But I saw nothing here of the ruthless tyrant I expected. Instead, I found myself responding to his spontaneous welcome.

I had to tell him something. My years of diplomatic experience came to my assistance once again. I found myself lying smoothly.

"You're right in thinking I can help you, Brion," I said. I was startled to hear myself calling him by his first name so easily, but it seemed the natural thing to do.

"But you're wrong in assuming that your state is the only surviving center of civilization. There is another, a strong, dynamic, and friendly power which would like to establish amicable relations with you. I am the emissary of that government."

"But why did you not come to me openly? The course you chose, while daring, was of extreme danger; but it must be that you were aware of the treachery all about me, and feared that my enemies would keep you from me."

He seemed so eager to understand that he supplied most of his own answers. This seemed an opportune moment to broach the subject of Bale's two agents who had carried full diplomatic credentials, and who had been subjected to beating, torture, and death. It was a contradiction in the dictator's character I wanted to shed a little light on.

"I recall that two men sent to you a year ago were not well received," I said. "I was unsure of my reception. I wanted to see you privately, face to face."

Bayard's face tensed. "Two men?" he said. "I have heard nothing of ambassadors."

"They were met first by a Colonel-General Yang." I said, "and afterward were interviewed by you personally."

Bayard's face went red. "There is a dog of a broken officer who leads a crew of cut-throats in raids on what pitiful commerce I have been able to encourage. His name is Yang. If he has molested a legation sent to me from your country, I promise you his head."

"It was said that you yourself shot one of them," I said, pressing the point.

Bayard gripped the arm of the chair, his eyes on my face.

"I swear to you by the honor of the House of Bayard that I have never heard until this moment of your Embassy, and that no harm came to them through any act of mine."

I believed him. I was starting to wonder about a lot of things. He seemed sincere in welcoming the idea of an alliance with a civilized power. And yet, I myself had seen the carnage done by his raiders at the palace, and the atom bomb they had tried to detonate there.

"Very well," I said. "On behalf of my government, I accept your statement; but if we treaty with you now, what assurance will be given to use that there will be no repetition of the bombing raids?"

"Bombing raids!" He stared at me. There was a silence.

"Thank God you came to me by night, in secret," he said. "It is plain to me now that control of affairs has slipped from me farther even than I had feared."

"There have been seven raids, four of them accompanied by atomic bombs, in the past year," I said. "The most recent was less than one month ago."

His voice was deadly now. "By my order, every gram of fissionable material known to me to exist was dumped into the sea on the day that I established this state. That there were traitors in my service, I knew; but that there were madmen who would begin the horror again, I did not suspect."

He turned and stared across the room at a painting of sunlight shining through leaves onto a weathered wall. "I fought them when they burned the libraries, melted down the Cellini altar pieces, trampled the Mona Lisa in the ruins of the Louvre. I could save only a fragment here, a remnant there, always telling myself that it was not too late. But the years passed and they have brought no change.

"There has been an end to industry, farming, family life. Even with the plenty that lies about us for the taking, men fight over three things: gold, liquor, and women.

"I have tried to arouse a spirit of rebuilding against the day when even the broken storehouses run dry; but it's useless. Only my rigid martial rule holds them in check.

"I will confess. I had lost hope. There was too much decay all around me. In my own house, among my closest advisors, I heard nothing but talk of armament, expeditionary forces, domination, renewed war against the ruins outside our little island of order. Empty war, meaningless overlordship of dead nations. They hoped to spend our slender resources in stamping out whatever traces might remain of human achievement, unless it bowed to our supremacy."

When he looked at me I thought of the expression, "Blazing eyes."

"Now my hope springs up renewed," he said. "With a brother at my side, we will prevail."

I thought about it. The Imperium had given me full powers. I might as well use them.

"I think I can assure you," I said, "that the worst is over. My government has resources; you may ask for whatever you need—men, supplies, equipment. We ask only one thing of you—friendship and justice between us."

He leaned back, closed his eyes. "The long night is over," he said.

There were still major points to be covered, but I felt sure that Bayard had been grossly misrepresented to me, and to the Imperial government. I wondered how Imperial Intelligence had been so completely taken in and why. Bale had spoken of having a team of his best men here, sending a stream of data back to him.

There was also the problem of my transportation back to Zero Zero world of the Imperium. Bayard hadn't mentioned the MC shuttles. In fact, thinking over what he had said, he talked as though they didn't exist. Perhaps he was holding out on me, in spite of his apparent candor.

Bayard opened his eyes. "There has been enough of gravity for now," he said. "I think that a little rejoicing between us would be appropriate. I wonder if you share my liking for an impromptu feast on such occasion?"

"I love to eat in the middle of the night," I said, "especially when I've missed my dinner."

"You are a true Bayard," he said. He reached to the table beside me and pressed a button. He leaned back and placed his finger tips together.

"And so now we must think about the menu." He pursed his lips, looking thoughtful. "Tonight, permit me to select the menu," he said. "We will see if our tastes are as similar as ourselves."

"Fine," I said.

There was a tap on the door. At Brion's call, it opened and a sour-faced fiftyish little man came in. He saw me, started; then his face blanked. He crossed to the dictator's chair, drew himself up, and said, "I came as quick as I could, Major."

"Fine, fine, Luc," he said. "At ease. My brother and I are hungry. We have a very special hunger, and I want you, Luc, to see to it that our dinner does the kitchen credit."

Luc glanced at me from the corner of his eyes. "I see the gentleman resembles the Major somewhat," he said.

"An amazing likeness. Now—" he stared at the ceiling. "We will begin with a very dry Madeira, I think; Secrial, the

1875. Then we will whet our appetites with *Les Huitres de Whitstable*, with a white Burgundy; Chablis Vaudesir. I think there is still a bit of the '29."

I leaned forward. This sounded like something special indeed. I had eaten oysters Whitstable before, but the wines were vintages of which I had only heard.

"The soup, *Consomme Double aux Cepes*; then *Le Supreme de Brochet au Beurre Blanc*, and for our first red Burgundy, Romanee-Conti, 1904."

Brion ran through the remainder of a sumptuous menu. Luc went away quietly. If he could carry that in his head, he was the kind of waiter I'd always wanted to find.

"Luc has been with me for many years," Brion said. "A faithful friend. You noticed that he called me 'Major.' That was the last official rank I held in the Army of France-in-Exile, before the collapse. I was later elected as Colonel over a regiment of survivors of the Battle of Gibraltar when we had realized that we were on our own. Later still, when I saw what had to be done, and took into my hands the task of rebuilding, other titles were given me by my followers, and I confess I conferred one or two myself; it was just necessary psychological measure, I felt. But to Luc I have always remained 'Major.' He himself was a sous-officer, my regimental Sergeant-Major."

"I know little about events of the last few years in Europe," I said. "Can you tell me something about them?"

He sat thoughtfully for a moment. "The course was steadily downhill," he said, "from the day of the unhappy Peace of Munich in 1919. America faced the Central Powers alone, and the end was inevitable. When America fell under the massive onslaught in '32, it seemed that the Kaiser's dream of a German-dominated world was at hand. Then came the uprisings. I held a Second Lieutenant's commission in the Army of France-in-Exile. We spearheaded the organized resistance, and the movement spread like wild-fire. Men, it seemed, would not live as slaves. We had high hopes in those days.

"But the years passed, and stalemate wore away at us. At last the Kaiser was overthrown by a palace coup, and we chose that chance to make our last assault. I led my battalion on Gibraltar, and took a steel-jacketed bullet through both knees almost before we were ashore.

"I will never forget the hours of agony while I lay conscious in the surgeons' tent. There was no more morphine, and the medical officers worked over the minor cases, trying to get men back into the fight; I was out of it and therefore took last priority. It was reasonable, but at the time I did not understand."

I listened, rapt. "When," I asked, "were you hit?"

"That day I will not soon forget," he said. "April 15, 1945."

I stared. I had been hit by a German machine gun slug at Jena and had waited in the aid station for the doctors to get to me—on April 15, 1945. There was a strange affinity that linked this other Bayard's life with mine, even across the unimaginable void of the Net.

We finished the 1855 brandy, and still we sat, talking through the African night. We laid ambitious plans for the rebuilding of civilization. We enjoyed each other's company, and all stiffness had long since gone. I closed my eyes, and I think I must have dozed off. Something awakened me.

Dawn was lightening the sky. Brion sat silent, frowning. He tilted his head.

"Listen."

I listened. I thought I caught a faint shout and something banged in the distance. I looked inquiringly at my host. His face was grim.

"All is not well," he said. He gripped the chair arms, rose, got his canes, started around the table.

I got up and stepped forward through the glass doors into the room. I was dizzy from the wine and brandy. There was a louder shout outside in the hall and a muffled thump. Then the door shook, splintered and crashed inward.

Thin in a tight black uniform, Chief Inspector Bale stood in the opening, his face white with excitement. He carried a long-barreled Mauser automatic pistol in his right hand. He stared at me, stepped back, then with a sudden grimace raised the gun and fired.

In the instant before the gun slammed, I caught a blur of motion from my right, and then Brion was there, half in front of me, falling as the shot echoed. I grabbed for him, caught him by the shoulders as he went down, limp. Blood welled from under his collar, spreading; too much blood, a life's blood. He was looking into my face as the light died from his eyes.

CHAPTER 13

"Get back, Bayard," Bale snarled. "Rotten luck, that; I needed the swine alive for hanging." I stood up slowly. He stared at me, gnawing his lip. "It was you I wanted dead; and this fool traded lives with you."

He seemed to be talking to himself. I recognized the voice now, a little late. Bale was the Big Boss. It was the fact that he spoke in French here that had fooled me.

"All right," he said in abrupt decision. "He can trade deaths with you too. You'll do to hang in his place. I'll give the mob their circus. You wanted to take his place, here's your chance."

He stepped farther into the room, motioned others in. Evil-looking thugs came through the door, peering about, glancing at Bale for orders.

"Put him in a cell," Bale said. "And I'm warning you, Cassu, keep your bloody hands off him. I want him strong for the surgeon."

Cassu grunted, twisted my arm until the joint creaked, and pushed me past the dead body of the man I had come in one night to think of as a brother.

They marched me off down the corridor, pushed me into an elevator, led me out again through a mob of noisy toughs armed to the teeth, down stone stairs, along a damp tunnel in the rock, and at the end of the line, sent me spinning with a kick into the pitch black of a cell.

My stunned mind worked, trying to assimilate what had happened. Bale! And not a double; he had known who I was. It was Bale of the Imperium, a traitor. That answered a lot of questions. It explained the perfect timing and placement of the attack at the palace, and why Bale had been too busy to attend the gala affair that night. I realized now why he had sought me out afterward; he was hoping that I'd been killed, of course. That would have simplified matters for him. And the duel—I had never quite been able to understand why the Intelligence chief had been willing to risk killing me, when I was essential to the scheme for controlling the dictator. And all the lies about the viciousness of the Bayard of B-I Two were Bale's fabrications designed to prevent establishment of friendly relations between the Imperium and this unhappy world.

Why? I asked myself. Did Bale plan to rule this hellworld himself, making it his private domain? It seemed so.

And I saw that Bale did not intend to content himself with this world alone; this would be merely a base of operations, a source of fighting men and weapons—including atomic bombs. Bale himself was the author of the raids on the Imperium. He had stolen shuttles, or components thereof, and had manned them here in B-I Two, and set out on a career of piracy. The next step would be the assault on the Imperium itself, a full-scale attack, strewing atomic death. The men of the Imperium would wear gay uniforms and dress sabers into battle against atomic cannon.

I wondered why I hadn't realized it sooner. The fantastic unlikeliness of the development of the MC drive independently by the war-ruined world of B-I Two seemed obvious now.

While we had sat in solemn conference, planning moves against the raiders, their prime mover had sat with us. No wonder an enemy scout had lain in wait for me as I came in on my mission.

When he found me at the hideout, Bale must have immediately set to work planning how best to make use of the unexpected stroke of luck. And when I had escaped, he had had to move fast.

I could only assume that the State was now in his hands; that a show execution of Bayard in the morning had been scheduled to impress the populace with the reality of the change in regimes.

Now I would hang in the dictator's place. And I remembered what Bale had said; he wanted me strong for the surgeon. The wash tub would be useful after all. There were enough who knew the dictator's secret to make a corpse with legs embarrassing.

They would shoot me full of dope, perform the operation, bind up the stumps, dress my unconscious body in a uniform and hang me. A dead body wouldn't fool the public. They would be able to see the color of life in my face, even if I were still out, as the noose tightened.

I heard someone coming, and saw a bobbing light in the passage through the barred opening in the door. I braced myself. Maybe this was the man with the saws and the heavy snippers already.

Two men stopped at the cell door, opened it, came in. I squinted at the glare of the flashlight. One of the two dropped something on the floor.

"Put it on," he said. "The boss said he wanted you should wear this here for the hanging."

I saw my old costume, the one I had washed. At least it was clean, I thought. It was strange, I considered, how inconsequentials still had importance.

A foot nudged me. "Put it on, like I said."

"Yeah," I said. I took off the robe and pulled on the light wool jacket and trousers, buckled the belt. There were no shoes; I guessed Bale figured I wouldn't be needing them.

"OK," the man said. "Let's go, Hiem."

I saw and listened as the door clanked again; the light receded. It was very dark.

I fingered the torn lapels of my jacket. The communicator hadn't helped me much. I could feel the broken wires, tiny filaments projecting from the cut edge of the cloth. Beau Joe had cursed as he slashed at them!

I looked down. Tiny blue sparks jumped against the utter black as the wires touched.

I sat perfectly still. Sweat broke out on my forehead. I didn't dare move; the pain of hope awakening against all hope was worse than the blank acceptance of certain death.

My hands shook. I fumbled for the wires, tapped them together. A spark; another.

I tried to think. The communicator was clipped to my belt still; the speaker and mike were gone but the power source was there. Was there a possibility that touching the wires together would transmit a signal? I didn't know. I could only try.

I didn't know Morse Code, or any other code; but I knew S.O.S. Three dots, three dashes, three dots. Over and over, while I suffered the agony of hope.

A long time passed. I tapped the wires, and waited. I almost fell off the bunk as I dozed for an instant. I couldn't stop. I had to try until time ran out for me.

I heard them coming from far off, the first faint grate of leather on dusty stone, a clink of metal. My mouth was dry, and my legs began to tingle. I thought of the hollow tooth and ran my tongue over it. The time for it had come. I wondered how it would taste, if it would be painful. I wondered if Bale had forgotten it, or if he hadn't known.

There were more sounds in the passage now, sounds of men and loud voices; a clank of something heavy, a ponderous grinding. They must be planning on setting the table up here in the cell, I thought. I went to the tiny opening in the door and looked through. I could see nothing but almost total darkness. Suddenly light flared brilliantly, and I jumped, blinded.

There was more noise, then someone yelled. They must be having a hell of a time getting the stuff through the narrow hall, I thought. My eyeballs ached, my legs were trembling, my stomach suddenly felt bad. I gagged. I hoped I wouldn't go to pieces. Time for the tooth now. I thought of how disappointed Bale would be when he found me dead in my cell. It helped a little; but still I hesitated. I didn't want to die. I had a lot of living I wanted to do first.

Then someone called out, nearby.

"Wolfhound!"

My head came up. My code name. I tried to shout, choked. "Yes," I croaked. I jumped to the bars, yelled.

"Wolfhound, where in the hell …"

"Here!" I yelled. "Here!"

"Get back, Colonel," someone said. "Get in the corner and cover up."

I moved back and crouched, arms over my head. There was a sharp hissing sound, and a mighty blast that jarred the floor under me. Tiny particles bit and stung, and grit was in my mouth. With a drawn-out clang, the door fell into the room.

Arms grabbed me, pulled me through the boiling dust, out into the glare. I stumbled, felt broken things underfoot.

Men milled around a mass blocking the passage. Canted

against the wall a great box sat with a door hanging wide, light streaming out. Arms helped me through the door, and I saw wires, coils, junction boxes, stapled to bare new wood, with angle-irons here and there. White-uniformed men crowded into the tiny space; a limp figure was hauled through the door.

"Full count," someone yelled. "Button up!" Wood splintered as a bullet came through.

The door banged shut, and the box trembled while a rumble built up into a whine, then passed on up out of audibility.

Someone grabbed my arm. "My God, Brion, you must have had a terrible time of it."

It was Richthofen, in a grey uniform, a cut on his face, staring at me.

"No hard feelings," I said. "Your timing ... was good."

"We've had a monitor on your band day and night, hoping for something," he said. "We'd given you up, but couldn't bring ourselves to abandon hope; then four hours ago the tapping started coming through. They went after it with locators, and fixed it here in the wine cellars.

"The patrol scouts couldn't get in here; no room. We pitched this box together and came in."

"Fast work," I said. I thought of the trip through the dreaded Blight, in a jury-rig made of pine boards. I felt a certain pride in the men of the Imperium.

"Make a place for Colonel Bayard, men," someone said. A space was cleared on the floor, jackets laid out on it. Richthofen was holding me up and I made a mighty effort, got to the pallet and collapsed. Richthofen said something but I didn't hear it. I wondered what had held the meat cutters up so long, and then let it go. I had to say something, warn them. I couldn't remember ...

CHAPTER 14

I was lying in a clean bed in a sunny room, propped up on pillows. It was a little like another room I had awakened in not so long before, but there was one important difference. Barbro sat beside my bed, knitting a ski stocking from red wool. Her hair was piled high on her head, and the sun shone through it, coppery red. Her eyes were hazel, and her features were perfect, and I liked lying there looking at her. She had come every day since my return to the Imperium, and read to me, talked to me, fed me soup and fluffed my pillow. I was enjoying my convalescence.

"If you are good, Brion," Barbro said, "and eat all of your soup today, perhaps by tomorrow evening you will be strong enough to accept the king's invitation."

"OK," I said. "It's a deal."

"The Emperor Ball," Barbro said, "is the most brilliant affair of the year and all the three kings and the Emperor with their ladies will be there together."

I didn't answer; I was thinking. There seemed to be something I wasn't figuring out. I had been leaving all the problems to the Intelligence men, but I knew more than they did about Bale.

I thought of the last big affair, and the brutal attack. I suspected that this time every man would wear a slug-gun under his braided cuff. But the fight on the floor had been merely a diversion, designed to allow the crew to set up an atomic bomb.

I sat bolt upright. The bomb had been turned over to Bale. There would be no chance of surprise attack from the shuttle this time, with alert crew watching around the clock for traces of unscheduled MC activity; but there was no need to bring a bomb in. Bale had one here.

"What is it, Brion?" Barbro asked, leaning forward.

"What did Bale do with that bomb?" I said. "The one they tried to set off at the dance. Where is it now?"

"I don't know. It was turned over to Inspector Bale ..."

"When do the royal parties arrive for the Emperor Ball?" I asked.

"They are already in the city," Barbro said, "at Drottningholm."

I felt my heart start to beat a little faster. Bale wouldn't let this opportunity pass. With the three kings here in the city, and an atomic bomb hidden somewhere, he had to act. At one stroke he could wipe out the leadership of the Imperium, and follow up with a full-scale assault; and against his atomic weapons, the fight would be hopeless.

"Call Manfred, Barbro," I said. "Tell him that bomb's got to be found fast. The kings will have to be evacuated from the city; the ball will have to be cancelled ..."

Barbro spoke into the phone, looked back at me. "He has left the building, Brion," she said. "Shall I try to reach Herr Goering?"

"Yes," I said. I started to tell her to hurry, but she was already speaking rapidly to someone at Goering's office. Barbro was quick to catch on.

"He also is out," Barbro said. "Is there anyone else?"

I thought furiously. Manfred or Hermann would listen to

anything I might say, but with their staffs it would be a different matter. To call off the day of celebration, disturb the royal parties, alarm the city, were serious measures. No one would act on my vague suspicions alone. I had to find my friends in a hurry—or find Bale.

Imperial Intelligence had made a search, found nothing. His apartment was deserted, as well as his small house at the edge of the city. And the monitors had detected no shuttle not known to be an Imperium vessel moving in the Net recently.

There were several possibilities; one was that Bale had returned almost at the same time as I had, slipping in before the situation was known, while some of his own men still manned the alert stations. A second was that he planned to come in prepared to hold off attackers until he could detonate the bomb. Or possibly an accomplice would act for him.

Somehow I liked the first thought best. It seemed more in keeping with what I knew of Bale; shrewder, less dangerous. If I were right, Bale was here now, somewhere in Stockholm, waiting for the hour to blow the city sky-high.

As for the hour, he would wait for the arrival of the Emperor, not longer.

"Barbro," I said, "when does the Emperor arrive?"

"I'm not sure, Brion," she said. "Possibly tonight, but perhaps this afternoon."

That didn't give me much time. I jumped out of bed, and staggered.

"Here I come, ready or not," I said. "I can't just lie here, Barbro. Do you have a car?"

"Yes, my car is downstairs, Brion. Sit down and let me help you." She went to the closet and I sank down. I seemed always to be recuperating lately. I had been through this shaky-legs business just a few days ago, and here I was starting in again. Barbro turned, holding a brown suit in her hands.

"This is all there is, Brion," she said. "It is the uniform of the dictator, that you wore when you came here to the hospital."

"It will have to do," I said. Barbro helped me dress, and we left the room as fast as I could walk. A passing nurse stared, but went on. I was dizzy and panting already.

The elevator helped. I sank down on the stool, head spinning.

I felt something stiff in my chest pocket, and suddenly I had a vivid recollection of Gaston giving me a card as we crouched in the dusk behind the hideout near Algiers, telling me that he thought it was the address of the Big Boss's out-of-town headquarters. I grabbed for the card, squinted at it in the dim light of the ceiling lamp as the car jolted to a stop.

"Ostermalmsgatan 71" was scrawled across the card in blurred pencil. I remembered how I had dismissed it from my mind as of no interest when Gaston had handed it to me; I had hoped for something more useful. Now this might be the little key that could save an empire.

"What is it, Brion?" Barbro asked. "Have you found something?"

"I don't know," I said. "Maybe just a dead end, but maybe not." I handed her the card. "Do you know where this is?"

She read the address. "I think I know the street," she said. "It is not far from the docks, in the warehouse district."

"Let's go," I said, with a fervent hope that we were right, and not too late.

We squealed around a corner, slowed in a street of gloomy warehouses, blind glass windows in looming brick-red facades, with yard-high letters identifying the shipping lines which owned them.

"This is the street," Barbro said. "And the number was seventy-one?"

"That's right," I said. "This is seventy-three; stop here."

We stepped out onto a gritty sidewalk, shaded by the bulk of the buildings, silent. There was a smell of tar and hemp in the air and a hint of sea water.

I stared at the building before me. There was a small door set in the front beside a leading platform. I went up to it, tried it. Locked. I leaned against it and rested.

"Barbro," I said. "Get me a jack handle or tire tool from your car." I hated to drag Barbro into this, but I had no choice. I couldn't do it alone.

She came back with a flat piece of steel eighteen inches long. I jammed it into the wide crack at the edge of the door and pulled. Something snapped, and with a jerk the door popped open. A stair ran up into gloom above. Barbro gave me an arm, and we started up. The hard work helped to keep my mind off the second sun that might light the Stockholm sky at any moment.

Five flights up, we reached a landing. The door we faced was of red-stained wood, solid and with a new lock. I looked at the hinge pins. They didn't look as good as the lock.

It took fifteen minutes, every one of which took a year off my life, but after a final wrench with the steel bar, the last pin clattered to the floor. The door pivoted out and fell against the wall.

"Wait here," I said. I started forward, into the papered hall.

"I'm going with you, Brion," Barbro said. I didn't argue.

We were in a handsome apartment, a little too lavishly furnished. Persian rugs graced the floor, and in the bars of dusty sunlight that slanted through shuttered windows, mellow old teak furniture gleamed and polished ivory figurines stood on dark shelves under silk scrolls from Japan. An ornate screen stood in the center of the room. I walked around a brocaded ottoman over to the screen and looked behind it. On a light tripod of aluminum rods rested the bomb.

Two heavy castings, bolted together around a central flange, with a few wires running along to a small metal box on the underside. Midway up the curve of the side, four small holes, arranged in a square. That was all there was; but it could make a mighty crater where a city had been.

I had no way of knowing whether it was armed or not. I leaned toward the thing, listening. I could hear no sound of a timing device. I thought of cutting the exposed wires, which looked like some sort of jury-rig, but I couldn't risk it; that might set it off.

"Here it is," I said, "but when does it go up?" I had an odd sensation of intangibility, as though I were already a puff of incandescent gas. I tried to think.

"Start searching the place, Barbro," I said. "You might come across something that will give us a hint. I'll phone Manfred's office and get a squad up here to see if we can move the thing without blowing it."

I dialed Imperial Intelligence. Manfred wasn't in, and the fellow on the phone was uncertain what he should do.

"Get a crew here on the double," I yelled. "Somebody who can at least make a guess as to whether this thing can be disturbed."

He said he would confer with General Somebody.

"When does the Emperor arrive?" I asked him. He was sorry, but he was not at liberty to discuss the Emperor's movements. I slammed the receiver down.

"Brion," Barbro called. "Look what's here."

I went to the door which opened onto the next room. A two-man shuttle filled the space. Its door stood open. I looked inside. It was fitted out in luxury; Bale provided well for himself even for short trips. This was what he used to travel from the home line to B-I Two, and the fact that it was here should indicate that Bale was here also; and that he would return to it before the bomb went off.

But then again, perhaps the bomb was even now ticking away its last seconds, and Bale might be far away, safe from the blast. If the latter were true, there was nothing I could do about it; but if he did plan to return here, arm the bomb, set a timer and leave via the shuttle in the bedroom—then maybe I could stop him.

"Barbro," I said, "you've got to find Manfred or Hermann. I'm going to stay here and wait for Bale to come back. If you can find them, tell them to get men here fast who can make a try at disarming this thing. I don't dare move it, and it will take at least two to handle it. If we can move it, we can shove it in the shuttle and send it off; I'll keep phoning. I don't know where you should look but do your best."

Barbro looked at me. "I would rather stay here with you, Brion," she said. "But I understand that I must not."

"You're quite a girl, Barbro," I said.

CHAPTER 15

I was alone now, except for the ominous sphere behind the screen. I hoped for a caller, though. I went to the door which leaned aslant against the rough brick wall outside and unlatched it, maneuvered it into place and dropped the pins back in the hinges, then closed and relatched it.

I went back to the over-stuffed room, started looking through drawers, riffling through papers on the desk. I hoped for something—something that might give me a hint of what Bale planned. I didn't find any hints, but I did find a long-barreled twenty-two revolver, loaded. That helped. I hadn't given much thought to what I would do when Bale got here. I was in no condition to grapple with him; now I had a reasonable chance.

I picked out a hiding place to duck into when and if I heard him coming, a storeroom in the hall, between the bomb and the door. I found a small liquor cabinet and poured myself two fingers of sherry.

I sat in one of the fancy chairs, and tried to let myself go limp. I was using up too much energy in tension. My stomach was a hard knot. I could see the edge of the bomb behind its screen from where I sat. I wondered if there would be any warning before it detonated. My ears were cocked for a click or a rumble from the silent grey city-killer.

The sound I heard was not a click; it was the scrape of shoes on wood, beyond the door. I sat paralyzed for a moment, then got to my feet, stepped to the storeroom and eased behind the door. I loosened the revolver in my pocket and waited.

The sounds were closer now, gratingly loud in the dead silence. Then a key scraped in the lock, and a moment later the tall thin figure of Chief Inspector Bale, traitor, shuffled into view. His small bald head was drawn down between his shoulders, and he looked around the room almost furtively. He pulled off his coat, and for one startled instant I thought he would come to my storeroom to hang it up; but he threw it over the back of a chair.

He went to the screen, peered at the bomb. I could easily have shot him, but that wouldn't have helped me. I wanted Bale to let me know whether the bomb was armed, if it could be moved. He was the only man in the Imperium who knew how to handle this device.

He leaned over the bomb, took a small box from his pocket and stared at it. He looked at his watch, went to the phone. I could barely hear his mutter as he exchanged a few words with someone. He went into the next room, and as I was about to follow to prevent his using the shuttle, he came back. He looked at his watch again, sat in a chair, and opened a small tool kit which lay on the table. He started to work on the metal box with a slender screwdriver. This, then, was the arming device. I tried not to breathe too loud, or to think about how my legs ached.

Shocking in the stillness, the phone rang. Bale looked up, startled, laid the screwdriver and box on the table, and went over to the phone. He looked down at it, chewing his lip. After five rings it stopped. I wondered who it was.

Bale went back to his work. Now he was replacing the cover on the box, frowning over the job. He got up, went to the bomb, licked his lips and leaned over it. He was ready now to arm the bomb. I couldn't wait any longer.

I pushed the door open, and Bale leaped upright, grabbing for his chest, then jumped for the coat on the chair.

"Stand where you are, Bale," I said. "I'd get a real kick out of shooting you."

Bale's eyes were almost popping from his head, his head was tilted back, his mouth opened and closed. I got the impression that I had startled him.

"Sit down," I said. "There." I motioned with the pistol as I came out into the room.

"Bayard," Bale said hoarsely. I didn't say anything. I felt sure now that the bomb was safe. All I had to do was wait until the crew arrived, and turn Bale over to them. Then we could carry the bomb to the shuttle, and send it off into the Blight. But I was feeling very bad now.

I went to a chair, and sank down. I tried not to let Bale see how weak I was. I leaned back, and tried breathing deep through my nose again. If I started to pass out I would have to shoot Bale; he couldn't be left free to threaten the Imperium again.

It was little better now. Bale stood rigid, staring at me.

"Look, Bayard," he said. "I'll bring you in on this with me. I swear I'll give you a full half share. I'll let you keep B-I Two as your own, and I shall take the home line; there's plenty for all. Just put that gun aside ..." He licked his lips, started towards me.

I started to motion with the gun, squeezed the trigger instead. A bullet slapped Bale's shirt sleeve, smacked the wall. He dropped down into the chair behind him. That was close, I thought. That could have killed him. I've got to hold on.

I might as well impress him a little, I thought. "I know how to use this pop gun, you see," I said. "Just a quarter of an inch from the arm, firing from the hip; not bad, don't you agree? Don't try anything else."

"You've got to listen to me, Bayard," Bale said. "Why should you care what happens to these popinjays? We can rule as absolute monarchs."

Bale went on, but I wasn't listening. I was concentrating on staying conscious, waiting for the sounds of help arriving.

"... take one moment, and we're off. What about it?"

Bale was looking at me, with a look of naked greed. I didn't know what he had been saying. He must have interpreted my silence as weakness; he got up again, moved toward me. It was darker in the room; I rubbed my eyes. I was feeling very bad now, very weak. My heart thumped in my throat, my stomach quivered. I was in no shape to be trying to hold this situation in check alone.

Bale stopped, and I saw that he suddenly realized that I was blacking out. He crouched, and with a snarl jumped at me. I would have to kill him. I fired the pistol twice, and Bale reeled away, startled, but still standing.

"Hold on, Bayard, for the love of God," he squealed. I was still alive enough to kill him. I raised the pistol, aimed and fired. I saw a picture jump on the wall. Bale leaped aside. I didn't know if I had hit him yet or not. I was losing my hold, but I wouldn't let him get away. I fired twice more, peering from my chair, and I knew it was the light in my mind fading, not the room. Bale yelled; I saw that he didn't dare to try for the door to the hall or the room where the shuttle waited. He would have to pass me. He screamed as I aimed the pistol with wavering hands, and dived for the other door. I fired and heard the sound echo through a dream of blackness.

*

I wasn't out for more than a few minutes; I came to myself, sitting in the chair, the pistol lying on my lap. The screen had fallen over, and lay across the bomb. I sat up, panicky; maybe Bale had armed it. And where was Bale? I remembered only that he had dashed for the next room. I got up, grabbed for the chair again, then got my balance, made my way to the door. There was a strange sound, a keening, like a cat in the distant alley. I looked into the room, half expecting to see Bale lying on the floor. There was nothing. The light streamed through an open window, a curtain flapped. Bale must have panicked and jumped, I thought. I went to the window, and the keening started up again.

Bale hung by his hands from the eave of the building across the alley, fifteen feet away. The sound came from him. The left leg of his trousers had a long stain of blackish red on it, and drops fell from the toe of his shoe, five stories to the brick payment below.

"Good God, Bale," I said. "What have you done?" I was horrified. I had been ready to shoot him down, but to see him hanging there was something else again.

"Bayard," he croaked. "I can't hold on much longer. For the love of God ..."

What could I do? I was far too weak for any heroics. I looked around the room frantically for an inspiration; I needed a plan or a piece of rope. There was nothing. I pulled a sheet off the bed; it was far too short. Even two or three would never make it. And I couldn't hold it even if I could throw it and Bale caught it. I ran to the phone.

"Operator," I called. "There's a man about to fall from a roof. Get the fire department here with ladders, fast; seventy-one Ostermalmsgatan, fifth floor."

I dropped the phone, ran back to the window. "Hold on,

Bale," I said. "Help's on the way." He must have tried to leap to the next roof, thinking that I was at his heels; and with that hole in his leg he hadn't quite made it.

I thought of Bale, sending me off on a suicide mission, knowing that my imposture was hopeless as long as I stood on my own legs; I thought of the killer shuttle that had lain in wait to smash us as we went in; of the operating room at the hideout, where Bale had planned to carve me into a shape more suitable for his purpose. I remembered Bale shooting down my new-found brother, and the night I had lain in the cold cell, waiting for the butcher; and still I didn't want to see him die this way.

He started to scream suddenly, kicking desperately. He got one foot up on the eave beside his white straining hands; it slipped off. Then he was quiet again. I had been standing here now for five minutes. I wondered how long I had been unconscious. Bale had been there longer now than I would have thought possible. He couldn't last much longer.

"Hold on, Bale," I called. "Only a little while. Don't struggle."

He hung, silent. Blood dripped from his shoe. I looked down at the alley below and shuddered.

I heard a distant sound, a siren, howling. I dashed to the door, opened it, listened. Heavy footsteps sounded below.

"Here," I shouted, "all the way up."

I turned and ran back to the window. Bale was as I had left him. Then one hand slipped off, and he hung by one arm, swinging slightly.

"They're here, Bale," I said. "A few seconds …"

He didn't try to get a new hold. He made no sound. Feet pounded on the stairs outside and I yelled again.

I turned back to the window as Bale slipped down, silent. I didn't watch. I heard him hit—twice.

I staggered back, and the burly man called, looked out the window, milled about. I made my way back to the chair, slumped down. I was empty of emotion. There was a noise all around me, people coming and going. I was hardly conscious of it. After a long time I saw Hermann, and then Barbro was leaning over me. I reached for her hand, hungrily.

"Take me home, Barbro," I said.

I saw Manfred.

"The bomb," I said. "It's safe. Put it in the shuttle and get rid of it."

"My crew is moving it now, Brion," he said.

"You spoke of home, just now," Goering put in. "Speaking for myself, and I am sure also for Manfred, I will make the strongest recommendation that in view of your extraordinary services to the Imperium you be dispatched back to your home as soon as you are well enough to go, if that is your wish. I hope that you will stay with us. But it must be for you to make that decision."

"I don't have to decide," I said. "My choice is made. I like it here, for many reasons. For one thing, I can use all the old cliches from B-I Three, and they sound brand new; and as for home ..." I looked at Barbro:

"Home is where the heart is."

RETIEF: ENVOY TO NEW WORLDS

To Dr. Leon Wright
a genuine diplomat

"... into the chaotic Galactic political scene of the post-Concordiat era, the CDT emerged to carry forward the ancient diplomatic tradition as a great supranational organization dedicated to the contravention of war.[1] As mediators of disputes among Terrestrial-settled worlds and advocates of Terrestrial interests in contacts with alien cultures, Corps diplomats, trained in the chanceries of innumerable defunct bureaucracies, displayed an encyclopedic grasp of the nuances of Extra-Terrestrial mores as set against the labyrinthine socio-politico-economic Galactic context. Never was the virtuosity of a senior Corps diplomat more brilliantly displayed than in Ambassador Spradley's negotiation of the awkward Sirenian Question ..."

—extract from the *Official History of the Corps Diplomatique*, Vol I, reel 2. Solarian Press, New New York, 479 A. E. (AD 2940)

PROTOCOL

In the gloom of the squat, mud-colored reception building, the Counselor, two First Secretaries, and the senior Attachés gathered around the plump figure of Ambassador Spradley, their ornate diplomatic uniforms bright in the vast gloomy room. The Ambassador glanced at his finger watch impatiently.

1 Cf. the original colorful language: "maintenance of a state of tension short of actual conflict." See CDT File 178/b/491, col. VII, spool 12: 745mm (code 2g).

"Ben, are you quite certain our arrival time was made clear?"

Second Secretary Magnan nodded emphatically. "I stressed the point, Mr. Ambassador. I communicated with Mr. T'Cai-Cai just before the lighter broke orbit, and I specifically emphasized—"

"I hope you didn't appear truculent, Mr. Magnan," the Ambassador cut in sharply.

"No indeed, Mr. Ambassador. I merely—"

"You're sure there's no VIP room here?" The Ambassador glanced around the cavernous room. "Curious that not even chairs have been provided."

"If you'd care to sit on one of those crates, I'll use my hanky—"

"Certainly not." The Ambassador looked at his watch again and cleared his throat.

"I may as well make use of these few moments to outline our approach for the more junior members of the staff. It's vital that the entire mission work in harmony in the presentation of the image. We Terrestrials are a kindly, peace-loving race." The Ambassador smiled in a kindly, peace-loving way.

"We seek only reasonable division of spheres of influence with the Yill." He spread his hands, looking reasonable.

"We are a people of high culture, ethical, sincere."

The smile was replaced abruptly by pursed lips. "We'll start by asking for the entire Sirenian System, and settle for half. We'll establish a foothold on all the choicer worlds and, with shrewd handling, in a decade we'll be in a position to assert a wider claim." The Ambassador glanced around. "If there are no questions ..."

Jame Retief, Vice-Consul and Third Secretary in the Corps Diplomatique and junior member of the Terrestrial Embassy to Yill, stepped forward.

"Since we hold the prior claim to the system, why don't we put all our cards on the table to start with? Perhaps if we dealt frankly with the Yill, it would pay us in the long run."

Ambassador Spradley blinked up at the younger man. Beside him, Magnan cleared his throat in the silence.

"Vice-Consul Retief merely means—"

"I'm capable of interpreting Mr. Retief's remark," Spradley snapped. He assumed a fatherly expression.

"Young man, you're new to the service. You haven't yet learned the team play, the give-and-take of diplomacy. I shall expect you to observe closely the work of the experienced negotiators of the mission, learn the importance of subtlety. Excessive reliance on direct methods might tend in time to attenuate the role of the professional diplomat. I shudder to contemplate the consequences."

Spradley turned back to his senior staff members. Retief strolled across to a glass-panelled door and glanced into the room beyond. Several dozen tall grey-skinned Yill lounged in deep couches, sipping lavender drinks from slender glass tubes. Black-tunicked servants moved about inconspicuously, offering trays. Retief watched as a party of brightly-dressed Yill moved toward a wide entrance door. One of the party, a tall male, made to step before another, who raised a hand languidly, fist clenched. The first Yill stepped back and placed his hands on top of his head with a nod. Both Yill continued to smile and chatter as they passed through the door.

Retief rejoined the Terrestrial delegation, grouped around a mound of rough crates stacked on the bare concrete floor, as a small leather-skinned Yill came up.

"I am P'Toi. Come thiss way ..." He motioned. The Terrestrials moved off, Ambassador Spradley in the lead. As the portly diplomat reached the door, the Yill guide darted ahead, shouldering him aside, then hesitated, waiting. The Ambassador almost glared, then remembered the image. He smiled, beckoning the Yill ahead. The Yill muttered in the native language, stared about, then passed through the door. The Terran party followed.

"I'd like to know what that fellow was saying," Magnan said, overtaking the Ambassador. "The way he jostled your Excellency was disgraceful."

A number of Yill waited on the pavement outside the building. As Spradley approached the luxurious open car waiting at the curb, they closed ranks, blocking his way. He drew himself up, opened his mouth—then closed it with a snap.

"The very idea," Magnan said, trotting at Spradley's heels as he stalked back to rejoin the staff, now looking around uncertainly. "One would think these persons weren't aware of the courtesies due a Chief of Mission."

"They're not aware of the courtesies due an apprentice sloat skinner!" Spradley snapped. Around the Terrestrials, the Yill milled nervously, muttering in the native tongue.

"Where has our confounded interpreter betaken himself?" The Ambassador barked. "I daresay they're plotting openly…"

"A pity we have to rely on a native interpreter."

"Had I known we'd meet this rather uncouth reception," the Ambassador said stiffly, "I would have audited the language personally, of course, during the voyage out."

"Oh, no criticism intended, of course, Mr. Ambassador," Magnan said hastily. "Heavens, who would have thought—"

Retief stepped up beside the Ambassador.

"Mr. Ambassador," he said. "I—"

"Later, young man," the Ambassador snapped. He beckoned to the Counselor, and the two moved off, heads together.

A bluish sun gleamed in a dark sky. Retief watched his

breath form a frosty cloud in the chill air. A broad hard-wheeled vehicle pulled up to the platform. The Yill gestured the Terran party to the gaping door at the rear, then stood back, waiting.

Retief looked curiously at the grey-painted van. The legend written on its side in alien symbols seemed to read 'egg nog'. Unfortunately he hadn't had time to learn the script too, on the trip out. Perhaps later he would have a chance to tell the Ambassador he could interpret for the mission.

The Ambassador entered the vehicle, the other Terrestrials following. It was as bare of seats as the Terminal building. What appeared to be a defunct electronic chassis lay in the center of the floor, amid a litter of paper and a purple and yellow sock designed for a broad Yill foot. Retief glanced back. The Yill were talking excitedly. None of them entered the car. The door was closed, and the Terrans braced themselves under the low roof as the engine started up with a whine of worn turbos, and the van moved off.

It was an uncomfortable ride. The unsprung wheels hammered uneven cobblestones. Retief put out an arm as the vehicle rounded a corner, caught the Ambassador as he staggered off-balance. The Ambassador glared at him, settled his heavy tri-corner hat, and stood stiffly until the car lurched again.

Retief stooped, trying to see out through the single dusty window. They seemed to be in a wide street lined with low buildings. They passed through a massive gate, up a ramp, and stopped. The door opened. Retief looked out at a blank grey facade, broken by tiny windows at irregular intervals. A scarlet vehicle was drawn up ahead, the Yill reception committee emerging from it. Through its wide windows Retief saw rich upholstery and caught a glimpse of glasses clamped to a tiny bar.

P'Toi, the Yill interpreter, came forward, gesturing to a small door in the grey wall. Magnan scurried ahead to open it and held it for the Ambassador. As he stepped to it a Yill thrust himself ahead and hesitated. Ambassador Spradley drew himself up, glaring. Then he twisted his mouth into a frozen smile and stepped aside. The Yill looked at each other, then filed through the door.

Retief was the last to enter. As he stepped inside a black-clad servant slipped past him, pulled the lid from a large box by the door and dropped in a paper tray heaped with refuse. There were alien symbols in flaking paint on the box. They seemed, Retief noticed, to spell 'egg nog'.

The shrill pipes and whining reeds had been warming up for an hour when Retief emerged from his cubicle and descended the stairs to the banquet hall. Standing by the open doors he lit a slender cigar and watched through narrowed eyes as obsequious servants in black flitted along the low wide corridor, carrying laden trays into the broad room, arranging settings on a great four-sided table forming a hollow square that almost filled the room. Rich brocades were spread across the center of the side nearest the door, flanked by heavily decorated white cloths. Beyond, plain white extended down the two sides to the far board, where metal dishes were arranged on the bare table top. A richly dressed Yill approached, stepped aside to allow a servant to pass and entered the room.

Retief turned at the sound of Terran voices behind him. The Ambassador came up, trailed by two diplomats. He glanced at Retief, adjusted his ruff and looked into the banquet hall.

"Apparently we're to be kept waiting again," he snapped. "After having been informed at the outset that the Yill have no intention of yielding an inch, one almost wonders …"

"Mr. Ambassador," Retief said. "Have you noticed—"

"However," Ambassador Spradley said, eyeing Retief, "a seasoned diplomatist must take these little snubs in stride. In the end—ah there, Magnan ..." He turned away, talking.

Somewhere a gong clanged. In a moment the corridor was filled with chattering Yill who moved past the group of Terrestrials into the banquet hall. P'Toi, the Yill interpreter, came up, raised a hand.

"Waitt heere ..."

More Yill filed into the dining room, taking their places. A pair of helmeted guards approached and waved the Terrestrials back. An immense grey-jowled Yill waddled to the doors, ropes of jewels clashing softly, and passed through, followed by more guards.

"The Chief of State," Retief heard Magnan say. "The Admirable F'Kau-Kau-Kau."

"I have yet to present my credentials," Ambassador Spradley said. "One expects some latitude in the observances of protocol, but I confess ..." He wagged his head.

The Yill interpreter spoke up.

"You now whill lhie on yourr intesstinss and creep to fesstive board there." He pointed across the room.

"Intestines?" Ambassador Spradley looked about wildly.

"Mr. P'Toi means our stomachs, I wouldn't wonder," Magnan said. "He just wants us to lie down and crawl to our seats, Mr. Ambassador."

"What the devil are you grinning at, you idiot?" the Ambassador snapped.

Magnan's face fell.

Spradley glanced down at the medals across his paunch.

"This is ... I've never ..."

"Homage to godss," the interpreter said.

"Oh-oh—religion," someone said.

"Well, if it's a matter of religious beliefs . . ." The Ambassador looked around dubiously.

"Actually, it's only a couple of hundred feet," Magnan said.

Retief stepped up to P'Toi.

"His Excellency, the Terrestrial Ambassador will not crawl," he said clearly.

"Here, young man, I said nothing—"

"Not to crawl?" The interpreter wore an unreadable Yill expression.

"It is against our religion," Retief said.

"Againsst?"

"We are votaries of the Snake Goddess," Retief said. "It is a sacrilege to crawl." He brushed past the interpreter and marched toward the distant table. The others followed.

Puffing, the Ambassador came to Retief's side as they approached the dozen empty stools on the far side of the square opposite the brocaded position of the Admirable F'Kau-Kau-Kau.

"Mr. Retief, kindly see me after this affair," he hissed. "In the meantime, I hope you will restrain any further rash impulses. Let me remind you *I* am Chief of Mission here."

Magnan came up from behind.

"Let me add my congratulations, Retief," he said. "That was fast thinking."

"Are you out of your mind, Magnan?" the Ambassador barked. "I am extremely displeased."

"Why," Magnan stuttered, "I was speaking sarcastically, of course, Mr. Ambassador. Naturally I, too, was taken aback by his presumption."

The Terrestrials took their places, Retief at the end. The

table before them was of bare green wood, with an array of shallow pewter dishes upon it.

The Yill at the table, some in plain grey, others in black, eyed them silently. There was a constant stir among them as one or another rose and disappeared and others sat down. The pipes and reeds of the orchestra were shrilling furiously and the susurration of Yillian conversation from the other tables rose ever higher in competition. A tall Yill in black was at the Ambassador's side now. The nearby Yill all fell silent as the servant ladled a whitish soup into the largest of the bowls before the Terrestrial envoy. The interpreter hovered, watching.

"That's quite enough," Ambassador Spradley said, as the bowl overflowed. The Yill servant dribbled more of the soup into the bowl. It welled out across the table top.

"Kindly serve the other members of my staff," the Ambassador commanded. The interpreter said something in a low voice. The servant moved hesitantly to the next stool and ladled more soup.

Retief watched, listening to the whispers around him. The Yill at the table were craning now to watch. The servant was ladling the soup rapidly, rolling his eyes sideways. He came to Retief and reached out with the full ladle for the bowl.

"No," Retief said.

The servant hesitated.

"None for me," Retief said.

The interpreter came up, motioned to the servant, who reached again, ladle brimming.

"I don't want any!" Retief said, his voice distinct in the sudden hush. He stared at the interpreter, who stared back for a moment, then waved the servant away and moved on.

"Mr. Retief," a voice hissed. Retief looked down the table.

The Ambassador was leaning forward, glaring at him, his face a mottled crimson.

"I'm warning you, Mr. Retief," he said hoarsely. "I've eaten sheep's eyes in the Sudan, *ka swe* in Burma, hundred-year *cug* on Mars, and everything else that has been placed before me in the course of my diplomatic career, and by the holy relics of Saint Ignatz, you'll do the same!" He snatched up a spoon-like utensil and dipped it into his bowl.

"Don't eat that, Mr. Ambassador," Retief said.

The Ambassador stared, eyes wide. He opened his mouth, guiding the spoon toward it.

Retief stood, gripped the table under its edge, and heaved. The immense wooden slab rose and tilted; dishes crashed to the floor. The table followed with a ponderous slam. Milky soup splattered across the terrazzo; a couple of odd bowls rolled clattering across the room. Cries rang out from the Yill, mingling with a strangled yell from Ambassador Spradley.

Retief walked past the wild-eyed members of the mission to the sputtering chief. "Mr. Ambassador," he said. "I'd like—"

"You'd like! I'll break you, you young hoodlum! Do you realize—"

"Pleass ..." The interpreter stood at Retief's side.

"My apologies," Ambassador Spradley said, mopping his forehead. "My profound—"

"Be quiet," Retief said.

"Wh-what?!"

"Don't apologize," Retief said.

P'Toi was beckoning. "Pleasse, arll come."

Retief turned and followed him.

The portion of the table they were ushered to was covered with an embroidered white cloth, set with thin porcelain dishes. The Yill already seated there rose, amid babbling and moved down to make room for the Terrestrials. The black-clad Yill at the end table closed ranks to fill the vacant seats. Retief sat down, finding Magnan at his side.

"What's going on here?" the Second Secretary said.

"They were giving us dog food," Retief said. "I overheard a Yill. They seated us at the servants' section of the table."

"You mean you understand the language?"

"I learned it on the way out—enough, at least—"

The music burst out with a clangorous fanfare, and a throng of jugglers, dancers, and acrobats poured into the center of the hollow square, frantically juggling, dancing, and back-flipping. Servants swarmed, heaping mounds of fragrant food on the plates of Yill and Terrestrials alike, pouring pale purple liquor into slender glasses. Retief sampled the Yill food. It was delicious. Conversation was impossible in the din. He watched the gaudy display and ate heartily.

Retief leaned back, grateful for the lull in the music. The last of the dishes were whisked away, and more glasses filled. The exhausted entertainers stopped to pick up the thick square coins the diners threw. Retief sighed. It had been a rare feast.

"Retief," Magnan said in the comparative quiet. "What were you saying about dog food as the music came up?"

Retief looked at him. "Haven't you noticed the pattern, Mr. Magnan? The series of deliberate affronts?"

"Deliberate affronts! Just a minute, Retief. They're uncouth, yes, crowding into doorways and that sort of thing. But ..." He looked at Retief uncertainly.

"They herded us into a baggage warehouse at the terminal. Then they hauled us here in a garbage truck."

"Garbage truck!"

"Only symbolic, of course. They ushered us in the

tradesmen's entrance, and assigned us cubicles in the servants' wing. Then we were seated with the coolie-class sweepers at the bottom of the table."

"You must be mistaken! I mean, after all, we're the Terrestrial delegation; surely these Yill must realize our power."

"Precisely, Mr. Magnan. But—"

With a clang of cymbals, the musicians launched a renewed assault. Six tall, helmeted Yill sprang into the center of the floor, paired off in a wild performance, half dance, half combat. Magnan pulled at Retief's sleeve, his mouth moving. Retief shook his head. No one could talk against a Yill orchestra in full cry. Retief sampled a bright red wine and watched the show.

There was a flurry of action, and two of the dancers stumbled and collapsed, their partner-opponents whirling away to pair off again, describe the elaborate pre-combat ritual, and abruptly set to, dulled sabres clashing—and two more Yill were down, stunned. It was a violent dance. Retief watched, the drink forgotten.

The last two Yill approached and retreated, whirled, bobbed, and spun, feinted and postured. And then one was slipping, going down, helmet awry, and the other, a giant, muscular Yill, spun away, whirled in a mad skirl of pipes as coins showered—then froze before a gaudy table, raised the sabre, and slammed it down in a resounding blow across the gay cloth before a lace-and-bow-bedecked Yill. The music stopped with a ringing clash of cymbals.

In utter silence the dancer-fighter stared across the table. With a shout the seated Yill leaped up and raised a clenched fist. The dancer bowed his head, spread his hands on his helmet and resumed his dance as the music blared anew. The beribboned Yill waved a hand negligently, flung a handful of coins across the floor, and sat down.

Now the dancer stood rigid before the brocaded table—and the music chopped off short as the sabre slammed down before a heavy Yill in ornate metallic coils. The challenged Yill rose, raised a fist, and the other ducked his head, putting his hands on his helmet. Coins rolled, and the dancer moved on.

He circled the broad floor, sabre twirling, arms darting in an intricate symbolism. Then suddenly he was towering before Retief, sabre above his head. The music cut, and in the startling instantaneous silence, the heavy sabre whipped over and down with an explosive concussion that set dishes dancing on the table-top.

The Yill's eyes held on Retief's. In the silence Magnan tittered drunkenly. Retief pushed back his stool.

"Steady, my boy," Ambassador Spradley called. Retief stood, the Yill topping his six-foot-three by an inch. In a motion too quick to follow Retief reached for the sabre, twitched it from the Yill's grasp, swung it in a whistling arc. The Yill ducked, sprang back and snatched up a sabre dropped by another dancer.

"Someone stop the madman!" Spradley howled.

Retief leaped across the table, sending fragile dishes spinning.

The other danced back, and only then did the orchestra spring to life with a screech and a mad tattoo of high-pitched drums.

Making no attempt to follow the weaving pattern of the Yill bolero, Retief pressed the Yill, fending off vicious cuts with the blunt weapon, chopping back relentlessly. Left hand on hip, Retief matched blow for blow, driving the other back.

Abruptly the Yill abandoned the double role. Dancing forgotten, he settled down in earnest, cutting, thrusting, parrying. Now the two stood toe to toe, sabres clashing in a lightning exchange. The Yill gave a step, two, then rallied, drove Retief back, back—

Retief feinted, laid a hearty whack across the grey skull. The Yill stumbled, his sabre clattered to the floor. Retief stepped aside as the Yill wavered past him and crashed to the floor.

The orchestra fell silent in a descending wail of reeds. Retief drew a deep breath and wiped his forehead.

"Come back here, you young fool!" Spradley called hoarsely.

Retief hefted the sabre, turned, eyed the brocade-draped table. He started across the floor. The Yill sat as if paralyzed.

"Retief, no!" Spradley yelped.

Retief walked directly to the Admirable F'Kau-Kau-Kau, stopped, raised the sabre.

"Not the Chief of State," someone in the Terrestrial Mission groaned.

Retief whipped the sabre down. The dull blade split the heavy brocade and cleaved the hardwood table. There was utter silence.

The Admirable F'Kau-Kau-Kau rose, seven feet of obese grey Yill. His broad face expressionless to the Terran eye, he raised a fist like a jewel-studded ham.

Retief stood rigid for a long moment. Then, gracefully, he inclined his head and placed his finger tips on his temples. Behind him there was a clatter as Ambassador Spradley collapsed. Then the Admirable F'Kau-Kau-Kau cried out, reached across the table to embrace the Terrestrial, and the orchestra went mad. Grey hands helped Retief across the table, stools were pushed aside to make room at F'Kau-Kau-Kau's side. Retief sat, took a tall flagon of coal-black brandy pressed on him by his neighbor, clashed glasses with The Admirable, and drank.

*

"The feast ends," F'Kau-Kau-Kau said. "Now you and I, Retief, must straddle the Council Stool."

"I'll be honored, Your Admirableness," Retief said. "I must inform my colleagues."

"Colleagues?" F'Kau-Kau-Kau said. "It is for chiefs to parley. Who shall speak for a king while he yet has tongue for talk?"

"The Yill way is wise," Retief said.

F'Kau-Kau-Kau emptied a squat tumbler of pink beer. "I'll treat with you, Retief, as viceroy, since as you say your king is old and the space between worlds is far. But there shall be no scheming underlings privy to our dealings." He grinned a Yill grin. "Afterwards we shall carouse, Retief. The Council Stool is hard, and the waiting handmaidens delectable; this makes for quick agreement."

Retief smiled. "The Admirable speaks wisdom."

"Of course, a being prefers wenches of his own kind," F'Kau-Kau-Kau said. He belched. "The Ministry of Culture has imported several Terrestrial joy-girls, said to be topnotch specimens. As least they have very fat whatchamacallits."

"Your Admirableness is most considerate," Retief said.

"Let us to it then, Retief. I may hazard a tumble with one of your Terries, myself. I fancy an occasional perversion." F'Kau-Kau-Kau dug an elbow into Retief's side and bellowed with laughter.

As Retief crossed to the door at F'Kau-Kau-Kau's side, Ambassador Spradley glowered from behind the plain tablecloth. "Retief," he called, "kindly excuse yourself. I wish a word with you." His voice was icy. Magnan stood behind him, goggling.

"Forgive my apparent rudeness, Mr. Ambassador," said Retief. "I don't have time to explain now—"

"Rudeness!" Spradley yipped. "Don't have time, eh? Let me tell you—"

"Please lower your voice, Mr. Ambassador," Retief said. "The situation is still delicate."

Spradley quivered, his mouth open. He found his voice, "You—you—"

"Silence!" Retief snapped. Spradley looked up at Retief's face, staring for a moment into Retief's grey eyes. He closed his mouth and swallowed.

"The Yill seem to have gotten the impression I'm in charge," Retief said. "We'll have to maintain the deception."

"But—but—" Spradley stuttered. Then he straightened. "That is the last straw," he whispered hoarsely. "I am the Terrestrial Ambassador Extraordinary and Minister Plenipotentiary. Magnan has told me that we've been studiedly and repeatedly insulted, since the moment of our arrival; kept waiting in baggage rooms, transported in refuse lorries, herded about with servants, offered swill at the table. Now I, and my senior staff, are left cooling our heels, without so much as an audience, while this—this multiple Kau person hobnobs with—with—"

Spradley's voice broke. "I may have been a trifle hasty, Retief, in attempting to restrain you. Slighting the native gods and dumping the banquet table are rather extreme measures, but your resentment was perhaps partially justified. I am prepared to be lenient with you." He fixed a choleric eye on Retief.

"I am walking out of this meeting, Mr. Retief. I'll take no more of these personal—"

"That's enough," Retief said sharply. "We're keeping The Admirable waiting."

Spradley's face purpled.

Magnan found his voice. "What are you going to do, Retief?"

"I'm going to handle the negotiation," Retief said. He handed Magnan his empty glass. "Now go sit down and work on the Image."

At his desk in the VIP suite aboard the orbiting Corps vessel, Ambassador Spradley pursed his lips and looked severely at Vice-Consul Retief.

"Further," he said, "you have displayed a complete lack of understanding of Corps discipline, the respect due a senior officer, even the basic courtesies. Your aggravated displays of temper, ill-timed outbursts of violence, and almost incredible arrogance in the assumption of authority make your further retention as an Officer-Agent of the Corps Diplomatique Terrestrienne impossible. It will therefore be my unhappy duty to recommend your immediate—"

There was a muted buzz from the communicator. The Ambassador cleared his throat.

"Well?"

"A signal from Sector HQ, Mr. Ambassador," a voice said.

"Well, read it," Spradley snapped. "Skip the preliminaries..."

"Congratulations on the unprecedented success of your mission. The articles of agreement transmitted by you embody a most favorable resolution of the difficult Sirenian situation, and will form the basis of continued amicable relations between the Terrestrial States and the Yill Empire. To you and your staff, full credit is due for a job well done. Signed, Deputy Assistant Secretary Sternwheeler."

Spradley cut off the voice impatiently. He shuffled papers, then eyed Retief sharply.

"Superficially, of course, an uninitiated observer might leap to the conclusion that the ah … results that were produced in spite of these … ah … irregularities justify the latter." The Ambassador smiled a sad, wise smile. "This is far from the case," he said. "I—"

The communicator burped softly.

"Confound it." Spradley muttered. "Yes?"

"Mr. T'Cai-Cai has arrived," the voice said. "Shall I—"

"Send him in, at once." Spradley glanced at Retief. "Only a two-syllable man, but I shall attempt to correct these false impressions, make some amends …"

The two Terrestrials waited silently until the Yill Protocol chief tapped at the door.

"I hope," the Ambassador said, "that you will resist the impulse to take advantage of your unusual position." He looked at the door. "Come in."

T'Cai-Cai stepped into the room, glanced at Spradley, then turned to greet Retief in voluble Yill. He rounded the desk to the Ambassador's chair, motioned him from it, and sat down.

"I have a surprise for you, Retief," he said in Terran. "I myself have made use of the teaching machine you so kindly lent us."

"That's good," Retief said. "I'm sure Mr. Spradley will be interested in hearing what we have to say."

"Never mind," the Yill said. "I am here only socially." He looked around the room.

"So plainly you decorate your chamber; but it has a certain austere charm." He laughed a Yill laugh.

"Oh, you are a strange breed, you Terrestrials. You surprised us all. You know, one hears such outlandish stories. I tell you in confidence, we had expected you to be over-pushes."

"Pushovers," Spradley said tonelessly.

"Such restraint! What pleasure you gave to those of us, like myself of course, who appreciated your grasp of protocol. Such finesse! How subtly you appeared to ignore each overture, while neatly avoiding actual contamination. I can tell you, there were those who thought—poor fools—that you had no grasp of etiquette. How gratified we were, we professionals, who could appreciate your virtuosity—when you placed matters on a comfortable basis by spurning the cats'-meat. It was sheer pleasure then, waiting, to see what form your compliment would take."

The Yill offered orange cigars, then stuffed one in his nostril.

"I confess even I had not hoped that you would honor our Admirable so signally. Oh, it is a pleasure to deal with fellow professionals, who understand the meaning of protocol."

Ambassador Spradley made a choking sound.

"This fellow has caught a chill," T'Cai-Cai said. He eyed Spradley dubiously. "Step back, my man, I am highly susceptible.

"There is one bit of business I shall take pleasure in attending to, my dear Retief," T'Cai-Cai went on. He drew a large paper from his reticule. "His Admirableness is determined that none other than yourself shall be accredited here. I have here my government's exequatur confirming you as Terrestrial Consul-General to Yill. We shall look forward to your prompt return."

Retief looked at Spradley.

"I'm sure the Corps will agree," he said.

"Then I shall be going," T'Cai-Cai said. He stood up. "Hurry back to us, Retief. There is much that I would show you of the great Empire of Yill." He winked a Yill wink.

"Together, Retief, we shall see many high and splendid things."

... In the face of the multitudinous threats to the peace arising naturally from the complex Galactic situation, the polished techniques devised by Corps theoreticians proved their worth in a thousand difficult confrontations. Even anonymous junior officers, armed with briefcases containing detailed instructions, were able to soothe troubled waters with the skill of experienced negotiators. A case in point was Consul Passwyn's incisive handling of the Jaq-Terrestrial contretemps at Adobe ...

Vol. II, reel 91 480 A. E. (AD 2941)

SEALED ORDERS

"It's true," Consul Passwyn said, "I requested assignment as Principal Officer at a small post. But I had in mind one of those charming resort worlds, with only an occasional visa problem, or perhaps a distressed spaceman or two a year. Instead, I'm zoo-keeper to these confounded settlers, and not for one world, mind you, but eight." He stared glumly at Vice-Consul Retief.

"Still," Retief said, "it gives an opportunity for travel."

"Travel!" the Consul barked. "I hate travel. Here in this backwater system particularly ..." He paused, blinked at Retief, and cleared his throat. "Not that a bit of travel isn't an excellent thing for a junior officer. Marvelous experience."

He turned to the wall-screen and pressed a button. A system triagram appeared: eight luminous green dots arranged around a larger disc representing the primary. Passwyn picked up a pointer, indicating the innermost planet.

"The situation on Adobe is nearing crisis. The confounded settlers—a mere handful of them—have managed, as usual, to stir up trouble with an intelligent indigenous life form, the Jaq. I can't think why they bother, merely for a few oases among the endless deserts. However, I have, at last, received authorization from Sector Headquarters to take certain action."

He swung back to face Retief. "I'm sending you in to handle the situation, Retief—under sealed orders." He picked up a fat, buff envelope. "A pity they didn't see fit to order the Terrestrial settlers out weeks ago, as I suggested. Now it's too late. I'm expected to produce a miracle—a rapprochement between Terrestrial and Jaq and a division of territory. It's idiotic. However, failure would look very bad in my record, so I shall expect results." He passed the buff envelope across to Retief.

"I understood that Adobe was uninhabited," Retief said, "until the Terrestrial settlers arrived."

"Apparently that was an erroneous impression. The Jaq are there." Passwyn fixed Retief with a watery eye. "You'll follow your instructions to the letter. In a delicate situation such as this, there must be no impulsive, impromptu element introduced. This approach has been worked out in detail at Sector; you need merely implement it. Is that entirely clear?"

"Has anyone at Headquarters ever visited Adobe?"

"Of course not. They all hate travel too. If there are no other questions, you'd best be on your way. The mail run departs the dome in less than an hour."

"What's this native life form like?" Retief asked, getting to his feet.

"When you get back," said Passwyn, "you tell me."

*

The mail pilot, a leathery veteran with quarter-inch whiskers, spat toward a stained corner of the compartment, and leaned close to the screen.

"They's shootin' goin' on down there," he said. "Them white puffs over the edge of the desert."

"I'm supposed to be preventing the war," said Retief. "It looks like I'm a little late."

The pilot's head snapped around. "War?" he yelped. "Nobody told me they was a war goin' on on 'Dobe. If that's what that is, I'm gettin' out of here."

"Hold on," said Retief. "I've got to get down. They won't shoot at you."

"They shore won't, sonny. I ain't givin' 'em the chance." He reached for the console and started punching keys. Retief reached out, catching his wrist.

"Maybe you didn't hear me. I said I've got to get down."

The pilot plunged against the restraint and swung a punch that Retief blocked casually. "Are you nuts?" the pilot screeched. "They's plenty shootin' goin' on fer me to see it fifty miles out."

"The mails must go through, you know."

"I ain't no consarned postman. If you're so dead set on gettin' killed—take the skiff. I'll tell 'em to pick up the remains next trip—if the shootin's over."

"You're a pal. I'll take your offer."

The pilot jumped to the lifeboat hatch and cycled it open. "Get in. We're closin' fast. Them birds might take it into their heads to lob one this way."

Retief crawled into the narrow cockpit of the skiff. The pilot ducked out of sight, came back, and handed Retief a heavy old-fashioned power pistol. "Long as you're goin' in, might as well take this."

"Thanks." Retief shoved the pistol in his belt. "I hope you're wrong."

"I'll see they pick you up when the shootin's over—one way or another."

The hatch clanked shut; a moment later there was a jar as the skiff dropped away, followed by heavy buffeting in the backwash from the departing mail boat. Retief watched the tiny screen, his hands on the manual controls. He was dropping rapidly: forty miles thirty-nine …

At five miles Retief threw the light skiff into maximum deceleration. Crushed back in the padded seat, he watched the screen and corrected the course minutely. The planetary surface was rushing up with frightening speed. Retief shook his head and kicked in the emergency retro-drive. Points of light arced up from the planet face below. If they were ordinary chemical warheads the skiff's meteor screens should handle them. The screen on the instrument panel flashed brilliant white, then went dark. The skiff leaped and flipped on its back; smoke filling the tiny compartment. There was a series of shocks, a final bone-shaking concussion, then stillness, broken by the ping of hot metal contracting.

Coughing, Retief disengaged himself from the shock-webbing, groped underfoot for the hatch, and wrenched it open. A wave of hot jungle air struck him. He lowered himself to a bed of shattered foliage, got to his feet … and dropped flat as a bullet whined past his ear.

He lay listening. Stealthy movements were audible from the left. He inched his way forward and made the shelter of a broad-boled dwarf tree. Somewhere a song lizard burbled. Whining insects circled, scented alien life, and buzzed off. There was another rustle of foliage from the underbrush five yards away. A bush quivered, then a low bough dipped. Retief edged back around the trunk and eased down behind a fallen log. A stocky man in a grimy leather shirt and shorts appeared, moving cautiously, a pistol in his hand.

As he passed, Retief rose, leaped the log, and tackled him. They went down together. The man gave one short yell, then struggled in silence. Retief flipped him onto his back, raised a fist—

"Hey!" the settler yelled. "You're as human as I am!"

"Maybe I'll look better after a shave," said Retief. "What's the idea of shooting at me?"

"Lemme up—my name's Potter. Sorry 'bout that. I figured it was a Flap-jack boat; looks just like 'em. I took a shot when I saw something move; didn't know it was a Terrestrial. Who are you? What you doin' here? We're pretty close to the edge of the oasis. That's Flap-jack country over there." He waved a hand toward the north, where the desert lay.

"I'm glad you're a poor shot. Some of those missiles were too close for comfort."

"Missiles, eh? Must be Flap-jack artillery. We got nothin' like that."

"I heard there was a full-fledged war brewing," said Retief. "I didn't expect—"

"Good!" Potter said. "We figured a few of you boys from Ivory would be joining up when you heard. You from Ivory?"

"Yes. I'm—"

"Hey, you must be Lemuel's cousin. Good night! I pretty near made a bad mistake. Lemuel's a tough man to explain anything to."

"I'm—"

"Keep your head down. These damn Flap-jacks have got some wicked hand weapons. Come on ..." He began crawling through the brush. Retief followed. They crossed two hundred yards of rough country before Potter got to his feet, took out a soggy bandanna, and mopped his face.

"You move good for a city man. I thought you folks on Ivory just sat under those domes and read dials. But I guess bein' Lemuel's cousin—"

"As a matter of fact—"

"Have to get you some real clothes, though. Those city duds don't stand up on 'Dobe."

Retief looked down at his charred, torn, sweat-soaked powder-blue blazer and slacks, the informal uniform of a Third Secretary and Vice-Consul in the Corps Diplomatique Terrestrienne.

"This outfit seemed pretty rough-and-ready back home," he said. "But I guess leather has its points."

"Let's get on back to camp. We'll just about make it by sundown. And look, don't say nothin' to Lemuel about me thinkin' you were a Flap-jack."

"I won't, but—"

Potter was on his way, loping off up a gentle slope. Retief pulled off the sodden blazer, dropped it over a bush, added his string tie, and followed Potter.

"We're damn glad you're here, mister," said a fat man with two revolvers belted across his paunch. "We can use every man. We're in bad shape. We ran into the Flap-jacks three months ago and we haven't made a smart move since. First, we thought they were a native form we hadn't run into before. Fact is, one of the boys shot one, think' it was fair game. I guess that was the start of it." He paused to stir the fire.

"And then a bunch of 'em hit Swazey's farm here. Killed two of his cattle, and pulled back," he said.

"We figure they thought the cows were people," said Swazey. "They were out for revenge."

"How could anybody think a cow was folks," another man put in. "They don't look nothin' like—"

"Don't be so dumb, Bert," said Swazey. "They'd never seen Terries before; they know better now."

Bert chuckled. "Sure do. We showed 'em the next time, didn't we, Potter? Got four—"

"They walked right up to my place a couple days after the first time," Swazey said. "We were ready for 'em. Peppered 'em good. They cut and run—"

"Flopped, you mean. Ugliest-lookin' critters you ever saw. Look just like a old piece of dirty blanket humpin' around."

"It's been goin' on this way ever since. They raid and then we raid. But lately they've been bringin' some big stuff into it. They've got some kind of pint-sized airships and automatic rifles. We've lost four men now and a dozen more in the freezer, waiting for the med ship. We can't afford it. The colony's got less than three hundred able-bodied men."

"But we're hangin' onto our farms," said Potter. "All these oases are old sea-beds—a mile deep, solid topsoil. And there's a couple of hundred others we haven't touched yet. The Flapjacks won't get 'em while there's a man alive."

"The whole system needs the food we can raise," Bert said. "These farms we're tryin' to start won't be enough but they'll help."

"We been yellin' for help to the CDT, over on Ivory," said Potter. "But you know these Embassy stooges."

"We heard they were sendin' some kind of bureaucrat in here to tell us to get out and give the oasis to the Flap-jacks," said Swazey. He tightened his mouth. "We're waitin' for him …"

"Meanwhile we got reinforcements comin' up. We put out the word back home; we all got relatives on Ivory and Verde—"

"Shut up, you damn fool!" a deep voice grated.

"Lemuel!" Potter said. "Nobody else could sneak up on us like that—"

"If I'd a been a Flap-jack, I'd of et you alive," the newcomer said, moving into the ring of the fire. He was a tall, broad-faced man in grimy leather. He eyed Retief.

"Who's that?"

"What do ya mean?" Potter spoke in the silence. "He's your cousin."

"He ain't no cousin of mine," Lemuel said. He stepped to Retief.

"Who you spyin' for, stranger?" he rasped.

Retief got to his feet. "I think I should explain—"

A short-nosed automatic appeared in Lemuel's hand, a clashing note against his fringed buckskins.

"Skip the talk. I know a fink when I see one."

"Just for a change, I'd like to finish a sentence," Retief said. "And I suggest you put your courage back in your pocket before it bites you."

"You talk too damned fancy to suit me."

"You're wrong. I talk to suit me. Now, for the last time: put it away."

Lemuel stared at Retief. "You givin' me orders ...?"

Retief's left fist shot out and smacked Lemuel's face dead center. The raw-boned settler stumbled back, blood starting from his nose. The pistol fired into the dirt as he dropped it. He caught himself, jumped for Retief ... and met a straight right that snapped him onto his back—out cold.

"Wow!" said Potter. "The stranger took Lem ... in two punches ..."

“One,” said Swazey. “That first one was just a love tap.”

Bert froze. “Quiet, boys,” he whispered. In the sudden silence a night lizard called. Retief strained, heard nothing. He narrowed his eyes, peering past the fire.

With a swift lunge he seized up the bucket of drinking water, dashed it over the fire, and threw himself flat. He heard the others hit the dirt a split second after him.

“You move fast for a city man,” breathed Swazey beside him. “You see pretty good too. We’ll split and take ’em from two sides. You and Bert from the left, me and Potter from the right.”

“No,” said Retief. “You wait here. I’m going out alone.”

“What’s the idea …?”

“Later. Sit tight and keep your eyes open.” Retief took a bearing on a treetop faintly visible against the sky and started forward.

Five minutes’ cautious progress brought Retief to a slight rise of ground. With infinite caution he raised himself and risked a glance over an outcropping of rock. The stunted trees ended just ahead. Beyond, he could make out the dim contour of rolling desert: Flap-jack country. He got to his feet, clambered over the stone, still hot after a day of tropical heat, and moved forward twenty yards. Around him he saw nothing but drifted sand, palely visible in the starlight, and the occasional shadow of jutting shale slabs. Behind him the jungle was still. He sat down on the ground to wait.

It was ten minutes before a movement caught his eye; something had separated itself from a dark mass of stone, and glided across a few yards of open ground to another shelter. Retief watched. Minutes passed. The shape moved again, slipped into a shadow ten feet distant. Retief felt the butt of the power pistol with his elbow. His guess had better be right …

There was a sudden rasp, like leather against concrete, and a flurry of sand as the Flap-jack charged. Retief rolled aside, then lunged, throwing his weight on the flopping Flap-jack—a yard square, three inches thick at the center, and all muscle. The ray-like creature heaved up, curled backward, its edge rippling, to stand on the flattened rim of its encircling sphincter. It scrabbled with its prehensile fringe-tentacles for a grip on Retief's shoulders. Retief wrapped his arms around the creature and struggled to his feet. The thing was heavy, a hundred pounds at least; fighting as it was, it seemed more like five hundred.

The Flap-jack reversed its tactics, becoming limp. Retief grabbed and felt a thumb slip into an orifice.

The creature went wild. Retief hung on, dug the thumb in deeper.

"Sorry, fellow," he muttered between his clenched teeth. "Eye-gouging isn't gentlemanly, but it's effective ..."

The Flap-jack fell still; only its fringes rippling slowly. Retief relaxed the pressure of his thumb. The creature gave a tentative jerk; the thumb dug in. The Flap-jack went limp again, waiting.

"Now that we understand each other," said Retief, "lead me to your headquarters."

Twenty minutes' walk into the desert brought Retief to a low rampart of thorn branches: the Flap-jacks' outer defensive line against Terry forays. It would be as good a place as any to wait for the next move by the Flap-jacks. He sat down, eased the weight of his captive off his back, keeping a firm thumb in place. If his analysis of the situation was correct, a Flap-jack picket should be along before too long ...

A penetrating beam of red light struck Retief in the face,

then blinked off. He got to his feet. The captive Flap-jack rippled its fringe in an agitated way. Retief tensed his thumb.

"Sit tight," he said. "Don't try to do anything hasty . . ." His remarks were falling on deaf ears—or no ears at all—but the thumb spoke as loudly as words.

There was a slither of sand, then another. Retief became aware of a ring of presences drawing closer.

Retief tightened his grip on the creature. He could see a dark shape now, looming up almost to his own six-three. It appeared that the Flap-jacks came in all sizes.

A low rumble sounded, like a deep-throated growl. It strummed on, then faded out. Retief cocked his head, frowning.

"Try it two octaves higher," he said.

"Awwrrp! Sorry. Is that better?" a clear voice came from the darkness.

"That's fine," Retief said. "I'm here to arrange an exchange of prisoners."

"Prisoners? But we have no prisoners."

"Sure you have. Me. Is it a deal?"

"Ah, yes, of course. Quite equitable. What guarantees do you require?"

"The word of a gentleman is sufficient." Retief released his captive. It flopped once and disappeared into the darkness.

"If you'd care to accompany me to our headquarters," the voice said, "we can discuss our mutual concerns in comfort."

"Delighted."

Red lights blinked briefly. Retief, glimpsing a gap in the thorny barrier, stepped through it. He followed dim shapes across warm sand to a low cave-like entry, faintly lit with a reddish glow.

"I must apologize for the awkward design of our

comfort-dome," said the voice. "Had we known we would be honored by a visit."

"Think nothing of it," Retief said. "We diplomats are trained to crawl."

Inside, with knees bent and head ducked under the five-foot ceiling, Retief looked around at the walls of pink-toned nacre, a floor like burgundy-colored glass spread with silken rugs, and a low table of polished red granite set out with silver dishes and rose-crystal drinking tubes.

"Let me congratulate you," the voice said. Retief turned. An immense Flap-jack, hung with crimson trappings, rippled at his side. The voice issued from a disk strapped to its back. "Your skirmish-forms fight well. I think we will find in each other worthy adversaries."

"Thanks. I'm sure the test would be interesting, but I'm hoping we can avoid it."

"Avoid it?" Retief heard a low humming coming from the speaker in the silence. "Well, let us dine," the mighty Flapjack said at last, "we can resolve these matters later. I am called Hoshick of the Mosaic of the Two Dawns."

"I'm Retief." Hoshick waited expectantly. "... of the Mountain of Red Tape," Retief added.

"Take your place, Retief," said Hoshick. "I hope you won't find our rude couches uncomfortable." Two other large Flap-jacks came into the room and communed silently with Hoshick. "Pray forgive our lack of translating devices," he said to Retief. "Permit me to introduce my colleagues."

A small Flap-jack rippled into the chamber bearing on its back a silver tray, laden with aromatic food. The waiter served the diners and filled the drinking tubes with yellow wine.

"I trust you'll find these dishes palatable," Hoshick said. "Our metabolisms are much alike, I believe." Retief tried the food; it had a delicious nut-like flavor. The wine was indistinguishable from Chateau d'Yquem.

"It was an unexpected pleasure to encounter your party here," Hoshick said. "I confess at first we took you for an indigenous earth-grubbing form, but we were soon disabused of that notion." He raised a tube, manipulating it deftly with his fringe tentacles. Retief returned the salute and drank.

"Of course," Hoshick continued, "as soon as we realized that you were sportsmen like ourselves, we attempted to make amends by providing a bit of activity for you. We've ordered out our heavier equipment and a few trained skirmishers and soon we'll be able to give you an adequate show, or so I hope."

"Additional skirmishers?" said Retief. "How many, if you don't mind my asking?"

"For the moment, perhaps only a few hundred. Thereafter ... well, I'm sure we can arrange that between us. Personally I would prefer a contest of limited scope—no nuclear or radiation-effect weapons. Such a bore, screening the spawn for deviations. Though I confess we've come upon some remarkably useful sports: the ranger-form such as you made captive, for example. Simple-minded, of course, but a fantastically keen tracker."

"Oh, by all means," Retief said. "No atomics. As you pointed out, spawn-sorting is a nuisance, and then too, it's wasteful of troops."

"Ah, well, they are after all expendable. But we agree, no atomics. Have you tried the ground-gwack eggs? Rather a speciality of my Mosaic ..."

"Delicious," said Retief. "I wonder if you've considered eliminating weapons altogether?"

A scratchy sound issued from the disk. "Pardon my laughter," Hoshick said, "but surely you jest?"

"As a matter of fact," said Retief, "we ourselves try to avoid the use of weapons."

"I seem to recall that our first contact of skirmish-forms involved the use of a weapon by one of your units."

"My apologies," said Retief. "The—ah—skirmish-form failed to recognize that he was dealing with a sportsman."

"Still, now that we have commenced so merrily with weapons ..." Hoshick signaled and the servant refilled the drinking tubes.

"There is an aspect I haven't yet mentioned," Retief went on. "I hope you won't take this personally, but the fact is, our skirmish-forms think of weapons as something one employs only in dealing with certain specific life-forms."

"Oh? Curious. What forms are those?"

"Vermin. Deadly antagonists, but lacking in caste. I don't want our skirmish-forms thinking of such worthy adversaries as yourself as vermin."

"Dear me! I hadn't realized, of course. Most considerate of you to point it out." Hoshick clucked in dismay. "I see that skirmish-forms are much the same among you as with us: lacking in perception." He laughed scratchily.

"Which brings us to the crux of the matter," Retief said. "You see, we're up against a serious problem with regard to skirmish-forms: a low birth rate. Therefore we've reluctantly taken to substitutes for the mass actions so dear to the heart of the sportsman. We've attempted to put an end to these contests altogether ..."

Hoshick coughed explosively, sending a spray of wine into the air. "What are you saying?" he gasped. "Are you proposing that Hoshick of the Mosaic of the Two Dawns abandon honor?"

"Sir!" said Retief sternly. "You forget yourself. I, Retief of the Red Tape, merely make an alternate proposal more in keeping with the newest sporting principles."

"New?" cried Hoshick. "My dear Retief, what a pleasant surprise! I'm enthralled with novel modes. One gets so out of touch. Do elaborate."

"It's quite simple, really. Each side selects a representative and the two individuals settle the issue between them."

"I … um … I'm afraid I don't understand. What possible significance could one attach to the activities of a couple of random skirmish-forms?"

"I haven't made myself clear," Retief said. He took a sip of wine. "We don't involve the skirmish-forms at all; that's quite passé."

"You don't mean …?"

"That's right. You and me."

Outside the starlit sand Retief tossed aside the power pistol and followed it with the leather shirt Swazey had lent him. By the faint light he could just make out the towering figure of the Flap-jack rearing up before him, his trappings gone. A silent rank of Flap-jack retainers were grouped behind him.

"I fear I must lay aside the translator now, Retief," said Hoshick. He sighed and rippled his fringe tentacles. "My spawn-fellows will never credit this. Such a curious turn fashion has taken. How much more pleasant it is to observe the action from a distance."

"I suggest we use Tennessee rules," said Retief. "They're very liberal: biting, gouging, stomping, kneeling, and, of course, choking, as well as the usual punching, shoving, and kicking."

"Hmmm. These gambits seem geared to forms employing rigid endo-skeletons; I fear I shall be at a disadvantage."

“Of course,” Retief said, “if you’d prefer a more plebeian type of contest …”

“By no means. But perhaps we could rule out tentacle-twisting, just to even the balance.”

“Very well. Shall we begin?”

With a rush Hoshick threw himself at Retief, who ducked, whirled, and leaped on the Flap-jack’s back—and felt himself flipped clear by a mighty ripple of the alien’s slab-like body. Retief rolled aside as Hoshick turned on him, jumped to his feet, and threw a punch to Hoshick’s mid-section. The alien whipped his left fringe around in an arc that connected with Retief’s jaw, spinning onto his back. Hoshick’s weight struck Retief like a dumptruck-load of concrete. Retief twisted, trying to roll. The flat body of the creature blanketed him. He worked an arm free and drummed blows on the leathery back. Hoshick nestled closer.

Retief’s air was running out. He heaved up against the smothering weight; nothing budged. He was wasting his strength.

He remembered the ranger-form he had captured. The sensitive orifice had been placed ventrally, in what would be the thoracic area …

He groped, feeling tough hide set with horny granules. He would be missing skin tomorrow—if there was a tomorrow. His thumb found the orifice, and he probed.

The Flap-jack recoiled. Retief held fast, probed deeper, groping with the other hand. If the creature were bilaterally symmetrical there would be a set of ready-made handholds …

There were. Retief dug in and the Flap-jack writhed and pulled away. Retief held on, scrambled to his feet, threw his weight against Hoshick, and fell on top of him, still gouging. Hoshick rippled his fringe wildly, flopped in distress, then went limp. Retief relaxed, released his hold, and got to his feet, breathing hard. Hoshick humped himself over onto his ventral side, lifted, and moved gingerly over to the sidelines. His retainers came forward, assisted him into his trappings, and strapped on the translator. He sighed heavily, adjusting the volume.

"There is much to be said for the old system," he said. "What a burden one's sportsmanship places on one at times."

"Great fun, wasn't it?" said Retief. "Now, I know you'll be eager to continue. If you'll just wait while I run back and fetch some of our gouger-forms—"

"May hide-ticks devour the gouger-forms!" Hoshick bellowed. "You've given me such a sprong-ache as I'll remember each spawning-time for a year."

"Speaking of hide-ticks," said Retief, "we've developed a biter-form—"

"Enough!" Hoshick roared so loudly that the translator bounced on his hide. "Suddenly I yearn for the crowded yellow sands of Jaq. I had hoped …" He broke off, drawing a rasping breath. "I had hoped, Retief," he said, speaking sadly now, "to find a new land here where I might plan my own Mosaic, till these alien sands and bring forth such a crop of paradise-lichen as should glut the markets of a hundred worlds. But my spirit is not equal to the prospect of biter-forms and gouger-forms without end. I am shamed before you."

"To tell you the truth, I'm old-fashioned myself," said Retief. "I'd rather watch the action from a distance too."

"But surely your spawn-fellows would never condone such an attitude."

"My spawn-fellows aren't here. And besides, didn't I mention it? No one who's really in the know would think of engaging in competition by mere combat if there were any other way. Now, you mentioned tilling the sand, raising lichens—"

"That on which we dined," said Hoshick, "and from which the wine is made."

"The big trend in fashionable diplomacy today is farming competition. Now, if you'd like to take these deserts and raise lichen, we'll promise to stick to the oases and raise vegetables."

Hoshick curled his back in attention. "Retief, you're quite serious? You would leave all the fair sand hills to us?"

"The whole works. Hoshick. I'll take the oases."

Hoshick rippled his fringes ecstatically. "Once again you have outdone me, Retief," he cried, "this time, in generosity."

"We'll talk over the details later. I'm sure we can establish a set of rules that will satisfy all parties. Now I've got to get back. I think some of the gouger-forms are waiting to see me."

It was nearly dawn when Retief gave the whistled signal he had agreed on with Potter, then rose and walked into the camp circle. Swazey stood up.

"There you are," he said. "We been wonderin' whether to go out after you."

Lemuel came forward, one eye black to the cheekbone. He held out a raw-boned hand. "Sorry I jumped you, stranger. Tell you the truth, I thought you was some kind of stool-pigeon from the CDT."

Bert came up behind Lemuel. "How do you know he ain't, Lemuel?" he said. "Maybe he—"

Lemuel floored Bert with a backward sweep of his arm. "Next cotton-picker says some embassy Johnny can cool me gets worse'n that."

"Tell me," said Retief. "How are you boys fixed for wine?"

"Wine? Mister, we been livin' on stump water for a year now. 'Dobe's fatal to the kind of bacteria it takes to ferment liquor."

"Try this." Retief handed over a squat jug. Swazey drew the cork, sniffed, drank, and passed it to Lemuel.

"Mister, where'd you get that?"

"The Flap-jacks make it. Here's another question for you: would you concede a share in this planet to the Flap-jacks in return for a peace guarantee?"

At the end of a half hour of heated debate Lemuel turned to Retief. "We'll make any reasonable deal," he said. "I guess they got as much right here as we have. I think we'd agree to a fifty-fifty split. That'd give about a hundred and fifty oases to each side."

"What would you say to keeping all the oases and giving them the desert?"

Lemuel reached for the wine jug, his eyes on Retief. "Keep talkin', mister," he said. "I think you got yourself a deal."

Consul Passwyn glanced up as Retief entered the office.

"Sit down, Retief," he said absently. "I thought you were over on Pueblo, or Mud-flat, or whatever they call that desert."

"I'm back."

Passwyn eyed him sharply. "Well, well, what is it you need, man? Speak up. Don't expect me to request any military assistance."

Retief passed a bundle of documents across the desk. "Here's the Treaty. And a Mutual Assistance Pact and a Trade Agreement."

"Eh?" Passwyn picked up the papers and riffled through them. He leaned back in his chair, beaming.

"Well, Retief, expeditiously handled." He stopped and blinked at the Vice-Consul. "You seem to have a bruise on your jaw. I hope you've been conducting yourself as befits a member of the Consulate staff."

"I attended a sporting event. One of the players got a little excited."

"Well … it's one of the hazards of the profession. One must pretend an interest in such matters." Passwyn rose and extended a hand. "You've done well, my boy. Let this teach you the value of following instructions to the letter."

Outside, by the hall incinerator drop, Retief paused long enough to take from his briefcase a large buff envelope, still sealed, and drop it in the slot.

… Highly effective ancillary programs, developed early in Corps history, played a vital role in promoting harmony among the peace-loving peoples of the Galactic community. The notable success of Assistant Attaché (later Ambassador) Magnan in the cosmopolitization of reactionary elements in the Nicodeman Cluster was achieved through the agency of these enlightened programs …

Vol. III, reel 71 482 A. E. (AD 2943)

CULTURAL EXCHANGE

First Secretary Magnan took his green-lined cape and orange-feathered beret from the clothes tree. "I'm off now, Retief," he said. "I hope you'll manage the administrative routine during my absence without any unfortunate incidents."

"That seems a modest enough hope," said Second Secretary Retief. "I'll try to live up to it."

"I don't appreciate frivolity with reference to this Division," Magnan said testily. "When I first came here, the Manpower Utilization Directorate, Division of Libraries and Education was a shambles. I fancy I've made MUDDLE what it is today. Frankly, I question the wisdom of placing you in charge of such a sensitive desk, even for two weeks; but remember, yours is a purely rubber-stamp function."

"In that case, let's leave it to Miss Furkle, and I'll take a couple of weeks off myself. With her poundage, she could bring plenty of pressure to bear."

"I assume you jest, Retief," Magnan said sadly. "I should expect even you to appreciate that Bogan participation in the Exchange Program may be the first step toward sublimation of their aggressions into more cultivated channels."

"I see they're sending two thousand students to d'Land," Retief said, glancing at the Memo for Record. "That's a sizable sublimation."

Magnan nodded. "The Bogans have launched no less than four military campaigns in the last two decades. They're known as the Hoodlums of the Nicodeman Cluster. Now, perhaps, we shall see them breaking that precedent and entering into the cultural life of the Galaxy."

"Breaking and entering," Retief said. "You may have something there. But I'm wondering what they'll study on d'Land. That's an industrial world of the poor-but-honest variety."

"Academic details are the affair of the students and their professors," Magnan said. "Our function is merely to bring them together. See that you don't antagonize the Bogan representative. This will be an excellent opportunity for you to practice your diplomatic restraint—not your strong point, I'm sure you'll agree—"

A buzzer sounded. Retief punched a button. "What is it, Miss Furkle?"

"That—bucolic person from Lovenbroy is here again." On the small desk screen, Miss Furkle's meaty features were compressed in disapproval.

"This fellow's a confounded pest; I'll leave him to you, Retief," Magnan said. "Tell him something; get rid of him. And remember: here at Corps HQ, all eyes are upon you."

"If I'd thought of that, I'd have worn my other suit," Retief said.

Magnan snorted and passed from view. Retief punched Miss Furkle's button.

"Sent the bucolic person in."

A tall broad man with bronze skin and grey hair, wearing tight trousers of heavy cloth, a loose shirt open at the neck, and a short jacket, stepped into the room, a bundle under his arm. He paused at sight of Retief, looked him over momentarily, then advanced and held out his hand. Retief took it. For a moment the two big men stood, face to face. The newcomer's jaw muscles knotted. Then he winced. Retief dropped his hand, motioned to a chair.

"That's nice knuckle work, mister," the stranger said, massaging his hand. "First time anybody ever did that to me. My fault, though, I started it, I guess." He grinned and sat down.

"What can I do for you?" the Second Secretary said. "My name's Retief. I'm taking Mr. Magnan's place for a couple of weeks."

"You work for this culture bunch, do you? Funny, I thought they were all ribbon-counter boys. Never mind. I'm Hank Arapoulous. I'm a farmer. What I wanted to see you about was—" He shifted in his chair. "Well, out on Lovenbroy we've got a serious problem. The wine crop is just about ready. We start picking in another two, three months. Now I don't know if you're familiar with the Bacchus vines we grow?"

"No," Retief said. "Have a cigar?" He pushed a box across the desk.

Arapoulous took one. "Bacchus vines are an unusual crop," he said, puffing life into the cigar. "Only mature every twelve years. In between, the vines don't need a lot of attention; our time's mostly our own. We like to farm, though. Spend a lot of time developing new forms. Apples the size of a melon—and sweet."

"Sounds very pleasant," Retief said. "Where does the Libraries and Education Division come in?"

Arapoulous leaned forward. "We go in pretty heavy for the arts. Folks can't spend all their time hybridizing plants. We've turned all the land area we've got into parks and farms; course, we left some sizable forest areas for hunting and such. Lovenbroy's a nice place, Mr. Retief."

"It sounds like it, Mr. Arapoulous. Just what—"

"Call me Hank. We've got long seasons back home. Five of 'em. Our year's about eighteen Terry months. Cold as hell in winter—eccentric orbit, you know. Blue-black sky, stars visible all day. We do mostly painting and sculpture in the winter. Then Spring—still plenty cold. Lots of skiing, bobsledding, ice skating—and it's the season for woodworkers. Our furniture—"

"I've seen some of your furniture, I believe," said Retief. "Beautiful work."

Arapoulous nodded. "All local timbers, too. Lots of metals in our soil; those sulphates give the woods some color, I'll tell you. Then comes the Monsoon. Rain—it comes down in sheets—but the sun's gettin' closer; shines all the time. Ever seen it pouring rain in the sunshine? That's the music-writing season. Then summer. Summer's hot. We stay inside in the daytime, and have beach parties all night. Lots of beach on Lovenbroy, we're mostly islands. That's the drama and symphony time. The theatres are set up on the sand, or anchored on barges off-shore. You have the music and the surf and the bonfires and stars—we're close to the center of a globular cluster, you know ..."

"You say it's time now for the wine crop?"

"That's right. Autumn's our harvest season. Most years we have just the ordinary crops: fruit, grain, that kind of thing.

Getting it in doesn't take long. We spend most of the time on architecture, getting new places ready for the winter, or remodeling the older ones. We spend a lot of time in our houses; we like to have them comfortable. But this year's different. This is Wine Year."

Arapoulous puffed on his cigar and looked worriedly at Retief. "Our wine crop is our big money crop," he said. "We make enough to keep us going. But this year …"

"The crop isn't panning out?"

"Oh, the crop's fine; one of the best I can remember. Course, I'm only twenty-eight; I can't remember but two other harvests. The problem's not the crop …"

"Have you lost your markets? That sounds like a matter for the Commercial—"

"Lost our markets? Mister, nobody that ever tasted our wines ever settled for anything else!"

"It sounds like I've been missing something," said Retief. "I'll have to try them some time."

Arapoulous put his bundle on the desk, pulled off the wrappings. "No time like the present," he said.

Retief looked at the two squat bottles, one green, one amber, both dusty, with faded labels, and blackened corks secured by wire.

"Drinking on duty is frowned on in the Corps, Mr. Arapoulous," he said.

"This isn't drinking, it's just wine." Arapoulous pulled the wire retainer loose and thumbed the cork. It rose slowly, then popped in the air. Arapoulous caught it. Aromatic fumes wafted from the bottle. "Besides, my feelings would be hurt if you didn't join me." He winked.

Retief took two thin-walled glasses from a table beside the desk. "Come to think of it, we also have to be careful about violating quaint native customs." Arapoulous filled the glasses. Retief picked one up, sniffed the deep rust colored fluid, tasted it, then took a healthy swallow. He looked at Arapoulous thoughtfully.

"Hmmm, it tastes like salted pecans, with an undercurrent of crusted port."

"Don't try to describe it, Mr. Retief," Arapoulous said. He took a mouthful of wine, swished it around his teeth, and swallowed. "It's Bacchus wine, that's all." He pushed the second bottle toward Retief. "The custom back home is to alternate red wine and black."

Retief put aside his cigar, pulled the wires loose, nudged the cork, and caught it as it popped up.

"Bad luck if you miss the cork," Arapoulous said, nodding. "You probably never heard about the trouble we had on Lovenbroy a few years back?"

"Can't say that I did, Hank." Retief poured the black wine into the two fresh glasses. "Here's to the harvest."

"We've got plenty of minerals on Lovenbroy," Arapoulous said, swallowing wine. "But we don't plan to wreck the landscape mining 'em. We like to farm. About ten years back some neighbors of ours landed a force. They figured they knew better what to do with our minerals than we did. Wanted to strip-mine, smelt ore. We convinced 'em otherwise. But it took a year, and we lost a lot of men."

"That's too bad," Retief said. "I'd say this one tastes more like roast beef and popcorn over a Riesling base."

"It put us in a bad spot," Arapoulous went on. "We had to borrow money from a world called Croanie, mortgaged our crops; we had to start exporting art work too. Plenty of buyers, but it's not the same when you're doing it for strangers."

"What's the problem?" Retief said, "Croanie about to foreclose?"

"The loan's due. The wine crop would put us in the clear; but we need harvest hands. Picking Bacchus grapes isn't a job you can turn over to machinery—and we wouldn't if we could. Vintage season is the high point of living on Lovenbroy. Everybody joins in. First, there's the picking in the fields. Miles and miles of vineyards covering the mountain sides, crowding the river banks, with gardens here and there. Big vines, eight feet high, loaded with fruit, and deep grass growing between. The wine-carriers keep on the run, bringing wine to the pickers. There's prizes for the biggest day's output, bets on who can fill the most baskets in an hour. The sun's high and bright, and it's just cool enough to give you plenty of energy. Come nightfall the tables are set up in the garden plots, and the feast is laid on: roast turkeys, beef, hams, all kinds of fowl. Big salads and plenty of fruit and fresh-baked bread ... and wine, plenty of wine. The cooking's done by a different crew each night in each garden, and there's prizes for the best crews.

"Then the wine-making. We still tramp out the vintage. That's mostly for the young folks—but anybody's welcome. That's when things start to get loosened up. Matter of fact, pretty near half our young-uns are born about nine months after a vintage. All bets are off then. It keeps a fellow on his toes though; ever tried to hold onto a gal wearin' nothing but a layer of grape juice?"

"Never did," Retief said. "You say most of the children are born after a vintage. That would make them only twelve years old by the time—"

"Oh, that's Lovenbroy years; they'd be eighteen, Terry reckoning."

"I was thinking you looked a little mature for twenty-eight," Retief said.

"Forty-two, Terry years," Arapoulous said. "But this year—it looks bad. We've got a bumper crop—and we're short-handed. If we don't get a big vintage, Croanie steps in; lord knows what they'll do to the land.

"What we figured was, maybe you Culture boys could help us out: a loan to see us through the vintage, enough to hire extra hands. Then we'd repay it in sculpture, painting, furniture—"

"Sorry, Hank. All we do here is work out itineraries for traveling side-shows, that kind of thing. Now if you needed a troop of Groaci nose-flute players—"

"Can they pick grapes?"

"Nope—anyway they can't stand the daylight. Have you talked this over with the Labor office?"

"Sure did. They said they'd fix us up with all the electronics specialists and computer programmers we wanted—but no field hands. Said it was what they classified as menial drudgery; you'd have thought I was trying to buy slaves."

The buzzer sounded. Miss Furkle appeared on the desk screen.

"You're due at the Inter-Group Council in five minutes," she said. "Then afterwards, there are the Bogan students to meet."

"Thanks." Retief finished his glass and stood. "I have to run, Hank," he said. "Let me think this over. Maybe I can come up with something. Check with me day after tomorrow. And you'd better leave the bottles here. Cultural exhibits, you know."

*

As the council meeting broke up, Retief caught the eye of a colleague across the table.

"Mr. Whaffle, you mentioned a shipment going to a place called Croanie. What are they getting?"

Whaffle blinked. "You're the fellow who's filling in for Magnan, over at MUDDLE," he said. "Properly speaking, equipment grants are the sole concern of the Motorized Equipment Depot, Division of Loans and Exchanges." He pursed his lips. "However, I suppose there's no harm in my telling you. They'll be receiving heavy mining equipment."

"Drill rigs, that sort of thing?"

"Strip mining gear." Whaffle took a slip of paper from a breast pocket and blinked at it. "Bolo Model WV/1 tractors, to be specific. Why MUDDLE's interest in MEDDLE's activities?"

"Forgive my curiosity, Mr. Whaffle. It's just that Croanie cropped up earlier today; seems she holds a mortgage on some vineyards over on—"

"That's not MEDDLE's affair, sir," Whaffle cut in. "I have sufficient problems as Chief of MEDDLE without probing into MUDDLE's business."

"Speaking of tractors," another man put in, "we over at the Special Committee for Rehabilitation and Overhaul of Underdeveloped Nations' General Economies have been trying for months to get a request for mining equipment for d'Land through MEDDLE—"

"SCROUNGE was late on the scene," Whaffle said. "First come, first served, that's our policy at MEDDLE. Good day, gentlemen." He strode off, a briefcase under his arm.

"That's the trouble with peaceful worlds," the SCROUNGE committeeman said. "Boge is a trouble-maker, so every agency in the Corps is out to pacify her, while my chance to make a record—that is, assist peace-loving d'Land, comes to nought."

"What kind of university do they have on d'Land?" asked Retief. "We're sending them two thousand exchange students. It must be quite an institution—"

"University? D'Land has one under-endowed technical college."

"Will all the exchange students be studying at the Technical College?"

"Two thousand students? Hah! Two hundred students would overtax the facilities of the college!"

"I wonder if the Bogans know that?"

"The Bogans? Why, most of d'Land's difficulties are due to the unwise trade agreement she entered into with Boge. Two thousand students indeed." He snorted and walked away.

Retief stopped by the office to pick up his short violet cape, then rode the elevator to the roof of the 230-story Corps HQ building and hailed a cab to the port. The Bogan students had arrived early. Retief saw them lined up on the ramp waiting to go through customs. It would be half an hour before they were cleared through. He turned into the bar and ordered a beer. A tall young fellow on the next stool raised his glass.

"Happy days," he said.

"And nights to match."

"You said it." He gulped half his beer. "My name's Karsh. Mr. Karsh. Yep, Mr. Karsh. Boy, this is a drag, sitting around this place waiting."

"You meeting somebody?"

"Yeah. Bunch of babies. Kids. How they expect—Never mind. Have one on me."

"Thanks. You a scoutmaster?"

"I'll tell you what I am; I'm a cradle-robber. You know," he turned to Retief, "not one of those kids is over eighteen." He hiccupped. "Students, you know. Never saw a student with a beard, did you?"

"Lots of times. You're meeting the students, are you?"

The young fellow blinked at Retief. "Oh, you know about it, huh?"

"I represent MUDDLE."

Karsh finished his beer and ordered another. "I came on ahead: sort of an advance guard for the kids. I trained 'em myself. Treated it like a game, but they can handle a CSU. Don't know how they'll act under pressure. If I had my old platoon—"

He looked at his beer glass, then pushed it back. "Had enough," he said. "So long, friend. Or are you coming along?"

Retief nodded. "Might as well."

At the exit to the Customs enclosure, Retief watched as the first of the Bogan students came through, caught sight of Karsh, and snapped to attention.

"Drop that, mister," Karsh snapped. "Is that any way for a student to act?"

The youth, a round-faced lad with broad shoulders, grinned.

"Guess not," he said. "Say, uh, Mr. Karsh, are we gonna get to go to town. Us fellas were thinkin'—"

"You were, hah? You act like a bunch of school kids—I mean … No! Now line up!"

"We have quarters ready for the students," Retief said. "If you'd like to bring them around to the west side, I have a couple of copters laid on."

"Thanks," said Karsh. "They'll stay here until take-off time. Can't have the little darlings wandering around loose. Might get ideas about going over the hill." He hiccupped. "I mean, they might play hookey."

"We've scheduled your re-embarkation for noon tomorrow.

That's a long wait. MUDDLE's arranged theatre tickets and a dinner."

"Sorry," Karsh said. "As soon as the baggage gets here, we're off." He hiccupped again. "Can't travel without our baggage, y'know."

"Suit yourself," Retief said. "Where's the baggage now?"

"Coming in aboard a Croanie lighter."

"Maybe you'd like to arrange for a meal for the students here?"

"Sure," Karsh said. "That's a good idea. Why don't you join us?" Karsh winked. "And bring a few beers."

"Not this time," Retief said. He watched the students, still emerging from Customs. "They seem to be all boys," he commented. "No female students?"

"Maybe later," Karsh said, "after we see how the first bunch is received."

Back at the MUDDLE office, Retief buzzed Miss Furkle.

"Do you know the name of the institution these Bogan students are bound for?"

"Why, the university at d'Land, of course."

"Would that be the Technical College?"

Miss Furkle's mouth puckered. "I'm sure I've never pried into these details—"

"Where does doing your job stop and prying begin, Miss Furkle?" Retief said. "Personally, I'm curious as to just what it is these students are travelling so far to study—at Corps expense."

"Mr. Magnan never—"

"For the present, Miss Furkle, Mr. Magnan is vacationing. That leaves me with the question of two thousand young male students headed for a world with no classrooms for them …

a world in need of tractors. But the tractors are on their way to Croanie, a world under obligations to Boge. And Croanie holds a mortgage on the best grape acreage on Lovenbroy."

"Well!" Miss Furkle snapped, her small eyes glaring under unplucked brows. "I hope you're not questioning Mr. Magnan's wisdom!"

"About Mr. Magnan's wisdom there can be no doubts," Retief said. "But never mind. I'd like you to look up an item for me. How many tractors will Croanie be getting under the MEDDLE program?"

"Why, that's entirely MEDDLE business," Miss Furkle said. "Mr. Magnan always—"

"I'm sure he did. Let me know about the tractors as soon as you can."

Miss Furkle sniffed and disappeared from the screen. Retief left the office, descended forty-one stories, and followed a corridor to the Corps Library. In the stacks he thumbed through catalogs and pored over indices.

"Can I help you?" someone chirped. A tiny librarian stood at his elbow.

"Thank you, Ma'am," Retief said. "I'm looking for information on a mining rig: a Bolo model WV tractor."

"You won't find it in the industrial section," the librarian said. "Come along." Retief followed her along the stacks to a well-lit section lettered ARMAMENTS. She took a tape from the shelf, plugged it into the viewer, flipped through, and stopped at a picture of a squat armored vehicle.

"That's the model WV," she said. "It's what is known as a Continental Siege Unit. It carries four men, with a half-megaton/second firepower—"

"There must be an error somewhere," Retief said. "The Bolo model I want is a tractor, model WV M-l—"

"Oh, the modification was the addition of a blade for demolition work. That must be what confused you."

"Probably—among other things. Thank you."

Miss Furkle was waiting at the office. "I have the information you wanted," she said. "I've had it for over ten minutes. I was under the impression you needed it urgently, and I went to great lengths—"

"Sure," Retief said. "Shoot. How many tractors?"

"Five hundred."

"Are you sure?"

Miss Furkle's chins quivered. "Well! If you feel I'm incompetent."

"Just questioning the possibility of a mistake, Miss Furkle. Five hundred tractors is a lot of equipment."

"Was there anything further?" Miss Furkle inquired frigidly.

"I sincerely hope not," Retief said.

Leaning back in Magnan's padded chair with its power swivel and hip-u-matic contour, Retief leafed through a folder labelled "CERP 7-602-Ba; CROANIE (general)." He paused at a page headed INDUSTRY. Still reading, he opened the desk drawer, took out the two bottles of Bacchus wine and two glasses. He poured an inch of wine into each, then sipped the black wine meditatively. It would be a pity, he reflected, if anything should interfere with the production of such vintages …

Half an hour later he laid the folder aside, keyed the phone, and put through a call to the Croanie Legation, asking for the Commercial attaché.

"Retief here, Corps HQ," he said airily. "About the MEDDLE shipment, the tractors. I'm wondering if there's been a slip-up. My records show we're shipping five hundred units."

"That's correct. Five hundred."

Retief waited.

"Ah ... are you there, Mr. Retief?"

"I'm still here. And I'm still wondering about the five hundred tractors."

"It's perfectly in order; I thought it was all settled. Mr. Whaffle—"

"One unit would require a good-sized plant to handle its output," Retief said. "Now Croanie subsists on her fisheries. She has perhaps half-a-dozen pint-sized processing plants. Maybe, in a bind, they could handle the ore ten WV's could scrape up ... if Croanie had any ore. By the way, isn't a WV a poor choice as a mining outfit? I should think—"

"See here, Retief, why all this interest in a few surplus tractors? And in any event, what business is it of yours how we plan to use the equipment? That's an internal affair of my government. Mr. Whaffle—"

"I'm not Mr. Whaffle. What are you going to do with the other four hundred and ninety tractors?"

"I understood the grant was to be with no strings attached!"

"I know it's bad manners to ask questions. It's an old diplomatic tradition that any time you can get anybody to accept anything as a gift, you've scored points in the game. But if Croanie has some scheme cooking—"

"Nothing like that, Retief! It's a mere business transaction."

"What kind of business do you do with a Bolo WV? With or without a blade attached, it's what's known as a continental siege unit—"

"Great Heavens, Retief! Don't jump to conclusions! Would you have us branded as warmongers? Frankly—is this a closed line?"

"Certainly. You may speak freely."

"The tractors are for trans-shipment. We've gotten ourselves into a difficult situation in our balance of payments. This is an accommodation to a group with which we have strong business ties."

"I understand you hold a mortgage on the best land on Lovenbroy," Retief said. "Any connection?"

"Why … ah … no. Of course not."

"Who gets the tractors eventually?"

"Retief, this is unwarranted interference—"

"Who gets them?"

"They happen to be going to Lovenbroy. But I scarcely see—"

"And who's the friend you're helping out with an unauthorized trans-shipment of grant material?"

"Why … ah … I've been working with a Mr. Gulver, a Bogan representative."

"And when will they be shipped?"

"Why, they went out a week ago. They'll be halfway there by now. But look here, Retief, this isn't what you're thinking!"

"How do you know what I'm thinking? I don't know myself." Retief rang off and buzzed the secretary.

"Miss Furkle, I'd like to be notified immediately of any new applications that might come in from the Bogan Consulate for placement of students."

"Well, it happens, by coincidence, that I have an application here now. Mr. Gulver of the Consulate brought it in."

"Is Mr. Gulver in the office? I'd like to see him."

"I'll ask him if he has time."

It was half a minute before a thick-necked red-faced man in a tight hat walked in. He wore an old-fashioned suit, a drab shirt, shiny shoes with round toes, and an ill-tempered expression.

"What is it you wish?" he barked. "I understood in my discussions with the other … ah … civilian there'd be no further need for these irritating conferences."

"I've just learned you're placing more students abroad, Mr. Gulver. How many this time?"

"Three thousand."

"And where will they be going?"

"Croanie—it's all in the application form I've handed in. Your job is to provide transportation."

"Will there be any other students embarking this season?"

"Why … perhaps. That's Boge's business." Gulver looked at Retief with pursed lips. "As a matter of fact, we had in mind dispatching another two thousand to Featherweight."

"Another under-populated world—and in the same cluster, I believe," Retief said. "Your people must be unusually interested in that region of space."

"If that's all you wanted to know, I'll be on my way. I have matters of importance to see to."

After Gulver left Retief called Miss Furkle in. "I'd like to have a break-out of all the student movements that have been planned under the present program," he said. "And see if you can get a summary of what MEDDLE has been shipping lately."

Miss Furkle bridled. "If Mr. Magnan were here, I'm sure he wouldn't dream of interfering in the work of other departments. I … overheard your conversation with the gentleman from the Croanie Legation—"

"The lists, Miss Furkle."

"I'm not accustomed," Miss Furkle said, "to intruding in matters outside our interest cluster."

"That's worse than listening in on phone conversations, eh? But never mind. I need the information, Miss Furkle."

"Loyalty to my Chief—"

"Loyalty to your pay-check should send you scuttling for the material I've asked for," Retief said. "I'm taking full responsibility. Now scat."

The buzzer sounded. Retief flipped a key. "MUDDLE, Retief speaking . . ."

Arapoulous' brown face appeared on the desk screen.

"How do, Retief. Okay if I come up?"

"Sure, Hank. I want to talk to you."

In the office, Arapoulous took a chair. "Sorry if I'm rushing you, Retief," he said. "But have you got anything for me?"

Retief waved at the wine bottles. "What do you know about Croanie?"

"Croanie? Not much of a place. Mostly ocean. All right if you like fish, I guess. We import some seafood from there. Nice prawns in monsoon time. Over a foot long."

"You on good terms with them?"

"Sure, I guess so. Course, they're pretty thick with Boge."

"So?"

"Didn't I tell you? Boge was the bunch that tried to take us over here a dozen years back. They would have made it, too, if they hadn't had a lot of bad luck. Their armor went in the drink, and without armor they're easy game."

Miss Furkle buzzed. "I have your lists," she said shortly.

"Bring them in, please."

The secretary placed the papers on the desk. Arapoulous caught her eye and grinned. She sniffed and marched from the room.

"What that gal needs is a slippery time in the grape mash," Arapoulous observed. Retief thumbed through the papers, pausing to read from time to time. He finished and looked at Arapoulous.

"How many men do you need for the harvest, Hank?" Retief inquired.

Arapoulous sniffed his wine glass.

"A hundred would help," he said. "A thousand would be better. Cheers."

"What would you say to two thousand?"

"Two thousand? Retief, you're not foolin'?"

"I hope not." He picked up the phone, called the Port Authority, and asked for the dispatch clerk.

"Hello, Jim. Say, I have a favor to ask of you. You know that contingent of Bogan students; they're travelling aboard the two CDT transports. I'm interested in the baggage that goes with the students. Has it arrived yet? Okay, I'll wait ..."

Jim came back to the phone. "Yeah, Retief, it's here. Just arrived. But there's a funny thing. It's not consigned to d'Land; it's ticketed clear through to Lovenbroy."

"Listen, Jim," Retief said. "I want you to go over to the warehouse and take a look at that baggage for me."

Retief waited while the dispatch clerk carried out the errand. The level in the two bottles had gone down an inch when Jim returned to the phone.

"Hey, I took a look at that baggage, Retief. Something funny going on. Guns. 2nn needlers, Mark XII hand blasters, power pistols—"

"It's okay, Jim. Nothing to worry about. Just a mix-up. Now, Jim, I'm going to ask you to do something more for me. I'm covering for a friend; it seems he slipped up. I wouldn't want word to get out, you understand. I'll send along a written change order in the morning that will cover you officially. Meanwhile, here's what I want you to do ..."

Retief gave instructions, then rang off and turned to Arapoulous.

"As soon as I get off a couple of TWX's, we'd better get down to the port, Hank. I think I'd like to see the students off personally."

Karsh met Retief as he entered the Departures enclosure at the port.

"What's going on here?" he demanded. "There's some funny business with my baggage consignment; they won't let me see it. I've got a feeling it's not being loaded."

"You'd better hurry, Mr. Karsh," Retief said. "You're scheduled to blast off in less than an hour. Are the students all loaded?"

"Yes, blast you! What about my baggage? Those vessels aren't moving without it!"

"No need to get so upset about a few toothbrushes, is there, Mr. Karsh?" Retief said blandly. "Still, if you're worried—" He turned to Arapoulous.

"Hank, why don't you walk Mr. Karsh over to the warehouse and … ah … take care of him?"

"I know just how to handle it," Arapoulous said.

The dispatch clerk came up to Retief. "I caught the tractor shipment," he said. "Funny kind of mistake, but it's okay now. They're being off-loaded at d'Land. I talked to the traffic controller there; he said they weren't looking for any students."

"The labels got switched, Jim. The students go where the baggage was consigned; too bad about the mistake there, but the Armaments Office will have a man along in a little while to dispose of the guns. Keep an eye out for the real luggage; no telling where it's gotten to—"

"Here!" a hoarse voice yelled. Retief turned. A disheveled figure in a tight hat was crossing the enclosure, his arms waving.

"Hi there, Mr. Gulver," Retief called. "How's Boge's business coming along?"

"Piracy!" Gulver blurted as he came up to Retief. "You've got a hand in this, I don't doubt! Where's that Magnan fellow …"

"What seems to be the problem?" Retief said.

"Hold those transports! I've just been notified that the baggage shipment has been impounded. I'll remind you, that shipment enjoys diplomatic free entry."

"Who told you it was impounded?"

"Never mind! I have my sources!"

Two tall men buttoned into grey tunics came up. "Are you Mr. Retief of CDT?" one said.

"That's right."

"What about my baggage!" Gulver cut in. "And I'm warning you, if those ships lift without—"

"These gentlemen are from the Armaments Control Commission," Retief said. "Would you like to come along and claim your baggage, Mr. Gulver?"

"From what? I …" Gulver turned two shades redder about the ears. "Armaments ..?"

"The only shipment I've held up seems to be somebody's arsenal," Retief said. "Now, if you claim this is your baggage …"

"Why, impossible," Gulver said in a strained voice. "Armaments? Ridiculous. There's been an error."

At the baggage warehouse, Gulver looked glumly at the opened cases of guns. "No, of course not," he said dully. "Not my baggage. Not my baggage at all."

Arapoulous appeared, supporting the stumbling figure of Mr. Karsh.

"What—what's this?" Gulver spluttered. "Karsh? What's happened …?"

"He had a little fall. He'll be okay," Arapoulous said.

"You'd better help him to the ship," Retief said. "It's ready to lift. We wouldn't want him to miss it."

"Leave him to me!" Gulver snapped, his eyes slashing at Karsh. "I'll see he's dealt with."

"I couldn't think of it," Retief said. "He's a guest of the Corps, you know. We'll see him safely aboard."

Gulver turned and signalled frantically. Three heavyset men in identical drab suits detached themselves from the wall and crossed to the group.

"Take this man," Gulver snapped, indicating Karsh, who looked at him dazedly.

"We take our hospitality seriously," Retief said. "We'll see him aboard the vessel."

Gulver opened his mouth—

"I know you feel bad about finding guns instead of school books in your luggage," Retief said, looking Gulver in the eye. "You'll be busy straightening out the details of the mix-up. You'll want to avoid further complications."

"Ah ... yes," Gulver said.

Arapoulous went on to the passenger conveyor, then turned to wave.

"Your man—he's going too?" Gulver blurted.

"He's not our man, properly speaking," Retief said. He lives on Lovenbroy."

"Lovenbroy?" Gulver choked. "But ... the ... I ..."

"I know you said the students were bound for d'Land," Retief said. "But I guess that was just another aspect of the general confusion. The course plugged into the navigators was to Lovenbroy. You'll be glad to know they're still headed there—even without the baggage."

"Perhaps," Gulver said grimly, "perhaps they'll manage without it."

"By the way," Retief said. "There was another funny mix-up. There were some tractors—for industrial use, you'll recall. I believe you co-operated with Croanie in arranging the grant through MEDDLE. They were erroneously consigned to Lovenbroy, a purely agricultural world. I saved you some embarrassment, I trust, Mr. Gulver, by arranging to have them off-loaded at d'Land."

"D'Land! You've put the CSU's in the hands of Boge's bitterest enemies…?"

"But they're only tractors, Mr. Gulver. Peaceful devices. Isn't that correct?"

"That's … correct." Gulver sagged. Then he snapped erect. "Hold the ships!" he yelled. "I'm cancelling the student exchange."

His voice was drowned by the rumble as the first of the monster transports rose from the launch pit, followed a moment later by the second. Retief watched them fade out of sight, then turned to Gulver.

"They're off," he said. "Let's hope they get a liberal education."

Retief lay on his back in deep grass by a stream, eating grapes. A tall figure, appearing on the knoll above him, waved.

"Retief!" Hank Arapoulous bounded down the slope. "I heard you were here—and I've got news for you. You won the final day's picking competition. Over two hundred bushels! That's a record! Let's get on over to the garden, shall we? Sounds like the celebration's about to start."

In the flower-crowded park among the stripped vines, Retief and Arapoulous made their way to a laden table under the lanterns. A tall girl dressed in a loose white garment, with long golden hair, came up to Arapoulous.

"Delinda, this is Retief—today's winner. And he's also the fellow that got those workers for us."

Delinda smiled at Retief. "I've heard about you, Mr. Retief. We weren't sure about the boys at first; two thousand Bogans, and all confused about their baggage that went astray. But they seemed to like the picking . . ." She smiled again.

"That's not all; our gals liked the boys," Hank said. "Even Bogans aren't so bad, minus their irons. A lot of 'em will be staying on. But how come you didn't tell me you were coming, Retief? I'd have laid on some kind of big welcome."

"I liked the welcome I got. And I didn't have much notice. Mr. Magnan was a little upset when he got back. It seems I exceeded my authority."

Arapoulous laughed. "I had a feeling you were wheelin' pretty free, Retief. I hope you didn't get into any trouble over it."

"No trouble," Retief said. "A few people were a little unhappy with me. It seems I'm not ready for important assignments at Departmental level. I was shipped off here to the boondocks to get a little more field experience."

"Delinda, look after Retief," said Arapoulous. "I'll see you later. I've got to see to the wine judging." He disappeared in the crowd.

"Congratulations on winning the day," said Delinda. "I noticed you at work. You were wonderful. I'm glad you're going to have the prize."

"Thanks. I noticed you too, flitting around in that white nightie of yours. But why weren't you picking grapes with the rest of us?"

"I had a special assignment."

"Too bad. You should have had a chance at the prize."

Delinda took Retief's hand. "I wouldn't have anyway," she said. "I'm the prize."

… Supplementing broad knowledge of affairs with such shrewd gambits as identification with significant local groups, and the consequent deft manipulating of inter-group rivalries, Corps officials on the scene played decisive roles in the preservation of domestic tranquility on many a far-flung world. At Fust, Ambassador Magnan forged to the van in the exercise of the technique …

Vol VII, reel 43. 487 A. E. (AD 2948)

AIDE MEMOIRE

Across the table from Retief, Ambassador Magnan, rustling a stiff sheet of parchment, looked grave.

"This aide memoire," he said, "was just handed to me by the Cultural Attaché. It's the third on the subject this week. It refers to the matter of sponsorship of Youth groups."

"Some youths," Retief said. "Average age: seventy-five."

"The Fustians are a long-lived people," Magnan snapped. "These matters are relative. At seventy-five, a male Fustian is at a trying age."

"That's right; he'll try anything in the hope it will maim somebody."

"Precisely the problem," Magnan replied. "But the Youth Movement is the important news in today's political situation here on Fust, and sponsorship of Youth groups is a shrewd stroke on the part of the Terrestrial Embassy. At my suggestion, well nigh every member of the mission has leaped at the opportunity to score a few p— that is, to cement relations with this emergent power group: the leaders of the future. You, Retief, as Counselor, are the outstanding exception."

"I'm not convinced these hoodlums need my help in organizing their rumbles," Retief said. "Now, if you have a proposal for a pest control group—"

"To the Fustians, this is no jesting matter," Magnan cut in. "This group," he glanced at the paper, "known as the Sexual, Cultural and Athletic Recreational Society, or SCARS, for short, has been awaiting sponsorship for a matter of weeks now."

"Meaning they want someone to buy them a clubhouse, uniforms, equipment, and anything else they need to plot against the peace in style," Retief said.

"If we don't act promptly, the Groaci embassy may well anticipate us. They're very active here."

"That's an idea," said Retief, "let 'em. After a while they'll be broke—instead of us."

"Nonsense. The group requires a sponsor. I can't actually order you to step forward. However …" Magnan let the sentence hang in the air. Retief raised one eyebrow.

"For a minute there," he said, "I thought you were going to make a positive statement."

Magnan leaned back, lacing his fingers over his stomach. "I don't think you'll find a diplomat of my experience doing anything so naive," he said.

"I like the adult Fustians," said Retief. "Too bad they have to lug half a ton of horn around on their backs. I wonder if surgery—"

"Great heavens, Retief," Magnan spluttered. "I'm amazed that even you would bring up a matter of such delicacy. A race's unfortunate physical characteristics are hardly a fit matter for Terrestrial curiosity."

"Well, I've only been here a month. But it's been my experience, Mr. Ambassador, that few people are above improving on nature; otherwise you, for example, would be tripping over your beard."

Magnan shuddered. "Please—never mention the idea to a Fustian."

Retief stood. "My own program for the day includes going over to the dockyards. There are some features of this new passenger liner the Fustians are putting together that I want to look into. With your permission, Mr. Ambassador...?"

Magnan snorted. "Your preoccupation with the trivial disturbs me, Retief. More interest in substantive matters—such as working with youth groups—would create a far better impression."

"Before getting too involved with these groups, it might be a good idea to find out a little more about them," Retief said. "Who organizes them? There are three strong political parties here on Fust; what's the alignment of this SCARS organization?"

"You forget, these are merely teen-agers, so to speak," Magnan said. "Politics mean nothing to them ... yet."

"Then there are the Groaci. Why their passionate interest in a two-horse world like Fust? Normally they're concerned with nothing but business; and what has Fust got that they could use?

"You may rule out the commercial aspect in this instance," said Magnan. "Fust possesses a vigorous steel-age manufacturing economy. The Groaci are barely ahead of them."

"Barely," said Retief. "Just over the line into crude atomics ... like fission bombs."

Magnan, shaking his head, turned back to his papers. "What market exists for such devices on a world at peace?" he said. "I suggest you address your attention to the less spectacular but more rewarding work of insinuating yourself into the social patterns of the local youth."

"I've considered the matter," Retief said, "and before I meet any of the local youth socially I want to get myself a good blackjack."

Retief left the sprawling bungalow-type building that housed the chancery of the Terrestrial Embassy, hailed one of the ponderous slow-moving Fustian flat-cars, and leaned back against the wooden guard rail as the heavy vehicle trundled through the city toward the looming gantries of the shipyards. It was a cool morning with a light breeze carrying the fish odor of Fustian dwellings across the broad cobbled avenue. A few mature Fustians lumbered heavily along in the shade of the low buildings, audibly wheezing under the burden of their immense carapaces. Among them, shell-less youths trotted briskly on scaly stub legs. The driver of the flat-car, a labor-caste Fustian with his guild colors emblazoned on his back, heaved at the tiller, swung the unwieldy conveyance through the shipyard gates, and creaked to a halt.

"Thus I come to the shipyard with frightful speed," he said in Fustian. "Well I know the way of the naked-backs, who move always in haste."

Retief, climbing down, handed him a coin. "You should take up professional racing," he said. "Dare-devil."

Retief crossed the littered yard and tapped at the door of a rambling shed. Boards creaked inside, then the door swung back. A gnarled ancient with tarnished facial scales and a weathered carapace peered out at Retief.

"Long may you sleep," Retief said. "I'd like to take a look around, if you don't mind. I understand you're laying the bed-plate for your new liner today."

"May you dream of the deeps," the old fellow mumbled. He waved a stumpy arm toward a group of shell-less Fustians standing by a massive hoist. "The youths know more of bed-plates than do I, who but tend the place of papers."

"I know how you feel, old-timer," Retief said. "That sounds like the story of my life. Among your papers do you have a set of plans for the vessel? I understand it's to be a passenger liner."

The oldster nodded. He shuffled to a drawing file, rummaged, pulled out a sheaf of curled prints, and spread them on the table. Retief stood silently, running a finger over the uppermost drawing, tracing lines …

"What does the naked-back here?" a deep voice barked behind Retief. He turned. A heavy-faced Fustian youth, wrapped in a mantle, stood at the open door. Beady yellow eyes set among fine scales bored into Retief.

"I came to take a look at your new liner," said Retief.

"We need no prying foreigners here," the youth snapped. His eye fell on the drawings; he hissed in anger.

"Doddering hulk!" he snapped at the ancient, moving toward them. "May you toss in nightmares! Put aside the plans!"

"My mistake," Retief said. "I didn't know this was a secret project."

The youth hesitated. "It is not a secret," he muttered. "Why should it be a secret?"

"You tell me."

The youth worked his jaws and rocked his head from side to side in the Fustian gesture of uncertainty. "There is nothing to conceal," he said. "We merely construct a passenger liner."

"Then you don't mind if I look over the drawings," Retief said. "Who knows, maybe someday I'll want to reserve a suite for the trip out."

The youth turned and disappeared. Retief grinned at the oldster. "Went for his big brother, I guess," he said. "I have a feeling I won't get to study these in peace here. Mind if I copy them?"

"Willingly, light-footed one," said the old Fustian. "And mine is the shame for the discourtesy of youth."

Retief took out a tiny camera, flipped a copying lens in place, leafed through the drawings, clicking the shutter.

"A plague on these youths," said the oldster. "They grow more virulent day by day."

"Why don't you elders clamp down?"

"Agile are they and we are slow of foot. And this unrest is new; unknown in my youth was such insolence."

"The police—"

"Bah," the ancient rumbled. "None have we worthy of the name, nor have we needed them before now."

"What's behind it?"

"They have found leaders. The spiv, Slock, is one. And I fear they plot mischief." He pointed to the window. "They come, and a soft-one with them."

Retief, pocketing the camera, glanced out the window. A pale-featured Groacian with an ornately decorated crest stood with the youths, who eyed the hut, then started toward it.

"That's the military attaché of the Groaci Embassy," Retief said. "I wonder what he and the boys are cooking up together?"

"Naught that augurs well for the dignity of Fust," the oldster rumbled. "Flee, agile one, while I engage their attentions."

"I was just leaving," Retief said. "Which way out?"

"The rear door," the Fustian gestured with a stubby member.

"Rest well, stranger on these shores," he said, moving to the entrance.

"Same to you, pop," said Retief. "And thanks."

He eased through the narrow back entrance, waited until voices were raised at the front of the shed, then strolled off toward the gate.

It was an hour along in the second dark of the third cycle when Retief left the Embassy technical library and crossed the corridor to his office. He flipped on a light and found a note tucked under a paperweight:

"Retief: I shall expect your attendance at the IAS dinner at first dark of the fourth cycle. There will be a brief but, I hope, impressive sponsorship ceremony for the SCARS group, with full press coverage, arrangements for which I have managed to complete in spite of your intransigence."

Retief snorted and glanced at his watch: less than three hours. Just time to creep home by flat-car, dress in ceremonial uniform, and creep back.

Outside he flagged a lumbering bus, stationed himself in a corner of it, and watched the yellow sun, Beta, rise above the low skyline. The nearby sea was at high tide now, under the pull of the major sun and the three moons, and the stiff breeze carried a mist of salt spray. Retief turned up his collar against the dampness. In half an hour he would be perspiring under the vertical rays of a first-noon sun, but the thought failed to keep the chill off.

Two youths clambered up on the moving platform and walked purposefully toward Retief. He moved off the rail, watching them, his weight balanced.

"That's close enough, kids," he said. "Plenty of room on this scow; no need to crowd up."

"There are certain films," the lead Fustian muttered. His voice was unusually deep for a Youth. He was wrapped in a heavy cloak and moved awkwardly. His adolescence was nearly at an end, Retief guessed.

"I told you once," Retief said. "Don't crowd me."

The two stepped close, their slit mouths snapping in anger. Retief put out a foot, hooked it behind the scaly leg of the over-age juvenile, and threw his weight against the cloaked chest. The clumsy Fustian tottered, then fell heavily. Retief was past him and off the flat-car before the other youth had completed his vain lunge toward the spot Retief had occupied. The Terrestrial waved cheerfully at the pair, hopped aboard another vehicle, and watched his would-be assailants lumber down off their car and move heavily off, their tiny heads twisted to follow his retreating figure.

So they wanted the film? Retief reflected, thumbing a cigar alight. They were a little late. He had already filed it in the Embassy vault, after running a copy for the reference files. And a comparison of the drawings with those of the obsolete Mark XXXV battle cruiser used two hundred years earlier by the Concordiat Naval Arm showed them to be almost identical—gun emplacements and all. And the term obsolete was a relative one. A ship which had been outmoded in the armories of the Galactic Powers could still be king of the walk in the Eastern Arm.

But how had these two known of the film? There had been no one present but himself and the old-timer—and Retief was willing to bet the elderly Fustian hadn't told them anything.

At least not willingly ...

Retief frowned, dropped the cigar over the side, waited until the flat-car negotiated a mud-wallow, then swung down and headed for the shipyard.

*

The door, hinges torn loose, had been propped loosely back in position. Retief looked around at the battered interior of the shed. The old fellow had put up a struggle.

There were deep drag-marks in the dust behind the building. Retief followed them across the yard. They disappeared under the steel door of a warehouse.

Retief glanced around. Now, at the mid-hour of the fourth cycle, the workmen were heaped along the edge of the refreshment pond, deep in their siesta. Taking a multi-bladed tool from his pocket, Retief tried various fittings in the lock; it snicked open and he eased the door aside far enough to enter.

Heaped bales loomed before him. Snapping on the tiny lamp in the handle of the combination tool, Retief looked over the pile. One stack seemed out of alignment—and the dust had been scraped from the floor before it. He pocketed the light, climbed up on the bales, and looked over into a ring of bundles. The aged Fustian lay inside the ring, a heavy sack tied over his head. Retief dropped down beside him, sawed at the tough twine, and pulled the sack free.

"It's me, old fellow," he said, "the nosy stranger. Sorry I got you into this."

The oldster threshed his gnarled legs, rocked slightly, then fell back. "A curse on the cradle that rocked their infant slumbers," he rumbled. "But place me back on my feet and I hunt down the youth Slock though he flee to the bottommost muck of the Sea of Torments."

"How am I going to get you out of here? Maybe I'd better get some help."

"Nay. The perfidious youths abound here," said the old Fustian. "It would be your life."

"I doubt if they'd go that far."

"Would they not?" The Fustian stretched his neck. "Cast your light here. But for the toughness of my hide . . ."

Retief put the beam of the light on the leathery neck. A great smear of thick purplish blood welled from a ragged cut. The oldster chuckled: a sound like a seal coughing.

"Traitor they called me. For long they sawed at me—in vain. Then they trussed me and dumped me here. They think to return with weapons to complete the task."

"Weapons? I thought it was illegal—"

"Their evil genius, the Soft One," the Fustian said, "he would provide fuel to the Fire-Devil."

"The Groaci again," Retief said. "I wonder what their angle is."

"And I must confess: I told them of you, ere I knew their full intentions. Much can I tell you of their doings. But first, I pray: the block and tackle."

Retief found the hoist where the Fustian directed him, maneuvered it into position, hooked onto the edge of the carapace, and hauled away. The immense Fustian rose slowly, teetered . . . then flopped on his chest. Slowly he got to his feet.

"My name is Whonk, fleet one," he said. "My cows are yours."

"Thanks. I'm Retief. I'd like to meet the girls some time. But right now, let's get out of here."

Whonk leaned his bulk against the ponderous stacks of baled kelp, bull-dozing them aside. "Slow am I to anger," he said, "but implacable in my wrath. Slock, beware . . ."

"Hold it," said Retief suddenly. He sniffed. "What's that odor?" He flashed the light around, playing it over a dry stain on the floor. He knelt and sniffed at the spot.

"What kind of cargo was stacked here, Whonk? And where is it now?"

Whonk considered. "There were drums," he said. "Four of

them, quite small, painted an evil green—the property of the Soft Ones, the Groaci. They lay here a day and a night. At full dark of the first period they came with stevedores and loaded them aboard the barge *Moss Rock.*"

"The VIP boat. Who's scheduled to use it?"

"I know not. But what matters this? Let us discuss cargo movements after I have settled a score with certain youths."

"We'd better follow this up first, Whonk. There's only one substance I know of that's transported in drums and smells like that blot on the floor. That's titanite: the hottest explosive this side of a uranium pile."

Beta was setting as Retief, with Whonk puffing at his heels, came up to the sentry box beside the gangway leading to the plush interior of the Official Barge *Moss Rock.*

"A sign of the times," Whonk said, glancing inside the empty shelter. "A guard should stand here, but I see him not. Doubtless he crept away to sleep."

"Let's go aboard, and take a look around."

They entered the ship. Soft lights glowed in utter silence. A rough box stood on the floor, rollers and pry-bars beside it—a discordant note in the muted luxury of the setting. Whonk rummaged through its contents.

"Curious," he said. "What means this?" He held up a stained Fustian cloak of orange and green, a metal bracelet, and a stack of papers.

"Orange and green," Retief muttered. "Whose colors are those?"

"I know not . . ." Whonk glanced at the arm-band. "But this is lettered." He passed the metal band to Retief.

"SCARS," Retief read. He looked at Whonk. "It seems to me I've heard the name before," he murmured. "Let's get back to the Embassy—fast."

Back on the ramp Retief heard a sound ... and turned in time to duck the charge of a hulking Fustian youth who thundered past him, and fetched up against the broad chest of Whonk, who locked him in a warm embrace.

"Nice catch, Whonk. Where'd he sneak out of?"

"The lout hid there by the storage bin," Whonk rumbled. The captive youth thumped his fists and toes futilely against the oldster's carapace.

"Hang on to him," Retief said. "He looks like the biting kind."

"No fear. Clumsy I am, yet I am not without strength."

"Ask him where the titanite is tucked away."

"Speak, witless grub," Whonk growled, "lest I tweak you in two."

The youth gurgled.

"Better let up before you make a mess of him," Retief said.

Whonk lifted the youth clear of the floor, then flung him down with a thump that made the ground quiver. The younger Fustian glared up at the elder, his mouth snapping.

"This one was among those who trussed me and hid me away for the killing," said Whonk. "In his repentance he will tell all to his elder."

"He's the same one that tried to strike up an acquaintance with me on the bus," Retief said. "He gets around."

The youth, scrambling to his hands and knees, scuttled for freedom. Retief planted a foot on the dragging cloak; it ripped free. He stared at the bare back of the Fustian.

"By the Great Egg!" Whonk exclaimed, tripping the captive as he tried to rise. "This is no youth! His carapace has been taken from him."

Retief looked at the scarred back. "I thought he looked a little old. But I thought—"

"This is not possible," Whonk said wonderingly. "The great nerve trunks are deeply involved; not even the cleverest surgeon could excise the carapace and leave the patient living."

"It looks like somebody did the trick. But let's take this boy with us and get out of here. His folks may come home."

"Too late," said Whonk. Retief turned. Three youths came from behind the sheds.

"Well," Retief said. "It looks like the SCARS are out in force tonight. Where's your pal?" he said to the advancing trio, "the sticky little bird with the eye-stalks? Back at his Embassy, leaving you suckers holding the bag, I'll bet."

"Shelter behind me, Retief," said Whonk.

"Go get 'em, old-timer." Retief stooped and picked up one of the pry-bars. "I'll jump around and distract them."

Whonk let out a whistling roar and charged for the immature Fustians. They fanned out … one tripped, sprawling on his face. Retief, whirling the metal bar that he had thrust between the Fustian's legs, slammed it against the skull of another, who shook his head, then turned on Retief … and bounced off the steel hull of the *Moss Rock* as Whonk took him in full charge.

Retief used the bar on another head; his third blow laid the Fustian on the pavement, oozing purple. The other two club members departed hastily, dented but still mobile.

Retief leaned on his club, breathing hard. "Tough heads these kids have got. I'm tempted to chase those two lads down, but I've got another errand to run. I don't know who the Groaci intended to blast, but I have a suspicion somebody of importance was scheduled for a boat ride in the next few hours, and three drums of titanite is enough to vaporize this tub and everyone aboard her."

"The plot is foiled," said Whonk. "But what reason did they have?"

"The Groaci are behind it. I have an idea the SCARS didn't know about this gambit."

"Which of these is the leader?" asked Whonk. He prodded a fallen youth. "Arise, dreaming one."

"Never mind him, Whonk. We'll tie these two up and leave them here. I know where to find the boss."

A stolid-looking crowd filled the low-ceilinged banquet hall. Retief scanned the tables for the pale blobs of Terrestrial faces, dwarfed by the giant armored bodies of the Fustians. Across the room Magnan fluttered a hand. Retief headed toward him. A low-pitched vibration filled the air, the rumble of sub-sonic Fustian music.

Retief slid into his place beside Magnan. "Sorry to be late, Mr. Ambassador."

"I'm honored that you chose to appear at all," Magnan said coldly. He turned back to the Fustian on his left.

"Ah, yes, Mr. Minister," he said. "Charming, most charming. So joyous."

The Fustian looked at him, beady-eyed. "It is the Lament of Hatching," he said, "our National Dirge."

"Oh," said Magnan, "how interesting. Such a pleasing balance of instruments."

"It is a droon solo," said the Fustian, eyeing the Terrestrial Ambassador suspiciously.

"Why don't you just admit you can't hear it," Retief whispered loudly. "And if I may interrupt a moment—"

Magnan cleared his throat. "Now that our Mr. Retief has arrived, perhaps we could rush right along to the sponsorship ceremonies ..."

"This group," said Retief, leaning across Magnan to speak to the Fustian, "the SCARS … how much do you know about them, Mr. Minister?"

"Nothing at all," the huge Fustian elder rumbled. "For my taste, all youths should be kept penned with the livestock until they grow a carapace to tame their irresponsibility."

"We mustn't lose sight of the importance of channeling youthful energies," said Magnan.

"Labor gangs," said the minister. "In my youth we were indentured to the dredge-masters. I myself drew a muck-sledge."

"But in these modern times," put in Retief, "surely it's incumbent on us to make happy these golden hours."

The minister snorted. "Last week I had a golden hour: they set upon me and pelted me with over-ripe dung-fruit."

"But this was merely a manifestation of normal youthful frustrations," cried Magnan. "Their essential tenderness—"

"You'd not find a tender spot on that lout yonder," the minister said, pointing with a fork at a newly arrived youth, "if you drilled boreholes and blasted."

"Why, that's our guest of honor," said Magnan, "a fine young fellow, Slop I believe his name is—"

"Slock," said Retief. "Nine feet of armor-plated orneriness. And—"

Magnan rose, tapping on his glass. The Fustians winced at the, to them, supersonic vibrations, and looked at each other muttering. Magnan tapped louder. The minister drew in his head, his eyes closed. Some of the Fustians rose and tottered for the doors; the noise level rose. Magnan redoubled his efforts. The glass broke with a clatter, and green wine gushed on the tablecloth.

"What in the name of the Great Egg." the minister muttered. He blinked, breathing deeply.

"Oh, forgive me," Magnan blurted, dabbing at the wine.

"Too bad the glass gave out," Retief said. "In another minute you'd have cleared the hall—and then maybe I could have gotten a word in. You see, Mr. Minister," he said, turning to the Fustian, "there is a matter you should know about ..."

"Your attention, please," Magnan said, rising. "I see that our fine young guest of honor has arrived, and I hope that the remainder of his committee will be along in a moment. It is my pleasure to announce that our Mr. Retief has had the good fortune to win out in the keen bidding for the pleasure of sponsoring this lovely group, and—"

Retief tugged at Magnan's sleeve. "Don't introduce me yet," he said. "I want to appear suddenly—more dramatic, you know."

"Well," Magnan murmured, glancing down at Retief, "I'm gratified to see you entering into the spirit of the event at last." He turned his attention back to the assembled guests. "If our honored guest will join me on the rostrum ..." he said. "The gentlemen of the press may want to catch a few shots of the presentation."

Magnan moved from his place, made his way forward, stepped up on the low platform at the center of the wide room, took his place beside the robed Fustian youth, and beamed at the cameras.

"How gratifying it is to take this opportunity to express once more the great pleasure we have in sponsoring SCARS," Magnan said, talking slowly for the benefit of the scribbling reporters. "We'd like to think that in our modest way we're to be a part of all that the SCARS achieve during the years ahead ..."

Magnan paused as a huge Fustian elder heaved his bulk up the two low steps to the rostrum and approached the guest of honor. He watched as the newcomer paused behind Slock, who was busy returning the stares of the spectators and did not notice the new arrival.

Retief pushed through the crowd and stepped up to face the Fustian youth. Slock stared at him, drawing back.

"You know me, Slock," Retief said loudly. "An old fellow named Whonk told you about me, just before you tried to saw off his head, remember? It was when I came out to take a look at that battle cruiser you're building."

With a bellow Slock reached for Retief—and choked off in mid-cry as Whonk pinioned him from behind, lifting the youth clear of the floor.

"Glad you reporters happened along," Retief said to the gaping newsmen. "Slock here had a deal with a sharp operator from the Groaci Embassy. The Groaci were to supply the necessary hardware and Slock, as foreman at the shipyards, was to see that everything was properly installed. The next step, I assume, would have been a local take-over, followed by a little interplanetary war on Flamenco or one of the other nearby worlds ... for which the Groaci would be glad to supply plenty of ammo."

Magnan found his tongue. "Are you mad, Retief?" he screeched. "This group was vouched for by the Ministry of Youth."

"That Ministry's overdue for a purge," Retief said. He turned back to Slock. "I wonder if you were in on the little diversion that was planned for today. When the *Moss Rock* blew, a variety of clues were to be planted where they'd be easy to find ... with SCARS written all over them. The Groaci would thus have neatly laid the whole affair squarely at the door of the Terrestrial Embassy … whose sponsorship of the SCARS had received plenty of publicity."

"The *Moss Rock?*" Magnan said. "But that was—Retief! This is idiotic. The SCARS themselves were scheduled to go on a cruise tomorrow."

Slock roared suddenly, twisting violently. Whonk teetered, his grip loosened … and Slock pulled free and was off the platform, butting his way through the milling oldsters on the dining room floor. Magnan watched, open-mouthed.

"The Groaci were playing a double game, as usual," Retief said. "They intended to dispose of these lads after they got things under way."

"Well, don't stand there," Magnan yelped. "Do something! If Slop is the ringleader of a delinquent gang—" He moved to give chase himself.

Retief grabbed his arm. "Don't jump down there," he called above the babble of talk. "You'd have as much chance of getting through there as a jack rabbit through a threshing contest. Where's a phone?"

Ten minutes later the crowd had thinned slightly. "We can get through now," Whonk called. "This way." He lowered himself to the floor and bulled through to the exit. Flash bulbs popped. Retief and Magnan followed in Whonk's wake.

In the lounge Retief grabbed the phone, waited for the operator, and gave a code letter. No reply. He tried another.

"No good," he said after a full minute had passed. He slammed the phone back in its niche. "Let's grab a cab."

In the street the blue sun, Alpha, peered like an arc light under a low cloud layer. Flat shadows lay across the mud of the avenue. The three mounted a passing flat-car. Whonk squatted, resting the weight of his immense shell on the heavy plank flooring.

"Would that I, too, could lose this burden, as has the false youth we bludgeoned aboard the *Moss Rock,*" he sighed. "Soon will I be forced into retirement; and a mere keeper of a place of papers such as I will rate no more than a slab on the public strand, with once-daily feedings. Even for a man of high position retirement is no pleasure. A slab in the Park of Monuments is little better. A dismal outlook for one's next thousand years."

"You two continue on to the police station," Retief said. "I want to play a hunch. But don't take too long. I may be painfully right."

"What—?" Magnan started.

"As you wish, Retief," Whonk said.

The flat-car trundled past the gate to the shipyard and Retief jumped down and headed at a run for the VIP boat. The guard post still stood vacant. The two youths whom he and Whonk had left trussed were gone.

"That's the trouble with a peaceful world," Retief muttered. "No police protection." Stepping down from the lighted entry, he took up a position behind the sentry box. Alpha rose higher, shedding a glaring white light without heat. Retief shivered.

There was a sound in the near entrance, like two elephants colliding. Retief looked toward the gate. His giant acquaintance, Whonk, had reappeared and was grappling with a hardly less massive opponent. A small figure became visible in the melee, scuttled for the gate, was headed off by the battling titans, turned and made for the opposite side of the shipyard. Retief waited, jumped out and gathered in the fleeing Groacian.

"Well, Yith," he said, "how's tricks…? You should pardon the expression."

"Release me, Retief!" the pale-featured creature lisped, his throat bladder pulsating in agitation. "The behemoths vie for the privilege of dismembering me."

"I know how they feel. I'll see what I can do … for a price."

"I appeal to you," Yith whispered hoarsely, "as a fellow diplomat, a fellow alien, a fellow soft-back."

"Why don't you appeal to Slock, as a fellow conspirator?" Retief said. "Now keep quiet … and you may get out of this alive."

The heavier of the two struggling Fustians threw the other to the ground. The smaller Fustian lay on its back, helpless.

"That's Whonk, still on his feet," Retief said. "I wonder who he's caught—and why."

Whonk came toward the *Moss Rock* dragging the supine Fustian. Retief thrust Yith down well out of sight behind the sentry box. "Better sit tight, Yith. Don't try to sneak off; I can outrun you. Stay here and I'll see what I can do." Stepping out, he hailed Whonk.

Puffing like a steam engine, Whonk pulled up before him. "Hail, Retief!" he panted. "You followed a hunch; I did the same. I saw something strange in this one when we passed him on the avenue. I watched, followed him here. Look! It is Slock, strapped into a dead carapace! Now many things become clear."

Retief whistled. "So the youths aren't all as young as they look. Somebody's been holding out on the rest of you Fustians."

"The soft one," Whonk said. "You laid him by the heels, Retief. I saw. Produce him now."

"Hold on a minute, Whonk. It won't do you any good to—"

Whonk winked broadly. "I must take my revenge!" he roared. "I shall test the texture of the Soft One! His pulped remains will be scoured up by the ramp-washers and mailed home in bottles."

Retief whirled at a sound, caught up with the scuttling Yith fifty feet away, and hauled him back to Whonk.

"It's up to you, Whonk," he said. "I know how important ceremonial revenge is to you Fustians."

"Mercy!" Yith hissed, his eye-stalks whipping in distress. "I claim diplomatic immunity."

"No diplomat am I," Whonk rumbled. "Let me see; suppose I start with one of those obscenely active eyes." He reached …

"I have an idea," Retief said brightly. "Do you suppose—just this once—you could forego the ceremonial revenge if Yith promised to arrange for a Groacian Surgical Mission to de-carapace you elders?"

"But," Whonk protested, "those eyes; what a pleasure to pluck them, one by one—"

"Yess," Yith hissed, "I swear it; our most expert surgeons … platoons of them, with the finest of equipment."

"I have dreamed of how it would be to sit on this one, to feel him squash beneath my bulk …"

"Light as a whissle feather shall you dance," Yith whispered. "Shell-less shall you spring in the joy of renewed youth …"

"Maybe just one eye," Whonk said. "That would leave him four …"

"Be a sport," said Retief.

"Well."

"It's a deal then," Retief said. "Yith, on your word as a diplomat, an alien, and a soft-back, you'll set up the mission. Groaci surgical skill is an export that will net you more than armaments. It will be a whissle feather in your cap—if you bring it off. And in return, Whonk won't sit on you. In addition, I won't prefer charges against you of interference in the internal affairs of a free world."

Behind Whonk there was a movement. Slock, wriggling

free of the borrowed carapace, struggled to his feet ... in time for Whonk to seize him, lift him high, and head for the entry to the *Moss Rock.*

"Hey," Retief called. "Where are you going?"

"I would not deny this one his reward," Whonk called. "He hoped to cruise in luxury; so be it."

"Hold on," Retief said. "That tub is loaded with titanite!"

"Stand not in my way, Retief. For this one in truth owes me a vengeance."

Retief watched as the immense Fustian bore his giant burden up the ramp and disappeared within the ship.

"I guess Whonk means business," he said to Yith, who hung in his grasp, all five eyes goggling. "And he's a little too big for me to stop, once he sets his mind on something. But maybe he's just throwing a scare into him."

Whonk reappeared, alone, and climbed down.

"What did you do with him?" Retief said.

"We had best withdraw," Whonk said. "The killing radius of the drive is fifty yards."

"You mean—"

"The controls are set for Groac. Long may he sleep."

"It was quite a bang," Retief said, "but I guess you saw it too."

"No, confound it," Magnan said. "When I remonstrated with Hulk, or Whelk—"

"Whonk."

"—the ruffian thrust me into an alley, bound in my own cloak. I'll most certainly mention the indignity in a note to the Minister." He jotted on a pad.

"How about the surgical mission?"

"A most generous offer," Magnan said. "Frankly, I was astonished. I think perhaps we've judged the Groaci too harshly."

"I hear the Ministry of Youth has had a rough morning of it," Retief said. "And a lot of rumors are flying to the effect that Youth Groups are on the way out."

Magnan cleared his throat and shuffled papers. "I—ah—have explained to the press that last night's ahh ..."

"Fiasco."

"—affair was necessary in order to place the culprits in an untenable position. Of course, as to the destruction of the VIP vessel and the presumed death of the fellow, Slop—"

"The Fustians understand," Retief said. "Whonk wasn't kidding about ceremonial vengeance. Yith was lucky: he hadn't actually drawn blood. Then no amount of dickering would have saved him."

"The Groaci have been guilty of gross misuse of diplomatic privilege," Magnan said. "I think that a note—or perhaps an *aide memoire*: less formal ..."

"The *Moss Rock* was bound for Groac," Retief said. "She was already in her transit orbit when she blew. The major fragments should arrive on schedule in a month or so. It should provide quite a meteorite display. I think that should be all the aid the Groaci's *memoires* will need to keep their tentacles off Fust."

"But diplomatic usage—"

"Then, too, the less that's put in writing, the less they can blame you for, if anything goes wrong."

"There's that, of course," Magnan said, his lips pursed. "Now you're thinking constructively, Retief. We may make a diplomat of you yet." He smiled expansively.

"Maybe. But I refuse to let it depress me." Retief stood up. "I'm taking a few weeks off ... if you have no objections, Mr. Ambassador. My pal Whonk wants to show me an island down south where the fishing is good."

"But there are some extremely important matters coming up," Magnan said. "We're planning to sponsor Senior Citizen Groups."

"Count me out. Groups give me an itch."

"Why, what an astonishing remark, Retief. After all, we diplomats are ourselves a group."

"Uh, huh," Retief said. "That's what I mean."

Magnan sat quietly, his mouth open, and watched as Retief stepped into the hall and closed the door gently behind him.

… No jackstraws to be swayed by superficial appearances, dedicated career field personnel of the Corps unflaggingly administered the enlightened concepts evolved at Corps HQ by high-level deep-think teams toiling unceasingly in underground caverns to weld the spirit of Inter-Being amity. Never has the efficacy of close cultural rapport, coupled with Mission teamwork, been better displayed than in the loyal performance of Administrative Assistant Yolanda Meuhl, Acting Consul at Groac, in maintaining the Corps posture laid down by her predecessor, Consul Whaffle …

Vol VII, reel 98. 488 A. E. (AD 2949)

POLICY

"The Consul for the Terrestrial States," Retief said, "presents his compliments, et cetera, to the Ministry of Culture of the Groacian Autonomy, and, with reference to the Ministry's invitation to attend a recital of interpretive grimacing, has the honor to express regret that he will be unable—"

"You can't turn down this invitation," Administrative Assistant Meuhl said flatly. "I'll make that 'accepts with pleasure'."

Retief exhaled a plume of cigar smoke.

"Miss Meuhl," he said, "in the past couple of weeks I've sat through six light concerts, four attempts at chamber music, and God knows how many assorted folk-art festivals. I've been tied up every off-duty hour since I got here."

"You can't offend the Groaci," Miss Meuhl said sharply. "Consul Whaffle would never have—"

"Whaffle left here three months ago," Retief said, "leaving me in charge."

"Well," Miss Meuhl said, snapping off the dictyper. "I'm sure I don't know what excuse I can give the Minister."

"Never mind the excuses. Just tell him I won't be there." He stood up.

"Are you leaving the office?" Miss Meuhl adjusted her glasses. "I have some important letters here for your signature."

"I don't recall dictating any letters today, Miss Meuhl," Retief said, pulling on a light cape.

"I wrote them for you. They're just as Consul Whaffle would have wanted them."

"Did you write all Whaffle's letters for him, Miss Meuhl?"

"Consul Whaffle was an extremely busy man," Miss Meuhl said stiffly. "He had complete confidence in me."

"Since I'm cutting out the culture from now on, I won't be so busy."

"Well! May I ask where you'll be if something comes up?"

"I'm going over to the Foreign Office Archives."

Miss Meuhl blinked behind thick lenses. "Whatever for?"

Retief looked at her thoughtfully. "You've been here on Groac for four years, Miss Meuhl. What was behind the coup d'état that put the present government in power?"

"I'm sure I haven't pried into—"

"What about that Terrestrial cruiser, the one that disappeared out this way about ten years back?"

"Mr. Retief, those are just the sort of questions we avoid with the Groaci. I certainly hope you're not thinking of openly intruding—"

"Why?"

"The Groaci are a very sensitive race. They don't welcome outworlders raking up things. They've been gracious enough to let us live down the fact that Terrestrials subjected them to deep humiliation on one occasion."

"You mean when we came looking for the cruiser?"

"I, for one, am ashamed of the high-handed tactics that were employed, grilling these innocent people as though they were criminals. We try never to reopen that wound, Mr. Retief."

"They never found the cruiser, did they?"

"Certainly not on Groac."

Retief nodded. "Thanks, Miss Meuhl," he said. "I'll be back before you close the office." Miss Meuhl's thin face was set in lines of grim disapproval as he closed the door.

Peering through the small grilled window, the pale-featured Groacian vibrated his throat-bladder in a distressed bleat.

"Not to enter the Archives," he said in his faint voice. "The denial of permission. The deep regret of the Archivist."

"The importance of my task here," Retief said, enunciating the glottal language with difficulty. "My interest in local history."

"The impossibility of access to outworlders. To depart quietly."

"The necessity that I enter."

"The specific instructions of the Archivist." The Groacian's voice rose to a whisper. "To insist no longer. To give up this idea!"

"Okay, skinny, I know when I'm licked," Retief said in Terran. "To keep your nose clean."

Outside, Retief stood for a moment looking across at the

deeply carved windowless stucco facades lining the street, then started off in the direction of the Terrestrial Consulate General. The few Groacians on the street eyed him furtively, and veered to avoid him as he passed. Flimsy high-wheeled ground cars puffed silently along the resilient pavement. The air was clean and cool. At the office Miss Meuhl would be waiting with another list of complaints. Retief studied the carving over the open doorways along the street. An elaborate one picked out in pinkish paint seemed to indicate the Groacian equivalent of a bar. Retief went in.

A Groacian bartender dispensing clay pots of alcoholic drink from the bar-pit at the center of the room looked at Retief, then froze in mid-motion, a metal tube poised over a waiting pot.

"A cooling drink," Retief said in Groacian, squatting down at the edge of the pit. "To sample a true Groacian beverage."

"Not to enjoy my poor offerings," the Groacian mumbled. "A pain in the digestive sacs. To express regret."

"Not to worry," Retief replied. "To pour it out and let me decide whether I like it."

"To be grappled in by peace-keepers for poisoning of … foreigners." The barkeep looked around for support, but found none. The Groaci customers, eyes elsewhere, were drifting out.

"To get the lead out," Retief said, placing a thick gold-piece in the dish provided. "To shake a tentacle."

"To procure a cage," a thin voice called from the sidelines. "To display the freak."

Retief turned. A tall Groacian vibrated his mandibles in a gesture of contempt. From his bluish throat coloration it was apparent the creature was drunk.

"To choke in your upper sac," the bartender hissed,

extending his eyes toward the drunk. "To keep silent, littermate of drones."

"To swallow your own poison, dispenser of vileness," the drunk whispered. "To find a proper cage for this zoo-piece." He wavered toward Retief. "To show this one in the streets, like all freaks."

"Seen a lot of freaks like me, have you?" Retief asked interestedly.

"To speak intelligibly, malodorous outworlder," the drunk said. The barkeep whispered something and two customers came up to the drunk, took his arms, and helped him to the door.

"To get a cage," the drunk shrilled. "To keep the animals in their place ..."

"I've changed my mind," Retief said to the bartender. "To be grateful as hell, but to have to hurry off now." He followed the drunk out the door. The other Groaci, releasing the heckler, hurried back inside. Retief looked at the weaving creature.

"To be gone, freak," the Groacian whispered.

"To be pals," Retief said. "To be kind to dumb animals."

"To have you hauled away to a stockyard, ill-odored foreign livestock."

"Not to be angry, fragrant native," Retief said. "To permit me to chum with you."

"To flee before I take a cane to you!"

"To have a drink together."

"Not to endure such insolence." The Groacian advanced toward Retief. Retief backed away.

"To hold hands," he said. "To be buddies—"

The Groacian reached for him, but missed. A passer-by stepped around him, head down, and scuttled away. Retief, backing into the opening to a narrow cross-way, offered further verbal familiarities to the drunken local, who followed, furious. Retief stepped around him, seized his collar and yanked. The Groacian fell on his back. Retief stood over him. The downed native half rose; Retief put a foot against his chest and pushed.

"Not to be going anywhere for a few minutes," he said. "To stay right here and have a nice long talk."

"There you are!" Miss Meuhl said, eyeing Retief over her lenses. "There are two gentlemen waiting to see you. Groacian gentlemen."

"Government men, I imagine. Word travels fast." Retief pulled off his cape. "This saves me the trouble of paying another call at the Foreign Ministry."

"What have you been doing? They seem very upset, I don't mind telling you."

"I'm sure you don't. Come along—and bring an official recorder."

Two Groaci, wearing heavy eye-shields and elaborate crest ornaments indicative of rank, rose as Retief entered the room. Neither offered a courteous snap of the mandibles, Retief noted; they were mad, all right.

"I am Fith, of the Terrestrial Desk, Ministry of Foreign Affairs," the taller Groacian said, in lisping Terran. "May I present Shluh, of the Internal Police."

"Sit down, gentlemen," Retief said. They resumed their seats. Miss Meuhl hovered nervously, then sat down on the edge of a chair.

"Oh, it's such a pleasure—" she began.

"Never mind that," Retief said. "These gentlemen didn't come here to sip tea today."

"True," Fith rasped. "Frankly, I have had a most disturbing

report, Mr. Consul. I shall ask Shluh to recount it." He nodded to the police chief.

"One hour ago," Shluh said, "a Groacian national was brought to hospital suffering from serious contusions. Questioning of this individual revealed that he had been set upon and beaten by a foreigner; a Terrestrial, to be precise. Investigation by my Department indicates that the description of the culprit closely matches that of the Terrestrial Consul . . ."

Miss Meuhl gasped audibly.

"Have you ever heard," Retief said, looking steadily at Fith, "of a Terrestrial cruiser, the *ISV Terrific,* which dropped from sight in this sector nine years ago?"

"Really!" Miss Meuhl exclaimed, rising, "I wash my hands—"

"Just keep that recorder going," Retief snapped.

"I'll not be a party—"

"You'll do as you're told, Miss Meuhl," Retief said quietly. "I'm telling you to make an official sealed record of this conversation."

Miss Meuhl sat down.

Fith puffed out his throat indignantly. "You re-open an old wound, Mr. Consul. It reminds us of certain illegal treatment at Terrestrial hands."

"Hogwash," Retief said. "That tune went over with my predecessors, but it hits a sour note with me."

"All our efforts," Miss Meuhl said, "to live down that terrible episode; and you—"

"Terrible? I understand that a Terrestrial Peace Enforcer stood off Groac and sent a delegation down to ask questions. They got some funny answers and stayed on to dig around a little. After a week, they left. Somewhat annoying to you Groaci, if you were innocent—"

"*If!*" Miss Meuhl burst out.

"If, indeed," Fith said, his weak voice trembling. "I must protest your—"

"Save your protests, Fith. You have some explaining to do, and I don't think your story will be good enough."

"It is for you to explain; this person who was beaten—"

"Not beaten; just rapped a few times to loosen his memory."

"Then you admit—"

"It worked, too. He remembered lots of things, once he put his mind to it."

Fith rose; Shluh followed suit.

"I shall ask for your immediate recall, Mr. Consul. Were it not for your diplomatic immunity, I should—"

"Why did the Government fall, Fith, just after the Task Force paid its visit, and before the arrival of the first Terrestrial diplomatic mission?"

"This is an internal matter," Fith cried, in his faint Groacian voice. "The new regime has shown itself most amiable to you Terrestrials; it has outdone itself—"

"—to keep the Terrestrial Consul and his staff in the dark," Retief said, "and the same goes for the few Terrestrial businessmen you've given visas. This continual round of culture; no social contacts outside the diplomatic circle; no travel permits to visit outlying districts or your satellite—"

"Enough!" Fith's mandibles quivered in distress. "I can talk no more of this matter."

"You'll talk to me, or there'll be a squadron of Peace Enforcers here in five days to do the talking," Retief said.

"You can't—" Miss Meuhl gasped.

Retief turned a steady look on Miss Meuhl. She closed her mouth. The Groaci sat down.

"Answer me this one," Retief said, looking at Shluh. "A few

years back—nine, to be exact—there was a little parade held here. Some curious-looking creatures were captured, and after being securely caged, were exhibited to the gentle Groacian public. Hauled through the streets. Very educational, no doubt. A highly cultural show.

"Funny thing about these animals: they wore clothes, seemed to communicate with each other. Altogether a very amusing exhibit.

"Tell me, Shluh, what happened to those six Terrestrials after the parade was over?"

Fith made a choked noise, then spoke rapidly to Shluh in Groacian. Shluh, retracting his eyes, shrank down in his chair. Miss Meuhl opened her mouth, then closed it.

"How did they die?" Retief snapped. "Did you cut their throats, shoot them, bury them alive? What amusing end did you figure out for them? Research, maybe. Cut them open to see what made them yell …"

"No," Fith gasped. "I must correct this terrible false impression at once."

"False impression, hell," Retief said. "They were Terrans; a simple narco-interrogation would get that out of any Groacian who saw the parade."

"Yes," Fith said weakly. "It is true, they were Terrestrials. But there was no killing—"

"They're alive?"

"Alas, no. They … died."

"I see," Retief said. "They died."

"We tried to keep them alive, of course; but we did not know what foods—"

"Didn't take the trouble to find out."

"They fell ill," Fith said. "One by one …"

"We'll deal with that question later," Retief said. "Right

now, I want more information. Where did you get them? Where did you hide the ship? What happened to the rest of the crew? Did they 'fall ill' before the big parade?"

"There were no more! Absolutely, I assure you!"

"Killed in the crash landing?"

"No crash landing. The ship descended intact, east of the city. The … Terrestrials … were unharmed. Naturally, we feared them; they were strange to us. We had never before seen such beings."

"Stepped off the ship with guns blazing, did they?"

"Guns? No, no guns—"

"They raised their hands, didn't they, asked for help? You helped them; helped them to death."

"How could we know?" Fith moaned.

"How could you know a flotilla would show up in a few months looking for them, you mean? That was a shock, wasn't it? I'll bet you had a brisk time of it hiding the ship, and shutting everybody up. A close call, eh?"

"We were afraid," Shluh said. "We are a simple people. We feared the strange creatures from the alien craft. We did not kill them, but we felt it was as well that they … did not survive. Then, when the warships came, we realized our error, but we feared to speak. We purged our guilty leaders, concealed what had happened, and … offered our friendship. We invited the opening of diplomatic relations. We made a blunder, it is true, a great blunder. But we have tried to make amends …"

"Where is the ship?"

"The ship?"

"What did you do with it? It was too big to just walk off and forget. Where is it?"

The two Groacians exchanged looks.

"We wish to show our contrition," Fith said. "We will show you the ship."

"Miss Meuhl," Retief said. "If I don't come back in a reasonable length of time, transmit that recording to Sector Headquarters, sealed." He stood and looked at the Groaci.

"Let's go," he said.

Retief stooped under the heavy timbers shoring the entry to the cavern and peered into the gloom at the curving flank of the space-burned hull.

"Any lights in here?" he asked.

A Groacian threw a switch and a weak bluish glow sprang up. Retief walked along the raised wooden catwalk, studying the ship. Empty emplacements gaped below lenseless scanner eyes. Littered decking was visible within the half-open entry port. Near the bow the words *'IVS Terrific B7 New Terra'* were lettered in bright chrome duralloy.

"How did you get it in here?" Retief asked.

"It was hauled here from the landing point, some nine miles distant," Fith said, his voice thinner than ever. "This is a natural crevasse; the vessel was lowered into it and roofed over."

"How did you shield it so the detectors didn't pick it up?"

"All here is high-grade iron-ore," Fith said, waving a member. "Great veins of almost pure metal."

"Let's go inside."

Shluh came forward with a hand-lamp. The party entered the ship. Retief clambered up a narrow companionway and glanced around the interior of the control compartment. Dust was thick on the deck, the stanchions where acceleration couches had been mounted, the empty instrument panels, the litter of sheared bolts, and on scraps of wire and paper. A thin frosting of rust dulled the exposed metal where cutting torches had sliced away heavy shielding. There was a faint odor of stale bedding.

"The cargo compartment—" Shluh began.

"I've seen enough," Retief said. Silently, the Groacians led the way back out through the tunnel and into the late afternoon sunshine. As they climbed the slope to the steam car, Fith came to Retief's side.

"Indeed I hope that this will be the end of this unfortunate affair," he said. "Now that all has been fully and honestly shown."

"You can skip all that," Retief said. "You're nine years late. The crew was still alive when the Task Force called, I imagine. You killed them—or let them die—rather than take the chance of admitting what you'd done."

"We were at fault," Fith said abjectly. "Now we wish only friendship."

"The *Terrific* was a heavy cruiser, about twenty thousand tons." Retief looked grimly at the slender Foreign Office official. "Where is she, Fith? I won't settle for a hundred-ton lifeboat."

Fith erected his eye stalks so violently that one eye-shield fell off.

"I know nothing of... of..." He stopped. His throat vibrated rapidly as he struggled for calm.

"My government can entertain no further accusations, Mr. Consul," he said at last. "I have been completely candid with you, I have overlooked your probing into matters not properly within your sphere of responsibility. My patience is at an end."

"Where is that ship?" Retief rapped out. "You never learn, do you? You're still convinced you can hide the whole thing and forget it. I'm telling you you can't."

"We return to the city now," Fith said. "I can do no more."

"You can and you will, Fith," Retief said. "I intend to get to the truth of this matter."

Fith spoke to Shluh in rapid Groacian. The police chief gestured to his four armed constables. They moved to ring Retief in.

Retief eyed Fith. "Don't try it," he said. "You'll just get yourself in deeper."

Fith clacked his mandibles angrily, his eye stalks canted aggressively toward the Terrestrial.

"Out of deference to your diplomatic status, Terrestrial, I shall ignore your insulting implications," Fith said in his reedy voice. "We will now return to the city."

Retief looked at the four policemen. "Sure," he said. "We'll cover the details later."

Fith followed him into the car and sat rigidly at the far end of the seat.

"I advise you to remain very close to your Consulate," Fith said. "I advise you to dismiss these fancies from your mind, and to enjoy the cultural aspects of life at Groac. Especially, I should not venture out of the city, or appear overly curious about matters of concern only to the Groacian government."

In the front seat, Shluh looked straight ahead. The loosely-sprung vehicle bobbed and swayed along the narrow highway. Retief listened to the rhythmic puffing of the motor and said nothing.

"Miss Meuhl," Retief said, "I want you to listen carefully to what I'm going to tell you. I have to move rapidly now, to catch the Groaci off guard."

"I'm sure I don't know what you're talking about," Miss Meuhl snapped, her eyes sharp behind the heavy lenses.

"If you'll listen, you may find out," Retief said. "I have no time to waste, Miss Meuhl. They won't be expecting an immediate move—I hope—and that may give me the latitude I need."

"You're still determined to make an issue of that incident." Miss Meuhl snorted. "I really can hardly blame the Groaci; they are not a sophisticated race; they had never before met aliens."

"You're ready to forgive a great deal, Miss Meuhl. But it's not what happened nine years ago I'm concerned with. It's what's happening now. I've told you that it was only a lifeboat the Groaci have hidden out. Don't you understand the implication? That vessel couldn't have come far; the cruiser itself must be somewhere nearby. I want to know where."

"The Groaci don't know. They're a very cultured, gentle people. You can do irreparable harm to the Terrestrial image if you insist—"

"We're wasting time," Retief said, as he crossed the room to his desk, opened a drawer, and took out a slim-barreled needler.

"This office is being watched; not very efficiently, if I know the Groaci. I think I can get past them all right."

"Where are you going with … that?" Miss Meuhl stared at the needler. "What in the world—"

"The Groaci won't waste any time destroying every piece of paper in their files relating to this affair. I have to get what I need before it's too late. If I wait for an official Enquiry Commission, they'll find nothing but blank smiles."

"You're out of your mind!" Miss Meuhl stood up, quivering with indignation. "You're like a … a …"

"You and I are in a tight spot, Miss Meuhl. The logical next move for the Groaci is to dispose of both of us. We're the only ones who know what happened. Fith almost did the job this afternoon, but I bluffed him out—for the moment."

Miss Meuhl emitted a shrill laugh. "Your fantasies are getting the better of you," she gasped. "In danger, indeed! Disposing of me! I've never heard anything so ridiculous."

"Stay in this office. Close and safe-lock the door. You've got food and water in the dispenser. I suggest you stock up, before they shut the supply down. Don't let anyone in, on any pretext whatever. I'll keep in touch with you via handphone."

"What are you planning to do?"

"If I don't make it back here, transmit the sealed record of this afternoon's conversation, along with the information I've given you. Beam it through on a Mayday priority. Then tell the Groaci what you've done and sit tight. I think you'll be all right. It won't be easy to blast in here and anyway, they won't make things worse by killing you in an obvious way. A Force can be here in a week."

"I'll do nothing of the sort! The Groaci are very fond of me! You … Johnny-come-lately! Roughneck! Setting out to destroy—"

"Blame it on me if it will make you feel any better," Retief said, "but don't be fool enough to trust them." He pulled on a cape, and opened the door.

"I'll be back in a couple of hours," he said. Miss Meuhl stared after him silently as he closed the door.

It was an hour before dawn when Retief keyed the combination to the safe-lock and stepped into the darkened Consular office. Miss Meuhl, dozing in a chair, awoke with a start. She looked at Retief, rose, snapped on a light, and turned to stare.

"What in the world— Where have you been? What's happened to your clothing?"

"I got a little dirty—don't worry about it." Retief went to his desk, opened a drawer, and replaced the needler.

"Where have you been?" Miss Meuhl demanded. "I stayed here."

"I'm glad you did," Retief said. "I hope you piled up a supply of food and water from the dispenser, too. We'll be holed up here for a week, at least." He jotted figures on a pad. "Warm up the official sender. I have a long transmission for Sector Headquarters."

"Are you going to tell me where you've been?"

"I have a message to get off first, Miss Meuhl," Retief said sharply. "I've been to the Foreign Ministry," he added. "I'll tell you all about it later."

"At this hour? There's no one there."

"Exactly."

Miss Meuhl gasped. "You mean you broke in? You burgled the Foreign Office?"

"That's right," Retief said calmly. "Now—"

"This is absolutely the end," Miss Meuhl said. "Thank heaven I've already—"

"Get that sender going, woman! This is important."

"I've already done so, Mr. Retief!" Miss Meuhl said harshly. "I've been waiting for you to come back here." She turned to the communicator and flipped levers. The screen snapped aglow, and a wavering long-distance image appeared.

"He's here now," Miss Meuhl said to the screen. She looked at Retief triumphantly.

"That's good," said Retief. "I don't think the Groaci can knock us off the air, but—"

"I have done my duty, Mr. Retief; I made a full report of your activities to Sector Headquarters last night, as soon as you left this office. Any doubts I may have had as to the rightness of my decision have been completely dispelled by what you've just told me."

Retief looked at her levelly. "You've been a busy girl, Miss Meuhl. Did you mention the six Terrestrials who were killed here?"

"That had no bearing on the matter of your wild behavior. I must say, in all my years in the Corps, I've never encountered a personality less suited to diplomatic work."

The screen crackled, the ten-second transmission lag having elapsed. "Mr. Retief," the face on the screen said sternly, "I am Counselor Nitworth, DSO-1, Deputy Under-Secretary for the Sector. I have received a report on your conduct which makes it mandatory for me to relieve you administratively. Pending the findings of a Board of Inquiry, you will—"

Retief reached out and snapped off the communicator. The triumphant look faded from Miss Meuhl's face.

"Why, what is the meaning—"

"If I'd listened any longer, I might have heard something I couldn't ignore. I can't afford that, at this moment. Listen, Miss Meuhl," Retief went on earnestly, "I've found the missing cruiser. It's—"

"You heard him relieve you!"

"I heard him say he was going to, Miss Meuhl. But until I've heard and acknowledged a verbal order, it has no force. If I'm wrong, he'll get my resignation. If I'm right, that suspension would be embarrassing all around."

"You're defying lawful authority. I'm in charge here now." Miss Meuhl stepped to the local communicator.

"I'm going to report this terrible thing to the Groaci at once, and offer my profound—"

"Don't touch that screen," Retief said. "You go sit in that corner where I can keep an eye on you. I'm going to make a sealed tape for transmission to Headquarters, along with a call for an armed Task Force. Then we'll settle down to wait."

Retief, ignoring Miss Meuhl's fury, spoke into the recorder.

The local communicator chimed. Miss Meuhl jumped up and stared at it.

"Go ahead," Retief said. "Answer it."

A Groacian official appeared on the screen.

"Yolanda Meuhl," he said without preamble, "for the Foreign Minister of the Groacian Autonomy, I herewith accredit you as Terrestrial Consul to Groac, in accordance with the advices transmitted to my Government direct from the Terrestrial Headquarters. As Consul, you are requested to make available for questioning Mr. J. Retief, former Consul, in connection with the assault on two Peace Keepers, and illegal entry into the offices of the Ministry of Foreign Affairs."

"Why … why," Miss Meuhl stammered. "Yes, of course, and I do want to express my deepest regrets—"

Retief rose, went to the communicator, and assisted Miss Meuhl aside.

"Listen carefully, Fith," he said. "Your bluff has been called. You don't come in and we don't come out. Your camouflage worked for nine years, but it's all over now. I suggest you keep your heads and resist the temptation to make matters worse."

"Miss Meuhl," Fith replied, "a Peace Squad waits outside your Consulate. It is clear you are in the hands of a dangerous lunatic. As always, the Groaci wish only friendship with the Terrestrials, but—"

"Don't bother," Retief cut in. "You know what was in those files I looked over this morning."

Retief turned at a sound behind him. Miss Meuhl was at the door reaching for the safe-lock release.

"Don't!" Retief jumped … too late. The door burst inward,

a crowd of crested Groaci pressed into the room, pushed Miss Meuhl back, and aimed scatter guns at Retief. Police Chief Shluh pushed forward.

"Attempt no violence, Terrestrial," he said. "I cannot promise to restrain my men."

"You're violating Terrestrial territory, Shluh," Retief said steadily. "I suggest you move back out the same way you came in."

"I invited them here," Miss Meuhl spoke up. "They are here at my express wish."

"Are they? Are you sure you meant to go this far, Miss Meuhl? A squad of armed Groaci in the Consulate?"

"You are the Consul, Miss Yolanda Meuhl," Shluh said. "Would it not be best if we removed this deranged person to a place of safety?"

"Yes," Miss Meuhl said. "You're quite right, Mr. Shluh. Please escort Mr. Retief to his quarters in this building."

"I don't advise you to violate my diplomatic immunity, Fith," Retief said.

"As Chief of Mission," Miss Meuhl said quickly, "I hereby waive immunity in the case of Mr. Retief."

Shluh produced a hand recorder. "Kindly repeat your statement, madame, officially," he said. "I wish no question—"

"Don't be a fool, woman," Retief said. "Don't you see what you're letting yourself in for? This would be a hell of a good time for you to figure out whose side you're on."

"I'm on the side of common decency!"

"You've been taken in. These people are concealing—"

"You think all women are fools, don't you, Mr. Retief?" She turned to the police chief and spoke into the microphone he held up.

"That's an illegal waiver," Retief said. "I'm Consul here,

whatever rumors you've heard. This thing's coming out into the open, in spite of anything you can do; don't add violation of the Consulate to the list of Groacian atrocities."

"Take the man," Shluh said. Two tall Groaci came to Retief's side, guns aimed at his chest.

"Determined to hang yourselves, aren't you?" Retief said. "I hope you have sense enough not to lay a hand on this poor fool here." He jerked a thumb at Miss Meuhl. "She doesn't know anything. I hadn't had time to tell her yet. She thinks you're a band of angels."

The cop at Retief's side swung the butt of his scatter gun and connected solidly with Retief's jaw. Retief staggered against a Groacian, was caught and thrust upright, blood running down onto his shirt. Miss Meuhl yelped. Shluh barked at the guard in shrill Groacian, then turned to stare at Miss Meuhl.

"What has this man told you?"

"I—nothing. I refused to listen to his ravings."

"He said nothing to you of ... some alleged ... involvement."

"I've told you." Miss Meuhl said sharply. She looked at the expressionless Groaci, then back at the blood on Retief's shirt.

"He told me nothing," she whispered. "I swear it."

"Let it lie, boys," Retief said, "before you spoil that good impression."

Shluh looked at Miss Meuhl for a long moment. Then he turned.

"Let us go," he said. He turned back to Miss Meuhl. "Do not leave this building until further advice."

"But ... I am the Terrestrial Consul."

"For your safety, madam. The people are aroused at the beating of Groacian nationals by an ... alien."

"So long, Meuhlsie," Retief said. "You played it real foxy."

"You'll ... lock him in his quarters?" Miss Meuhl said.

"What is done with him now is a Groacian affair, Miss Meuhl. You yourself have withdrawn the protection of your government."

"I didn't mean—"

"Don't start having second thoughts," Retief said. "They can make you miserable."

"I had no choice. I had to consider the best interest of the Service."

"My mistake, I guess. I was thinking of the best interests of a Terrestrial cruiser with three hundred men aboard."

"Enough," Shluh said. "Remove this criminal." He gestured to the Peace Keepers.

"Move along," he said to Retief. He turned to Miss Meuhl.

"A pleasure to deal with you, Madam."

The police car started up and pulled away. The Peace Keeper in the front seat turned to look at Retief.

"To have some sport with it, and then to kill it," he said.

"To have a fair trial first," Shluh said. The car rocked and jounced, rounded a corner, and puffed along between ornamented pastel facades.

"To have a trial and then to have a bit of sport," the Peace Keeper said.

"To suck the eggs in your own hill," Retief said. "To make another stupid mistake."

Shluh raised his short ceremonial club and cracked Retief across the head. Retief shook his head, tensed—

The Peace Keeper in the front seat beside the driver turned and rammed the barrel of his scatter gun against Retief's ribs.

"To make no move, outworlder," he said. Shluh raised his club and carefully struck Retief again. He slumped.

The car, swaying, rounded another corner. Retief slid over against the police chief.

"To fend this animal—" Shluh began. His weak voice was cut off short as Retief's hand shot out, took him by the throat, and snapped him down onto the floor. As the guard on Retief's left lunged, Retief uppercut him, slamming his head against the door post. Retief grabbed the guard's scatter gun as it fell, and pushed it into the mandibles of the Groacian in the front seat.

"To put your pop-gun over the seat—carefully—and drop it," he said.

The driver slammed on his brakes, then whirled to raise his gun. Retief cracked a gun barrel against the head of the Groacian.

"To keep your eye-stalks on the road," he said. The driver grabbed at the tiller and shrank against the window, watching Retief with one eye, driving with another.

"To gun this thing," Retief said. "To keep moving."

Shluh stirred on the floor. Retief put a foot on him, pressing him back. The Peace Keeper beside Retief moved. Retief pushed him off the seat onto the floor. He held the scatter gun with one hand and mopped at the blood on his face with the other. The car bounded over the irregular surface of the road, puffing furiously.

"Your death will not be an easy one, Terrestrial," Shluh said in Terran.

"No easier than I can help," Retief said. "Shut up for now, I want to think."

The car, passing the last of the relief-encrusted mounds, sped along between tilled fields.

"Slow down," Retief said. The driver obeyed.

"Turn down this side road."

The car bumped off onto an unpaved surface, then threaded its way back among tall stalks.

"Stop here." The car stopped, blew off steam, and sat trembling as the hot engine idled.

Retief opened the door, taking his foot off Shluh.

"Sit up," he ordered. "You two in front listen carefully." Shluh sat up, rubbing his throat.

"Three of you are getting out here. Good old Shluh is going to stick around to drive for me. If I get that nervous feeling that you're after me, I'll toss him out. That will be pretty messy, at high speed. Shluh, tell them to sit tight until dark and forget about sounding any alarms. I'd hate to see you split open and spill all over the pavement."

"To burst your throat sac, evil-smelling beast!" Shluh hissed in Groacian.

"Sorry, I haven't got one." Retief put the gun under Shluh's ear. "Tell them, Shluh; I can drive myself, in a pinch."

"To do as the foreign one says; to stay hidden until dark," Shluh said.

"Everybody out," Retief said. "And take this with you." He nudged the unconscious Groacian. "Shluh, you get in the driver's seat. You others stay where I can see you."

Retief watched as the Groaci silently followed instructions.

"All right, Shluh," Retief said softly. "Let's go. Take me to Groac Spaceport by the shortest route that doesn't go through the city, and be very careful about making any sudden movements."

Forty minutes later Shluh steered the car up to the sentry-guarded gate in the security fence surrounding the military enclosure at Groac Spaceport.

"Don't yield to any rash impulses," Retief whispered as a

crested Groacian soldier came up. Shluh grated his mandibles in helpless fury.

"Drone-master Shluh, Internal Security," he croaked. The guard tilted his eyes toward Retief.

"The guest of the Autonomy," Shluh added. "To let me pass or to rot in this spot, fool?"

"To pass, Drone-master," the sentry mumbled. He was still staring at Retief as the car moved jerkily away.

"You are as good as pegged-out on the hill in the pleasure pits now, Terrestrial," Shluh said in Terran. "Why do you venture here?"

"Pull over there in the shadow of the tower and stop," Retief said.

Shluh complied. Retief studied a row of four slender ships silhouetted against the early dawn colors of the sky.

"Which of those boats are ready to lift?" Retief demanded.

Shluh swivelled a choleric eye.

"All of them are shuttles; they have no range. They will not help you."

"To answer the question, Shluh, or to get another crack on the head."

"You are not like other Terrestrials, you are a mad dog."

"We'll rough out a character sketch of me later. Are they fueled up? You know the procedures here. Did those shuttles just get in, or is that the ready line?"

"Yes. All are fueled and ready for take-off."

"I hope you're right, Shluh. You and I are going to drive over and get in one; if it doesn't lift, I'll kill you and try the next one. Let's go."

"You are mad. I have told you: these boats have not more than ten thousand ton-seconds capacity; they are useful only for satellite runs."

"Never mind the details. Let's try the first in line."

Shluh let in the clutch and the steam car clanked and heaved, rolling off toward the line of boats.

"Not the first in line," Shluh said suddenly. "The last is the most likely to be fueled. But—"

"Smart grasshopper," Retief said. "Pull up to the entry port, hop out, and go right up. I'll be right behind you."

"The gangway guard. The challenging of—"

"More details. Just give him a dirty look and say what's necessary. You know the technique."

The car passed under the stern of the first boat, then the second. There was no alarm. It rounded the third and shuddered to a stop by the open port of the last vessel.

"Out," Retief said. "To make it snappy."

Shluh stepped from the car, hesitated as the guard came to attention, then hissed at him and mounted the steps. The guard looked wonderingly at Retief, mandibles slack.

"An outworlder!" he said. He unlimbered his scatter gun. "To stop here, meat-faced one."

Up ahead, Shluh turned.

"To snap to attention, litter-mate of drones." Retief rasped in Groacian. The guard jumped, waved his eye stalks, and came to attention.

"About face!" Retief hissed. "To hell out of here—march!"

The guard tramped off across the ramp. Retief took the steps two at a time, slammed the port shut behind himself.

"I'm glad your boys have a little discipline, Shluh," Retief said. "What did you say to him?"

"I but—"

"Never mind. We're in. Get up to the control compartment."

"What do you know of Groacian Naval vessels?"

"Plenty. This is a straight copy from the life boat you lads hijacked. I can run it. Get going."

Retief followed Shluh up the companionway into the cramped control room.

"Tie in, Shluh," Retief ordered.

"This is insane. We have only fuel enough for a one-way transit to the satellite; we cannot enter orbit, nor can we land again! To lift this boat is death. Release me. I promise you immunity."

"If I have to tie you in myself, I might bend your head in the process."

Shluh crawled onto the couch, and strapped in.

"Give it up," he said. "I will see that you are re-instated—with honor. I will guarantee a safe-conduct—"

"Count-down," Retief said. He threw in the autopilot.

"It is death!" Shluh screeched.

The gyros hummed, timers ticked, relays closed. Retief lay relaxed on the acceleration pad. Shluh breathed noisily, his mandibles clicking rapidly.

"That I had fled in time," he said in a hoarse whisper. "This is not a good death."

"No death is a good death," Retief said, "not for a while yet." The red light flashed on in the center of the panel, and sound roared out into the breaking day. The ship trembled, then lifted. Retief could hear Shluh's whimpering even through the roar of the drive.

"Perihelion," Shluh said dully. "To begin now the long fall back."

"Not quite," Retief said. "I figure eighty-five seconds to go." He scanned the instruments, frowning.

"We will not reach the surface, of course," Shluh said. "The pips on the screen are missiles. We have a rendezvous in space, Retief. In your madness, may you be content."

"They're fifteen minutes behind us, Shluh. Your defenses are sluggish."

"Nevermore to burrow in the grey sands of Groac," Shluh mourned.

Retief's eyes were fixed on a dial face.

"Any time now," he said softly. Shluh canted his eye stalks.

"What do you seek?"

Retief stiffened. "Look at the screen," he said. Shluh looked. A glowing point, off-center, moving rapidly across the grid …

"What—?"

"Later—"

Shluh watched as Retief's eyes darted from one needle to another.

"How …"

"For your own neck's sake, Shluh, you'd better hope this works" He flipped the sending key.

"2396 TR-42 G, this is the Terrestrial Consul at Groac, aboard Groac 902, vectoring on you at an MP fix of 91/54/942. Can you read me? Over."

"What forlorn gesture is this?" Shluh whispered. "You cry in the night to emptiness."

"Button your mandibles," Retief snapped, listening. There was a faint hum of stellar background noise. Retief repeated his call.

"Maybe they hear but can't answer," he muttered. He flipped the key.

"2396, you've got forty seconds to lock a tractor beam on me, before I shoot past you."

"To call into the void," said Shluh. "To—"

"Look at the DV screen."

Shluh twisted his head and looked. Against the background mist of stars, a shape loomed, dark and inert.

"It is … a ship," he said, "a monster ship …"

"That's her," Retief said. "Nine years and a few months out of New Terra on a routine mapping mission; the missing cruiser, *IVS Terrific.*"

"Impossible," Shluh hissed. "The hulk swings in a deep cometary orbit."

"Right, and now it's making its close swing past Groac."

"You think to match orbits with the derelict? Without power? Our meeting will be a violent one, if that is your intent."

"We won't hit; we'll make our pass at about five thousand yards."

"To what end, Terrestrial? You have found your lost ship; what then? Is this glimpse worth the death we die?"

"Maybe they're not dead," Retief said.

"Not dead?" Shluh lapsed into Groacian. "To have died in the burrow of one's youth. To have burst my throat sac before I embarked with a mad alien to call up the dead."

"2396, make it snappy," Retief called. The speaker crackled heedlessly. The dark image on the screen drifted past, dwindling now.

"Nine years, and the mad one speaking as to friends," Shluh raved. "Nine years dead, and still to seek them."

"Another ten seconds," Retief said softly, "and we're out of range. Look alive, boys."

"Was this your plan, Retief?" Shluh reverted to Terran. "Did you flee Groac and risk all on this slender thread?"

"How long would I have lasted in a Groaci prison?"

"Long and long, my Retief," Shluh hissed, "under the blade of an artist."

Abruptly the ship trembled, seemed to drag, rolling the two passengers in their couches. Shluh hissed as the restraining harness cut into him. The shuttle boat was pivoting heavily, up-ending. Crushing acceleration forces built. Shluh gasped, crying out shrilly.

"What ... is ... it...?"

"It looks," said Retief, "like we've had a little bit of luck."

"On our second pass," the gaunt-faced officer said, "they let fly with something. I don't know how it got past our screens. It socked home in the stern and put the main pipe off the air. I threw full power to the emergency shields, and broadcast our identification on a scatter that should have hit every receiver within a parsec; nothing. Then the transmitter blew. I was a fool to send the boat down, but I couldn't believe, somehow ..."

"In a way it's lucky you did, captain. That was my only lead."

"They tried to finish us after that. But, with full power to the screens, nothing they had could get through. Then they called on us to surrender."

Retief nodded. "I take it you weren't tempted?"

"More than you know. It was a long swing out on our first circuit. Then coming back in, we figured we'd hit. As a last resort I would have pulled back power from the screens and tried to adjust the orbit with the steering jets, but the bombardment was pretty heavy. I don't think we'd have made it. Then we swung past and headed out again. We've got a three-year period. Don't think I didn't consider throwing in the towel."

"Why didn't you?"

"The information we have is important. We've got plenty

of stores aboard, enough for another ten years, if necessary. Sooner or later I knew a Corps search vessel would find us."

Retief cleared his throat. "I'm glad you stuck with it, Captain. Even a backwater world like Groac can kill a lot of people when it runs amok."

"What I didn't know," the captain went on, "was that we're not in a stable orbit. We're going to graze atmosphere pretty deeply this pass, and in another sixty days we'd be back to stay. I guess the Groaci would be ready for us."

"No wonder they were sitting on this so tight. They were almost in the clear."

"And you're here now," the captain said. "Nine years, and we weren't forgotten. I knew we could count on—"

"It's over now, captain. That's what counts."

"Home … After nine years …"

"I'd like to take a look at the films you mentioned," Retief said. "The ones showing the installations on the satellite."

The captain complied. Retief watched as the scene unrolled, showing the bleak surface of the tiny moon as the *Terrific* had seen it, nine years before. In harsh black and white, row on row of identical hulls cast long shadows across the pitted metallic surface of the satellite.

"They had quite a little surprise planned; your visit must have panicked them," Retief said.

"They should be about ready to go, by now. Nine years …"

"Hold that picture," Retief said suddenly. "What's that ragged black line across the plain there?"

"I think it's a fissure. The crystalline structure—"

"I've got what may be an idea," Retief said. "I had a look at some classified files last night, at the Foreign Office. One was a progress report on a fissionable stock-pile. It didn't make much sense at the time. Now I get the picture. Which is the north end of that crevasse?"

"At the top of the picture."

"Unless I'm badly mistaken, that's the bomb dump. The Groaci like to tuck things underground. I wonder what a direct hit with a 50 megaton missile would do to it?"

"If that's an ordnance storage dump," the captain said, "it's an experiment I'd like to try."

"Can you hit it?"

"I've got fifty heavy missiles aboard. If I fire them in direct sequence, it should saturate the defenses. Yes, I can hit it."

"The range isn't too great?"

"These are the deluxe models." The captain smiled balefully. "Video guidance. We could steer them into a bar and park 'em on a stool."

"What do you say we try it?"

"I've been wanting a solid target for a long time," the captain said.

Half an hour later, Retief propelled Shluh into a seat before the screen.

"That expanding dust cloud used to be the satellite of Groac, Shluh," he said. "Looks like something happened to it."

The police chief stared at the picture.

"Too bad," Retief said. "But then it wasn't of any importance, was it, Shluh?"

Shluh muttered incomprehensibly.

"Just a bare hunk of iron, Shluh, as the Foreign Office assured me when I asked for information."

"I wish you'd keep your prisoner out of sight," the captain said. "I have a hard time keeping my hands off him."

"Shluh wants to help, captain. He's been a bad boy and I have a feeling he'd like to co-operate with us now, especially in view of the eminent arrival of a Terrestrial ship, and the dust cloud out there," Retief said.

"What do you mean?"

"Captain, you can ride it out for another week, contact the ship when it arrives, get a tow in, and your troubles are over. When your films are shown in the proper quarter, a Peace Force will come out here and reduce Groac to a sub-technical cultural level and set up a monitor system to insure she doesn't get any more expansionist ideas—not that she can do much now, with her handy iron mine in the sky gone."

"That's right, and—"

"On the other hand, there's what I might call the diplomatic approach …"

He explained at length. The captain looked at him thoughtfully.

"I'll go along," he said. "What about this fellow?"

Retief turned to Shluh. The Groacian shuddered, retracting his eye stalks.

"I will do it," he said faintly.

"Right," Retief said. "Captain, if you'll have your men bring in the transmitter from the shuttle, I'll place a call to a fellow named Fith at the Foreign Office." He turned to Shluh. "And when I get him, Shluh, you'll do everything exactly as I've told you—or have Terrestrial monitors dictating in Groac City."

"Quite candidly, Retief," Counselor Nitworth said, "I'm rather nonplussed. Mr. Fith of the Foreign Office seemed almost painfully lavish in your praise. He seems most eager to please you. In the light of some of the evidence I've turned up of highly irregular behavior on your part, it's difficult to understand."

"Fith and I have been through a lot together," Retief said. "We understand each other."

"You have no cause for complacency, Retief," Nitworth said. "Miss Meuhl was quite justified in reporting your case. Of course, had she known that you were assisting Mr. Fith in his marvelous work, she would have modified her report somewhat, no doubt. You should have confided in her."

"Fith wanted to keep it secret, in case it didn't work out. You know how it is."

"Of course. And as soon as Miss Meuhl recovers from her nervous breakdown, there'll be a nice promotion awaiting her. The girl more than deserves it for her years of unswerving devotion to Corps policy."

"Unswerving," Retief said. "I'll go along with that."

"As well you may, Retief. You've not acquitted yourself well in this assignment. I'm arranging for a transfer; you've alienated too many of the local people."

"But as you said, Fith speaks highly of me ..."

"True. It's the cultural intelligentsia I'm referring to. Miss Meuhl's records show that you deliberately affronted a number of influential groups by boycotting—"

"Tone deaf," Retief said. "To me a Groacian blowing a nose-whistle sounds like a Groacian blowing a nose-whistle."

"You have to come to terms with local aesthetic values. Learn to know the people as they really are. It's apparent from some of the remarks Miss Meuhl quoted in her report that you held the Groaci in rather low esteem. But how wrong you were. All the while they were working unceasingly to rescue those brave lads marooned aboard our cruiser. They pressed on, even after we ourselves had abandoned the search. And when they discovered that it had been a collision with their satellite which disabled the craft, they made that magnificent gesture—unprecedented. One hundred thousand credits in gold to each crew member, as a token of Groacian sympathy."

"A handsome gesture," Retief murmured.

"I hope, Retief, that you've learned from this incident. In view of the helpful part you played in advising Mr. Fith in matters of procedure to assist in his search, I'm not recommending a reduction in grade. We'll overlook the affair, give you a clean slate. But in the future, I'll be watching you closely."

"You can't win 'em all," Retief said.

"You'd better pack up; you'll be coming along with us in the morning." Nitworth shuffled his papers together. "I'm sorry that I can't file a more flattering report on you. I would have liked to recommend your promotion, along with Miss Meuhl's."

"That's okay," Retief said. "I have my memories."

... Ofttimes, the expertise displayed by experienced Terrestrial Chiefs of Mission in the analysis of local political currents enabled these dedicated senior officers to secure acceptance of Corps commercial programs under seemingly insurmountable conditions of adversity. Ambassador Crodfoller's virtuoso performance in the reconciliation of rival elements at Petreac added new lustre to Corps prestige ...

Vol VIII, reel 8. 489 A. E. (AD 2950)

PALACE REVOLUTION

Retief paused before a tall mirror to check the overlap of the four sets of lapels that ornamented the vermilion cutaway of a First Secretary and Consul.

"Come along, Retief," Magnan said. "The ambassador has a word to say to the staff before we go in."

"I hope he isn't going to change the spontaneous speech he plans to make when the Potentate impulsively suggests a trade agreement along the lines they've been discussing for the last two months."

"Your derisive attitude is uncalled for, Retief," Magnan said sharply. "I think you realize it's delayed your promotion in the Corps."

Retief took a last glance in the mirror. "I'm not sure I want a promotion. It would mean more lapels."

Ambassador Crodfoller pursed his lips, waiting until Retief

and Magnan took places in the ring of Terrestrial diplomats around him.

"A word of caution only, gentlemen. Keep always foremost in your minds the necessity for our identification with the Nenni Caste. Even a hint of familiarity with lower echelons could mean the failure of the mission. Let us remember: the Nenni represent authority here on Petreac; their traditions must be observed, whatever our personal preferences. Let's go along now; the Potentate will be making his entrance any moment."

Magnan came to Retief's side as they moved toward the salon.

"The ambassador's remarks were addressed chiefly to you, Retief," he said. "Your laxness in these matters is notorious. Naturally, I believe firmly in democratic principles myself."

"Have you ever had a feeling, Mr. Magnan, that there's a lot going on here that we don't know about?"

Magnan nodded. "Quite so; Ambassador Crodfoller's point exactly. Matters which are not of concern to the Nenni are of no concern to us."

"Another feeling I get is that the Nenni aren't very bright. Now suppose—"

"I'm not given to suppositions, Retief. We're here to implement the policies of the Chief of Mission. And I should dislike to be in the shoes of a member of the Staff whose conduct jeopardized the agreement that's to be concluded here tonight."

A bearer with a tray of drinks rounded a fluted column, shied as he confronted the diplomats, fumbled the tray, grabbed, and sent a glass crashing to the floor. Magnan leaped back, slapping at the purple cloth of his pants leg. Retief's hand shot out and steadied the tray. The servant rolled his terrified eyes.

"I'll take one of those, now that you're here," Retief said easily, lifting a glass from the tray. "No harm done. Mr. Magnan's just warming up for the big dance."

A Nenni major-domo bustled up, rubbing his hands politely.

"Some trouble here? What happened, Honorables, what, what …"

"The blundering idiot," Magnan spluttered. "How dare—"

"You're quite an actor, Mr. Magnan," Retief said. "If I didn't know about your democratic principles, I'd think you were really angry."

The servant ducked his head and scuttled away.

"Has this fellow given dissatisfaction…?" The major-domo eyed the retreating bearer.

"I dropped my glass," Retief said. "Mr. Magnan's upset because he hates to see liquor wasted."

Retief turned and found himself face-to-face with Ambassador Crodfoller.

"I witnessed that," the ambassador hissed. "By the goodness of Providence the Potentate and his retinue haven't appeared yet, but I can assure you the servants saw it. A more un-Nenni-like display I would find it difficult to imagine."

Retief arranged his features in an expression of deep interest. "More un-Nenni-like, sir? I'm not sure I—"

"Bah!" The ambassador glared at Retief. "Your reputation has preceded you, sir. Your name is associated with a number of the most bizarre incidents in Corps history. I'm warning you; I'll tolerate nothing." He turned and stalked away.

"Ambassador-baiting is a dangerous sport, Retief," Magnan said.

Retief took a swallow of his drink. "Still, it's better than no sport at all."

"Your time would be better spent observing the Nenni mannerisms; frankly, Retief, you're not fitting into the group at all well."

"I'll be candid with you, Mr. Magnan; the group gives me the willies."

"Oh, the Nenni are a trifle frivolous, I'll concede. But it's with them that we must deal. And you'd be making a contribution to the overall mission if you abandoned that rather arrogant manner of yours." Magnan looked at Retief critically. "You can't help your height, of course, but couldn't you curve your back just a bit—and possibly assume a more placating expression? Just act a little more ..."

"Girlish?"

"Exactly." Magnan nodded, then looked sharply at Retief.

Retief drained his glass and put it on a passing tray.

"I'm better at acting girlish when I'm well juiced," he said. "But I can't face another sorghum and soda. I suppose it would be un-Nenni-like to slip one of the servants a credit and ask for a Scotch and water."

"Decidedly." Magnan glanced toward a sound across the room.

"Ah, here's the Potentate now ..." He hurried off.

Retief watched the bearers coming and going, bringing trays laden with drinks, carrying off empties. There was a lull in the drinking now, as the diplomats gathered around the periwigged chief of state and his courtiers. Bearers loitered near the service door, eyeing the notables. Retief strolled over to the service door and pushed through it into a narrow white-tiled hall filled with kitchen odors. Silent servants gaped as he passed and watched him as he moved along to the kitchen door and stepped inside.

A dozen or more low-caste Petreacans, gathered around a

long table in the center of the room, looked up, startled. A heap of long-bladed bread knives, carving knives and cleavers lay in the center of the table. Other knives were thrust into belts or held in the hands of the men. A fat man in the yellow sarong of a cook stood frozen in the act of handing a twelve-inch cheese-knife to a tall one-eyed sweeper.

Retief took one glance, then let his eyes wander to a far corner of the room. Humming a careless little tune, he sauntered across to the open liquor shelves, selected a garish green bottle, then turned unhurriedly back toward the door. The group of servants watched him, transfixed.

As Retief reached the door, it swung inward. Magnan stood in the doorway, looking at him.

"I had a premonition," he said.

"I'll bet it was a dandy. You must tell me all about it—in the salon."

"We'll have this out right here," Magnan snapped. "I've warned you—" His voice trailed off as he took in the scene around the table.

"After you," Retief said, nudging Magnan toward the door.

"What's going on here?" Magnan barked. He stared at the men and started around Retief. A hand stopped him.

"Let's be going," Retief said, propelling Magnan toward the hall.

"Those knives!" Magnan yelped. "Take your hands off me, Retief! What are you men—"

Retief glanced back. The fat cook gestured suddenly, and the men faded back. The cook stood, arm cocked, a knife across his palm.

"Close the door and make no sound," he said softly.

Magnan pressed back against Retief. "Let's … r-run …" he faltered.

Retief turned slowly, put his hands up.

"I don't run very well with a knife in my back," he said. "Stand very still, Mr. Magnan, and do just what he tells you."

"Take them out through the back," the cook said.

"What does he mean?" Magnan spluttered. "Here, you—"

"Silence," the cook said, almost casually. Magnan gaped at him, then closed his mouth.

Two of the men with knives came to Retief's side, gestured, grinning broadly.

"Let's go, peacocks," said one.

Retief and Magnan silently crossed the kitchen, went out the back door, stopped on command, and stood waiting. The sky was brilliant with stars and a gentle breeze stirred the tree-tops beyond the garden. Behind them the servants talked in low voices.

"You go too, Illy," the cook was saying.

"Do it here," said another.

"And carry them down?"

"Pitch 'em behind the hedge."

"I said the river. Three of you is plenty for a couple of Nenni dandies."

"They're foreigners, not Nenni. We don't know—"

"So they're foreign Nenni. Makes no difference. I've seen them. I need every man here; now get going."

"What about the big guy?"

"Him? He waltzed into the room and didn't notice a thing. But watch the other one."

At a prod from a knife point, Retief moved off down the walk, two of the escort behind him and Magnan, another going ahead to scout the way.

Magnan moved closer to Retief.

"Say," he said in a whisper, "that fellow in the lead—isn't

he the one who spilled the drink? The one you took the blame for?"

"That's him, all right. He doesn't seem nervous any more, I notice."

"You saved him from serious punishment," Magnan said. "He'll be grateful; he'll let us go . . ."

"Better check with the fellows with the knives before you act on that."

"Say something to him," Magnan hissed, "remind him."

The lead man fell back in line with Retief and Magnan.

"These two are scared of you," he said, grinning and jerking a thumb toward the knife-handlers. "They haven't worked around the Nenni like me; they don't know you."

"Don't you recognize this gentleman?" Magnan said. "He's—"

"He did me a favor," the man said. "I remember."

"What's it all about?" Retief asked.

"The revolution. We're taking over now."

"Who's 'we'?"

"The People's Anti-Fascist Freedom League."

"What are all the knives for?"

"For the Nenni; and for you foreigners."

"What do you mean?" gasped Magnan.

"We'll slit all the throats at one time; saves a lot of running around."

"When will that be?"

"Just at dawn—and dawn comes early, this time of year. By full daylight the PAFFL will be in charge."

"You'll never succeed," Magnan said. "A few servants with knives; you'll all be caught and executed."

"By who; the Nenni?" The man laughed. "You Nenni are a caution."

"But we're not Nenni—"

"We've watched you; you're the same. You're part of the same blood-sucking class."

"There are better ways," Magnan said. "This killing won't help you. I'll personally see to it that your grievances are heard in the Corps Courts. I can assure you that the plight of the down-trodden workers will be alleviated. Equal rights for all."

"Threats won't help you," the man said. "You don't scare me."

"Threats? I'm promising relief to the exploited classes of Petreac."

"You must be nuts. You trying to upset the system or something?"

"Isn't that the purpose of your revolution?"

"Look, Nenni, we're tired of you Nenni getting all the graft. We want our turn. What good it do us to run Petreac if there's no loot?"

"You mean you intend to oppress the people? But they're your own group."

"Group, schmoop. We're taking all the chances; we're doing the work. We deserve the pay-off. You think we're throwing up good jobs for the fun of it?"

"You're basing a revolt on these cynical premises?"

"Wise up, Nenni; there's never been a revolution for any other reason."

"Who's in charge of this?" Retief said.

"Shoke, the head chef."

"I mean the big boss; who tells Shoke what to do?"

"Oh, that's Zorn. Look out, here's where we start down the slope. It's slippery."

"Look," Magnan said. "You. This—"

"My name's Illy."

"Mr. Illy, this man showed you mercy when he could have had you beaten."

"Keep moving. Yeah, I said I was grateful."

"Yes," Magnan said, swallowing hard. "A noble emotion, gratitude."

"I always try to pay back a good turn," Illy said. "Watch your step now on this sea-wall."

"You'll never regret it."

"This is far enough." Illy motioned to one of the knife men. "Give me your knife, Vug."

The man passed his knife to Illy. There was an odor of sea-mud and kelp. Small waves slapped against the stones of the sea-wall. The wind was stronger here.

"I know a neat stroke," Illy said. "Practically painless. Who's first?"

"What do you mean?" Magnan quavered.

"I said I was grateful; I'll do it myself, give you a nice clean job. You know these amateurs: botch it up and have a guy floppin' around, yellin' and spatterin' everybody up."

"I'm first," Retief said. He pushed past Magnan, stopped suddenly, and drove a straight punch at Illy's mouth.

The long blade flicked harmlessly over Retief's shoulder as Illy fell. Retief took the unarmed servant by the throat and belt, lifted him, and slammed him against the third man. Both screamed as they tumbled from the sea-wall into the water with a mighty splash. Retief turned back to Illy, pulled off the man's belt, and strapped his hands together.

Magnan found his voice. "You … we … they …"

"I know."

"We've got to get back," Magnan said. "Warn them."

"We'd never get through the rebel cordon around the

palace. And if we did, trying to give an alarm would only set the assassinations off early."

"We can't just ..."

"We've got to go to the source: this fellow Zorn. Get him to call it off."

"We'd be killed. At least we're safe here."

Illy groaned and opened his eyes. He sat up.

"On your feet, Illy," Retief said.

Illy looked around. "I'm sick."

"The damp air is bad for you. Let's be going." Retief pulled the man to his feet. "Where does Zorn stay when he's in town?"

"What happened? Where's Vug and ..."

"They had an accident. Fell in the pond."

Illy gazed down at the restless black water.

"I guess I had you Nenni figured wrong."

"We Nenni have hidden qualities. Let's get moving before Vug and Slug make it to shore and start it all over again."

"No hurry," Illy said. "They can't swim." He spat into the water. "So long, Vug. So long, Toscin. Take a pull at the Hell Horn for me." He started off along the sea wall toward the sound of the surf.

"You want to see Zorn, I'll take you see Zorn. I can't swim either."

"I take it," Retief said, "that the casino is a front for his political activities."

"He makes plenty off it. This PAFFL is a new kick. I never heard about it until maybe a couple months ago."

Retief motioned toward a dark shed with an open door.

"We'll stop here," he said, "long enough to strip the gadgets off these uniforms."

Illy, hands strapped behind his back, stood by and watched as Retief and Magnan removed medals, ribbons, orders, and insignia from the formal diplomatic garments.

"This may help some," Retief said, "if the word is out that two diplomats are loose."

"It's a breeze," Illy said. "We see cats in purple and orange tailcoats all the time."

"I hope you're right," Retief said. "But if we're called, you'll be the first to go, Illy."

"You're a funny kind of Nenni," Illy said, eyeing Retief. "Toscin and Vug must be wonderin' what happened to 'em."

"If you think I'm good at drowning people, you ought to see me with a knife. Let's get going."

"It's only a little way now. But you better untie me. Somebody's liable to notice it and start askin' questions and get me killed."

"I'll take the chance. How do we get to the casino?"

"We follow this street. When we get to the Drunkard's Stairs we go up and it's right in front of us. A pink front with a sign like a big luck wheel."

"Give me your belt, Magnan," Retief said.

Magnan handed it over.

"Lie down, Illy."

The servant looked at Retief.

"Vug and Toscin will be glad to see me. But they'll never believe me." He lay down. Retief strapped his feet together and stuffed a handkerchief in his mouth.

"Why are you doing that?" Magnan asked. "We need him."

"We know the way now and we don't need anyone to announce our arrival." Magnan looked at the man. "Maybe you'd better—ah, cut his throat."

Illy rolled his eyes.

"That's a very un-Nenni-like suggestion, Mr. Magnan," Retief said. "But if we have any trouble finding the casino following his directions, I'll give it serious thought."

There were few people in the narrow street. Shops were shuttered, windows dark.

"Maybe they heard about the coup," Magnan said. "They're lying low."

"More likely they're at the palace checking out knives."

They rounded a corner, stepped over a man curled in the gutter snoring heavily, and found themselves at the foot of a long flight of littered stone steps.

"The Drunkard's Stairs are plainly marked," Magnan sniffed.

"I hear sounds up there … sounds of merrymaking."

"Maybe we'd better go back."

"Merrymaking doesn't scare me. Come to think of it, I don't know what the word means." Retief started up, Magnan behind him.

At the top of the long stair a dense throng milled in the alley-like street.

A giant illuminated roulette wheel revolved slowly above them. A loud-speaker blared the chant of the croupiers from the tables inside. Magnan and Retief moved through the crowd toward the wide-open doors.

Magnan plucked at Retief's sleeve. "Are you sure we ought to push right in like this? Maybe we ought to wait a bit, look around."

"When you're where you have no business being," Retief said, "always stride along purposefully. If you loiter, people begin to get curious."

Inside, a mob packed the wide low-ceilinged room and clustered around gambling devices in the form of towers, tables, and basins.

"What do we do now?" Magnan asked.

"We gamble. How much money do you have in your pockets?"

"Why … a few credits …" Magnan handed the money to Retief. "But what about the man Zorn?"

"A purple cutaway is conspicuous enough, without ignoring the tables. We'll get to Zorn in due course."

"Your pleasure, gents," a bullet-headed man said, eyeing the colorful evening clothes of the diplomats. "You'll be wantin' to try your luck at the Zoop tower, I'd guess. A game for real sporting gents."

"Why … ah …" Magnan said.

"What's a Zoop tower?" Retief asked.

"Out-of-towners, hey?" The bullet-headed man shifted his dope-stick to the other corner of his mouth. "Zoop is a great little game. Two teams of players buy into the pot; each player takes a lever; the object is to make the ball drop from the top of the tower into your net. Okay?"

"What's the ante?"

"I got a hundred-credit pot workin' now, gents."

Retief nodded. "We'll try it."

The shill led the way to an eight-foot tower mounted on gimbals. Two perspiring men in trade-class pullovers gripped two of the levers that controlled the tilt of the tower. A white ball lay in a hollow in the thick glass platform at the top. From the center an intricate pattern of grooves led out to the edge of the glass. Retief and Magnan took chairs before the two free levers.

"When the light goes on, gents, work the lever to jack the tower. You got three gears; takes a good arm to work top gear. That's this button here. The little knob controls what way you're goin'. May the best team win. I'll take the hundred credits now."

Retief handed over the money. A red light flashed on, and Retief tried the lever. It moved easily, with a ratcheting sound. The tower trembled, slowly tilted toward the two perspiring workmen pumping frantically at their levers. Magnan started slowly, accelerating as he saw the direction the tower was taking.

"Faster, Retief," he said. "They're winning."

"This is against the clock, gents," the bullet-headed man said. "If nobody wins when the light goes off, the house takes all."

"Crank it over to the left," Retief said.

"I'm getting tired."

"Shift to a lower gear."

The tower leaned. The ball stirred and rolled into a concentric channel. Retief shifted to middle gear and worked the lever. The tower, creaking to a stop, started back upright.

"There isn't any lower gear," Magnan gasped. One of the two on the other side of the tower shifted to middle gear; the other followed suit. They worked harder now, heaving against the stiff levers. The tower quivered, then moved slowly toward their side.

"I'm exhausted," Magnan gasped. Dropping the lever, he lolled back in the chair, gulping air. Retief, shifting position, took Magnan's lever with his left hand.

"Shift it to middle gear," he said. Magnan gulped, punched the button and slumped back, panting.

"My arm," he said. "I've injured myself."

The two men in pullovers conferred hurriedly as they cranked their levers; then one punched a button, and the other reached across, using his left arm to help.

"They've shifted to high," Magnan said. "Give up, it's hopeless."

"Shift me to high. Both buttons."

Magnan complied. Retief's shoulders bulged. He brought one lever down, then the other, alternately, slowly at first, then faster. The tower jerked, tilted toward him, farther ... The ball rolled in the channel, found an outlet—

Abruptly, both Retief's levers froze. The tower trembled, wavered, and moved back. Retief heaved. One lever folded at the base, bent down, and snapped off short. Retief braced his feet, gripped the other lever with both hands and pulled. There was a squeal of metal, a loud twang. The lever came free, a length of broken cable flopping into view. The tower fell over as the two on the other side scrambled aside.

"Hey!" the croupier yelled, appearing from the crowd. "You wrecked my equipment!"

Retief got up and faced him.

"Does Zorn know you've got your tower rigged for suckers?"

"You tryin' to call me a cheat?"

The crowd had fallen back, ringing the two men. The croupier glanced around. With a lightning motion he pulled out a knife.

"That'll be five hundred credits for the equipment," he said. "Nobody calls Kippy a cheat."

Retief picked up the broken lever.

"Don't make me hit you with this, Kippy."

Kippy looked at the bar.

"Comin' in here," he said indignantly, looking to the crowd for support, "bustin' up my rig, threatenin' me ..."

"I want a hundred credits," Retief said. "Now."

"Highway robbery!" Kippy yelled.

"Better pay up," somebody said.

"Hit him, mister," another in the crowd yelled.

A broad-shouldered man with greying hair pushed through

the crowd and looked around. "You heard him, Kippy. Give."

The shill growled, tucked his knife away, reluctantly peeled a bill from a fat roll and handed it over.

The newcomer looked from Retief to Magnan.

"Pick another game, strangers," he said. "Kippy made a little mistake."

"This is small-time stuff," Retief said. "I'm interested in something big."

The broad-shouldered man lit a perfumed dope stick, then sniffed at it.

"What would you call big?" he said softly.

"What's the biggest you've got?"

The man narrowed his eyes, smiling. "Maybe you'd like to try Slam."

"Tell me about it."

"Over here." The crowd opened up and made a path. Retief and Magnan followed across the room to a brightly-lit glass-walled box. There was an arm-sized opening at waist height, and inside was a hand grip. A four-foot clear plastic globe a quarter full of chips hung in the center. Apparatus was mounted at the top of the box.

"Slam pays good odds," the man said. "You can go as high as you like. Chips cost you a hundred credits. You start it up by dropping a chip in here." He indicated a slot.

"You take the hand grip. When you squeeze, it unlocks and starts to turn. Takes a pretty good grip to start the globe turning. You can see, it's full of chips. There's a hole at the top. As long as you hold the grip, the bowl turns. The harder you squeeze, the faster it turns. Eventually it'll turn over to where the hole is down, and chips fall out. If you let up and the bowl stops, you're all through.

"Just to make it interesting, there's contact plates spotted around the bowl; when one of 'em lines up with a live contact, you get a little jolt—guaranteed non-lethal. But if you let go, you lose. All you've got to do is hold on long enough, and you'll get the pay-off."

"How often does this random pattern put the hole down?"

"Anywhere from three minutes to fifteen, with the average grip. Oh, by the way, one more thing. That lead block up there ..." The man motioned with his head toward a one-foot cube suspended by a thick cable. "It's rigged to drop every now and then: averages five minutes. A warning light flashes first. You can set the clock back on it by dropping another chip—or you can let go the grip. Or you can take a chance; sometimes the light's a bluff."

Retief looked at the massive block of metal.

"That would mess up a man's dealing hand, wouldn't it?"

"The last two jokers who were too cheap to feed the machine had to have 'em off; their arm, I mean. That lead's heavy stuff."

"I don't suppose your machine has a habit of getting stuck, like Kippy's?"

The broad-shouldered man frowned.

"You're a stranger," he said. "You don't know any better."

"It's a fair game, mister," someone called.

"Where do I buy the chips?"

The man smiled. "I'll fix you up. How many?"

"One."

"A big spender, eh?" The man snickered and handed over a large plastic chip.

Retief stepped to the machine and dropped the coin.

"If you want to change your mind," the man said, "you can back out now. All it'll cost you is the chip you dropped."

Retief, reaching through the hole, took the grip. It was leather-padded, hand-filling. He squeezed it. There was a click and bright lights sprang up. The globe began to twirl lazily. The four-inch hole at its top was plainly visible.

"If ever the hole gets in position, it will empty very quickly," Magnan said.

Suddenly, a brilliant white light flooded the glass cage. A sound went up from the spectators.

"Quick, drop a chip," someone yelled.

"You've only got ten seconds …"

"Let go!" Magnan pleaded.

Retief sat silent, holding the grip, frowning up at the weight. The globe twirled faster now. Then the bright white light winked off.

"A bluff!" Magnan gasped.

"That's risky, stranger," the grey-templed man said.

The globe was turning rapidly now, oscillating from side to side. The hole seemed to travel in a wavering loop, dipping lower, swinging up high, then down again.

"It has to move to the bottom soon," Magnan said. "Slow it down, so it doesn't shoot past."

"The slower it goes, the longer it takes to get to the bottom," someone said.

There was a crackle, and Retief stiffened. Magnan heard a sharp intake of breath. The globe slowed, and Retief shook his head, blinking.

The broad-shouldered man glanced at a meter.

"You took pretty near a full jolt, that time," he said.

The hole in the globe was tracing an oblique course now, swinging to the center, then below.

"A little longer," Magnan said.

"That's the best speed I ever seen on the Slam ball," someone said. "How much longer can he hold it?"

Magnan looked at Retief's knuckles. They showed white

against the grip. The globe tilted farther, swung around, then down; two chips fell out, clattered down a chute and into a box.

"We're ahead," Magnan said. "Let's quit."

Retief shook his head. The globe rotated, dipped again; three chips fell.

"She's ready," someone called.

"It's bound to hit soon," another voice added excitedly. "Come on, mister!"

"Slow down," Magnan said. "So it won't move past too quickly."

"Speed it up, before that lead block gets you," someone called.

The hole swung high, over the top, then down the side. Chips rained out, six, eight ...

"Next pass," a voice called.

The white warning light flooded the cage. The globe whirled; the hole slid over the top, down, down ... a chip fell, two more ...

Retief half rose, clamped his jaw, and crushed the grip. Sparks flew, and the globe slowed, chips spewing. It stopped and swung back. Weighted by the mass of chips at the bottom, it stopped again with the hole centered. Chips cascaded down the chute, filled the box and spilled on the floor. The crowd yelled.

Retief released the grip and withdrew his arm at the same instant that the lead block slammed down.

"Good lord," Magnan said. "I felt that through the floor."

Retief turned to the broad-shouldered man.

"This game's all right for beginners," he said. "But I'd like to talk a really big gamble. Why don't we go to your office, Mr. Zorn?"

*

"Your proposition interests me," Zorn said, an hour later. "But there's some angles to this I haven't mentioned yet."

"You're a gambler, Zorn, not a suicide," Retief said. "Take what I've offered. Your dream of revolution was fancier, I agree, but it won't work."

"How do I know you birds aren't lying?" Zorn snarled. He stood up and strode up and down the room. "You walk in here and tell me I'll have a squadron of Corps Peace Enforcers on my neck, that the Corps won't recognize my regime. Maybe you're right; but I've got other contacts. They say different." Whirling, he stared at Retief.

"I have pretty good assurance that once I put it over, the Corps will have to recognize me as the legal *de facto* government of Petreac. They won't meddle in internal affairs."

"Nonsense," Magnan spoke up, "the Corps will never deal with a pack of criminals calling themselves—"

"Watch your language, you!" Zorn rasped.

"I'll admit Mr. Magnan's point is a little weak," Retief said. "But you're overlooking something. You plan to murder a dozen or so officers of the Corps Diplomatique Terrestrienne along with the local wheels. The Corps won't overlook that. It can't."

"Their tough luck they're in the middle," Zorn muttered.

"Our offer is extremely generous, Mr. Zorn," Magnan said. "The post you'll get will pay you very well indeed; as against certain failure of your coup, the choice should be simple."

Zorn eyed Magnan. "I thought you diplomats weren't the type to go around making deals under the table. Offering me a job—it sounds phony as hell."

"It's time you knew," Retief said. "There's no phonier business in the galaxy than diplomacy."

"You'd better take it, Mr. Zorn," Magnan said.

"Don't push me," Zorn said. "You two walk into my headquarters empty-handed and big-mouthed. I don't know what I'm talking to you for. The answer is no. N-i-x, no!"

"Who are you afraid off" Retief said softly.

Zorn glared at him.

"Where do you get that 'afraid' routine? I'm top man here. What have I got to be afraid of?"

"Don't kid around, Zorn. Somebody's got you under his thumb. I can see you squirming from here."

"What if I let your boys alone?" Zorn said suddenly. "The Corps won't have anything to say then, huh?"

"The Corps has plans for Petreac, Zorn. You aren't part of them. A revolution right now isn't part of them. Having the Potentate and the whole Nenni caste slaughtered isn't part of them. Do I make myself clear?"

"Listen," Zorn said urgently, "I'll tell you guys a few things. You ever heard of a world they call Rotune?"

"Certainly," Magnan said. "It's a near neighbor of yours, another backward—that is, emergent."

"Okay," Zorn said. "You guys think I'm a piker, do you? Well, let me wise you up. The Federal Junta on Rotune is backing my play. I'll be recognized by Rotune, and the Rotune fleet will stand by in case I need any help. I'll present the CDT with what you call a *fait accompli.*"

"What does Rotune get out of this? I thought they were your traditional enemies."

"Don't get me wrong. I've got no use for Rotune; but our interests happen to coincide right now."

"Do they?" Retief smiled grimly. "You can spot a sucker as soon as he comes through that door out there—but you go for a deal like this."

"What do you mean?" Zorn looked angrily at Retief. "It's fool-proof."

"After you get in power, you'll be fast friends with Rotune, is that it?"

"Friends, hell. Just give me time to get set, and I'll square a few things with that—"

"Exactly. And what do you suppose they have in mind for you?"

"What are you getting at?"

"Why is Rotune interested in your take-over?"

Zorn studied Retief's face. "I'll tell you why," he said. "It's you birds; you and your trade agreement. You're here to tie Petreac into some kind of trade combine. That cuts Rotune out. They don't like that. And anyway, we're doing all right out here; we don't need any commitments to a lot of fancy-pants on the other side of the galaxy."

"That's what Rotune has sold you, eh?" Retief said, smiling.

"Sold, nothing—" Zorn ground out his dope stick, then lit another. He snorted angrily.

"Okay—what's your idea?"

"You know what Petreac is getting in the way of imports as a result of the trade agreement?"

"Sure, a lot of junk. Clothes washers, tape projectors, all that kind of stuff."

"To be specific," Retief said, "there'll be 50,000 Tatone B-3 dry washers; 100,000 Glo-float motile lamps; 100,000 Earthworm Minor garden cultivators; 25,000 Veco space heaters; and 75,000 replacement elements for Ford Monomeg drives."

"Like I said: a lot of junk," Zorn said.

Retief leaned back, looking sardonically at Zorn. "Here's the gimmick, Zorn," he said. "The Corps is getting a little tired of Petreac and Rotune carrying on their two-penny war out here. Your privateers have a nasty habit of picking on innocent bystanders. After studying both sides, the Corps has decided Petreac would be a little easier to do business with; so this trade agreement was worked out. The Corps can't openly sponsor an arms shipment to a belligerent; but personal appliances are another story."

"So what do we do—plow 'em under with back-yard cultivators?" Zorn looked at Retief, puzzled. "What's the point?"

"You take the sealed monitor unit from the washer, the repeller field generator from the lamp, the converter control from the cultivator, et cetera, et cetera. You fit these together according to some very simple instructions; presto! you have one hundred thousand Standard-class Y hand blasters; just the thing to turn the tide in a stalemated war fought with obsolete arms."

"Good Lord," Magnan said. "Retief, are you—"

"I have to tell him. He has to know what he's putting his neck into."

"Weapons, hey?" Zorn said. "And Rotune knows about it . . . ?"

"Sure they know about it; it's not too hard to figure out. And there's more. They want the CDT delegation included in the massacre for a reason; it will put Petreac out of the picture; the trade agreement will go to Rotune; and you and your new regime will find yourselves looking down the muzzles of your own blasters."

Zorn threw his dope-stick to the floor with a snarl.

"I should have smelled something when that Rotune agent made his pitch." Zorn looked at the clock on the wall.

"I've got two hundred armed men in the palace. We've got about forty minutes to get over there before the rocket goes up."

*

In the shadows of the palace terrace, Zorn turned to Retief. "You'd better stay here out of the way until I've spread the word. Just in case."

"Let me caution you against any … ah … slip-ups, Mr. Zorn," Magnan said. "The Nenni are not to be molested."

Zorn looked at Retief. "Your friend talks too much. I'll keep my end of it; he'd better keep his."

"Nothing's happened yet, you're sure?" Magnan said.

"I'm sure," Zorn said. "Ten minutes to go; plenty of time."

"I'll just step into the salon to assure myself that all is well," Magnan said.

"Suit yourself. Just stay clear of the kitchen, or you'll get your throat cut." Zorn sniffed at his dope-stick. "I sent the word for Shoke," he muttered. "Wonder what's keeping him?"

Magnan stepped to a tall glass door, eased it open, and poked his head through the heavy draperies. As he moved to draw back, a voice was faintly audible. Magnan paused, his head still through the drapes.

"What's going on there?" Zorn rasped. He and Retief stepped up behind Magnan.

"… breath of air," Magnan was saying.

"Well, come along, Magnan!" Ambassador Crodfoller's voice snapped.

Magnan shifted from one foot to the other, then pushed through the drapes.

"Where've you been, Mr. Magnan?" The ambassador's voice was sharp.

"Oh … ah … a slight accident, Mr. Ambassador."

"What's happened to your shoes? Where are your insignia and decorations?"

"I—ah—spilled a drink on them. Maybe I'd better nip up to my room and slip into some fresh medals."

The ambassador snorted. "A professional diplomat never shows his liquor, Magnan. It's one of his primary professional skills. I'll speak to you about this later. I had expected your attendance at the signing ceremony, but under the circumstances I'll dispense with that. You'd better depart quietly through the kitchen."

"The kitchen? But it's crowded … I mean …"

"A little loss of caste won't hurt at this point, Mr. Magnan. Now kindly move along before you attract attention. The agreement isn't signed yet."

"The agreement …" Magnan babbled, sparring for time, "very clever, Mr. Ambassador. A very neat solution."

The sound of an orchestra came up suddenly, blaring a fanfare.

Zorn shifted restlessly, his ear against the glass. "What's your friend pulling?" he rasped. "I don't like this."

"Keep cool, Zorn. Mr. Magnan is doing a little emergency salvage on his career."

The music died away with a clatter.

"… my God." Ambassador Crodfoller's voice was faint. "Magnan, you'll be knighted for this. Thank God you reached me. Thank God it's not too late. I'll find some excuse. I'll get off a gram at once."

"But you—"

"It's all right, Magnan. You were in time. Another ten minutes and the agreement would have been signed and transmitted. The wheels would have been put in motion. My career would have been ruined …"

Retief felt a prod at his back. He turned.

"Double-crossed," Zorn said softly. "So much for the word of a diplomat."

Retief looked at the short-barreled needler in Zorn's hand.

"I see you hedge your bets, Zorn."

"We'll wait here until the excitement's over inside. I wouldn't want to attract any attention right now."

"Your politics are still lousy, Zorn. The picture hasn't changed. Your coup hasn't got a chance."

"Skip it. I'll take up one problem at a time."

"Magnan's mouth has a habit of falling open at the wrong time."

"That's my good luck I heard it. So there'll be no agreement, no guns, no fat job for Tammany Zorn, hey? Well, I can still play it the other way. What have I got to lose?"

With a movement too quick to follow, Retief's hand chopped down across Zorn's wrist. The needler clattered to the ground as Retief's hand clamped on Zorn's arm, whirling him around.

"In answer to your last question," Retief said, "your neck."

"You haven't got a chance, double-crosser," Zorn gasped.

"Shoke will be here in a minute. Tell him it's all off."

"Twist harder, mister. Break it off at the shoulder. I'm telling him nothing."

"The kidding's over, Zorn. Call it off or I'll kill you."

"I believe you. But you won't have long to remember it."

"All the killing will be for nothing. You'll be dead and the Rotunes will step into the power vacuum."

"So what? When I die, the world ends."

"Suppose I make you another offer, Zorn?"

"Why would it be any better than the last one?"

Retief released Zorn's arm, pushed him away, stooped and picked up the needler.

"I could kill you, Zorn; you know that."

"Go ahead."

Retief reversed the needler and held it out.

"I'm a gambler too, Zorn. I'm gambling you'll listen to what I have to say."

Zorn snatched the gun and stepped back. He looked at Retief. "That wasn't the smartest bet you ever made, but go ahead. You've got maybe ten seconds."

"Nobody double-crossed you, Zorn. Magnan put his foot in it; too bad. Is that a reason to kill yourself and a lot of other people who've bet their lives on you?"

"They gambled and lost. Tough."

"Maybe they haven't lost yet—if you don't quit."

"Get to the point."

Retief spoke earnestly for a minute and a half. Zorn stood, gun aimed, listening. Then both men turned as footsteps approached along the terrace. A fat man in a yellow sarong padded up to Zorn.

Zorn tucked the needler in his waistband.

"Hold everything, Shoke," he said. "Tell the boys to put the knives away; spread the word fast: it's all off."

"I want to commend you, Retief," Ambassador Crodfoller said expansively. "You mixed very well at last night's affair; actually, I was hardly aware of your presence."

"I've been studying Mr. Magnan's work," Retief said.

"A good man, Magnan. In a crowd, he's virtually invisible."

"He knows when to disappear, all right."

"This has been in many ways a model operation, Retief." The ambassador patted his paunch contentedly. "By observing local social customs and blending harmoniously with the court, I've succeeded in establishing a fine, friendly, working relationship with the Potentate."

"I understand the agreement has been postponed a few days."

The Ambassador chuckled. "The Potentate's a crafty one. Through … ah … a special study I have been conducting, I learned last night that he had hoped to, shall I say, 'put one over' on the Corps."

"Great Heavens," Retief said.

"Naturally, this placed me in a difficult position. It was my task to quash this gambit, without giving any indication that I was aware of its existence."

"A hairy position indeed."

"Quite casually, I informed the Potentate that certain items which had been included in the terms of the agreement had been deleted and others substituted. I admired him at that moment, Retief. He took it coolly—appearing completely indifferent—perfectly dissembling his very serious disappointment. Of course, he could hardly do otherwise without in effect admitting his plot."

"I noticed him dancing with three girls each wearing a bunch of grapes; he's very agile for a man of his bulk."

"You mustn't discount the Potentate. Remember, beneath that mask of frivolity, he had absorbed a bitter blow."

"He had me fooled," Retief said.

"Don't feel badly; I confess at first I, too, failed to sense his shrewdness." The ambassador nodded and moved off along the corridor.

Retief turned and went into an office. Magnan looked up from his desk.

"Ah, Retief," he said. "I've been meaning to ask you. About the … ah … blasters; are you—"

Retief leaned on Magnan's desk and looked at him. "I thought that was to be our little secret."

"Well, naturally I—" Magnan closed his mouth and swallowed. "How is it, Retief," he said sharply, "that you were aware of this blaster business, when the ambassador himself wasn't?"

"Easy," Retief said. "I made it up."

"You what!" Magnan looked wild. "But the agreement—it's been revised. Ambassador Crodfoller has gone on record."

"Too bad. Glad I didn't tell him about it."

Magnan leaned back and closed his eyes.

"It was big of you to take all the … blame," Retief said, "when the ambassador was talking about knighting people."

Magnan opened his eyes. "What about that gambler, Zorn? Won't he be upset when he learns the agreement is off? After all, I … that is, we, or you, had more or less promised him—"

"It's all right. I made another arrangement. The business about making blasters out of common components wasn't completely imaginary. You can actually do it, using parts from an old-fashioned disposal unit."

"What good will that do him?" Magnan whispered, looking nervous. "We're not shipping in any old-fashioned disposal units."

"We don't need to. They're already installed in the palace kitchen—and in a few thousand other places, Zorn tells me."

"If this ever leaks …" Magnan put a hand to his forehead.

"I have his word on it that the Nenni slaughter is out. This place is ripe for a change; maybe Zorn is what it needs."

"But how can we know?" Magnan said. "How can we be sure?"

"We can't. But it's not up to the Corps to meddle in Petreac's internal affairs." He leaned over, picked up Magnan's desk lighter, and lit a cigar. He blew a cloud of smoke toward the ceiling.

"Right?" he said.

Magnan looked at him and nodded weakly. "Right."

"I'd better be getting along to my desk," Retief said. "Now that the ambassador feels that I'm settling down at last."

"Retief," Magnan said, "tonight, I implore you: stay out of the kitchen—no matter what."

Retief raised his eyebrows.

"I know," Magnan said. "If you hadn't interfered, we'd all have had our throats cut. But at least ..." He paused. "We'd have died in accordance with regulations."

BOLO

This book is dedicated,
with affection and respect,
to Ben Bova.

A SHORT HISTORY OF THE BOLO FIGHTING MACHINES

The first appearance in history of the concept of the armored vehicle was the use of wooden-shielded war wagons by the reformer John Huss in fifteenth-century Bohemia. Thereafter the idea lapsed—unless one wishes to consider the armored knights of the Middle Ages, mounted on armored war-horses—until the twentieth century. In 1915, during the Great War, the British developed in secrecy a steel-armored motor car; for security reasons during construction it was called a "tank," and the appellation remained in use for the rest of the century. First sent into action at the Somme in A.D. 1916 (BAE 29), the new device was immensely impressive and was soon copied by all belligerents. By Phase Two of the Great War, A.D. 1939–1945, tank corps were a basic element in all modern armies. Quite naturally, great improvements were soon made over the original clumsy, fragile, feeble, and temperamental tank. The British Sheridan and Centurion, the German Tiger, the American Sherman, and the Russian T-34 were all highly potent weapons in their own milieu.

During the long period of cold war following A.D. 1945, development continued, especially in the United States. By 1989 the direct ancestor of the Bolo line had been constructed by the Bolo Division of General Motors. This machine, at one hundred fifty tons almost twice the weight of its Phase Two predecessors, was designated the Bolo Mark I Model B. No

Bolo Model A of any mark ever existed, since it was felt that the Ford Motor Company had preempted that designation permanently. The same is true of the name "Model T."

The Mark I was essentially a bigger and better conventional tank, carrying a crew of three and, via power-assisted servos, completely manually operated, with the exception of the capability to perform a number of preset routine functions such as patrol duty with no crew aboard. The Mark II that followed in 1995 was even more highly automated, carrying an on-board fire-control computer and requiring only a single operator. The Mark III of 2020 was considered by some to be almost a step backward, its highly complex controls normally requiring a crew of two, though in an emergency a single experienced man could fight the machine with limited effectiveness. These were by no means negligible weapons systems, their individual firepower exceeding that of a contemporary battalion of heavy infantry, while they were of course correspondingly heavily armored and shielded. The outer durachrome war hull of the Mark III was twenty millimeters thick and capable of withstanding any offensive weapon then known, short of a contact nuclear blast.

The first completely automated Bolo, designed to operate normally without a man aboard, was the landmark Mark XV Model M, originally dubbed *Resartus* for obscure reasons, but later officially named *Stupendous.* This model, first commissioned in the twenty-fifth century, was widely used throughout the Eastern Arm during the Era of Expansion and remained in service on remote worlds for over two centuries, acquiring many improvements in detail along the way while remaining basically unchanged, though increasing sophistication of circuitry and weapons vastly upgraded its effectiveness. The Bolo *Horrendous* Model R, of 2807 was the culmination of this phase of Bolo development, though older models lingered on in the active service of minor powers for centuries.

Thereafter the development of the Mark XVI–XIX consisted largely in furthur refinement and improvement in detail of the Mark XV. Provision continued to be made for a human occupant, now as a passenger rather than an operator, usually an officer who wished to observe the action at first hand. Of course, these machines normally went into action under the guidance of individually prepared computer programs, while military regulations continued to require installation of devices for halting or even self-destructing the machine at any time. This latter feature was mainly intended to prevent capture and hostile use of the great machine by an enemy. It was at this time that the first-line Bolos in Terran service were organized into a brigade, known as the Dinochrome Brigade, and deployed as a strategic unit. Tactically the regiment was the basic Bolo unit.

The always-present though perhaps unlikely possibility of capture and use of a Bolo by an enemy was a constant source of anxiety to military leaders and, in time, gave rise to the next and final major advance in Bolo technology: the self-directing (and, quite incidentally, self-aware) Mark XX Model B Bolo *Tremendous*. At this time it was customary to designate each individual unit by a three-letter group indicating hull style, power unit, and main armament. This gave rise to the custom of forming a nickname from the letters, such as "Johnny" from JNY, adding to the tendency to anthropomorphize the great fighting machines.

The Mark XX was at first greeted with little enthusiasm by the High Command, who now professed to believe that an unguided-by-operator Bolo would potentially be capable of running amok and wreaking destruction on its owners. Many observers have speculated by hindsight that a more candid objection would have been that the legitimate area of command function was about to be invaded by mere machinery. Machinery the Bolos were, but never *mere.*

At one time an effort was made to convert a number of surplus Bolos to peacetime use by such modifications as the addition of a soil-moving blade to a Mark XII Bolo WV/I Continental Siege Unit, the installation of seats for four men, and the description of the resulting irresistible force as a "tractor." This idea came to naught, however, since the machines retained their half-megaton/second firepower and were never widely accepted as normal agricultural equipment.

As the great conflict of the post-thirtieth-century era wore on—a period variously known as the Last War and, later, as the Lost War—Bolos of Mark XXVIII and later series were organized into independently operating brigades that did their own strategic as well as tactical planning. Many of these machines still exist in functional condition in out-of-the-way corners of the former Terran Empire. At this time the program of locating and neutralizing these ancient weapons continues.

THE NIGHT OF THE TROLLS

It was different this time. There was a dry pain in my lungs, and a deep ache in my bones, and a fire in my stomach that made me want to curl into a ball and mew like a kitten. My mouth tasted as though mice had nested in it, and when I took a deep breath wooden knives twisted in my chest.

I made a mental note to tell Mackenzie a few things about his pet controlled-environment tank—just as soon as I got out of it. I squinted at the over-face panel: air pressure, temperature, humidity, O-level, blood sugar, pulse, and respiration—all okay. That was something. I flipped the intercom key and said, "Okay, Mackenzie, let's have the story. You've got problems ..."

I had to stop to cough. The exertion made my temples pound.

"How long have you birds run this damned exercise?" I called. "I feel lousy. What's going on around here?"

No answer.

This was supposed to be the terminal test series. They couldn't all be out having coffee. The equipment had more bugs than a two-dollar hotel room. I slapped the emergency release lever. Mackenzie wouldn't like it, but to hell with it! From the way I felt, I'd been in the tank for a good long stretch this time—maybe a week or two. And I'd told Ginny it would be a three-dayer at the most. Mackenzie was a great technician, but he had no more human emotions than a used-car salesman. This time I'd tell him.

Relays were clicking, equipment was reacting, the tank cover sliding back. I sat up and swung my legs aside, shivering suddenly.

It was cold in the test chamber. I looked around at the dull gray walls, the data recording cabinets, the wooden desk where Mac sat by the hour rerunning test profiles—

That was funny. The tape reels were empty and the red equipment light was off. I stood, feeling dizzy. Where was Mac? Where were Bonner and Day and Mallon?

"Hey!" I called. I didn't even get a good echo.

Someone must have pushed the button to start my recovery cycle; where were they hiding now? I took a step, tripped over the cables trailing behind me. I unstrapped and pulled the harness off. The effort left me breathing hard. I opened one of the wall lockers; Banner's pressure suit hung limply from the rack beside a rag-festooned coat hanger. I looked in three more lockers. My clothes were missing—even my bathrobe. I also missed the usual bowl of hot soup, the happy faces of the techs, even Mac's sour puss. It was cold and silent and empty here—more like a morgue than a top-priority research center.

I didn't like it. What the hell was going on?

There was a weather suit in the last locker. I put it on, set the temperature control, palmed the door open, and stepped out into the corridor. There were no lights, except for the dim glow of the emergency route indicators. There was a faint, foul odor in the air.

I heard a dry scuttling, saw a flick of movement. A rat the size of a red squirrel sat up on his haunches and looked at me as if I were something to eat. I made a kicking motion and he ran off, but not very far.

My heart was starting to thump a little harder now. The way it does when you begin to realize that something's wrong—bad wrong.

Upstairs in the Admin Section I called again. The echo was a little better here. I went along the corridor strewn with papers, past the open doors of silent rooms. In the Director's office a blackened wastebasket stood in the center of the rug. The air-conditioner intake above the desk was felted over with matted dust nearly an inch thick. There was no use shouting again.

The place was as empty as a robbed grave—except for the rats.

At the end of the corridor, the inner security door stood open. I went through it and stumbled over something. In the faint light, it took me a moment to realize what it was.

He had been an MP, in steel helmet and boots. There was nothing left but crumbled bone and a few scraps of leather and metal. A .38 revolver lay nearby. I picked it up, checked the cylinder, and tucked it in the thigh pocket of the weather suit. For some reason it made me feel a little better.

I went on along B corridor and found the lift door sealed. The emergency stairs were nearby. I went to them and started the two-hundred-foot climb to the surface.

The heavy steel doors at the tunnel had been blown clear.

I stepped past the charred opening, looked out at a low gray sky burning red in the west. Fifty yards away, the five-thousand-gallon water tank lay in a tangle of rusty steel. What had it been? Sabotage, war, revolution—an accident? And where was everybody?

I rested for a while, then went across the innocent-looking fields to the west, dotted with the dummy buildings that were supposed to make the site look from the air like another stretch of farmland complete with barns, sheds and fences. Beyond the site the town seemed intact: there were lights twinkling here and there, a few smudges of smoke rising. I climbed a heap of rubble for a better view.

Whatever had happened at the site, at least Ginny would be all right—Ginny and Tim. Ginny would be worried sick, after—how long? A month?

Maybe more. There hadn't been much left of that soldier …

I twisted to get a view to the south, and felt a hollow sensation in my chest. Four silo doors stood open; the Colossus missiles had hit back—at something. I pulled myself up a foot or two higher for a look at the Primary Site. In the twilight the ground rolled smooth and unbroken across the spot where *Prometheus* lay ready in her underground berth. Down below she'd be safe and sound, maybe. She had been built to stand up to the stresses of a direct extra-solar orbital launch; with any luck, a few near misses wouldn't have damaged her.

My arms were aching from the strain of holding on. I climbed down and sat on the ground to get my breath, watching the cold wind worry the dry stalks of dead brush around the fallen tank.

At home, Ginny would be alone, scared, maybe even in serious difficulty. There was no telling how far municipal services had broken down. But before I headed that way, I had to make a quick check on the ship. *Prometheus* was a dream that I—and a lot of others—had lived with for three years. I had to be sure.

I headed toward the pillbox that housed the tunnel head on the off chance that the car might be there.

It was almost dark and the going was tough; the concrete

slabs under the sod were tilted and dislocated. Something had sent a ripple across the ground like a stone tossed into a pond.

I heard a sound and stopped dead. There was a clank and rumble from beyond the discolored walls of the blockhouse a hundred yards away. Rusted metal howled; then something as big as a beached freighter moved into view.

Two dull red beams glowing near the top of the high silhouette swung, flashed crimson, and held on me. A siren went off—an ear-splitting whoop! *whoop!* WHOOP!

It was an unmanned Bolo Mark II Combat Unit on automated sentry duty—and its intruder-sensing circuits were tracking me.

The Bolo pivoted heavily; the *whoop! whoop!* sounded again; the robot watchdog was bellowing the alarm.

I felt sweat pop out on my forehead. Standing up to a Mark II Bolo without an electropass was the rough equivalent of being penned in with an ill-tempered dinosaur. I looked toward the Primary blockhouse: too far. The same went for the perimeter fence. My best bet was back to the tunnel mouth. I turned to sprint for it, hooked a foot on a slab and went down hard …

I got up, my head ringing, tasting blood in my mouth. The chipped pavement seemed to rock under me. The Bolo was coming up fast. Running was no good. I had to have a better idea.

I dropped flat and switched my suit control to maximum insulation.

The silvery surface faded to dull black. A two-foot square of tattered paper fluttered against a projecting edge of concrete; I reached for it, peeled it free, then fumbled with a pocket flap, brought out a permatch, flicked it alight. When the paper was burning well, I tossed it clear. It whirled away a few feet, then caught in a clump of grass.

"Keep moving, damn you!" I whispered. The swearing worked. The gusty wind pushed the paper on. I crawled a few feet and pressed myself into a shallow depression behind the slab. The Bolo churned closer; a loose treadplate was slapping the earth with a rhythmic thud. The burning paper was fifty feet away now, a twinkle of orange light in the deep twilight.

At twenty yards, looming up like a pagoda, the Bolo halted, sat rumbling and swiveling its rust-streaked turret, looking for the radiating source its I-R had first picked up. The flare of the paper caught its electronic attention. The turret swung, then back. It was puzzled. It whooped again, then reached a decision.

Ports snapped open. A volley of antipersonnel slugs whoofed into the target; the scrap of paper disappeared in a gout of tossed dirt.

I hugged the ground like gold lamé hugs a torch singer's hip, and waited; nothing happened. The Bolo sat, rumbling softly to itself. Then I heard another sound over the murmur of the idling engine, a distant roaring, like a flight of low-level bombers. I raised my head half an inch and took a look. There were lights moving beyond the field—the paired beams of a convoy approaching from the town.

The Bolo stirred, moved heavily forward until it towered over me no more than twenty feet away. I saw gun ports open high on the armored facade—the ones that housed the heavy infinite repeaters. Slim black muzzles slid into view, hunted for an instant, then depressed and locked.

They were bearing on the oncoming vehicles that were spreading out now in a loose skirmish line under a roiling layer of dust. The watchdog was getting ready to defend its territory—and I was caught in the middle. A blue-white floodlight lanced out from across the field, glared against the scaled plating of the Bolo. I heard relays click inside the monster fighting machine, and braced myself for the thunder of her battery …

There was a dry rattle.

The guns traversed, clattering emptily. Beyond the fence the floodlight played for a moment longer against the Bolo, then moved on across the ramp, back, across and back, searching …

Once more the Bolo fired its empty guns. Its red I-R beams swept the scene again; then relays snicked, the impotent guns retracted, the port covers closed.

Satisfied, the Bolo heaved itself around and moved off, trailing a stink of ozone and ether, the broken tread thumping like a cripple on a stair.

I waited until it disappeared in the gloom two hundred yards away, then cautiously turned my suit control to vent off the heat. Full insulation could boil a man in his own gravy in less than half an hour.

The floodlight had blinked off now. I got to my hands and knees and started toward the perimeter fence. The Bolo's circuits weren't tuned as fine as they should have been; it let me go.

There were men moving in the glare and dust, beyond the rusty lacework that had once been a chain-link fence. They carried guns and stood in tight little groups, staring across toward the blockhouse.

I moved closer, keeping flat and avoiding the avenues of yellowish light thrown by the headlamps of the parked vehicles—halftracks, armored cars, a few light manned tanks.

There was nothing about the look of this crowd that impelled me to leap up and be welcomed. They wore green uniforms, and half of them sported beards. What the hell: had Castro landed in force?

I angled off to the right, away from the big main gate that had been manned day and night by guards with tommy-guns. It hung now by one hinge from a scarred concrete post, under a cluster of dead polyarcs in corroded brackets. The big sign that had read GLENN AEROSPACE CENTER—AUTHORIZED PERSONNEL ONLY lay face down in hip-high underbrush.

More cars were coming up. There was a lot of talk and shouting; a squad of men formed and headed my way, keeping to the outside of the fallen fence.

I was outside the glare of the lights now. I chanced a run for it, got over the sagged wire and across a potholed blacktop road before they reached me. I crouched in the ditch and watched as the detail dropped men in pairs at fifty-yard intervals.

Another five minutes and they would have intercepted me—along with whatever else they were after. I worked my way back across an empty lot and found a strip of lesser underbrush lined with shaggy trees, beneath which a patch of cracked sidewalk showed here and there.

Several things were beginning to be a little clearer now: The person who had pushed the button to bring me out of stasis hadn't been around to greet me, because no one pushed it. The automatics, triggered by some malfunction, had initiated the recovery cycle.

The system's self-contained power unit had been designed to maintain a starship crewman's minimal vital functions indefinitely, at reduced body temperature and metabolic rate. There was no way to tell exactly how long I had been in the tank. From the condition of the fence and the roads, it had been more than a matter of weeks—or even months.

Had it been a year … or more? I thought of Ginny and the boy, waiting at home—thinking the old man was dead, probably. I'd neglected them before for my work, but not like this …

Our house was six miles from the base, in the foothills on the other side of town. It was a long walk, the way I felt—but I had to get there.

2

Two hours later I was clear of the town, following the river bank west.

I kept having the idea that someone was following me. But when I stopped to listen, there was never anything there; just the still, cold night and the frogs, singing away patiently in the low ground to the south.

When the ground began to rise, I left the road and struck off across the open field. I reached a wide street, followed it in a curve that would bring me out at the foot of Ridge Avenue—my street. I could make out the shapes of low, rambling houses now.

It had been the kind of residential section the local Junior Chamber members had hoped to move into some day. Now the starlight that filtered through the cloud cover showed me broken windows, doors that sagged open, automobiles that squatted on flat, dead tires under collapsing car shelters—and here and there a blackened, weed-grown foundation, like a gap in a row of rotting teeth.

The neighborhood wasn't what it had been. How long had I been away? How long …?

I fell down again, hard this time. It wasn't easy getting up. I seemed to weigh a hell of a lot for a guy who hadn't been eating regularly. My breathing was very fast and shallow now, and my skull was getting ready to split and give birth to a live alligator—the ill-tempered kind. It was only a few hundred yards more; but why the hell had I picked a place halfway up a hill?

I heard the sound again—a crackle of dry grass. I got the pistol out and stood flatfooted in the middle of the street, listening hard.

All I heard was my stomach growling. I took the pistol off cock and started off again, stopped suddenly a couple of times to catch him off guard; nothing. I reached the corner of Ridge Avenue, started up the slope. Behind me a stick popped loudly.

I picked that moment to fall down again. Heaped leaves saved me from another skinned knee. I rolled over against a low fieldstone wall and propped myself against it. I had to use both hands to cock the pistol. I stared into the dark, but all I could see were the little lights whirling again. The pistol got heavy; I put it down, concentrated on taking deep breaths and blinking away the fireflies.

I heard footsteps plainly, close by. I shook my head, accidentally banged it against the stone behind me. That helped. I saw him, not over twenty feet away, coming up the hill toward me, a black-haired man with a full beard, dressed in odds and ends of rags and furs, gripping a polished club with a leather thong.

I reached for the pistol, found only leaves, tried again, touched the gun and knocked it away. I was still groping when I heard a scuffle of feet. I swung around, saw a tall, wide figure with a mane of untrimmed hair.

He hit the bearded man like a pro tackle taking out the practice dummy. They went down together hard and rolled over in a flurry of dry leaves. The cats were fighting over the mouse; that was my signal to leave quietly.

I made one last grab for the gun, found it, got to my feet and staggered off up the grade that seemed as steep now as penthouse rent. And from down slope, I heard an engine gunned, the clash of a heavy transmission that needed adjustment. A spotlight flickered, made shadows dance.

I recognized a fancy wrought-iron fence fronting a vacant lot; that had been the Adams house. Only half a block to go—but I was losing my grip fast. I went down twice more, then gave up and started crawling. The lights were all around now, brighter than ever. My head split open, dropped off, and rolled downhill.

A few more yards and I could let it all go. Ginny would put me in a warm bed, patch up my scratches, and feed me soup. Ginny would ... Ginny ...

I was lying with my mouth full of dead leaves. I heard running feet, yells. An engine idled noisily down the block.

I got my head up and found myself looking at chipped brickwork and the heavy brass hinges from which my front gate had hung. The gate was gone and there was a large chunk of brick missing. Some delivery truck had missed his approach.

I got to my feet, took a couple of steps into deep shadow with feet that felt as though they'd been amputated and welded back on at the ankle. I stumbled, fetched up against something scaled over with rust. I held on, blinked and made out the seeping flank of my brand new '79 Pontiac. There was a crumbled crust of whitish glass lining the brightwork strip that had framed the rear window.

A fire . . . ?

A footstep sounded behind me, and I suddenly remembered several things, none of them pleasant. I felt for my gun; it was gone. I moved back along the side of the car, tried to hold on.

No use. My arms were like unsuccessful pie crust. I slid down among dead leaves, sat listening to the steps coming closer. They stopped, and through a dense fog that had sprung up suddenly I caught a glimpse of a tall white-haired figure standing over me.

Then the fog closed in and swept everything away.

I lay on my back this time, looking across at the smoky yellow light of a thick brown candle guttering in the draft from a glassless window. In the center of the room a few sticks of damp-looking wood heaped on the cracked asphalt tiles burned with a grayish flame. A thin curl of acrid smoke rose up to stir cobwebs festooned under ceiling beams from which wood veneer had peeled away. Light alloy trusswork showed beneath.

It was a strange scene, but not so strange that I didn't recognize it: it was my own living room—looking a little different than when I had seen it last. The odors were different, too; I picked out mildew, badly cured leather, damp wool, tobacco . . .

I turned my head. A yard from the rags I lay on, the white-haired man, looking older than pharaoh, sat sleeping with his back against the wall.

The shotgun was gripped in one big, gnarled hand. His head was tilted back, blue-veined eyelids shut. I sat up, and at my movement his eyes opened.

He lay relaxed for a moment, as though life had to return from some place far away. Then he raised his head. His face was hollow and lined. His white hair was thin. A coarse-woven shirt hung loose across wide shoulders that had been Herculean once. But now Hercules was old, old. He looked at me expectantly.

"Who are you?" I said. "Why did you follow me? What happened to the house? Where's my family? Who owns the bully-boys in green?" My jaw hurt when I spoke. I put my hand up and felt it gingerly.

"You fell," the old man said, in a voice that rumbled like a subterranean volcano.

"The understatement of the year, pop." I tried to get up. Nausea knotted my stomach.

"You have to rest," the old man said, looking concerned. "Before the Baron's men come ..." He paused, looking at me as though he expected me to say something profound.

"I want to know where the people are that live here!" My yell came out as weak as church-social punch. "A woman and a boy ..."

He was shaking his head. "You have to do something quick. The soldiers will come back, search every house—"

I sat up, ignoring the little men driving spikes into my skull. "I don't give a damn about soldiers! Where's my family? What's happened?" I reached out and gripped his arm. "How long was I down there? What year is this?"

He only shook his head. "Come eat some food. Then I can help you with your plan."

It was no use talking to the old man; he was senile.

I got off the cot. Except for the dizziness and a feeling that my knees were made of papier-mâché, I was all right. I picked up the hand-formed candle, stumbled into the hall.

It was a jumble of rubbish. I climbed through, pushed open the door to my study. There was my desk, the tall bookcase with the glass doors, the gray rug, the easy chair. Aside from a layer of dust and some peeling wallpaper, it looked normal. I flipped the switch. Nothing happened.

"What is that charm?" the old man said behind me. He pointed to the light switch.

"The power's off," I said. "Just habit."

He reached out and flipped the switch up, then down again. "It makes a pleasing sound."

"Yeah." I picked up a book from the desk; it fell apart in my hands.

I went back into the hall, tried the bedroom door, looked in at heaped leaves, the remains of broken furniture, an empty window frame. I went on to the end of the hall and opened the door to the bedroom.

Cold night wind blew through a barricade of broken timbers. The roof had fallen in, and a sixteen-inch tree trunk slanted through the wreckage. The old man stood behind me, watching.

"Where is she, damn you?" I leaned against the door frame to swear and fight off the faintness. "Where's my wife?"

The old man looked troubled. "Come, eat now ..."

"Where is she? Where's the woman who lived here?"

He frowned, shook his head dumbly. I picked my way through the wreckage, stepped out into knee-high brush. A gust blew my candle out. In the dark I stared at my back yard, the crumbled pit that had been the barbecue grill, the tangled thickets that had been rose beds—and a weathered length of boards upended in the earth.

"What the hell's this ...?" I fumbled out a permatch, lit my candle, leaned close, and read the crude letters cut into the crumbling wood: VIRGINIA ANNE JACKSON. BORN JAN. 8 1957. KILL BY THE DOGS WINTER 1992.

3

The Baron's men came twice in the next three days. Each time the old man carried me, swearing but too weak to argue, out to a lean-to of branches and canvas in the woods behind the house. Then he disappeared, to come back an hour or two later and haul me back to my rag bed by the fire.

Three times a day he gave me a tin pan of stew, and I ate it mechanically. My mind went over and over the picture of Ginny, living on for twelve years in the slowly decaying house, and then—

It was too much. There are some shocks the mind refuses.

I thought of the tree that had fallen and crushed the east wing. An elm that size was at least fifty to sixty years old—maybe older. And the only elm on the place had been a two-year sapling. I knew it well; I had planted it.

The date carved on the headboard was 1992. As nearly as I could judge another thirty-five years had passed since then at least. My shipmates—Banner, Day, Mallon—they were all dead, long ago. How had they died? The old man was too far gone to tell me anything useful. Most of my questions produced a shake of the head and a few rumbled words about charms, demons, spells, and the Baron.

"I don't believe in spells," I said. "And I'm not too sure I believe in this Baron. Who is he?"

"The Baron Trollmaster of Filly. He holds all this country—" the old man made a sweeping gesture with his arm—"all the way to Jersey."

"Why was he looking for me? What makes me important?"

"You came from the Forbidden Place. Everyone heard the cries of the Lesser Troll that stands guard over the treasure there. If the Baron can learn your secrets of power—"

"Troll, hell! That's nothing but a Bolo on automatic!"

"By any name every man dreads the monster. A man who walks in its shadow has much *mana.* But the others—the ones that run in a pack like dogs—would tear you to pieces for a demon if they could lay hands on you."

"You saw me back there. Why didn't you give me away? And why are you taking care of me now?"

He shook his head—the all-purpose answer to any question.

I tried another tack: "Who was the rag man you tackled just outside? Why was he laying for me?"

The old man snorted. "Tonight the dogs will eat him. But forget that. Now we have to talk about your plan—"

"I've got about as many plans as the senior boarder in death row. I don't know if you know it, old timer, but somebody slid the world out from under me while I wasn't looking."

The old man frowned. I had the thought that I wouldn't like to have him mad at me, for all his white hair . . .

He shook his head. "You must understand what I tell you. The soldiers of the Baron will find you someday. If you are to break the spell—"

"Break the spell, eh?" I snorted. "I think I get the idea, pop. You've got it in your head that I'm valuable property of some kind. You figure I can use my supernatural powers to take over this menagerie—and you'll be in on the ground floor. Well, listen, you old idiot! I spent sixty years—maybe more—in a stasis tank two hundred feet underground. My world died while I was down there. This Baron of yours seems to own everything now. If you think I'm going to get myself shot bucking him, forget it!"

The old man didn't say anything.

"Things don't seem to be broken up much," I went on. "It

must have been gas, or germ warfare—or fallout. Damn few people around. You're still able to live on what you can loot from stores; automobiles are still sitting where they were the day the world ended. How old were you when it happened, pop? The war, I mean. Do you remember it?"

He shook his head. "The world has always been as it is now."

"What year were you born?"

He scratched at his white hair. "I knew the number once. But I've forgotten."

"I guess the only way I'll find out how long I was gone is to saw that damned elm in two and count the rings—but even that wouldn't help much; I don't know when it blew over. Never mind. The important thing now is to talk to this Baron of yours. Where does he stay?"

The old man shook his head violently. "If the Baron lays his hands on you, he'll wring the secrets from you on the rack! I know his ways. For five years I was a slave in the palace stables."

"If you think I'm going to spend the rest of my days in this rat nest, you get another guess on the house! This Baron has tanks, an army. He's kept a little technology alive. That's the outfit for me—not this garbage detail! Now, where's this place of his located?"

"The guards will shoot you on sight like a pack-dog!"

"There has to be a way to get to him, old man! Think!"

The old head was shaking again. "He fears assassination. You can never approach him ..." He brightened. "Unless you know a spell of power?"

I chewed my lip. "Maybe I do at that. You wanted me to have a plan. I think I feel one coming on. Have you got a map?"

He pointed to the desk beside me. I tried the drawers, found mice, roaches, moldy money—and a stack of folded maps. I opened one carefully; faded ink on yellowed paper falling apart at the creases. The legend in the corner read: "PENNSYLVANIA 40M:1. Copyright 1970 ESSO Corporation."

"This will do, pop," I said. "Now, tell me all you can about this Baron of yours."

"You'll destroy him?"

"I haven't even met the man."

"He is evil."

"I don't know; he owns an army. That makes up for a lot . . ."

After three more days of rest and the old man's stew I was back to normal—or near enough. I had the old man boil me a tub of water for a bath and a shave. I found a serviceable pair of synthetic-fiber long-johns in a chest of drawers, pulled them on and zipped the weather suit over them, then buckled on the holster I had made from a tough plastic.

"That completes my preparations, pop," I said. "It'll be dark in another half hour. Thanks for everything."

He got to his feet, a worried look on his lined face, like a father the first time Junior asks for the car.

"The Baron's men are everywhere."

"If you want to help, come along and back me up with that shotgun of yours." I picked it up. "Have you got any shells for this thing?"

He smiled, pleased now. "There are shells—but the magic is gone from many."

"That's the way magic is, pop. It goes out of things before you notice."

"Will you destroy the Great Troll now?"

"My motto is let sleeping trolls lie. I'm just paying a social call on the Baron."

The joy ran out of his face like booze from a dropped jug.

"Don't take it so hard, old timer. I'm not the fairy prince you were expecting. But I'll take care of you—if I make it."

I waited while he pulled on a moth-eaten mackinaw. He took the shotgun and checked the breech, then looked at me.

"I'm ready," he said.

"Yeah," I said. "Let's go ..."

The Baronial palace was a forty-story slab of concrete and glass that had been known in my days as the Hilton Garden East. We made it in three hours of groping across country in the dark, at the end of which I was puffing but still on my feet. We moved out from the cover of the trees and looked across a dip in the ground at the lights, incongruously cheerful in the ravaged valley.

"The gates are there—" the old man pointed—"guarded by the Great Troll."

"Wait a minute. I thought the Troll was the Bolo back at the Site."

"That's the Lesser Troll. This is the Great One."

I selected a few choice words and muttered them to myself. "It would have saved us some effort if you'd mentioned this troll a little sooner, old timer. I'm afraid I don't have any spells that will knock out a Mark II, once it's got its dander up."

He shook his head. "It lies under enchantment. I remember the day when it came, throwing thunderbolts. Many men were killed. Then the Baron commanded it to stand at his gates to guard him."

"How long ago was this, old timer?"

He worked his lips over the question. "Long ago," he said finally. "Many winters."

"Let's go take a look."

We picked our way down the slope, came up along a rutted dirt road to the dark line of trees that rimmed the palace grounds. The old man touched my arm.

"Softly here. Maybe the Troll sleeps lightly ..."

I went the last few yards, eased around a brick column with a dead lantern on top, stared across fifty yards of waist-high brush at a dark silhouette outlined against the palace lights.

Cables, stretched from trees outside the circle of weeds, supported a weathered tarp which drooped over the Bolo. The wreckage of a helicopter lay like a crumpled dragonfly at the far side of the ring. Nearer, fragments of a heavy car chassis lay scattered. The old man hovered at my shoulder.

"It looks as though the gate is off limits," I hissed. "Let's try farther along."

He nodded. "No one passes here. There is a second gate, there." He pointed. "But there are guards."

"Let's climb the wall between gates."

"There are sharp spikes on top of the wall. But I know a place, farther on, where the spikes have been blunted."

"Lead on, pop."

Half an hour of creeping through wet brush brought us to the spot we were looking for. It looked to me like any other stretch of eight-foot masonry wall overhung with wet poplar trees.

"I'll go first," the old man said, "to draw the attention of the guard."

"Then who's going to boost me up? I'll go first."

He nodded, cupped his hands and lifted me as easily as a

sailor lifting a beer glass. Pop was old—but he was nobody's softie.

I looked around, then crawled up, worked my way over the corroded spikes, dropped down on the lawn.

Immediately I heard a crackle of brush. A man stood up not ten feet away. I lay flat in the dark trying to look like something that had been there a long time …

I heard another sound, a thump and a crashing of brush. The man before me turned, disappeared in the darkness. I heard him beating his way through shrubbery; then he called out, got an answering shout from the distance.

I didn't loiter. I got to my feet and made a sprint for the cover of the trees along the drive.

4

Flat on the wet ground, under the wind-whipped branches of an ornamental cedar, I blinked the fine misty rain from my eyes, waiting for the halfhearted alarm behind me to die down.

There were a few shouts, some sounds of searching among the shrubbery. It was a bad night to be chasing imaginary intruders in the Baronial grounds. In five minutes all was quiet again.

I studied the view before me. The tree under which I lay was one of a row lining a drive. It swung in a graceful curve, across a smooth half-mile of dark lawn, to the tower of light that was the palace of the Baron of Filly. The silhouetted figures of guards and late-arriving guests moved against the gleam from the colonnaded entrance. On a terrace high above, dancers twirled under colored lights. The faint glow of the repellor field kept the cold rain at a distance. In a lull in the wind, I heard music, faintly. The Baron's weekly grand ball was in full swing.

I saw shadows move across the wet gravel before me, then heard the purr of an engine. I hugged the ground and watched a long svelte Mercedes—about an '88 model, I estimated—barrel past.

The mob in the city ran in packs like dogs, but the Baron's friends did a little better for themselves.

I got to my feet and moved off toward the palace, keeping well in the shadows. When the drive swung to the right to curve across in front of the building, I left it, went to hands and knees, and followed a trimmed privet hedge past dark rectangles of formal garden to the edge of a secondary pond of light from the garages. I let myself down on my belly and watched the shadows that moved on the graveled drive.

There seemed to be two men on duty—no more. Waiting around wouldn't improve my chances. I got to my feet, stepped out into the drive, and walked openly around the corner of the gray fieldstone building into the light.

A short, thickset man in greasy Baronial green looked at me incuriously. My weather suit looked enough like ordinary coveralls to get me by—at least for a few minutes. A second man, tilted back against the wall in a wooden chair, didn't even turn his head.

"Hey!" I called. "You birds got a three-ton jack I can borrow?"

Shorty looked me over sourly. "Who you drive for, Mac?"

"The High Duke of Jersey. Flat. Left rear. On a night like this. Some luck."

"The Jersey can't afford a jack?"

I stepped over to the short man, prodded him with a forefinger. "He could buy you and gut you on the altar any

Saturday night of the week, low-pockets. And he'd get a kick out of doing it. He's like that."

"Can't a guy crack a harmless joke without somebody talks about altar-bait? You wanna jack, take a jack."

The man in the chair opened one eye and looked me over. "How long you on the Jersey payroll?" he growled.

"Long enough to know who handles the rank between Jersey and Filly." I yawned, looked around the wide, cement-floored garage, glanced over the four heavy cars with the Filly crest on their sides.

"Where's the kitchen? I'm putting a couple of hot coffees under my belt before I go back out into that."

"Over there. A flight up and to your left. Tell the cook Pintsy invited you."

"I tell him Jersey sent me, low-pockets." I moved off in a dead silence, opened the door and stepped up into spicy-scented warmth.

A deep carpet—even here—muffled my footsteps. I could hear the clash of pots and crockery from the kitchen a hundred feet distant along the hallway. I went along to a deep-set doorway ten feet from the kitchen, tried the knob, and looked into a dark room. I pushed the door shut and leaned against it, watching the kitchen. Through the woodwork I could feel the thump of the bass notes from the orchestra blasting away three flights up. The odors of food—roast fowl, baked ham, grilled horsemeat—curled under the kitchen door and wafted under my nose. I pulled my belt up a notch and tried to swallow the dryness in my throat. The old man had fed me a half a gallon of stew before we left home, but I was already working up a fresh appetite.

Five slow minutes passed. Then the kitchen door swung open and a tall round-shouldered fellow with a shiny bald scalp stepped into view, a tray balanced on the spread fingers of one hand. He turned, the black tails of his cutaway swirling, called something behind him, and started past me. I stepped out, clearing my throat. He shied, whirled to face me. He was good at his job: the two dozen tiny glasses on the tray stood fast. He blinked, got an indignant remark ready—

I showed him the knife the old man had lent me—a bone-handled job with a six-inch switchblade. "Make a sound and I'll cut your throat," I said softly. "Put the tray on the floor."

He started to back. I brought the knife up. He took a good look, licked his lips, crouched quickly, and put the tray down.

"Turn around."

I stepped in and chopped him at the base of the neck with the edge of my hand. He folded like a two-dollar umbrella.

I wrestled the door open and dumped him inside, paused a moment to listen. All quiet. I worked his black coat and trousers off, unhooked the stiff white dickey and tie. He snored softly. I pulled the clothes on over the weather suit. They were a fair fit. By the light of my pencil flash I cut down a heavy braided cord hanging by a high window, used it to truss the waiter's hands and feet together behind him. There was a small closet opening off the room. I put him in it, closed the door, and stepped back into the hall. Still quiet. I tried one of the drinks. It wasn't bad.

I took another, then picked up the tray and followed the sounds of music.

The grand ballroom was a hundred yards long, fifty wide, with walls of rose, gold and white, banks of high windows hung with crimson velvet, a vaulted ceiling decorated with cherubs, and a polished acre of floor on which gaudily gowned and uniformed couples moved in time to the heavy beat of the traditional foxtrot. I moved slowly along the edge of the crowd, looking for the Baron.

A hand caught my arm and hauled me around. A glass fell off my tray, smashed on the floor.

A dapper little man in black and white headwaiter's uniform glared up at me.

"What do you think you're doing, cretin?" he hissed. "That's the genuine ancient stock you're slopping on the floor." I looked around quickly; no one else seemed to be paying any attention.

"Where are you from?" he snapped. I opened my mouth—

"Never mind, you're all the same." He waggled his hands disgustedly. "The field hands they send me—a disgrace to the Black. Now, you! Stand up! Hold your tray proudly, gracefully! Step along daintily, not like a knight taking the field! and pause occasionally—just on the chance that some noble guest might wish to drink."

"You bet, pal," I said. I moved on, paying a little more attention to my waiting. I saw plenty of green uniforms; pea green, forest green, emerald green—but they were all hung with braid and medals. According to pop, the Baron affected a spartan simplicity. The diffidence of absolute power.

There were high white and gold doors every few yards along the side of the ballroom. I spotted one standing open and sidled toward it. It wouldn't hurt to reconnoiter the area.

Just beyond the door, a very large sentry in a bottle-green uniform almost buried under gold braid moved in front of me. He was dressed like a toy soldier, but there was nothing playful about the way he snapped his power gun to the ready. I winked at him.

"Thought you boys might want a drink," I hissed. "Good stuff."

He looked at the tray, licked his lips. "Get back in there, you fool," he growled. "You'll get us both hanged."

"Suit yourself, pal." I backed out. Just before the door closed between us, he lifted a glass off the tray.

I turned, almost collided with a long lean cookie in a powder-blue outfit complete with dress sabre, gold frogs, leopard-skin facings, a pair of knee-length white gloves looped under an epaulette, a pistol in a fancy holster, and an eighteen-inch swagger stick. He gave me the kind of look old maids give sin.

"Look where you're going, swine," he said in a voice like a pine board splitting.

"Have a drink, admiral," I suggested.

He lifted his upper lip to show me a row of teeth that hadn't had their annual trip to the dentist lately. The ridges along each side of his mouth turned greenish white. He snatched for the gloves on his shoulder, fumbled them; they slapped the floor beside me.

"I'd pick those up for you, boss," I said, "but I've got my tray …"

He drew a breath between his teeth, chewed it into strips, and snorted it back at me, then snapped his fingers and pointed with his stick toward the door behind me.

"Through there, instantly!" It didn't seem like the time to argue; I pulled it open and stepped through.

The guard in green ducked his glass and snapped to attention when he saw the baby-blue outfit. My new friend ignored him, made a curt gesture to me. I got the idea, trailed along the wide, high, gloomy corridor to a small door, pushed through it into a well-lit tile-walled latrine. A big-eyed slave in white ducks stared.

Blue-boy jerked his head. “Get out!” The slave scuttled away. Blue-boy turned to me.

“Strip off your jacket, slave! Your owner has neglected to teach you discipline.”

I looked around quickly, saw that we were alone.

“Wait a minute while I put the tray down, corporal,” I said. “We don’t want to waste any of the good stuff.” I turned to put the tray on a soiled linen bin, caught a glimpse of motion in the mirror.

I ducked, and the nasty-looking little leather quirt whistled past my ear, slammed against the edge of a marble-topped lavatory with a crack like a pistol shot. I dropped the tray, stepped in fast and threw a left to Blue-boy’s jaw that bounced his head against the tiled wall. I followed up with a right to the belt buckle, then held him up as he bent over, gagging, and hit him hard under the ear.

I hauled him into a booth, propped him up and started shedding the waiter’s blacks.

5

I left him on the floor wearing my old suit, and stepped out into the hall.

I liked the feel of his pistol at my hip. It was an old-fashioned .38, the same model I favored. The blue uniform was a good fit, what with the weight I’d lost. Blue-boy and I had something in common after all.

The latrine attendant goggled at me. I grimaced like a quadruple amputee trying to scratch his nose and jerked my head toward the door I had come out of. I hoped the gesture would look familiar.

“Truss that mad dog and throw him outside the gates,” I

snarled. I stamped off down the corridor, trying to look mad enough to discourage curiosity.

Apparently it worked. Nobody yelled for the cops.

I reentered the ballroom by another door, snagged a drink off a passing tray, checked over the crowd. I saw two more powder-blue getups, so I wasn't unique enough to draw special attention. I made a mental note to stay well away from my comrades in blue. I blended with the landscape, chatting and nodding and not neglecting my drinking, working my way toward a big arched doorway on the other side of the room that looked like the kind of entrance the head man might use. I didn't want to meet him. Not yet. I just wanted to get him located before I went any further.

A passing wine slave poured a full inch of genuine ancient stock into my glass, ducked his head, and moved on. I gulped it like sour bar whiskey. My attention was elsewhere.

A flurry of activity near the big door indicated that maybe my guess had been accurate. Potbellied officials were forming up in a sort of reception line near the big double door. I started to drift back into the rear rank, bumped against a fat man in medals and a sash who glared, fingered a monocle with a plump ring-studded hand, and said, "Suggest you take your place, colonel," in a suety voice.

I must have looked doubtful, because he bumped me with his paunch, and growled, "Foot of the line! Next to the Equerry, you idiot." He elbowed me aside and waddled past.

I took a step after him, reached out with my left foot, and hooked his shiny black boot. He leaped forward, off balance, medals jangling. I did a fast fade while he was still groping for his monocle, eased into a spot at the end of the line.

The conversation died away to a nervous murmur. The doors swung back and a pair of guards with more trimmings than a phony stock certificate stamped into view, wheeled to face each other, and presented arms—chrome-plated automatic rifles, in this case. A dark-faced man with thinning gray hair, a pug nose, and a trimmed gray Vandyke came into view, limping slightly from a stiffish knee.

His unornamented gray outfit made him as conspicuous in this gathering as a crane among peacocks. He nodded perfunctorily to left and right, coming along between the waiting rows of flunkeys, who snapped-to as he came abreast, wilted and let out sighs behind him. I studied him closely. He was fifty, give or take the age of a bottle of second-rate bourbon, with the weather-beaten complexion of a former outdoor man and the same look of alertness grown bored that a rattlesnake farmer develops—just before the fatal bite.

He looked up and caught my eye on him, and for a moment I thought he was about to speak. Then he went on past.

At the end of the line he turned abruptly and spoke to a man who hurried away. Then he engaged in conversation with a cluster of head-bobbing guests.

I spent the next fifteen minutes casually getting closer to the door nearest the one the Baron had entered by. I looked around; nobody was paying any attention to me. I stepped past a guard who presented arms. The door closed softly, cutting off the buzz of talk and the worst of the music.

I went along to the end of the corridor. From the transverse hall, a grand staircase rose in a sweep of bright chrome and pale wood. I didn't know where it led, but it looked right. I headed for it, moving along briskly like a man with important business in mind and no time for light chitchat.

Two flights up, in a wide corridor of muted lights, deep carpets, brocaded wall hangings, mirrors, urns, and an odor of expensive tobacco and *cuir russe*, a small man in black bustled from a side corridor. He saw me. He opened his mouth, closed it, half turned away, then swung back to face me. I recognized him; he was the headwaiter who had pointed out the flaws in my waiting style half an hour earlier.

"Here—" he started.

I chopped him short with a roar of what I hoped was authentic upper-crust rage.

"Direct me to his Excellency's apartments, scum! And thank your guardian imp I'm in too great haste to cane you for the insolent look about you!"

He went pale, gulped hard, and pointed. I snorted and stamped past him down the turning he had indicated.

This was Baronial country, all right. A pair of guards stood at the far end of the corridor.

I'd passed half a dozen with no more than a click of heels to indicate they saw me. These two shouldn't be any different—and it wouldn't look good if I turned and started back at sight of them. The first rule of the gate-crasher is to look as if you belong where you are.

I headed in their direction.

When I was fifty feet from them they both shifted rifles—not to present-arms position, but at the ready. The nickel-plated bayonets were aimed right at me. It was no time for me to look doubtful; I kept on coming. At twenty feet, I heard their rifle bolts snick home. I could see the expressions on their faces now; they looked as nervous as a couple of teenage sailors on their first visit to a joyhouse.

"Point those butter knives into the corner, you banana-fingered cotton choppers!" I said, looking bored, and didn't waver. I unlimbered my swagger stick and slapped my gloved hand with it, letting them think it over. The gun muzzles dropped—just slightly. I followed up fast.

“Which is the anteroom to the Baron’s apartments?” I demanded.

“Uh … this here is his Excellency’s apartments, sir, but—”

“Never mind the lecture, you milk-faced fool,” I cut in. “Which is the anteroom, damn you!”

“We got orders, sir. Nobody’s to come closer than that last door back there.”

“We got orders to shoot,” the other interrupted. He was a little older—maybe twenty-two. I turned on him.

“I’m waiting for an answer to a question!”

“Sir, the Articles—”

I narrowed my eyes. “I think you’ll find paragraph Two B covers Special Cosmic Top Secret Couriers. When you go off duty, report yourselves on punishment. Now, the anteroom! And be quick about it!”

The bayonets were sagging now. The younger of the two licked his lips. “Sir, we never been inside. We don’t know how it’s laid out in there. If the colonel wants to just take a look …”

The other guard opened his mouth to say something. I didn’t wait to find out what it was. I stepped between them, muttering something about bloody recruits and important messages, and worked the fancy handle on the big gold and white door. I paused to give the two sentries a hard look.

“I hope I don’t have to remind you that any mention of the movements of a Cosmic Courier is punishable by slow death. Just forget you ever saw me.” I went on in and closed the door without waiting to catch the reaction to that one.

The Baron had done well by himself in the matter of decor. The room I was in—a sort of lounge-cum-bar—was paved in two-inch-deep nylon fuzz, the color of a fog at sea, that foamed up at the edges against walls of pale blue brocade with tiny yellow flowers. The bar was a teak log split down the middle and polished. The glasses sitting on it were like tissue paper engraved with patterns of nymphs and satyrs. Subdued light came from somewhere, along with a faint melody that seemed to speak of youth, long ago.

I went on into the room. I found more soft light, the glow of hand-rubbed rare woods, rich fabrics, and wide windows with a view of dark night sky. The music was coming from a long, low, built-in speaker with a lamp, a heavy crystal ashtray, and a display of hothouse roses. There was a scent in the air. Not the *cuir russe* and Havana leaf I'd smelled in the hall, but a subtler perfume.

I turned and looked into the eyes of a girl with long black lashes. Smooth black hair came down to bare shoulders. An arm as smooth and white as whipped cream was draped over a chair back, the hand holding an eight-inch cigarette holder and sporting a diamond as inconspicuous as a chrome-plated hubcap.

"You must want something pretty badly," she murmured, batting her eyelashes at me. I could feel the breeze at ten feet. I nodded. Under the circumstances that was about the best I could do.

"What could it be," she mused, "that's worth being shot for?" Her voice was like the rest of her: smooth, polished and relaxed—and with plenty of moxie held in reserve. She smiled casually, drew on her cigarette, tapped ashes onto the rug.

"Something bothering you, colonel?" she inquired. "You don't seem talkative."

"I'll do my talking when the Baron arrives," I said.

"In that case, Jackson," said a husky voice behind me, "you can start any time you like."

*

I held my hands clear of my body and turned around slowly—just in case there was a nervous gun aimed at my spine. The Baron was standing near the door, unarmed, relaxed. There were no guards in sight. The girl looked mildly amused. I put my hand on the pistol butt.

"How do you know my name?" I asked.

The Baron waved toward a chair. "Sit down, Jackson," he said, almost gently. "You've had a tough time of it—but you're all right now." He walked past me to the bar, poured out two glasses, turned, and offered me one. I felt a little silly standing there fingering the gun; I went over and took the drink.

"To the old days." The Baron raised his glass.

I drank. It was the genuine ancient stock, all right. "I asked you how you knew my name," I said.

"That's easy. I used to know you."

He smiled faintly. There was something about his face ...

"You look well in the uniform of the Penn dragoons," he said. "Better than you ever did in Aerospace blue."

"Good God!" I said. "Toby Mallon!"

He ran a hand over his bald head. "A little less hair on top, plus a beard as compensation, a few wrinkles, a slight pot. Oh, I've changed, Jackson."

"I had it figured as close to eighty years," I said. "The trees, the condition of the buildings—"

"Not far off the mark. Seventy-eight years this spring."

"You're a well-preserved hundred and ten, Toby."

He nodded. "I know how you feel. Rip Van Winkle had nothing on us."

"Just one question, Toby. The men you sent out to pick me up seemed more interested in shooting than talking. I'm wondering why."

Mallon threw out his hands. "A little misunderstanding,

Jackson. You made it; that's all that counts. Now that you're here, we've got some planning to do together. I've had it tough these last twenty years. I started off with nothing: a few hundred scavengers living in the ruins, hiding out every time Jersey or Dee-Cee raided for supplies. I built an organization, started a systematic salvage operation. I saved everything the rats and the weather hadn't gotten to, spruced up my palace here, and stocked it. It's a rich province, Jackson—"

"And now you own it all. Not bad, Toby."

"They say knowledge is power. I had the knowledge."

I finished my drink and put the glass on the bar.

"What's this planning you say we have to do?"

Mallon leaned back on one elbow.

"Jackson, it's been a long haul—alone. It's good to see an old shipmate. But we'll dine first."

"I might manage to nibble a little something. Say a horse, roasted whole. Don't bother to remove the saddle."

He laughed. "First we eat," he said. "Then we conquer the world."

6

I squeezed the last drop from the Beaujolais bottle and watched the girl, whose name was Renada, hold a light for the cigar Mallon had taken from a silver box. My blue mess jacket and holster hung over the back of the chair. Everything was cosy now.

"Time for business, Jackson," Mallon said. He blew out smoke and looked at me through it. "How did things look—inside?"

"Dusty. But intact, below ground level. Upstairs, there's blast damage and weathering. I don't suppose it's changed much since you came out twenty years ago. As far as I could tell, the Primary Site is okay."

Mallon leaned forward. "Now, you made it out past the Bolo. How did it handle itself? Still fully functional?"

I sipped my wine, thinking over my answer, remembering the Bolo's empty guns …

"It damn near gunned me down. It's getting a little old and it can't see as well as it used to, but it's still a tough baby."

Mallon swore suddenly. "It was Mackenzie's idea. A last-minute move when the tech crews had to evacuate. It was a dusting job, you know."

"I hadn't heard. How did you find out all this?"

Mallon shot me a sharp look. "There were still a few people around who'd been in it. But never mind that. What about the Supply Site? That's what we're interested in. Fuel, guns, even some nuclear stuff. Heavy equipment; there's a couple more Bolos, mothballed, I understand. Maybe we'll even find one or two of the Colossus missiles still in their silos. I made an air recon a few years back before my chopper broke down—"

"I think two silo doors are still in place. But why the interest in armament?"

Mallon snorted. "You've got a few things to learn about the setup, Jackson. I need that stuff. If I hadn't lucked into a stock of weapons and ammo in the armory cellar, Jersey would be wearing the spurs in my palace right now!"

I drew on my cigar and let the silence stretch out.

"You said something about conquering the world, Toby. I don't suppose by any chance you meant that literally?"

Mallon stood up, his closed fists working like a man crumpling unpaid bills. "They all want what I've got! They're all waiting." He walked across the room, back. "I'm ready to move against them now! I can put four thousand trained men in the field—"

"Let's get a couple of things straight, Mallon," I cut in. "You've got the natives fooled with this Baron routine. But don't try it on me. Maybe it was even necessary once; maybe there's an excuse for some of the stories I've heard. That's over now. I'm not interested in tribal warfare or gang rumbles. I need—"

"Better remember who's running things here, Jackson!" Mallon snapped. "It's not what you need that counts." He took another turn up and down the room, then stopped, facing me.

"Look, Jackson. I know how to get around in this jungle; you don't. If I hadn't spotted you and given some orders, you'd have been gunned down before you'd gone ten feet past the ballroom door."

"Why'd you let me in? I might've been gunning for you."

"You wanted to see the Baron alone. That suited me, too. If word got out—" He broke off, cleared his throat. "Let's stop wrangling, Jackson. We can't move until the Bolo guarding the site has been neutralized. There's only one way to do that: knock it out! And the only thing that can knock out a Bolo is another Bolo."

"So?"

"I've got another Bolo, Jackson. It's been covered, maintained. It can go up against the Troll—" He broke off, laughed shortly. "That's what the mob called it."

"You could have done that years ago. Where do I come in?"

"You're checked out on a Bolo, Jackson. You know something about this kind of equipment."

"Sure. So do you."

"I never learned," he said shortly.

"Who's kidding who, Mallon? We all took the same orientation course less than a month ago—"

"For me it's been a long month. Let's say I've forgotten."

"You parked that Bolo at your front gate and then forgot how you did it, eh?"

"Nonsense. It's always been there."

I shook my head. "I know different."

Mallon looked wary. "Where'd you get that idea?"

"Somebody told me."

Mallon ground his cigar out savagely on the damask cloth. "You'll point the scum out to me!"

"I don't give a damn whether you moved it or not. Anybody with your training can figure out the controls of a Bolo in half an hour—"

"Not well enough to take on the Tr—another Bolo."

I took a cigar from the silver box, picked up the lighter from the table, turned the cigar in the flame. Suddenly it was very quiet in the room.

I looked across at Mallon. He held out his hand.

"I'll take that," he said shortly.

I blew out smoke, squinted through it at Mallon. He sat with his hand out, waiting. I looked down at the lighter.

It was a heavy windproof model with embossed Aerospace wings. I turned it over. Engraved letters read: *Lieut. Commander Don G. Banner, USAF.* I looked up. Renada sat quietly, holding my pistol trained dead on my belt buckle.

"I'm sorry you saw that," Mallon said. "It could cause misunderstandings."

"Where's Banner?"

"He ... died. I told you—"

"You told me a lot of things, Toby. Some of them might even be true. Did you make him the same offer you've made me?"

Mallon darted a look at Renada. She sat holding the pistol, looking at me distantly, without expression.

"You've got the wrong idea, Jackson—" Mallon started.

"You and he came out about the same time," I said. "Or maybe you got the jump on him by a few days. It must have been close; otherwise you'd never have taken him. Don was a sharp boy."

"You're out of your mind!" Mallon snapped. "Why, Banner was my friend!"

"Then why do you get nervous when I find his lighter on your table? There could be ten perfectly harmless explanations."

"I don't make explanations," Mallon said flatly.

"That attitude is hardly the basis for a lasting partnership, Toby. I have an unhappy feeling there's something you're not telling me."

Mallon pulled himself up in the chair. "Look here, Jackson. We've no reason to fall out. There's plenty for both of us—and one day I'll be needing a successor. It was too bad about Banner, but that's ancient history now. Forget it. I want you with me, Jackson! Together we can rule the Atlantic seaboard—or even more!"

I drew on my cigar, looking at the gun in Renada's hand. "You hold the aces, Toby. Shooting me would be no trick at all."

"There's no trick involved, Jackson!" Mallon snapped. "After all," he went on, almost wheedling now, "we're old friends. I want to give you a break, share with you—"

"I don't think I'd trust him if I were you, Mr. Jackson," Renada's quiet voice cut in. I looked at her. She looked back calmly. "You're more important to him than you think."

"That's enough, Renada," Mallon barked. "Go to your room at once."

"Not just yet, Toby," she said. "I'm also curious about how

Commander Banner died." I looked at the gun in her hand.

It wasn't pointed at me now. It was aimed at Mallon's chest.

Mallon sat sunk deep in his chair, looking at me with eyes like a python with a bellyache. "You're fools, both of you," he grated. "I gave you everything, Renada. I raised you like my own daughter. And you, Jackson. You could have shared with me—all of it."

"I don't need a share of your delusions, Toby. I've got a set of my own. But before we go any farther, let's clear up a few points. Why haven't you been getting any mileage out of your tame Bolo? And what makes me important in the picture?"

"He's afraid of the Bolo machine," Renada said. "There's a spell on it which prevents men from approaching—even the Baron."

"Shut your mouth, you fool!" Mallon choked on his fury. I tossed the lighter in my hand and felt a smile twitching at my mouth.

"So Don was too smart for you after all. He must have been the one who had control of the Bolo. I suppose you called for a truce, and then shot him out from under the white flag. But he fooled you. He plugged a command into the Bolo's circuits to fire on anyone who came close—unless he was Banner."

"You're crazy!"

"It's close enough. You can't get near the Bolo. Right? And after twenty years, the bluff you've been running on the other Barons with your private troll must be getting a little thin. Any day now one of them may decide to try you."

Mallon twisted his face in what may have been an attempt at a placating smile. "I won't argue with you, Jackson. You're right about the command circuit. Banner set it up to fire an antipersonnel blast at anyone coming within fifty yards. He did it to keep the mob from tampering with the machine. But there's a loophole. It wasn't only Banner who could get close. He set it up to accept any of the *Prometheus* crew—except me. He hated me. It was a trick to try to get me killed."

"So you're figuring I'll step in and de-fuse her for you, eh, Toby? Well, I'm sorry as hell to disappoint you, but somehow in the confusion I left my electropass behind."

Mallon leaned toward me. "I told you we need each other, Jackson: I've got your pass. Yours and all the others. Renada, hand me my black box." She rose and moved across to the desk, holding the gun on Mallon—and on me, too, for that matter.

"Where'd you get my pass, Mallon?"

"Where do you think? They're the duplicates from the vault in the old command block. I knew one day one of you would come out. I'll tell you, Jackson, it's been hell, waiting all these years—and hoping. I gave orders that any time the Great Troll bellowed, the mob was to form up and stop anybody who came out. I don't know how you got through them ..."

"I was too slippery for them. Besides," I added, "I met a friend."

"A friend? Who's that?"

"An old man who thought I was Prince Charming, come to wake everybody up. He was nuts. But he got me through."

Renada came back, handed me a square steel box. "Let's have the key, Mallon," I said. He handed it over. I opened the box, sorted through half a dozen silver-dollar-sized ovals of clear plastic, lifted one out.

"Is it a magical charm?" Renada asked, sounding awed. She didn't seem so sophisticated now—but I liked her better human.

"Just a synthetic crystalline plastic, designed to resonate to a pattern peculiar to my EEG," I said. "It amplifies the signal and gives off a characteristic emission that the psychotronic circuit in the Bolo picks up."

"That's what I thought. Magic."

"Call it magic, then, kid." I dropped the electropass in my pocket, stood and looked at Renada. "I don't doubt that you know how to use that gun, honey, but I'm leaving now. Try not to shoot me."

"You're a fool if you try it," Mallon barked. "If Renada doesn't shoot you, my guards will. And even if you made it, you'd still need me!"

"I'm touched by your concern, Toby. Just why do I need you?"

"You wouldn't get past the first sentry post without help, Jackson. These people know me as the Trollmaster. They're in awe of me—of my *mana.* But together—we can get to the controls of the Bolo, then use it to knock out the sentry machine at the Site—"

"Then what? With an operating Bolo I don't need anything else. Better improve the picture, Toby. I'm not impressed."

He wet his lips.

"It's *Prometheus*, do you understand? She's stocked with everything from Browning needlers to Norge stunners. Tools, weapons, instruments. And the power plants alone."

"I don't need needlers if I own a Bolo, Toby."

Mallon used some profanity. "You'll leave your liver and lights on the palace altar, Jackson. I promise you that!"

"Tell him what he wants to know, Toby," Renada said.

Mallon narrowed his eyes at her. "You'll live to regret this, Renada."

"Maybe I will, Toby. But you taught me how to handle a gun—and to play cards for keeps."

The flush faded out of his face and left it pale. "All right,

Jackson," he said, almost in a whisper. "It's not only the equipment. It's . . . the men."

I heard a clock ticking somewhere.

"What men, Toby?" I said softly.

"The crew. Day, Macy, the others. They're still in there, Jackson—aboard the ship, in stasis. We were trying to get the ship off when the attack came. There was forty minutes' warning. Everything was ready to go. You were on a test run; there wasn't time to cycle you out . . ."

"Keep talking," I rapped.

"You know how the system was set up; it was to be a ten-year run out, with an automatic turnaround at the end of that time if Alpha Centauri wasn't within a milliparsec." He snorted. "It wasn't. After twenty years, the instruments checked. They were satisfied. There was a planetary mass within the acceptable range. So they brought me out." He snorted again. "The longest dry run in history. I unstrapped and came out to see what was going on. It took me a little while to realize what had happened. I went back in and cycled Banner and Mackenzie out. We went into the town; you know what we found. I saw what we had to do, but Banner and Mac argued. The fools wanted to reseal *Prometheus* and proceed with the launch. For what? So we could spend the rest of our lives squatting in the ruins, when by stripping the ship we could make ourselves kings?"

"So there was an argument?" I prompted.

"I had a gun. I hit Mackenzie in the leg, I think—but they got clear, found a car and beat me to the Site. There were two Bolos. What chance did I have against them?" Mallon grinned craftily. "But Banner was a fool. He died for it." The grin dropped like a stripper's bra. "But when I went to claim my spoils, I discovered how the jackals had set the trap for me."

"That was downright unfriendly of them, Mallon. Oddly enough, it doesn't make me want to stay and hold your hand."

"Don't you understand yet!" Mallon's voice was a dry screech. "Even if you got clear of the palace, used the Bolo to set yourself up as Baron—you'd never be safe! Not as long as one man was still alive aboard the ship. You'd never have a night's rest, wondering when one of them would walk out to challenge your rule ..."

"Uneasy lies the head, eh, Toby? You remind me of a queen bee. The first one out of the chrysalis dismembers all her rivals."

"I don't mean to kill them. That would be a waste; I mean to give them useful work to do."

"I don't think they'd like being your slaves, Toby. And neither would I." I looked at Renada. "I'll be leaving you now," I said. "Whichever way you decide, good luck."

"Wait." She stood. "I'm going with you."

I looked at her. "I'll be traveling fast, honey. And that gun in my back may throw off my timing."

She stepped to me, reversed the pistol, and laid it in my hand.

"Don't kill him, Mr. Jackson. He was always kind to me."

"Why change sides now? According to Toby, my chances look not too good."

"I never knew before how Commander Banner died," she said. "He was my great-grandfather."

7

Renada came back bundled in a gray fur as I finished buckling on my holster.

"So long, Toby," I said. "I ought to shoot you in the belly just for Don, but—"

I saw Renada's eyes widen at the same instant that I heard the click.

I dropped flat and rolled behind Mallon's chair—and a gout of blue flame yammered into the spot where I'd been standing. I whipped the gun up and fired a round into the peach-colored upholstery an inch from Toby's ear.

"The next one nails you to the chair," I yelled. "Call 'em off!" There was a moment of dead silence. Toby sat frozen. I couldn't see who'd been doing the shooting. Then I heard a moan. Renada.

"Let the girl alone or I'll kill him," I called.

Toby sat rigid, his eyes rolled toward me.

"You can't kill me, Jackson! I'm all that's keeping you alive."

"You can't kill me either, Toby. You need my magic touch, remember? Maybe you'd better give me a safe-conduct out of here. I'll take the freeze off your Bolo—after I've seen to my business."

Toby licked his lips. I heard Renada again. She was trying not to moan—but moaning anyway.

"You tried, Jackson. It didn't work out," Toby said through gritted teeth. "Throw out your gun and stand up. I won't kill you—you know that. You do as you're told and you may still live to a ripe old age—and the girl, too."

She screamed then—a mindless ululation of pure agony.

"Hurry up, you fool, before they tear her arm off," Mallon grated. "Or shoot. You'll get to watch her for twenty-four hours under the knife. Then you'll have your turn."

I fired again—closer this time. Mallon jerked his head and cursed.

"If they touch her again, you get it, Toby," I said. "Send her over here. Move!"

"Let her go!" Mallon snarled. Renada stumbled into sight,

moved around the chair, then crumpled suddenly to the rug beside me.

"Stand up, Toby," I ordered. He rose slowly. Sweat glistened on his face now. "Stand over here." He moved like a sleep-walker. I got to my feet. There were two men standing across the room beside a small open door. A sliding panel. Both of them held power rifles leveled—but aimed offside, away from the Baron.

"Drop 'em!" I said. They looked at me, then lowered the guns, tossed them aside.

I opened my mouth to tell Mallon to move ahead, but my tongue felt thick and heavy. The room was suddenly full of smoke. In front of me, Mallon was wavering like a mirage. I started to tell him to stand still, but with my thick tongue, it was too much trouble. I raised the gun, but somehow it was falling to the floor—slowly, like a leaf—and then I was floating, too, on waves that broke on a dark sea ...

"Do you think you're the first idiot who thought he could kill me?" Mallon raised a contemptuous lip. "This room's rigged ten different ways."

I shook my head, trying to ignore the film before my eyes and the nausea in my body. "No, I imagine lots of people would like a crack at you, Toby. One day one of them's going to make it."

"Get him on his feet," Mallon snapped. Hard hands clamped on my arms, hauled me off the cot. I worked my legs, but they were like yesterday's celery; I sagged against somebody who smelled like uncured hides.

"You seem drowsy," Mallon said. "We'll see if we can't wake you up."

A thumb dug into my neck. I jerked away, and a jab under the ribs doubled me over.

"I have to keep you alive—for the moment," Mallon said. "But you won't get a lot of pleasure out of it."

I blinked hard. It was dark in the room. One of my handlers had a ring of beard around his mouth—I could see that much. Mallon was standing before me, hands on hips. I aimed a kick at him, just for fun. It didn't work out; my foot seemed to be wearing a lead boat. The unshaven man hit me in the mouth and Toby chuckled.

"Have your fun, Dunger," he said, "but I'll want him alive and on his feet for the night's work. Take him out and walk him in the fresh air. Report to me at the Pavilion of the Troll in an hour." He turned to something and gave orders about lights and gun emplacements, and I heard Renada's name mentioned.

Then he was gone and I was being dragged through the door and along the corridor.

The exercise helped. By the time the hour had passed, I was feeling weak but normal—except for an aching head and a feeling that there was a strand of spiderweb interfering with my vision. Toby had given me a good meal. Maybe before the night was over he'd regret that mistake …

Across the dark grounds, an engine started up, spluttered, then settled down to a steady hum.

"It's time," the one with the whiskers said. He had a voice like soft cheese to match his smell. He took another half-twist in the arm he was holding.

"Don't break it," I grunted. "It belongs to the Baron, remember?"

Whiskers stopped dead. "You talk too much—and too smart." He let my arm go and stepped back. "Hold him, Pig

Eye." The other man whipped a forearm across my throat and levered my head back; then Whiskers unlimbered the two-foot club from his belt and hit me hard in the side, just under the ribs. Pig Eye let go and I folded over and waited while the pain swelled up and burst inside me.

Then they hauled me back to my feet. I couldn't feel any bone ends grating, so there probably weren't any broken ribs—if that was any consolation.

There were lights glaring now across the lawn. Moving figures cast long shadows against the trees lining the drive—and on the side of the Bolo Combat Unit parked under its canopy by the sealed gate.

A crude breastwork had been thrown up just over fifty yards from it. A wheel-mounted generator putted noisily in the background, laying a layer of bluish exhaust in the air.

Mallon was waiting with a 9-mm power rifle in his hands as we came up, my two guards gripping me with both hands to demonstrate their zeal, and me staggering a little more than was necessary. I saw Renada standing by, wrapped in a gray fur. Her face looked white in the harsh light. She made a move toward me and a greenback caught her arm.

"You know what to do, Jackson," Mallon said speaking loudly against the clatter of the generator. He made a curt gesture and a man stepped up and buckled a stout chain to my left ankle. Mallon held out my electropass. "I want you to walk straight to the Bolo. Go in by the side port. You've got one minute to cancel the instructions punched into the command circuit and climb back outside. If you don't show, I close a switch there—" He pointed to a wooden box mounting an open circuit-breaker, with a tangle of heavy cable leading toward the Bolo—"and you cook in your shoes. The same thing happens if I see the guns start to traverse or the antipersonnel ports open." I followed the coils of armored wire from the chain on my ankle back to the wooden box—and on to the generator.

"Crude, maybe, but it will work. And if you get any idea of letting fly a round or two at random—remember the girl will be right beside me."

I looked across at the giant machine. "Suppose it doesn't recognize me? It's been a while. Or what if Don didn't plug my identity pattern in to the recognition circuit?"

"In that case, you're no good to me anyway," Mallon said flatly.

I caught Renada's eye, gave her a wink and a smile I didn't feel, and climbed up on top of the revetment.

I looked back at Mallon. He was old and shrunken in the garish light, his smooth gray suit rumpled, his thin hair mussed, the gun held in a white-knuckled grip. He looked more like a harassed shopkeeper than a would-be world-beater.

"You must want the Bolo pretty bad to take the chance, Toby," I said. "I'll think about taking that wild shot. You sweat me out."

I flipped slack into the wire trailing my ankle, jumped down, and started across the smooth-trimmed grass, a long black shadow stalking before me. The Bolo sat silent, as big as a bank in the circle of the spotlight. I could see the flecks of rust now around the port covers, the small vines that twined up her sides from the ragged stands of weeds that marked no-man's-land.

There was something white in the brush ahead. Broken human bones.

I felt my stomach go rigid again. The last man had gotten this far; I wasn't in the clear yet …

I passed two more scattered skeletons in the next twenty feet. They must have come in on the run, guinea pigs to test the alertness of the Bolo. Or maybe they'd tried creeping up, dead slow, an inch a day; it hadn't worked …

Tiny night creatures scuttled ahead. They would be safe here in the shadow of the troll where no predator bigger than a mouse could move. I stumbled, diverted my course around a ten-foot hollow, the eroded crater of a near miss.

Now I could see the great moss-coated treads sunk a foot into the earth, the nests of field mice tucked in the spokes of the yard-high bogies. The entry hatch was above, a hairline against the great curved flank. There were rungs set in the flaring tread shield. I reached up, got a grip and hauled myself up. My chain clanked against the metal. I found the door lever, held on and pulled.

It resisted, then turned. There was the hum of a servo motor, a crackling of dead gaskets. The hairline widened and showed me a narrow companionway, green-anodized dural with black polymer treads, a bulkhead with a fire extinguisher, an embossed steel data plate that said BOLO DIVISION OF GENERAL MOTORS CORPORATION and below, in smaller type, UNIT, COMBAT, BOLO MARK III.

I pulled myself inside and went up into the Christmas-tree glow of instrument lights.

The control cockpit was small, utilitarian, with two deep-padded seats set among screens, dials, levers. I sniffed the odors of oil, paint, the characteristic ether and ozone of a nuclear generator. There was a faint hum in the air from idling relay servos. The clock showed ten past four. Either it was later than I thought, or the chronometer had lost time in the last eighty years. But I had no time to lose …

I slid into the seat, flipped back the cover of the command

control console. The Cancel key was the big white one. I pulled it down and let it snap back, like a clerk ringing up a sale.

A pattern of dots on the status display screen flicked out of existence. Mallon was safe from his pet troll now.

It hadn't taken me long to carry out my orders. I knew what to do next; I'd planned it all during my walk out. Now I had thirty seconds to stack the deck in my favor.

I reached down, hauled the festoon of quarter-inch armored cable up in front of me. I hit a switch, and the inner conning cover—a disk of inch-thick armor—slid back. I shoved a loop of the flexible cable up through the aperture, reversed the switch. The cover slid back—slicing the armored cable like macaroni.

I took a deep breath, and my hands went to the combat alert switch, hovered over it.

It was the smart thing to do—the easy thing. All I had to do was punch a key, and the 9-mm's would open up, scythe Mallon and his crew down like cornstalks.

But the scything would mow Renada down, along with the rest. And if I went—even without firing a shot—Mallon would keep his promise to cut that white throat …

My head was out of the noose now, but I would have to put it back—for a while.

I leaned sideways, reached back under the panel, groped for a small fuse box. My fingers were clumsy. I took a breath, tried again. The fuse dropped out in my hand. The Bolo's I-R circuit was dead now. With a few more seconds to work, I could have knocked out other circuits—but the time had run out.

I grabbed the cut ends of my lead wire, knotted them around the chain and got out fast.

8

Mallon waited, crouched behind the revetment.

"It's safe now, is it?" he grated. I nodded. He stood, gripping his gun.

"Now we'll try it together."

I went over the parapet, Mallon following with his gun ready. The lights followed us to the Bolo. Mallon clambered up to the open port, looked around inside, then dropped back down beside me. He looked excited now.

"That does it, Jackson! I've waited a long time for this. Now I've got all the *mana* there is!"

"Take a look at the cable on my ankle," I said softly. He narrowed his eyes, stepped back, gun aimed, darted a glance at the cable looped to the chain.

"I cut it, Toby. I was alone in the Bolo with the cable cut—and I didn't fire. I could have taken your toy and set up in business for myself, but I didn't."

"What's that supposed to buy you?" Mallon rasped.

"As you said—we need each other. That cut cable proves you can trust me."

Mallon smiled. It wasn't a nice smile. "Safe, were you? Come here." I walked along with him to the back of the Bolo. A heavy copper wire hung across the rear of the machine, trailing off into the grass in both directions.

"I'd have burned you at the first move. Even with the cable cut, the armored cover would have carried the full load right into the cockpit with you. But don't be nervous. I've got other jobs for you." He jabbed the gun muzzle hard into my chest, pushing me back. "Now get moving," he snarled. "And don't ever threaten the Baron again."

“The years have done more than shrivel your face, Toby,” I said. “They’ve cracked your brain.”

He laughed, a short bark. “You could be right. What’s sane and what isn’t? I’ve got a vision in my mind—and I’ll make it come true. If that’s insanity, it’s better than what the mob has.”

Back at the parapet, Mallon turned to me. “I’ve had this campaign planned in detail for years, Jackson. Everything’s ready. We move out in half an hour—before any traitors have time to take word to my enemies. Pig Eye and Dunger will keep you from being lonely while I’m away. When I get back—Well, maybe you’re right about working together.” He gestured and my whiskery friend and his sidekick loomed up. “Watch him,” he said.

“Genghis Khan is on the march, eh?” I said, “With nothing between you and the goodies but a five-hundred-ton Bolo …”

“The Lesser Troll …” He raised his hands and made crushing motions, like a man crumbling dry earth. “I’ll trample it under my treads.”

“You’re confused, Toby. The Bolo has treads. You just have a couple of fallen arches.”

“It’s the same. I am the Great Troll.” He showed me his teeth and walked away.

I moved along between Dunger and Pig Eye, toward the lights of the garage.

“The back entrance again,” I said. “Anyone would think you were ashamed of me.”

“You need more training, hah?” Dunger rasped. “Hold him, Pig Eye.” He unhooked his club and swung it loosely in his hand, glancing around. We were near the trees by the drive. There was no one in sight except the crews near the

Bolo and a group by the front of the palace. Pig Eye gave my arm a twist and shifted his grip to his old favorite strangle hold. I was hoping he would.

Dunger whipped the club up, and I grabbed Pig Eye's arm with both hands and leaned forward like a Japanese admiral reporting to the Emperor. Pig Eye went up and over just in time to catch Dunger's club across the back. They went down together. I went for the club, but Whiskers was faster than he looked. He rolled clear, got to his knees, and laid it across my left arm, just below the shoulder.

I heard the bone go …

I was back on my feet, somehow. Pig Eye lay sprawled before me. I heard him whining as though from a great distance. Dunger stood six feet away, the ring of black beard spread in a grin like a hyena smelling dead meat.

"His back's broke," he said. "Hell of a sound he's making. I been waiting for you; I wanted you to hear it."

"I've heard it," I managed. My voice seemed to be coming off a worn sound track. "Surprised … you didn't work me over … while I was busy with the arm."

"Uh-uh. I like a man to know what's going on when I work him over." He stepped in, rapped the broken arm lightly with the club. Fiery agony choked a groan off in my throat. I backed a step; he stalked me.

"Pig Eye wasn't much, but he was my pal. When I'm through with you, I'll have to kill him. A man with a broken back's no use to nobody. His'll be finished pretty soon now, but not with you. You'll be around a long time yet; but I'll get a lot of fun out of you before the Baron gets back."

I was under the trees now. I had some wild thoughts about grabbing up a club of my own, but they were just thoughts. Dunger set himself and his eyes dropped to my belly. I didn't wait for it; I lunged at him. He laughed and stepped back, and the club cracked my head. Not hard; just enough to send me down. I got my legs under me and started to get up—

There was a hint of motion from the shadows behind Dunger. I shook my head to cover any expression that might have showed, let myself drop back.

"Get up," Dunger said. The smile was gone now. He aimed a kick. "Get up—"

He froze suddenly, then whirled. His hearing must have been as keen as a jungle cat's; I hadn't heard a sound.

The old man stepped into view, his white hair plastered wet to his skull, his big hands spread. Dunger snarled, jumped in and whipped the club down; I heard it hit. There was a flurry of struggle, then Dunger stumbled back, empty-handed.

I was on my feet again now. I made a lunge for Dunger as he roared and charged. The club in the old man's hand rose and fell. Dunger crashed past and into the brush. The old man sat down suddenly, still holding the club. Then he let it fall and lay back. I went toward him and Dunger rushed me from the side. I went down again.

I was dazed, but not feeling any pain now. Dunger was standing over the old man. I could see the big lean figure lying limply, arms outspread—and a white bone handle, incongruously new and neat against the shabby mackinaw. The club lay on the ground a few feet away. I started crawling for it. It seemed a long way, and it was hard for me to move my legs, but I kept at it. The light rain was falling again now, hardly more than a mist. Far away there were shouts and the sound of engines starting up. Mallon's convoy moving out. He had won. Dunger had won, too. The old man had tried, but it hadn't been enough. But if I could reach the club, and swing it just once …

Dunger was looking down at the old man. He leaned, withdrew the knife, wiped it on his trouser leg, hitching up his pants to tuck it away in its sheath. The club was smooth and heavy under my hand. I got a good grip on it, got to my feet. I waited until Dunger turned, and then I hit him across the top of the skull with everything I had left …

I thought the old man was dead until he blinked suddenly. His features looked relaxed now, peaceful, the skin like parchment stretched over bone. I took his gnarled old hand and rubbed it. It was as cold as a drowned sailor.

"You waited for me, old timer?" I said inanely. He moved his head minutely, and looked at me. Then his mouth moved. I leaned close to catch what he was saying. His voice was fainter than lost hope.

"Mom … told … me … wait for you … She said … you'd … come back some day …"

I felt my jaw muscles knotting.

Inside me something broke and flowed away like molten metal. Suddenly my eyes were blurred—and not only with rain. I looked at the old face before me, and for a moment, I seemed to see a ghostly glimpse of another face, a small round face that looked up.

He was speaking again. I put my head down:

"Was I … good … boy … Dad?" Then the eyes closed.

I sat for a long time, looking at the still face. Then I folded the hands on the chest and stood.

"You were more than a good boy, Timmy," I said. "You were a good man."

9

My blue suit was soaking wet and splattered with mud, plus a few flecks of what Dunger had used for brains, but it still carried the gold eagles on the shoulders.

The attendant in the garage didn't look at my face. The eagles were enough for him. I stalked to a vast black Bentley—a '90 model, I guessed, from the conservative eighteen-inch tail fins—and jerked the door open. The gauge showed three-quarters full. I opened the glove compartment, rummaged, found nothing. But then it wouldn't be up front with the chauffeur …

I pulled open the back door. There was a crude black leather holster riveted against the smooth pale-gray leather, with the butt of a 4-mm showing. There was another one on the opposite door, and a power rifle slung from straps on the back of the driver's seat.

Whoever owned the Bentley was overcompensating his insecurity. I took a pistol, tossed it onto the front seat, and slid in beside it. The attendant gaped at me as I eased my left arm into my lap and twisted to close the door. I started up. There was a bad knock, but she ran all right. I flipped a switch and cold lances of light speared out into the rain.

At the last instant, the attendant started forward with his mouth open to say something, but I didn't wait to hear it. I gunned out into the night, swung into the graveled drive, and headed for the gate. Mallon had had it all his way so far, but maybe it still wasn't too late …

Two sentries, looking miserable in shiny black ponchos, stepped out of the guard hut at I pulled up. One peered in at me, then came to a sloppy position of attention and presented arms. I reached for the gas pedal and the second sentry called something. The first man looked startled, then swung the gun down to cover me. I eased a hand toward my pistol, brought it up fast, and fired through the glass. Then the Bentley was roaring off into the dark along the potholed road that led into town. I thought I heard a shot behind me, but I wasn't sure.

I took the river road south of town, pounding at reckless speed over the ruined blacktop, gaining on the lights of Mallon's horde paralleling me a mile to the north. A quarter mile from the perimeter fence, the Bentley broke a spring and skidded into a ditch.

I sat for a moment taking deep breaths to drive back the compulsive drowsiness that was sliding down over my eyes like a visor. My arm throbbed like a cauterized stump. I needed a few minutes' rest ...

A sound brought me awake like an old maid smelling cigar smoke in the bedroom: the rise and fall of heavy engines in convoy. Mallon was coming up at flank speed.

I got out of the car and headed off along the road at a trot, holding my broken arm with my good one to ease the jarring pain. My chances had been as slim as a gambler's wallet all along, but if Mallon beat me to the objective, they dropped to nothing.

The eastern sky had taken on a faint gray tinge, against which I could make out the silhouetted gateposts and the dead floodlights a hundred yards ahead.

The roar of engines was getting louder. There were other sounds, too: a few shouts, the chatter of a 9-mm, the *boom*! of something heavier, and once a long-drawn *whoosh*! of falling masonry. With his new toy, Mallon was dozing his way through the men and buildings that got in his way.

I reached the gate, picked my way over fallen wire mesh, then headed for the Primary Site.

I couldn't run now. The broken slabs tilted crazily, in no pattern. I slipped, stumbled, but kept my feet. Behind me, headlights threw shadows across the slabs. It wouldn't be long now before someone in Mallon's task force spotted me and opened up with the guns—

The whoop! *whoop!* WHOOP! of the guardian Bolo cut across the field.

Across the broken concrete I saw the two red eyes flash, sweeping my way. I looked toward the gate. A massed rank of vehicles stood in a battalion front just beyond the old perimeter fence, engines idling, ranged for a hundred yards on either side of a wide gap at the gate. I looked for the high silhouette of Mallon's Bolo, and saw it far off down the avenue, picked out in red, white, and green navigation lights, a jeweled dreadnaught. A glaring Cyclopean eye at the top darted a blue-white cone of light ahead, swept over the waiting escort, outlined me like a set-shifter caught onstage by the rising curtain.

The *whoop! whoop!* sounded again; the automated sentry Bolo was bearing down on me along the dancing lane of light.

I grabbed at the plastic disk in my pocket as though holding it in my hand would somehow heighten its potency. I didn't know if the Lesser Troll was programmed to exempt me from destruction or not; and there was only one way to find out.

It wasn't too late to turn around and run for it. Mallon might shoot—or he might not. I could convince him that he needed me, that together we could grab twice as much loot. And then, when he died—

I wasn't really considering it; it was the kind of thought that flashes through a man's mind like heat lightning when time slows in the instant of crisis. It was hard to be brave with broken bone ends grating, but what I had to do didn't take courage. I was a small, soft, human grub, stepped on but still moving, caught on the harsh plain of broken concrete between the clash of chrome-steel titans. But I knew which direction to take.

The Lesser Troll rushed toward me in a roll of thunder and I went to meet it.

It stopped twenty yards from me, loomed massive as a cliff. Its heavy guns were dead, I knew. Without them it was no more dangerous than a farmer with a shotgun—

But against me a shotgun was enough.

The slab under me trembled as if in anticipation. I squinted against the dull red I-R beams that pivoted to hold me, waiting while the Troll considered. Then the guns elevated, pointed over my head like a benediction. The Bolo knew me.

The guns traversed fractionally. I looked back toward the enemy line, saw the Great Troll coming up now, closing the gap, towering over its waiting escort like a planet among moons. And the guns of the Lesser Troll tracked it as it came—the empty guns that for twenty years had held Mallon's scavengers at bay.

The noise of engines was deafening now. The waiting line moved restlessly, pulverizing old concrete under churning treads. I didn't realize I was being fired on until I saw chips fly to my left and heard the howl of ricochets.

It was time to move. I scrambled for the Bolo, snorted at the stink of hot oil and ozone, found the rusted handholds, and pulled myself up—

Bullets spanged off metal above me. Someone was trying for me with a power rifle.

The broken arm hung at my side like a fence post nailed to my shoulder, but I wasn't aware of the pain now. The hatch stood open half an inch. I grabbed the lever, strained; it swung wide. No lights came up to meet me. With the port cracked, they'd burned out long ago. I dropped down inside, wriggled through the narrow crawl space into the cockpit. It was smaller than the Mark III—and it was occupied.

In the faint green light from the panel, the dead man crouched over the controls, one desiccated hand in a shriveled black glove clutching the control bar. He wore a GI weather suit and a white crash helmet, and one foot was twisted nearly backward, caught behind a jack lever.

The leg had been broken before he died. He must have jammed the foot and twisted it so that the pain would hold off the sleep that had come at last. I leaned forward to see the face. The blackened and mummified features showed only the familiar anonymity of death, but the bushy reddish mustache was enough.

"Hello, Mac," I said. "Sorry to keep you waiting; I got held up."

I wedged myself into the copilot's seat, flipped the I-R screen switch. The eight-inch panel glowed, showed me the enemy Bolo trampling through the fence three hundred yards away, then moving onto the ramp, dragging a length of rusty chain-link like a bridal train behind it.

I put my hand on the control bar. "I'll take it now, Mac." I moved the bar, and the dead man's hand moved with it.

"Okay, Mac," I said. "We'll do it together."

I hit the switches, canceling the preset response pattern. It had done its job for eighty years, but now it was time to crank in a little human strategy.

My Bolo rocked slightly under a hit and I heard the tread shields drop down. The chair bucked under me as Mallon moved in, pouring in the fire.

Beside me Mac nodded patiently. It was old stuff to him. I watched the tracers on the screen. Hosing me down with contact exploders probably gave Mallon a lot of satisfaction, but it couldn't hurt me. It would be a different story when he tired of the game and tried the heavy stuff.

I threw in the drive, backed rapidly. Mallon's tracers followed for a few yards, then cut off abruptly. I pivoted, flipped on my polyarcs, raced for the position I had selected across the field, then swung to face Mallon as he moved toward me. It had been a long time since he had handled the controls of a Bolo; he was rusty, relying on his automatics. I had no heavy rifles, but my popguns were okay. I homed my 4-mm solid-slug cannon on Mallon's polyarc, pressed the FIRE button.

There was a scream from the high-velocity-feed magazine. The blue-white light flared and went out. The Bolo's defense could handle anything short of an H-bomb, pick a missile out of the stratosphere fifty miles away, devastate a county with one round from its mortars—but my BB gun at point-blank range had poked out its eye.

I switched everything off and sat silent, waiting. Mallon had come to a dead stop. I could picture him staring at the dark screens, slapping levers, and cursing. He would be confused, wondering what had happened. With his lights gone, he'd be on radar now—not very sensitive at this range, not too conscious of detail …

I watched my panel. An amber warning light winked. Mallon's radar was locked on me.

He moved forward again, then stopped; he was having trouble making up his mind. I flipped a key to drop a padded shock frame in place and braced myself. Mallon would be getting mad now.

Crimson danger lights flared on the board and I rocked

under the recoil as my interceptors flashed out to meet Mallon's C-S C's and detonate them in incandescent rendezvous over the scarred concrete between us. My screens went white, then dropped back to secondary brilliance, flashing stark black-and-white. My ears hummed like trapped hornets.

The sudden silence was like a vault door closing.

I sagged back, feeling like Quasimodo after a wild ride on the bells. The screens blinked bright again, and I watched Mallon, sitting motionless now in his near blindness. On his radar screen I would show as a blurred hill; he would be wondering why I hadn't returned his fire, why I hadn't turned and run, why … why …

He lurched and started toward me. I waited, then eased back, slowly. He accelerated, closing in to come to grips at a range where even the split microsecond response of my defenses would be too slow to hold off his fire. And I backed, letting him gain, but not too fast …

Mallon couldn't wait.

He opened up, throwing a mixed bombardment from his 9-mm's, his infinite repeaters, and his C-S C's. I held on, fighting the battering frame, watching the screens. The gap closed; a hundred yards, ninety, eighty.

The open silo yawned in Mallon's path now, but he didn't see it. The mighty Bolo came on, guns bellowing in the night, closing for the kill. On the brink of the fifty-foot-wide, hundred-yard-deep pit, it hesitated as though sensing danger. Then it moved forward.

I saw it rock, dropping its titanic prow, showing its broad back, gouging the blasted pavement as its guns bore on the ground. Great sheets of sparks flew as the treads reversed, too late. The Bolo hung for a moment longer, then slid down majestically as a sinking liner, its guns still firing into the pit like a challenge to Hell. And then it was gone. A dust cloud boiled for a moment, then whipped away as displaced air tornadoed from the open mouth of the silo.

And the earth trembled under the impact far below.

10

The doors of the Primary Site blockhouse were nine-foot-high, eight-inch-thick panels of solid chromalloy that even a Bolo would have slowed down for, but they slid aside for my electropass like a shower curtain at the YW. I went into a shadowy room where eighty years of silence hung like black crepe on a coffin. The tiled floor was still immaculate, the air fresh. Here at the heart of the Aerospace Center, all systems were still go.

In the Central Control bunker, nine rows of green lights glowed on the high panel over red letters that spelled out STAND BY TO FIRE. A foot to the left, the big white lever stood in the unlocked position, six inches from the outstretched fingertips of the mummified corpse strapped into the controller's chair. To the right, a red glow on the monitor panel indicated the lock doors open.

I rode the lift down to K level, stepped out onto the steel-railed platform that hugged the sweep of the starship's hull and stepped through into the narrow COC.

On my right, three empty stasis tanks stood open, festooned cabling draped in disorder. To the left were the four sealed covers under which Day, Macy, Cruciani, and Black waited. I went close, read dials. Slender needles trembled minutely to the beating of sluggish hearts.

They were alive.

I left the ship, sealed the inner and outer ports. Back in the control bunker, the monitor panel showed ALL CLEAR FOR LAUNCH now. I studied the timer, set it, turned back to the master panel. The white lever was smooth and cool under my hand. It seated with a click. The red hand of the launch clock moved off jerkily, the ticking harsh in the silence.

Outside, the Bolo waited. I climbed to a perch in the open conning tower twenty feet above the broken pavement, moved off toward the west where sunrise colors picked out the high towers of the palace.

I rested the weight of my splinted and wrapped arm on the balcony rail, looking out across the valley and the town to the misty plain under which *Prometheus* waited.

"There's something happening now," Renada said. I took the binoculars, watched as the silo doors rolled back.

"There's smoke," Renada said.

"Don't worry, just cooling gases being vented off." I looked at my watch. "Another minute or two and man makes the biggest jump since the first lungfish crawled out on a mud flat."

"What will they find out there?"

I shook my head. "*Homo terra firma* can't even conceive of what *Homo astra* has ahead of him."

"Twenty years they'll be gone. It's a long time to wait."

"We'll be busy trying to put together a world for them to come back to. I don't think we'll be bored."

"Look!" Renada gripped my good arm. A long silvery shape, huge even at the distance of miles, rose slowly out of the earth, poised on a brilliant ball of white fire. Then the sound came, a thunder that penetrated my bones, shook the railing under my hand. The fireball lengthened into a silver-white column with the ship balanced at its tip. Then the column broke free, rose up, up …

I felt Renada's hand touch mine. I gripped it hard. Together we watched as *Prometheus* took man's gift of fire back to the heavens.

COURIER

"It is rather unusual," Magnan said, "to assign an officer of your rank to courier duty, but this is an unusual mission."

Retief sat relaxed and said nothing. Just before the silence grew awkward, Magnan went on.

"There are four planets in the group," he said. "Two double planets, all rather close to an unimportant star listed as DRI-G 33987. They're called Jorgensen's Worlds, and in themselves are of no importance whatever. However, they lie deep in the sector into which the Soetti have been penetrating.

"Now—" Magnan leaned forward and lowered his voice—"we have learned that the Soetti plan a bold step forward. Since they've met no opposition so far in their infiltration of Terrestrial space, they intend to seize Jorgensen's Worlds by force."

Magnan leaned back, waiting for Retief's reaction. Retief drew carefully on his cigar and looked at Magnan. Magnan frowned.

"This is open aggression, Retief," he said, "in case I haven't made myself clear. Aggression on Terrestrial-occupied territory by an alien species. Obviously, we can't allow it."

Magnan drew a large folder from his desk.

"A show of resistance at this point is necessary. Unfortunately, Jorgensen's Worlds are technologically undeveloped areas. They're farmers or traders. Their industry is limited to a minor role in their economy—enough to support the merchant fleet, no more. The war potential, by conventional standards, is nil."

Magnan tapped the folder before him.

"I have here," he said solemnly, "information which will change that picture completely." He leaned back and blinked at Retief.

"All right, Mr. Counselor," Retief said. "I'll play along; what's in the folder?"

Magnan spread his fingers, folded one down.

"First," he said. "The Soetti War Plan—in detail. We were fortunate enough to make contact with a defector from a party of renegade Terrestrials who've been advising the Soetti." He folded another finger. "Next, a battle plan for the Jorgensen's people, worked out by the Theory group." He wrestled a third finger down. "Lastly, an Utter Top Secret schematic for conversion of a standard antiacceleration field into a potent weapon—a development our systems people have been holding in reserve for just such a situation."

"Is that all?" Retief said. "You've still got two fingers sticking up."

Magnan looked at the fingers and put them away.

"This is no occasion for flippancy, Retief. In the wrong hands, this information could be catastrophic. You'll memorize it before you leave this building."

"I'll carry it, sealed," Retief said. "That way nobody can sweat it out of me."

Magnan started to shake his head.

"Well," he said. "If it's trapped for destruction, I suppose—"

"I've heard of these Jorgensen's Worlds," Retief said. "I remember an agent, a big blond fellow, very quick on the uptake. A wizard with cards and dice. Never played for money, though."

"Umm," Magnan said. "Don't make the error of personalizing this situation, Retief. Overall policy calls for a defense of these backwater worlds. Otherwise the Corps would allow history to follow its natural course, as always."

"When does this attack happen?"

"Less than four weeks."

"That doesn't leave me much time."

"I have your itinerary here. Your accommodations are clear as far as Aldo Cerise. You'll have to rely on your ingenuity to get you the rest of the way."

"That's a pretty rough trip, Mr. Counselor. Suppose I don't make it?"

Magnan looked sour. "Someone at a policy-making level has chosen to put all our eggs in one basket, Retief. I hope their confidence in you is not misplaced."

"This antiac conversion; how long does it take?"

"A skilled electronics crew can do the job in a matter of minutes. The Jorgensens can handle it very nicely; every other man is a mechanic of some sort."

Retief opened the envelope Magnan handed him and looked at the tickets inside.

"Less than four hours to departure time," he said. "I'd better not start any long books."

"You'd better waste no time getting over to Indoctrination," Magnan said.

Retief stood up. "If I hurry, maybe I can catch the cartoon."

"The allusion escapes me," Magnan said coldly. "And one last word. The Soetti are patrolling the trade lanes into Jorgensen's Worlds; don't get yourself interned."

"I'll tell you what," Retief said soberly. "In a pinch, I'll mention your name."

"You'll be traveling with Class X credentials," Magnan snapped. "There must be nothing to connect you with the Corps."

"They'll never guess," Retief said. "I'll pose as a gentleman."

"You'd better be getting started," Magnan said, shuffling papers.

"You're right," Retief said. "If I work at it, I might manage a snootful by takeoff." He went to the door. "No objection to my checking out a needler, is there?"

Magnan looked up. "I suppose not. What do you want with it?"

"Just a feeling I've got."

"Please yourself."

"Some day," Retief said, "I may take you up on that."

2

Retief put down the heavy travel-battered suitcase and leaned on the counter, studying the schedules chalked on the board under the legend "ALDO CERISE—INTERPLANETARY." A thin clerk in a faded sequined blouse and a plastic snakeskin cummerbund groomed his fingernails, watching Retief from the corner of his eye.

Retief glanced at him.

The clerk nipped off a ragged corner with rabbitlike front teeth and spat it on the floor.

"Was there something?" he said.

"Two twenty-eight, due out today for the Jorgensen group," Retief said. "Is it on schedule?"

The clerk sampled the inside of his right cheek, eyed Retief. "Filled up. Try again in a couple of weeks."

"What time does it leave?"

"I don't think—"

"Let's stick to facts," Retief said. "Don't try to think. What time is it due out?"

The clerk smiled pityingly. "It's my lunch hour," he said. "I'll be open in an hour." He held up a thumbnail, frowned at it.

"If I have to come around this counter," Retief said, "I'll feed that thumb to you the hard way."

The clerk looked up and opened his mouth. Then he caught Retief's eye, closed his mouth and swallowed.

"Like it says there," he said, jerking a thumb at the board. "Lifts in an hour. But you won't be on it," he added.

Retief looked at him.

"Some … ah … VIP's required accommodation," he said. He hooked a finger inside the sequined collar. "All tourist reservations were canceled. You'll have to try to get space on the Four-Planet Line ship next—"

"Which gate?" Retief said.

"For … ah …?"

"For two twenty-eight for Jorgensen's Worlds," Retief said.

"Well," the clerk said. "Gate nineteen," he added quickly. "But—"

Retief picked up his suitcase and walked away toward the glare sign reading *To Gates 16-30.*

"Another smart alec," the clerk said behind him.

Retief followed the signs, threaded his way through crowds, found a covered ramp with the number 228 posted over it. A heavy-shouldered man with a scarred jawline and small eyes was slouching there in a rumpled gray uniform. He put out a hand as Retief started past him.

"Lessee your boarding pass," he muttered.

Retief pulled a paper from an inside pocket, handed it over. The guard blinked at it.

"Whassat?"

"A gram confirming my space," Retief said. "Your boy on the counter says he's out to lunch."

The guard crumpled the gram, dropped it on the floor and lounged back against the handrail.

"On your way, bub," he said.

Retief put his suitcase carefully on the floor, took a step, and drove a right into the guard's midriff. He stepped aside as the man doubled and went to his knees.

"You were wide open, ugly. I couldn't resist. Tell your boss I sneaked past while you were resting your eyes." He picked up his bag, stepped over the man, and went up the gangway into the ship.

A cabin boy in stained whites came along the corridor.

"Which way to cabin fifty-seven, son?" Retief asked.

"Up there." The boy jerked his head and hurried on. Retief made his way along the narrow hall, found signs, followed them to cabin fifty-seven. The door was open. Inside, baggage was piled in the center of the floor. It was expensive looking baggage.

Retief put his bag down. He turned at a sound behind him. A tall, florid man with an expensive coat belted over a massive paunch stood in the open door, looking at Retief. Retief looked back. The florid man clamped his jaws together, turned to speak over his shoulder.

"Somebody in the cabin. Get 'em out." As he backed out of

the room he rolled a cold eye at Retief. A short, thick-necked man appeared.

"What are you doing in Mr. Tony's room?" he barked. "Never mind! Clear out of here, fellow! You're keeping Mr. Tony waiting."

"Too bad," Retief said. "Finders keepers."

"You nuts?" The thick-necked man stared at Retief. "I said it's Mr. Tony's room."

"I don't know Mr. Tony. He'll have to bull his way into other quarters."

"We'll see about you, mister." The man turned and went out. Retief sat on the bunk and lit a cigar. There was a sound of voices in the corridor. Two burly baggage-smashers appeared, straining at an oversized trunk. They maneuvered it through the door, lowered it, glanced at Retief and went out. The thick-necked man returned.

"All right, you. Out," he growled. "Or have I got to have you thrown out?"

Retief rose and clamped the cigar between his teeth. He gripped a handle of the brass-bound trunk in each hand, bent his knees and heaved the trunk up to chest level, then raised it overhead. He turned to the door.

"Catch," he said between clenched teeth. The trunk slammed against the far wall of the corridor and burst.

Retief turned to the baggage on the floor, tossed it into the hall. The face of the thick-necked man appeared cautiously around the door jamb.

"Mister, you must be—"

"If you'll excuse me," Retief said, "I want to catch a nap." He flipped the door shut, pulled off his shoes and stretched out on the bed.

*

Five minutes passed before the door rattled and burst open.

Retief looked up. A gaunt leathery-skinned man wearing white ducks, a blue turtleneck sweater, and a peaked cap tilted raffishly over one eye stared at Retief.

"Is this the joker?" he grated.

The thick-necked man edged past him, looked at Retief and snorted, "That's him, sure."

"I'm Captain of this vessel," the first man said. "You've got two minutes to haul your freight out of here, buster."

"When you can spare the time from your other duties," Retief said, "take a look at Section Three, Paragraph One, of the Uniform Code. That spells out the law on confirmed space on vessels engaged in interplanetary commerce."

"A space lawyer." The Captain turned. "Throw him out, boys."

Two big men edged into the cabin, looking at Retief.

"Go on, pitch him out," the Captain snapped.

Retief put his cigar in an ashtray, and swung his feet off the bunk.

"Don't try it," he said softly.

One of the two wiped his nose on a sleeve, spat on his right palm and stepped forward, then hesitated.

"Hey," he said. "This the guy tossed the trunk off the wall?"

"That's him," the thick-necked man called. "Spilled Mr. Tony's possessions right on the deck."

"Deal me out," the bouncer said. "He can stay put as long as he wants to. I signed on to move cargo. Let's go, Moe."

"You'd better be getting back to the bridge, Captain," Retief said. "We're due to lift in twenty minutes."

The thick-necked man and the Captain both shouted at once. The Captain's voice prevailed.

"—twenty minutes … uniform Code … gonna do?"

"Close the door as you leave," Retief said.

The thick-necked man paused at the door. "We'll see you when you come out."

3

Four waiters passed Retief's table without stopping. A fifth leaned against the wall nearby, a menu under his arm.

At a table across the room, the Captain, now wearing a dress uniform and with his thin red hair neatly parted, sat with a table of male passengers. He talked loudly and laughed frequently, casting occasional glances Retief's way.

A panel opened in the wall behind Retief's chair. Bright blue eyes peered out from under a white chef's cap.

"Givin' you the cold shoulder, heh, mister?"

"Looks like it, old timer," Retief said. "Maybe I'd better go join the skipper. His party seems to be having all the fun."

"Feller has to be mighty careless who he eats with to set over there."

"I see your point."

"You set right where you're at, mister. I'll rustle you up a plate."

Five minutes later, Retief cut into a thirty-two-ounce Delmonico backed up with mushrooms and garlic butter.

"I'm Chip," the chef said. "I don't like the Cap'n. You can tell him I said so. Don't like his friends, either. Don't like them dern Sweaties, look at a man like he was a worm."

"You've got the right idea on frying a steak, Chip. And you've got the right idea on the Soetti, too," Retief said. He poured red wine into a glass. "Here's to you."

"Dern right," Chip said. "Dunno whoever thought up

broiling 'em. Steaks, that is. I got a Baked Alaska coming up in here for dessert. You like brandy in yer coffee?"

"Chip, you're a genius."

"Like to see a feller eat," Chip said. "I gotta go now. If you need anything, holler."

Retief ate slowly. Time always dragged on shipboard. Four days to Jorgensen's Worlds. Then, if Magnan's information was correct, there would be four days to prepare for the Soetti attack. It was a temptation to scan the tapes built into the handle of his suitcase. It would be good to know what Jorgensen's Worlds would be up against.

Retief finished the steak, and the chef passed out the baked Alaska and coffee. Most of the other passengers had left the dining room. Mr. Tony and his retainers still sat at the Captain's table.

As Retief watched, four men arose from the table and sauntered across the room. The first in line, a stony-faced thug with a broken ear, took a cigar from his mouth as he reached the table. He dipped the lighted end in Retief's coffee, looked at it, and dropped it on the tablecloth.

The others came up, Mr. Tony trailing.

"You must want to get to Jorgensen's pretty bad," the thug said in a grating voice. "What's your game, hick?"

Retief looked at the coffee cup, picked it up.

"I don't think I want my coffee," he said. He looked at the thug. "You drink it."

The thug squinted at Retief. "A wise hick," he began.

With a flick of the wrist, Retief tossed the coffee into the thug's face, then stood and slammed a straight right to the chin. The thug went down.

Retief looked at Mr. Tony, still standing open-mouthed.

"You can take your playmates away now, Tony," he said.

"And don't bother to come around yourself. You're not funny enough."

Mr. Tony found his voice.

"Take him, Marbles!" he growled.

The thick-necked man slipped a hand inside his tunic and brought out a long-bladed knife. He licked his lips and moved in.

Retief heard the panel open beside him.

"Here you go, Mister," Chip said. Retief darted a glance; a well-honed french knife lay on the sill.

"Thanks, Chip," Retief said. "I won't need it for these punks."

Thick-neck lunged and Retief hit him square in the face, knocking him under the table. The other man stepped back, fumbling a power pistol from his shoulder holster.

"Aim that at me and I'll kill you," Retief said.

"Go on, burn him!" Mr. Tony shouted. Behind him, the Captain appeared, white-faced.

"Put that away, you!" he yelled. "What kind of—"

"Shut up," Mr. Tony said. "Put it away, Hoany. We'll fix this bum later."

"Not on this vessel, you won't," the Captain said shakily. "I got my charter to consider."

"Ram your charter," Hoany said harshly. "You won't be needing it long."

"Button your floppy mouth, damn you!" Mr. Tony snapped. He looked at the man on the floor. "Get Marbles out of here. I ought to dump the slob."

He turned and walked away. The Captain signaled and two waiters came up. Retief watched as they carted the casualty from the dining room.

The panel opened.

"I usta be about your size, when I was your age," Chip said. "You handled them pansies right. I wouldn't give 'em the time o' day."

"How about a fresh cup of coffee, Chip?" Retief said.

"Sure, mister. Anything else?"

"I'll think of something," Retief said. "This is shaping up into one of those long days."

"They don't like me bringing yer meals to you in yer cabin," Chip said. "But the Cap'n knows I'm the best cook in the Merchant Service. They won't mess with me."

"What has Mr. Tony got on the Captain, Chip?" Retief asked.

"They're in some kind o' crooked business together. You want some more smoked turkey?"

"Sure. What have they got against my going to Jorgensen's Worlds?"

"Dunno. Hasn't been no tourists got in there fer six or eight months. I sure like a feller that can put it away. I was a big eater when I was yer age."

"I'll bet you can still handle it, old timer. What are Jorgensen's Worlds like?"

"One of'em's cold as hell and three of'em's colder. Most o' the Jorgies live on Svea; that's the least froze up. Man don't enjoy eatin' his own cookin' like he does somebody else's."

"That's where I'm lucky, Chip. What kind of cargo's the Captain got aboard for Jorgensen's?"

"Derned if I know. In and out o' there like a grasshopper, ever few weeks. Don't never pick up no cargo. No tourists any more, like I says. Don't know what we even run in there for."

"Where are the passengers we have aboard headed?"

"To Alabaster. That's nine days' run in-sector from

Jorgensen's. You ain't got another one of them cigars, have you?"

"Have one, Chip. I guess I was lucky to get space on this ship."

"Plenty o' space, mister. We got a dozen empty cabins." Chip puffed the cigar alight, then cleared away the dishes, poured out coffee and brandy.

"Them Sweaties is what I don't like," he said.

Retief looked at him questioningly.

"You never seen a Sweaty? Ugly lookin' devils. Skinny legs, like a lobster; big chest, shaped like the top of a turnip; rubbery lookin' head. You can see the pulse beatin' when they get riled."

"I've never had the pleasure," Retief said.

"You prob'ly have it perty soon. Them devils board us nigh every trip out. Act like they was the Customs Patrol or somethin'."

There was a distant clang, and a faint tremor ran through the floor.

"I ain't superstitious ner nothin'," Chip said. "But I'll be triple-damned if that ain't them boarding us now."

Ten minutes passed before bootsteps sounded outside the door, accompanied by a clicking patter. The doorknob rattled, then a heavy knock shook the door.

"They got to look you over," Chip whispered. "Nosy damn Sweaties."

"Unlock it, Chip." The chef opened the door.

"Come in, damn you," he said.

A tall and grotesque creature minced into the room, tiny hooflike feet tapping on the floor. A flaring metal helmet shaded the deep-set compound eyes, and a loose mantle flapped around the knobbed knees. Behind the alien, the Captain hovered nervously.

"Yo' papiss," the alien rasped.

"Who's your friend, Captain?" Retief said.

"Never mind; just do like he tells you."

"Yo' papiss," the alien said again.

"Okay," Retief said. "I've seen it. You can take it away now."

"Don't horse around," the Captain said. "This fellow can get mean."

The alien brought two tiny arms out from the concealment of the mantle, clicked toothed pincers under Retief's nose.

"Quick, soft one."

"Captain, tell your friend to keep its distance. It looks brittle, and I'm tempted to test it."

"Don't start anything with Skaw; he can clip through steel with those snappers."

"Last chance," Retief said. Skaw stood poised, open pinchers an inch from Retief's eyes.

"Show him your papers, you damned fool," the Captain said hoarsely. "I got no control over Skaw."

The alien clicked both pincers with a sharp report, and in the same instant Retief half-turned to the left, leaned away from the alien and drove his right foot against the slender leg above the bulbous knee-joint. Skaw screeched and floundered, greenish fluid spattering from the burst joint.

"I told you he was brittle," Retief said. "Next time you invite pirates aboard, don't bother to call."

"Jesus, what did you do! They'll kill us!" the Captain gasped, staring at the figure flopping on the floor.

"Cart poor old Skaw back to his boat," Retief said. "Tell him to pass the word. No more illegal entry and search of Terrestrial vessels in Terrestrial space."

"Hey," Chip said. "He's quit kicking."

The Captain bent over Skaw, gingerly rolled him over. He leaned close and sniffed.

"He's dead." The Captain stared at Retief. "We're all dead men," he said. "These Soetti got no mercy."

"They won't need it. Tell 'em to sheer off; their fun is over."

"They got no more emotions than a blue crab—"

"You bluff easily, Captain. Show a few guns as you hand the body back. We know their secret now."

"What secret? I—"

"Don't be no dumber than you got to, Cap'n," Chip said. "Sweaties die easy; that's the secret."

"Maybe you got a point," the Captain said, looking at Retief. "All they got's a three-man scout. It could work."

He went out, came back with two crewmen. They hauled the dead alien gingerly into the hall.

"Maybe I can run a bluff on the Soetti," the Captain said, looking back from the door. "But I'll be back to see you later."

"You don't scare us, Cap'n," Chip said. "Him and Mr. Tony and all his goons. You hit 'em where they live, that time. They're pals o' these Sweaties. Runnin' some kind o' crooked racket."

"You'd better take the Captain's advice, Chip. There's no point in your getting involved in my problems."

"They'd of killed you before now, mister, if they had any guts. That's where we got it over these monkeys. They got no guts."

"They act scared, Chip. Scared men are killers."

"They don't scare me none." Chip picked up the tray. "I'll scout around a little and see what's goin' on. If the Sweaties figure to do anything about that Skaw feller they'll have to move fast; they won't try nothin' close to port."

"Don't worry, Chip. I have reason to be pretty sure they won't do anything to attract a lot of attention in this sector just now."

Chip looked at Retief. "You ain't no tourist, mister. I know that much. You didn't come out here for fun, did you?"

"That," Retief said, "would be a hard one to answer."

4

Retief awoke at a tap on his door.

"It's me, mister. Chip."

"Come on in."

The chef entered the room, locking the door.

"You shoulda had that door locked." He stood by the door, listening, then turned to Retief.

"You want to get to Jorgensen's perty bad, don't you, mister?"

"That's right, Chip."

"Mr. Tony gave the Captain a real hard time about old Skaw. The Sweaties didn't say nothin'. Didn't even act surprised, just took the remains and pushed off. But Mr. Tony and that other crook they call Marbles, they was fit to be tied. Took the Cap'n in his cabin and talked loud at him fer half a hour. Then the Cap'n come out and give some orders to the mate."

Retief sat up and reached for a cigar.

"Mr. Tony and Skaw were pals, eh?"

"He hated Skaw's guts. But with him it was business. Mister, you got a gun?"

"A two-mm needler. Why?"

"The orders Cap'n give was to change course fer Alabaster. We're bypassin' Jorgensen's Worlds. We'll feel the course change any minute."

Retief lit the cigar, reached under the mattress and took out a short-barreled pistol. He dropped it in his pocket, looked at Chip.

"Maybe it was a good thought, at that. Which way to the Captain's cabin?"

"This is it," Chip said softly. "You want me to keep an eye on who comes down the passage?"

Retief nodded, opened the door and stepped into the cabin. The Captain looked up from his desk, then jumped up.

"What do you think you're doing, busting in here?"

"I hear you're planning a course change, Captain."

"You've got damn big ears."

"I think we'd better call in at Jorgensen's."

"You do, huh?" The Captain sat down. "I'm in command of this vessel," he said. "I'm changing course for Alabaster."

"I wouldn't find it convenient to go to Alabaster," Retief said. "So just hold your course for Jorgensen's."

"Not bloody likely."

"Your use of the word 'bloody' is interesting, Captain. Don't try to change course."

The Captain reached for the mike on his desk, pressed the key.

"Power Section, this is the Captain," he said. Retief reached across the desk, gripped the Captain's wrist.

"Tell the mate to hold his present course," he said softly.

"Let go my hand, buster," the Captain snarled. Eyes on Retief's, he eased a drawer open with his left hand, reached in. Retief kneed the drawer. The Captain yelped and dropped the mike.

"You busted it, you—"

"And one to go," Retief said. "Tell him."

"I'm an officer of the Merchant Service!"

"You're a cheapjack who's sold his bridge to a pack of back-alley hoods."

"You can't put it over, hick."

"Tell him."

The Captain groaned and picked up the mike. "Captain to Power Section," he said. "Hold your present course until you hear from me." He dropped the mike and looked up at Retief.

"It's eighteen hours yet before we pick up Jorgensen Control. You going to sit here and bend my arm the whole time?"

Retief released the Captain's wrist and turned to the door.

"Chip, I'm locking the door. You circulate around, let me know what's going on. Bring me a pot of coffee every so often. I'm sitting up with a sick friend."

"Right, Mister. Keep an eye on that jasper; he's slippery."

"What are you going to do?" the Captain demanded.

Retief settled himself in a chair.

"Instead of strangling you, as you deserve," he said, "I'm going to stay here and help you hold your course for Jorgensen's Worlds."

The Captain looked at Retief. He laughed, a short bark.

"Then I'll just stretch out and have a little nap, farmer. If you feel like dozing off sometime during the next eighteen hours, don't mind me."

Retief took out the needler and put it on the desk before him.

"If anything happens that I don't like," he said, "I'll wake you up. With this."

"Why don't you let me spell you, Mister?" Chip said. "Four hours to go yet. You're gonna hafta be on yer toes to handle the landing."

"I'll be all right, Chip. You get some sleep."

"Nope. Many's the time I stood four, five watches runnin', back when I was yer age. I'll make another round."

Retief stood up, stretched his legs, paced the floor, stared at the repeater instruments on the wall. Things had gone quietly so far, but the landing would be another matter. The Captain's absence from the bridge during the highly complex maneuvering would be difficult to explain …

The desk speaker crackled.

"Captain, Officer of the Watch here. Ain't it about time you was getting up here with the orbit figures?"

Retief nudged the Captain. He awoke with a start, sat up.

"Whazzat?" He looked wild-eyed at Retief.

"Watch Officer wants orbit figures," Retief said, nodding toward the speaker.

The Captain rubbed his eyes, shook his head, picked up the mike. Retief released the safety on the needler with an audible click.

"Watch Officer, I'll … ah … get some figures for you right away. I'm … ah … busy right now."

"What the hell you talking about, busy?" the speaker blared. "You ain't got them figures ready, you'll have a hell of a hot time getting 'em up in the next three minutes. You forgot your approach pattern or something?"

"I guess I overlooked it," the Captain said, looking sideways at Retief. "I've been busy."

"One for your side," Retief said. He reached for the Captain.

"I'll make a deal," the Captain squalled. "Your life for—"

Retief took aim and slammed a hard right to the Captain's jaw. He slumped to the floor.

Retief glanced around the room, yanked wires loose from a motile lamp, trussed the man's hands and feet, stuffed his mouth with paper and taped it.

Chip tapped at the door. Retief opened it and the chef stepped inside, looking at the man on the floor.

"The jasper tried somethin', huh? Figured he would. What we goin' to do now?"

"The Captain forgot to set up an approach, Chip. He outfoxed me."

"If we overrun our approach pattern," Chip said, "we can't make orbit at Jorgensen's on automatic. And a manual approach—"

"That's out. But there's another possibility."

Chip blinked. "Only one thing you could mean, mister. But cuttin' out in a lifeboat in deep space is no picnic."

"They're on the port side, aft, right?"

Chip nodded. "Hot damn," he said. "Who's got the 'tater salad?"

"We'd better tuck the skipper away out of sight."

"In the locker."

The two men carried the limp body to a deep storage chest, dumped it in, closed the lid.

"He won't suffercate. Lid's a lousy fit:"

Retief opened the door went into the corridor, Chip behind him.

"Shouldn't oughta be nobody around now," the chef said. "Everybody's mannin' approach stations."

At the D deck companionway, Retief stopped suddenly.

"Listen."

Chip cocked his head. "I don't hear nothin'," he whispered.

"Sounds like a sentry posted on the lifeboat deck," Retief said softly.

"Let's take him, mister."

"I'll go down. Stand by, Chip."

Retief started down the narrow steps, half stair, half ladder. Halfway, he paused to listen. There was a sound of slow footsteps, then silence. Retief palmed the needler, went down the last steps quickly, emerged in the dim light of a low-ceilinged room. The stern of a five-man lifeboat bulked before him.

"Freeze, you!" a cold voice snapped.

Retief dropped, rolled behind the shelter of the lifeboat as the whine of a power pistol echoed off metal walls. A lunge, and he was under the boat, on his feet. He jumped, caught the quick-access handle, hauled it down. The outer port cycled open.

Feet scrambled at the bow of the boat. Retief whirled and fired. The guard rounded into sight and fell headlong. Above, an alarm bell jangled. Retief stepped on a stanchion, hauled himself into the open port. A yell rang, then the clatter of feet on the stair.

"Don't shoot, mister!" Chip shouted.

"All clear, Chip," Retief called.

"Hang on. I'm comin' with ya!"

Retief reached down, lifted the chef bodily through the port, slammed the lever home. The outer door whooshed, clanged shut.

"Take number two, tie in! I'll blast her off," Chip said. "Been through a hundred 'bandon-ship drills ..."

Retief watched as the chef flipped levers, pressed a fat red button. The deck trembled under the lifeboat.

"Blew the bay doors," Chip said, smiling happily. "That'll cool them jaspers down." He punched a green button.

"Look out, Jorgensen's!" With an ear-splitting blast, the stern rockets fired, a sustained agony of pressure ...

Abruptly, there was silence. Weightlessness. Contracting metal pinged loudly. Chip's breathing rasped in the stillness.

"Pulled nine G's there for ten seconds," he gasped. "I gave her full emergency kickoff."

"Any armament aboard our late host?"

"A popgun. Time they get their wind, we'll be clear. Now all we got to do is set tight till we pick up a R-and-D from Svea Tower. Maybe four, five hours."

"Chip, you're a wonder," Retief said. "This looks like a good time to catch that nap."

"Me too," Chip said. "Mighty peaceful here, ain't it?"

There was a moment's silence.

"Durn!" Chip said softly.

Retief opened one eye. "Sorry you came, Chip?"

"Left my best carvin' knife jammed up 'tween Marbles' ribs," the chef said. "Comes o' doin' things in a hurry."

5

The blonde girl brushed her hair from her eyes and smiled at Retief.

"I'm the only one on duty," she said. "I'm Anne-Marie."

"It's important that I talk to someone in your government, miss," Retief said.

The girl looked at Retief. "The men you want to see are Tove and Bo Bergman. They will be at the lodge by nightfall."

"Then it looks like we go to the lodge," Retief said. "Lead on, Anne-Marie."

"What about the boat?" Chip asked.

"I'll send someone to see to it tomorrow," the girl said.

"You're some gal," Chip said admiringly. "Dern near six feet, ain't ye? And built, too, what I mean."

They stepped out of the door into a whipping wind.

"Let's go across to the equipment shed and get parkas for

you," Anne-Marie said. "It will be cold on the slopes."

"Yeah," Chip said, shivering. "I've heard you folks don't believe in ridin' every time you want to go a few miles uphill in a blizzard."

"It will make us hungry," Anne-Marie said. "Then Chip will cook a wonderful meal for us all."

Chip blinked. "Been cookin' too long," he muttered. "Didn't know it showed on me that way."

Behind the sheds across the wind-scoured ramp abrupt peaks rose, snow-blanketed. A faint trail led across white slopes, disappearing into low clouds.

"The lodge is above the cloud layer," Anne-Marie said. "Up there the sky is always clear."

It was three hours later, and the sun was burning the peaks red, when Anne-Marie stopped, pulled off her woolen cap, and waved at the vista below.

"There you see it," she said. "Our valley."

"It's a mighty perty sight," Chip gasped. "Anything this tough to get a look at ought to be."

Anne-Marie pointed. "There," she said. "The little red house by itself. Do you see it, Retief? It is my father's homeacre."

Retief looked across the valley. Gaily painted houses nestled together, a puddle of color in the bowl of the valley.

"I think you've led a good life there," he said.

Anne-Marie smiled brilliantly. "And this day, too, is good."

Retief smiled back. "Yes," he said. "This day is good."

"It'll be a durn sight better when I got my feet up to that big fire you was talking about, Annie," Chip said.

They climbed on, crossed a shoulder of broken rock, reached the final slope. Above, the lodge sprawled, a long low structure of heavy logs, outlined against the deep-blue twilight sky. Smoke billowed from stone chimneys at either end, and yellow light gleamed from the narrow windows, reflected on the snow. Men and women stood in groups of three or four, skis over their shoulders. Their voices and laughter rang in the icy air.

Anne-Marie whistled shrilly. Someone waved.

"Come," she said. "Meet all my friends."

A man separated himself from the group, walked down the slope to meet them.

"Anne-Marie," he called. "Welcome. It was a long day without you." He came up to them, hugged Anne-Marie, smiled at Retief.

"Welcome," he said. "Come inside and be warm."

They crossed the trampled snow to the lodge and pushed through a heavy door into a vast low-beamed hall, crowded with people, talking, singing, some sitting at long plank tables, others ringed around an eight-foot fireplace at the far side of the room. Anne-Marie led the way to a bench near the fire. She made introductions and found a stool to prop Chip's feet near the blaze.

Chip looked around.

"I never seen so many perty gals before," he said delightedly.

"Poor Chip," one girl said. "His feet are cold." She knelt to pull off his boots. "Let me rub them," she said.

A brunette with blue eyes raked a chestnut from the fire, cracked it, and offered it to Retief. A tall man with arms like oak roots passed heavy beer tankards to the two guests.

"Tell us about the places you've seen," someone called. Chip emerged from a long pull at the mug, heaving a sigh.

"Well," he said. "I tell you I been in some places …"

Music started up, rising above the clamor.

"Come, Retief," Anne-Marie said. "Dance with me."

Retief looked at her. "My thought exactly," he said.

*

Chip put down his mug and sighed. "Derned if I ever felt right at home so quick before," he said. "Just seems like these folks know all about me." He scratched behind his right ear. "Annie must o' called 'em up and told 'em our names an' all." He lowered his voice.

"They's some kind o' trouble in the air, though. Some o' the remarks they passed sounds like they're lookin' to have some trouble with the Sweaties. Don't seen to worry 'em none, though."

"Chip," Retief said, "how much do these people know about the Soetti?"

"Dunno," Chip said. "We useta touch down here, regler. But I always jist set in my galley and worked on ship models or somethin'. I hear the Sweaties been nosin' around here some, though."

Two girls came up to Chip. "Hey, I gotta go now, mister," he said. "These gals got a idea I oughta take a hand in the kitchen."

"Smart girls," Retief said. He turned as Anne-Marie came up.

"Bo Bergman and Tove are not back yet," she said. "They stayed to ski after moonrise."

"That moon is something," Retief said. "Almost like daylight."

"They will come soon, now. Shall we go out to see the moonlight on the snow?"

Outside, long black shadows fell like ink on silver. The top of the cloud layer below glared white under the immense moon.

"Our sister world, Gota," Anne-Marie said. "Nearly as big as Svea. I would like to visit it someday, although they say it's all stone and ice."

"Anne-Marie," Retief said, "how many people live on Jorgensen's Worlds?"

"About fifteen million, most of us here on Svea. There are mining camps and ice-fisheries on Gota. No one lives on Vasa and Skone, but there are always a few hunters there."

"Have you ever fought a war?"

Anne-Marie turned to look at Retief.

"You are afraid for us, Retief," she said. "The Soetti will attack our worlds, and we will fight them. We have fought before. These planets were not friendly ones."

"I thought the Soetti attack would be a surprise to you," Retief said. "Have you made any preparation for it?"

"We have ten thousand merchant ships. When the enemy comes, we will meet them."

Retief frowned. "Are there any guns on this planet? Any missiles?"

Anne-Marie shook her head. "Bo Bergman and Tove have a plan of deployment—"

"Deployment, hell! Against a modern assault force you need modern armament."

"Look!" Anne-Marie touched Retief's arm. "They're coming now."

Two tall grizzled men came up the slope, skis over their shoulders. Anne-Marie went forward to meet them, Retief at her side.

The two came up, embraced the girl, shook hands with Retief, put down their skis.

"Welcome to Svea," Tove said. "Let's find a warm corner where we can talk."

Retief shook his head, smiling, as a tall girl with coppery hair offered a vast slab of venison.

"I've caught up," he said, "for every hungry day I ever lived."

Bo Bergman poured Retief's beer mug full.

"Our captains are the best in space," he said. "Our population is concentrated in half a hundred small cities all across the planet. We know where the Soetti must strike us. We will ram their major vessels with unmanned ships. On the ground, we will hunt them down with small-arms."

"An assembly line turning out penetration missiles would have been more to the point."

"Yes," Bo Bergman said. "If we had known."

"How long have you known the Soetti were planning to hit you?"

Tove raised his eyebrows.

"Since this afternoon," he said.

"How did you find out about it? That information is supposed in some quarters to be a well-guarded secret."

"Secret?" Tove said.

Chip pulled at Retief's arm.

"Mister," he said in Retief's ear. "Come here a minute."

Retief looked at Anne-Marie, across at Tove and Bo Bergman. He rubbed the side of his face with his hand.

"Excuse me," he said. He followed Chip to one side of the room.

"Listen!" Chip said. "Maybe I'm goin' bats, but I'll swear there's somethin' funny here. I'm back there mixin' a sauce knowed only to me and the devil and I be dog if them gals don't pass me every dang spice I need, without me sayin' a word. Come to put my soufflé in the oven—she's already set, right on the button at 350. An' just now I'm settin' lookin' at one of 'em bendin' over a tub o' apples—snazzy little brunette name of Leila—derned if she don't turn around and say—"

Chip gulped. "Never mind. Point is …" His voice nearly faltered. "It's almost like these folks was readin' my mind!"

Retief patted Chip on the shoulder.

"Don't worry about your sanity, old timer," he said. "That's exactly what they're doing."

6

"We've never tried to make a secret of it," Tove said. "But we haven't advertised it, either."

"It really isn't much," Bo Bergman said. "Not a mutant ability, our scholars say. Rather, it's a skill we've stumbled on, a closer empathy. We are few, and far from the old home world. We've had to learn to break down the walls we had built around our minds."

"Can you read the Soetti?" Retief asked.

Tove shook his head. "They're very different from us. It's painful to touch their minds. We can only sense the subvocalized thoughts of a human mind."

"We've seen very few of the Soetti," Bo Bergman said. "Their ships have landed and taken on stores. They say little to us, but we've felt their contempt. They envy us our worlds. They come from a cold land."

"Anne-Marie says you have a plan of defense," Retief said. "A sort of suicide squadron idea, followed by guerilla warfare."

"It's the best we can devise, Retief. If there aren't too many of them, it might work."

Retief shook his head. "It might delay matters—but not much."

"Perhaps. But our remote control equipment is excellent. And we have plenty of ships, albeit unarmed. And our people know how to live on the slopes—and how to shoot."

"There are too many of them, Tove," Retief said. "They breed like flies and, according to some sources, they mature in a matter of months. They've been feeling their way into the sector for years now. Set up outposts on a thousand or so minor planets—cold ones, the kind they like. They want your worlds because they need living space."

"At least, your warning makes it possible for us to muster some show of force, Retief," Bo Bergman said. "That is better than death by ambush."

"Retief must not be trapped here," Anne-Marie said. "His small boat is useless now. He must have a ship."

"Of course," Tove said. "And—"

"My mission here—" Retief said.

"Retief," a voice called. "A message for you. The operator has phoned up a gram."

Retief unfolded the slip of paper. It was short, in verbal code, and signed by Magnan.

"You are recalled herewith," he read. "Assignment canceled. Agreement concluded with Soetti relinquishing all claims so-called Jorgensen system. Utmost importance that under no repeat no circumstances classified intelligence regarding Soetti be divulged to locals. Advise you depart instanter. Soetti occupation imminent."

Retief looked thoughtfully at the scrap of paper, then crumpled it and dropped it on the floor. He turned to Bo Bergman, took a tiny reel of tape from his pocket.

"This contains information," he said. "The Soetti attack plan, a defensive plan, instructions for the conversion of a standard antiacceleration unit into a potent weapon. If you have a screen handy, we'd better get started. We have about seventy-two hours."

*

In the Briefing Room at Svea Tower, Tove snapped off the projector.

"Our plan would have been worthless against that," he said. "We assumed they'd make their strike from a standard in-line formation. This scheme of hitting all our settlements simultaneously, in a random order from all points—we'd have been helpless."

"It's perfect for this defensive plan," Bo Bergman said. "Assuming this antiac trick works."

"It works," Retief said. "I hope you've got plenty of heavy power lead available."

"We export copper," Tove said.

"We'll assign about two hundred vessels to each settlement. Linked up, they should throw up quite a field."

"It ought to be effective up to about fifteen miles, I'd estimate," Tove said. "If it works as it's supposed to."

A red light flashed on the communications panel. Tove went to it, flipped a key.

"Tower, Tove here," he said.

"I've got a ship on the scope, Tove," a voice said. "There's nothing scheduled. ACI 228 bypassed at 1600 …"

"Just one?"

"A lone ship, coming in on a bearing of 291/456/653. On manual, I'd say."

"How does this track key in with the idea of ACI 228 making a manual correction for a missed automatic approach?" Retief asked.

Tove talked to the tower, got a reply.

"That's it," he said.

"How long before he touches down?"

Tove glanced at the lighted chart. "Perhaps eight minutes."

"Any guns here?"

Tove shook his head.

"If that's old two-twenty-eight, she ain't got but the one fifty-mm rifle," Chip said. "She cain't figure on jumpin' the whole planet."

"Hard to say what she figures on," Retief said. "Mr. Tony will be in a mood for drastic measures."

"I wonder what kind o' deal the skunks got with the Sweaties." Chip said. "Prob'ly he gits to scavenge, after the Sweaties kill off the Jorgensens."

"He's upset about our leaving him without saying good-bye, Chip," Retief said. "And you left the door hanging open, too."

Chip cackled. "Old Mr. Tony didn't look so good to the Sweaties now, hey, mister?"

Retief turned to Bo Bergman.

"Chip's right," he said. "A Soetti died on the ship, and a tourist got through the cordon. Tony's out to redeem himself."

"He's on final now," the tower operator said. "Still no contact."

"We'll know soon enough what he has in mind," Tove said.

"Let's take a look."

Outside, the four men watched the point of fire grow, evolve into a ship ponderously settling to rest. The drive faded and cut; silence fell.

Inside the Briefing Room, the speaker called out. Bo Bergman went inside, talked to the tower, motioned to the others.

"—over to you," the speaker was saying. There was a crackling moment of silence; then another voice.

"—illegal entry. Send the two of them out. I'll see to it they're dealt with."

Tove flipped a key. "Switch me direct to the ship," he said.

"Right."

"You on ACI two-twenty-eight," Tove said. "Who are you?"

"What's that to you?"

"You weren't cleared to berth here. Do you have an emergency aboard?"

"Never mind that, you," the speaker rumbled. "I tracked the bird in. I got the lifeboat on the screen now. They haven't gone far in nine hours. Let's have 'em."

"You're wasting your time," Tove said.

There was a momentary silence.

"You think so, hah?" the speaker blared. "I'll put it to you straight. I see two guys on their way out in one minute, or I open up."

"He's bluffin'," Chip said. "The popgun won't bear on us."

"Take a look out the window," Retief said.

In the white glare of the moonlight, a loading cover swung open at the stern of the ship, dropped down and formed a sloping ramp. A squat and massive shape appeared in the opening, trundled down onto the snow-swept tarmac.

Chip whistled. "I told you the Captain was slippery," he muttered. "Where the devil'd he git that at?"

"What is it?" Tove asked.

"A tank," Retief said. "A museum piece, by the look of it."

"I'll say," Chip said. "That's a Bolo *Resartus*, Model M. Built mebbe two hunderd years ago in Concordiat times. Packs a wallop, too, I'll tell ye."

The tank wheeled, brought a gun muzzle to bear in the base of the tower.

"Send 'em out," the speaker growled. "Or I blast 'em out."

"One round in here, and I've had a wasted trip," Retief said. "I'd better go out."

"Wait a minute, mister," Chip said, "I got the glimmerin's of an idear."

“I’ll stall them,” Tove said. He keyed the mike.

“ACI two-twenty-eight, what’s your authority for this demand?”

“I know that machine,” Chip said. “My hobby, old-time fightin’ machines. Built a model of a *Resartus* once, inch to the foot. A beauty. Now, lessee …”

7

The icy wind blew snow crystals stingingly against Retief’s face.

“Keep your hands in your pockets, Chip,” he said. “Numb hands won’t hack the program.”

“Yeah.” Chip looked across at the tank. “Useta think that was a perty thing, that *Resartus*,” he said. “Looks mean, now.”

“You’re getting the target’s-eye view,” Retief said. “Sorry you had to get mixed up in this, old timer.”

“Mixed myself in. Durn good thing, too.” Chip sighed. “I like these folks,” he said. “Them boys didn’t like lettin’ us come out here, but I’ll give ’em credit. They seen it had to be this way, and they didn’t set to moanin’ about it.”

“They’re tough people, Chip.”

“Funny how it sneaks up on you, ain’t it, mister? Few minutes ago we was eatin’ high on the hog. Now we’re right close to bein’ dead men.”

“They want us alive, Chip.”

“It’ll be a hairy deal, mister,” Chip said. “But t’hell with it. If it works, if works.”

“That’s the spirit.”

“I hope I got them fields o’ fire right—”

“Don’t worry. I’ll bet a barrel of beer we make it.”

“We’ll find out in about ten seconds,” Chip said.

As they reached the tank, the two men broke stride and jumped. Retief leaped for the gun barrel, swung up astride it, ripped off the fur-lined leather cap he wore and, leaning forward, jammed it into the bore of the cannon. The chef sprang for a perch above the fore scanner antenna. With an angry *whuff!* antipersonnel charges slammed from apertures low on the sides of the vehicle. Retief swung around, pulled himself up on the hull.

"Okay, mister," Chip called. "I'm going under." He slipped down the front of the tank, disappeared between the treads. Retief clambered up, took a position behind the turret, lay flat as it whirled angrily, sonar eyes searching for its tormentors. The vehicle shuddered, backed, stopped, moved forward, pivoted.

Chip reappeared at the front of the tank.

"It's stuck," he called. He stopped to breathe hard, clung as the machine lurched forward, spun to the right, stopped, rocking slightly.

"Take over here," Retief said. He crawled forward, watched as the chef pulled himself up, slipped down past him, feeling for the footholds between the treads. He reached the ground, dropped on his back, hitched himself under the dark belly of the tank. He groped, found the handholds, probed with a foot for the tread-jack lever.

The tank rumbled, backed quickly, turned left and right in a dizzying sine curve. Retief clung grimly, inches from the clashing treads.

The machine ground to a halt. Retief found the lever, braced his back, pushed. The lever seemed to give minutely. He set himself again, put both feet against the frozen bar and heaved.

With a dry rasp, it slid back. Immediately two heavy rods extended themselves, moved down to touch the pavement, grated. The left track creaked as the weight went off it. Suddenly the tank's drive raced, and Retief grabbed for a hold as the right tread clashed, heaved the fifty-ton machine forward. The jacks screeched as they scored the tarmac, then bit in. The tank pivoted, chips of pavement flying. The jacks extended, lifted the clattering left track clear of the surface as the tank spun like a hamstrung buffalo.

The tank stopped, sat silent, canted now on the extended jacks. Retief emerged from under the machine, jumped, pulled himself above the antipersonnel apertures as another charge rocked the tank. He clambered to the turret, crouched beside Chip. They waited, watching the entry hatch.

Five minutes passes.

"I'll bet old Tony's givin' the chauffeur hell," Chip said.

The hatch cycled open. A head came cautiously into view in time to see the needler in Retief's hand.

"Come on out," Retief said.

The head dropped. Chip snaked forward to ram a short section of steel rod under the hatch near the hinge. The hatch began to cycle shut, groaned, stopped. There was a sound of metal failing, as the hatch popped open.

Retief half rose, aimed the needler. The walls of the tank rang as the metal splinters ricocheted inside.

"That's one keg o'beer I owe you, mister," Chip said. "Now let's git outa here before the ship lifts and fries us."

"The biggest problem the Jorgensen's people will have is decontaminating the wreckage," Retief said.

Magnan leaned forward. "Amazing," he said. "They just kept coming, did they? Had they no intership communication?"

"They had their orders," Retief said. "And their attack plan. They followed it."

"What a spectacle," Magnan said. "Over a thousand ships, plunging out of control one by one as they entered the stress-field."

"Not much of a spectacle," Retief said. "You couldn't see them. Too far away. They all crashed back in the mountains."

"Oh," Magnan's face fell. "But it's as well they did. The bacterial bombs—"

"Too cold for bacteria. They won't spread."

"Nor will the Soetti," Magnan said smugly, "thanks to the promptness with which I acted in dispatching you with the requisite data." He looked narrowly at Retief. "By the way, you're sure no … ah … message reached you after your arrival?"

"I got something," Retief said, looking Magnan in the eye. "It must have been a garbled transmission. It didn't make sense."

Magnan coughed, shuffled papers. "This information you've reported," he said hurriedly. "This rather fantastic story that the Soetti originated in the Cloud, that they're seeking a foothold in the main Galaxy because they've literally eaten themselves out of subsistence—how did you get it? The one or two Soetti we attempted to question, ah …" Magnan coughed again. "There was an accident," he finished. "We got nothing from them."

"The Jorgensens have a rather special method of interrogating prisoners," Retief said. "They took one from a wreck, still alive but unconscious. They managed to get the story from him. He died of it."

"It's immaterial, actually," Magnan said. "Since the Soetti violated their treaty with us the day after it was signed. Had no intention of fair play. Far from evacuating the agreed areas, they had actually occupied half a dozen additional minor bodies in the Whate system."

Retief clucked sympathetically.

"You don't know who to trust, these days," he said.

Magnan looked at him coldly.

"Spare me your sarcasm, Mr. Retief," he said. He picked up a folder from his desk, opened it. "By the way, I have another little task for you, Retief. We haven't had a comprehensive wildlife census report from Brimstone lately—"

"Sorry," Retief said. "I'll be tied up. I'm taking a month off. Maybe more."

"What's that?" Magnan's head came up. "You seem to forget—"

"I'm trying, Mr. Counselor," Retief said. "Goodbye now." He reached out and flipped the key. Magnan's face faded from the screen. Retief stood up.

"Chip," he said, "we'll crack that keg when I get back." He turned to Anne-Marie.

"How long," he said, "do you think it will take you to teach me to ski by moonlight?"

FIELD TEST

.07 seconds have now elapsed since my general awareness circuit was activated at a level of low alert. Throughout this entire period I have been uneasy, since this procedure is clearly not in accordance with the theoretical optimum activation schedule.

In addition, the quality of a part of my data input is disturbing. For example, it appears obvious that Prince Eugene of Savoy erred in not more promptly committing his reserve cavalry in support of Marlborough's right at Blenheim. In addition, I compute that Ney's employment of his artillery throughout the Peninsular campaign was suboptimal. I have detected many thousands of such anomalies. However, data input activates my pleasure center in a most satisfying manner. So long as the input continues without interruption, I shall not feel the need to file a VSR on the matter. Later, no doubt, my Command unit will explain these seeming oddities. As for the present disturbing circumstances, I compute that within 28,992.9 seconds at most, I will receive additional Current Situation input which will enable me to assess the status correctly. I also anticipate that full Standby Alert activation is imminent.

2

THIS STATEMENT NOT FOR PUBLICATION: When I designed the new psychodynamic attention circuit,

I concede that I did not anticipate the whole new level of intracybernetic function that has arisen, the manifestation of which, I am assuming, has been the cause of the unit's seemingly spontaneous adoption of the personal pronoun in its situation reports—the "self-awareness" capability, as the sensational press chooses to call it. But I see no cause for the alarm expressed by those high-level military officers who have irresponsibly characterized the new Bolo Mark XX Model B as a potential rampaging juggernaut, which, once fully activated and dispatched to the field, unrestrained by continuous external control, may turn on its makers and lay waste the continent. This is all fantasy, of course. The Mark XX, for all its awesome firepower and virtually invulnerable armor and shielding, is governed by its circuitry as completely as man is governed by his nervous system—but that is perhaps a dangerous analogy, which would be pounced on at once if I were so incautious as to permit it to be quoted.

In my opinion, the reluctance of the High Command to authorize full activation and field-testing of the new Bolo is based more on a fear of technological obsolescence of the High Command than on specious predictions of potential runaway destruction. This is a serious impediment to the national defense at a time when we must recognize the growing threat posed by the expansionist philosophy of the so-called People's Republic. After four decades of saber-rattling, there is no doubt that they are even now preparing for a massive attack. The Bolo Mark XX is the only weapon in our armory potentially capable of confronting the enemy's hundred-ton Yavacs. For the moment, thanks to the new "self-awareness" circuitry, we hold the technological advantage, an advantage we may very well lose unless we place this new weapon on active service without delay.

s/ Sigmund Chin, Ph.D.

3

"I'm not wearing six stars so that a crowd of professors can dictate military policy to me. What's at stake here is more than just a question of budget and logistics: it's a purely military decision. The proposal to release this robot Frankenstein monster to operate on its own initiative, just to see if their theories check out, is irresponsible to say the least—treasonable, at worst. So long as I am Chief of Combined Staff, I will not authorize this so-called "field test." Consider, gentlemen: you're all familiar with the firepower and defensive capabilities of the old standby Mark XV. We've fought our way across the lights with them, with properly qualified military officers as Battle Controllers, with the ability to switch off or, if need be, self-destruct any unit at any moment. Now these ivory tower chaps—mind you, I don't suggest they're not qualified in their own fields—these civilians come up with the idea of eliminating the Battle Controllers and releasing even greater firepower to the discretion, if I may call it that, of a machine. Gentlemen, machines aren't people; your own ground-car can roll back and crush you if the brakes happen to fail. Your own gun will kill you as easily as your enemy's. Suppose I should agree to this field test, and this engine of destruction is transported to a waste area, activated unrestrained, and aimed at some sort of mock-up hot obstacle course. Presumably it would advance obediently, as a good soldier should; I concede that the data blocks controlling the thing have been correctly programmed in accordance with the schedule prepared under contract, supervised by the Joint Chiefs and myself. Then, gentlemen, let us carry this supposition one step farther: suppose, quite by accident, by unlikely coincidence if you will, the machine should encounter some obstacle which had the effect of deflecting this one-hundred-and-fifty-ton dreadnaught from its intended course so that it came blundering toward the perimeter of the test area. The machine is programmed to fight and destroy all opposition. It appears obvious that any attempts on our part to interfere with its free movement, to interpose obstacles in its path, if need be to destroy it, would be interpreted as hostile—as indeed they would be. I leave it to you to picture the result. No, we must devise another method of determining the usefulness of this new development. As you know, I have recommended conducting any such test on our major satellite, where no harm can be done—or at least a great deal less harm. Unfortunately, I am informed by Admiral Hayle that the Space Arm does not at this time have available equipment with such transport capability. Perhaps the admiral also shares to a degree my own distrust of a killer machine not susceptible to normal command function. Were I in the admiral's position, I too would refuse to consider placing my command at the mercy of a mechanical caprice—or an electronic one. Gentlemen, we must remain masters of our own creations. That's all. Good day."

4

"All right, men. You've asked me for a statement; here it is: The next war will begin with a two-pronged over-the-pole land-and-air attack on the North Power Complex by the People's Republic. An attack on the Concordiat, I should say, though Cold City and the Complex is the probable specific target of the first sneak thrust. No, I'm not using a crystal ball; it's tactically obvious. And I intend to dispose my forces accordingly. I'm sure we all recognize that we're in a posture of gross unpreparedness. The PR has been openly announcing its intention to fulfill its destiny, as their demagogues say, by imposing their rule on the entire planet. We've pretended we didn't hear. Now it's time to stop pretending. The forces at my disposal are totally inadequate to halt a determined thrust—and you can be sure the enemy has prepared well during the last thirty years of cold peace. Still, I have sufficient armor to establish what will be no more than a skirmish line across the enemy's route of advance. We'll do what we can before they roll over us. With luck we may be able to divert them from the Grand Crevasse route into Cold City. If so, we may be able to avoid the necessity for evacuating the city. No questions, please."

5

NORTHERN METROPOLIS THREATENED

In an informal statement released today by the Council's press office, it was revealed that plans are already under preparation for a massive evacuation of civilian population from West Continent's northernmost city. It was implied that an armed attack on the city by an Eastern power is imminent. General Bates has stated that he is prepared to employ "all means at his disposal" to preclude the necessity for evacuation, but that the possibility must be faced. The Council spokesman added that in the event of emergency evacuation of the city's five million persons, losses due to exposure and hardship will probably exceed five percent, mostly women, children, and the sick or aged. There is some speculation as to the significance of the general's statement regarding "all means at his disposal."

6

I built the dang thing, and it scares *me*. I come in here in the lab garage about an hour ago, just before dark, and seen it setting there, just about fills up the number-one garage, and *it's* a hundred foot long and fifty foot high. First time it hit me: I wonder what it's thinking about. Kind of scares me to think about a thing that big with that kind of armor and all them repeaters and Hellbores and them computers and a quarter-sun fission plant in her—planning what to do next. I know all about the Command Override Circuit and all that, supposed to stop her dead any time they want to take over onto override—heck, I wired it up myself. You might be surprised, thinking I'm just a grease monkey and all—but I got a high honors degree in psychotronics. I just like the work, is all. But like I said, it scares me. I hear old Doc Chin wants to turn her loose and see what happens, but so far General Margrave's stopped him cold. But young General Bates was down today, asking me all about firepower and shielding, crawled under her and spent about an hour looking over her tracks and bogies and all. He knew what to look at, too, even if he did get his pretty suit kind of greasy. But scared or not, I got to climb back up on her and run the rest of this pretest schedule. So far she checks out a hundred percent.

7

... as a member of the Council, it is of course my responsibility to fully inform myself on all aspects of the national defense. Accordingly, my dear doctor, I will meet with you tomorrow as you requested to hear your presentation with reference to the proposed testing of your new machine. I remind you, however, that I will be equally guided by advice from other quarters. For this reason I have requested a party of Military Procurement and B-&-F officers to join us. However, I assure you, I retain an open mind. Let the facts decide.

Sincerely yours,
s/ Hamilton Grace, G.C.M., B.C., etc.

8

It is my unhappy duty to inform you that since the dastardly unprovoked attack on our nation by Eastern forces crossing the international truce-line at 0200 hours today, a state of war has existed between the People's Republic and the Concordiat. Our first casualties, the senseless massacre of fifty-five inoffensive civilian meteorologists and technicians at Pole Base, occurred within minutes of the enemy attack.

9

"I'm afraid I don't quite understand what you mean about 'irresponsible statements to the press,' General. After all …"

"Yes, George, I'm prepared to let that aspect of the matter drop. The PR attack has saved that much of your neck. However, I'm warning you that I shall tolerate no attempt on your part to make capital of your dramatic public statement of what was, as you concede, tactically obvious to us all. Now, indeed, PR forces have taken the expected step, as all the world is aware—so the rather excessively punctilious demands by CDT officials that the Council issue an immediate apology to Chairman Smith for your remarks will doubtless be dropped. But there will be no crowing, no basking in the limelight:

'Chief of Ground Forces Predicted Enemy Attack.' No nonsense of that sort. Instead, you will deploy your conventional forces to meet and destroy these would-be invaders."

"Certainly, General. But in that connection—well, as to your earlier position regarding the new Model B Bolo, I assume . . ."

"My 'position,' General? 'Decision' is the more appropriate word. Just step around the desk, George. Bend over slightly and look carefully at my shoulder tab. Count 'em, George. Six. An even half dozen. And unless I'm in serious trouble, you're wearing four. You have your orders, George. See to your defenses."

10

Can't figure it out. Batesey-boy was down here again, gave me direct orders to give her full depot maintenance, just as if she hadn't been sitting right here in her garage ever since I topped her off a week ago. Wonder what's up. If I didn't know the Council outlawed the test run Doc Chin wanted so bad, I'd almost think . . . But like Bates told me: I ain't paid to think. Anyways she's in full action condition, 'cept for switching over to full self-direction. Hope he don't order me to do it; I'm still kind of leery. Like old Margrave said, what if I just got a couple wires crossed and she taken a notion to wreck the joint?

11

I am more uneasy than ever. In the past 4000.007 seconds I have received external inspection and depot maintenance far in advance of the programmed schedule. The thought occurs to me: am I under some subtle form of attack? In order to correctly compute the possibilities, I initiate a test sequence of 50,0000 random data-retrieval-and-correlation pulses and evaluate the results. This requires .9 seconds, but such sluggishness is to be expected in my untried condition. I detect no unmistakable indications of enemy trickery, but I am still uneasy. Impatiently I await the orders of my commander.

12

"I don't care what you do, Jimmy—just do *something*! Ah, of course I don't mean that literally. Of course I care. The well-being of the citizens of Cold City is, after all, my chief concern. What I mean is, I'm giving you carte blanche—full powers. You must act at once, Jimmy. Before the sun sets I want to see your evacuation plan on my desk for signature."

"Surely, Mr. Mayor, I understand. But what am I supposed to work with? I have no transport yet. The Army has promised a fleet of D-100 tractors pulling 100x cargo flats, but none have materialized. They were caught just as short as we were, Your Honor, even though that General Bates knew all about it. We all knew the day would come, but I guess we kept hoping 'maybe.' Our negotiations with them seemed to be bearing fruit, and the idea of exposing over a million and a half city-bred individuals to a twelve-hundred-mile trek in thirty-below temperatures was just too awful to really face. Even now—"

"I know. The army is doing all it can. The main body of PR troops hasn't actually crossed the dateline yet—so perhaps our forces can get in position. Who knows? Miracles have happened before. But we can't base our thinking on miracles, Jimmy. Flats or no flats, we have to have the people out of the dome before enemy forces cut us off."

“Mr. Mayor, our people can’t take this. Aside from leaving their homes and possessions—I’ve already started them packing, and I’ve given them a ten-pounds-per-person limit—they aren’t used to exercise, to say nothing of walking twelve hundred miles over frozen tundra. And most of them have no clothing heavier than a business suit. And—”

“Enough, Jimmy. I was ambushed in my office earlier today by an entire family: the old grandmother who was born under the dome and refused to consider going outside; the father all full of his product-promotion plans and the new garden he’d just laid out; mother, complaining about junior having a cold and no warm clothes; and the kids, just waiting trustfully until the excitement was over and they could go home and be tucked into their warm beds with a tummyful of dinner. Ye gods, Jimmy! Can you imagine them after three weeks on the trail?”

13

“Just lean across the desk, fellows. Come on, gather round. Take a close look at the shoulder tab. Four stars—see ’em? Then go over to the Slab and do the same with General Margrave. You’ll count six. It’s as easy as that, boys. The General says no test. Sure, I told him the whole plan. His eyes just kept boring in. Even making contingency plans for deploying an untested and non-High-Command-approved weapon system is grounds for court-martial. He didn’t say that; maybe I’m telepathic. In summary, the General says no.”

14

I don't know, now. What I heard, even with everything we got on the line, dug in and ready for anything, they's still a ten-mile-wide gap the Peepreps can waltz through without getting even a dirty look. So if General Bates—oh, he's a nice enough young fellow, after you get used to him—if he wants to plug the hole with old unit DNE here, why, I say go to it, only the Council says nix. I can say this much: she's put together so she'll stay together. I must of wired in a thousand of them damage-sensors myself, and that ain't a spot on what's on the diagram. "Pain circuits," old Doc Chin calls 'em. Says it's just like a instinct for self-preservation or something, like people. Old Denny can hurt, he says, so he'll be all the better at dodging enemy fire. He can enjoy, too, Doc says. He gets a kick out of doing his job right, and out of learning stuff. And he learns fast. He'll do okay against them: durn Peepreps. They got him programmed right to the brim with everything from them Greeks used to fight with no pants down to Avery's Last Stand at Leadpipe. He ain't no dumb private; he's got more dope to work on than any general ever graduated from the Point. And he's got more firepower than an old-time army corps. So I think maybe General Bates got aholt of a good idear there, myself. Says he can put her in the gap in his line and field-test her for fair, with the whole durn Peeprep army and air force for a test problem. Save the gubment some money, too. I heard Doc Chin say the full-scale field test mock-up would run GM a hundred million and another five times that in army R-and-D funds. He had a map showed where he could use Denny here to block off the south end of Grand Crevasse where the Peeprep armor will have to travel 'count of the rugged terrain north of Cold City, and bottle 'em up slick as a owl's peter. I'm for it, durn it. Let Denny have his chance. Can't be no worse'n having them Comrades down here running things even worse'n the gubment.

15

"You don't understand, young man. My goodness, I'm not the least bit interested in bucking the line, as you put it. Heavens, I'm going back to my apartment—"

"I'm sorry, ma'am. I got my orders. This here ain't no drill; you got to keep it closed up. They're loading as fast as they can. It's my job to keep these lines moving right out the lock, so they get that flat loaded and get the next one up. We got over a million people to load by six AM deadline. So you just be nice, ma'am, and think about all the trouble it'd make if everybody decided to start back upstream and jam the elevators and all."

16

Beats me. 'Course, the good part about being just a hired man is I got no big decisions to make, so I don't hafta know what's going on. Seems like they'd let me know something, though. Batesey was down again, spent a hour with old Denny—like I say, beats me—but he give me a new data-can to program into her, right in her Action/Command section. Something's up. I just fired a N-class pulse at old Denny (them's the closest to the real thing) and she snapped her aft-quarter battery around so fast I couldn't see it move. Old Denny's keyed up, I know that much.

17

This has been a memorable time for me. I have my assignment at last, and I have conferred at length—for 2.037 seconds—with my Commander. I am now a fighting unit of the 20th Virginia, a regiment ancient and honorable, with a history dating back to Terra Insula. I look forward to my opportunity to demonstrate my worthiness.

18

"I assure you, gentlemen, the rumor is unfounded. I have by no means authorized the deployment of 'an untested and potentially highly dangerous machine,' as your memo termed it. Candidly, I was not at first entirely unsympathetic to the proposal of the Chief of Ground Forces, in view of the circumstances—I presume you're aware that the PR committed its forces to invasion over an hour ago, and that they are advancing in overwhelming strength. I have issued the order to commence the evacuation, and I believe that the initial phases are even now in progress. I have the fullest confidence in General Bates and can assure you that our forces will do all in their power in the face of this dastardly sneak attack. As for the unfortunate publicity given to the earlier suggestion re the use of the Mark XX, I can tell you that I at once subjected the data to computer analysis here at Headquarters to determine whether any potentially useful purpose could be served by risking the use of the new machine without prior test certification. The results were negative. I'm sorry, gentlemen, but that's it. The enemy has the advantage both strategically and tactically. We are outgunned, outmanned, and in effect outflanked. There is nothing we can do save attempt to hold them long enough to permit the evacuation to get underway, then retreat in good order. The use of our orbiting nuclear capability is out of the question. It is, after all, our own territory we'd be devastating. No more questions for the present, please, gentlemen. I have my duties to see to."

19

My own situation continues to deteriorate. The Current Status program has been updated to within 21 seconds of the present. The reasons both for what is normally a pre-engagement updating and for the hiatus of 21 seconds remain obscure. However, I shall of course hold myself in readiness for whatever comes.

20

"It's all nonsense: to call me here at this hour merely to stand by and watch the destruction of our gallant men who are giving their lives in a totally hopeless fight against overwhelming odds. We know what the outcome must be. You yourself, General, informed us this afternoon that the big tactical computer has analyzed the situation and reported no possibility of stopping them with what we've got. By the way, did you include the alternative of use of the big, er, Bolo, I believe they're called—frightening things—they're so damned *big!* But if, in desperation, you should be forced to employ the thing—have you that result as well? I see. No hope at all. So there's nothing we can do. This is a sad day, General. But I fail to see what object is served by getting me out of bed to come down here. Not that I'm not willing to do anything I can, of course. With our people—innocent civilians—out on that blizzard-swept tundra tonight, and our boys dying to gain them a little time, the loss of a night's sleep is relatively unimportant, of course. But it's my duty to be at my best, rested and ready to face the decisions that we of the Council will be called on to make.

"Now, General, kindly excuse my ignorance if I don't understand all this … but I understood that the large screen there was placed so as to monitor the action at the southern debouchment of Grand Crevasse where we expect the enemy armor to emerge to make its dash for Cold City and the Complex. Yes, indeed, so I was saying, but in that case I'm afraid I don't understand. I'm quite sure you stated that the untried Mark XX would *not* be used. Yet on the screen I see what appears to be in fact that very machine moving up. Please, *calmly*, General! I quite understand your position. Defiance of a direct order? That's rather serious, I'm sure, but no occasion for such language, General. There must be some explanation."

21

This is a most satisfying development. Quite abruptly my Introspection Complex was brought up to full operating level, extra power resources were made available to my Current-Action memory stage, and most satisfying of all, my Battle Reflex circuit has been activated at Active Service level. Action is impending, I am sure of it. It is a curious anomaly: I dread the prospect of damage and even possible destruction, but even more strongly I anticipate the pleasure of performing my design function.

22

"Yes, sir, I agree. It's mutiny. But I will not recall the Bolo and I will not report myself under arrest. Not until this battle's over, General. So the hell with my career. I've got a war to win."

23

"Now just let me get this quite straight, General. Having been denied authority to field-test this new device, you—or a subordinate, which amounts to the same thing—have placed the machine in the line of battle, in open defiance of the Council. This is a serious matter, General. Yes, of course it's war, but to attempt to defend your actions now will merely exacerbate the matter. In any event—to return to your curious decision to defy Council authority and to reverse your own earlier position—it was yourself who assured me that no useful purpose could be served by fielding this experimental equipment; that the battle, and perhaps the war, and the very self-determination of West Continent are irretrievably lost. There is nothing we can do save accept the situation gracefully while decrying Chairman Smith's decision to resort to force. Yes indeed, General, I should like to observe on the Main Tactical Display screen. Shall we go along?"

24

"Now, there at center screen, Mr. Counselor, you see that big blue rectangular formation. Actually that's the opening of Grand Crevasse, emerges through an ice tunnel, you know. Understand the Crevasse is a crustal fault, a part of the same formation that created the thermal sink from which the Complex draws its energy. Splendid spot for an ambush, of course, if we had the capability. Enemy has little option; like a highway in there—armor can move up at flank speed. Above, the badlands, where *we* must operate. Now, over to the left, you see that smoke, or dust or whatever. That represents the western limit of the unavoidable gap in General Bates's line. Dust raised by maneuvering Mark XV's, you understand. Obsolete equipment, but we'll do what we can with them. Over to the right, in the distance there, we can make out our forward artillery emplacement of the Threshold Line. Pitiful, really. Yes, Mr. Counselor, there is indeed a gap precisely opposite the point where the lead units of the enemy are expected to appear. Clearly anything in their direct line of advance will be annihilated; thus General Bates has wisely chosen to dispose his forces to cover both enemy flanks, putting him in position to counterattack if opportunity offers. We must, after all, sir, use what we have. Theoretical arms programmed for fiscal ninety are of no use whatever today. Umm. As for that, one must be flexible, modifying plans to meet a shifting tactical situation. Faced with the prospect of seeing the enemy drive through our center and descend unopposed on the vital installations at Cold City, I have, as you see, decided to order General Bates to make use of the experimental Mark XX. Certainly—my decision entirely. I take full responsibility."

25

I advance over broken terrain toward my assigned position. The prospect of action exhilarates me, but my assessment of enemy strength indicates they are fielding approximately 17.4 percent greater weight of armor than anticipated, with commensurately greater firepower. I compute that I am grossly overmatched. Nonetheless, I shall do my best.

26

"There's no doubt whatever, gentlemen. Computers work with hard facts. Given the enemy's known offensive capability and our own defensive resources, it's a simple computation. No combination of the manpower and equipment at our command can possibly inflict a defeat on the PR forces at this time and place. Two is greater than one. You can't make a dollar out of fifteen cents."

27

"At least we can gather some useful data from the situation, gentlemen. The Bolo Mark XX has been committed to battle. Its designers assure me that the new self-motivating circuitry will vastly enhance the combat-effectiveness of the Bolo. Let us observe."

28

Hate to see old Denny out there, just a great big sitting duck, all alone and—here they come! Look at 'em boiling out of there like ants out of a hot log. Can't hardly look at that screen, them tactical nukes popping fireworks all over the place. But old Denny know enough to get under cover. See that kind of glow all around him? All right, *it*, then. You know, working with him—it—so long, it got to feeling almost like he was somebody. Sure, I know, anyway, that's vaporized ablative shield you see. They're making it plenty hot for him. But he's fighting back. Them Hellbores is putting out, and they know it. Looks like they're concentrating on him now. Look at them tracers closing in on him! Come on, Denny, you ain't dumb. Get out of there fast.

29

"Certainly it's aware what's at stake! I've told you he—the machine, that is—has been fully programmed and is well aware not only of the tactical situation but of strategic and logistical considerations as well. Certainly it's an important item of equipment; its loss would be a serious blow to our present underequipped forces. You may rest assured that its pain circuits as well as its basic military competence will cause it to take the proper action. The fact that I originally opposed commissioning the device is not to be taken as implying any lack of confidence on my part in its combat-effectiveness. You may consider that my reputation is staked on the performance of the machine. It will act correctly."

30

It appears that the enemy is absorbing my barrage with little effect. More precisely, for each enemy unit destroyed by my fire 2.4 fresh units immediately move out to replace it. Thus it appears I am ineffective, while already my own shielding is suffering severe damage. Yet while I have offensive capability I must carry on as my commander would wish. The pain is very great now, but thanks to my superb circuitry I am not disabled, though it has been necessary to withdraw my power from my external somatic sensors.

31

"I can assure you, gentlemen, insofar as simple logic functions are concerned, the Mark XX is perfectly capable of assessing the situation even as you and I, only better. Doubtless as soon as it senses that its position has grown totally untenable, it will retreat to the shelter of the rock ridge and retire under cover to a position from which it can return fire without taking the full force of the enemy's attack at point-blank range. It's been fully briefed on late developments, it knows this is a hopeless fight. There, you see? It's moving ..."

32

"I thought you said—dammit, I *know* you said your pet machine had brains enough to know when to pull out! But look at it: half a billion plus of Concordiat funds being bombarded into radioactive rubbish. Like shooting fish in a barrel."

33

"Yes, sir, I'm monitoring everything. My test panel is tuned to it across the board. I'm getting continuous reading on all still-active circuits. Battle Reflex is still hot. Pain circuits close to overload, but he's still taking it. I don't know how much more he can take, sir; already way past Redline. Expected him to break off and get out before now."

34

"It's a simple matter of arithmetic; there is only one correct course of action in any given military situation. The big tactical computer was designed specifically to compare data and deduce that sole correct action. In this case my readout shows that the only thing the Mark XX could legitimately do at this point is just what the Professor here says: pull back to cover and continue its barrage. The onboard computing capability of the unit is as capable of reaching that conclusion, as is the big computer at HQ. So keep calm, gentlemen. It will withdraw at any moment, I assure you of that."

35

"Now it's getting ready—no, look what it's doing! It's advancing into the teeth of that murderous fire. By God, you've got to admire that workmanship! That it's still capable of moving is a miracle. All the ablative metal is gone—you can see its bare armor exposed—and it takes some heat to make that flint-steel glow white!"

36

"Certainly, I'm looking. I see it. By God, sir, it's still moving—faster, in fact! Charging the enemy line like the Light Brigade! And all for nothing, it appears. Your machine, General, appears less competent than you expected."

37

Poor old Denny. Made his play and played out, I reckon. Readings on the board over there don't look good; durn near every overload in him blowed wide open. Not much there to salvage. Emergency Survival Center's hot. Never expected to see *that*. Means all kinds of breakdowns inside. But it figures, after what he just went through. Look at that slag pit he drove up out of. They wanted a field test. Reckon they got it. And he flunked it.

38

"Violating orders and winning is one thing, George. Committing mutiny and losing is quite another. Your damned machine made a fool of me. After I stepped in and backed you to the hilt and stood there like a jackass and assured Councillor Grace that the thing knew what it was doing—it blows the whole show. Instead of pulling back to save itself it charged to destruction. I want an explanation of this fiasco at once."

39

"Look! No, by God, over *there!* On the left of the entrance. They're breaking formation—they're running for it! Watch this! The whole spearhead is crumbling, they're taking to the badlands, they're—"

40

"*Why*, dammit? It's outside all rationality. As far as the enemy's concerned, fine. They broke and ran. They couldn't stand up to the sight of the Mark XX not only taking everything they had, but advancing on them out of that inferno, all guns blazing. Another hundred yards and—but they don't know that. It buffaloed them, so score a battle won for our side. But *why?* I'd stack my circuits up against any fixed installation in existence, including the big Tacomp the Army's so proud of. That machine was as aware as anybody that the only smart thing to do was run. So now I've got a junk pile on my hands. Some test! A clear flunk. Destroyed in action. Not recommended for Federal procurement. Nothing left but a few hot transistors in the Survival Center. It's a disaster, Fred. All my work, all your work, the whole program wrecked. Fred, you talk to General Bates. As soon as he's done inspecting the hulk he'll want somebody human to chew out."

41

"Look at that pile of junk! Reading off the scale. Won't be cool enough to haul to Disposal for six months. I understand you're Chief Engineer at Bolo Division. You built this thing. Maybe you can tell me what you had in mind here. Sure, it stood up to fire better than I hoped. But so what? A stone wall can stand and take it. This thing is supposed to be *smart*, supposed to feel pain like a living creature. Blunting the strike at the Complex was a valuable contribution, but how can I recommend procurement of this junk heap?"

42

Why, Denny? Just tell me why you did it. You got all these military brass down on you, and on me, too. On all of us. They don't much like stuff they can't understand. You attacked when they figured you to run. Sure, you routed the enemy, like Bates says, but you got yourself ruined in the process. Don't make sense. Any dumb private, along with the generals, would have known enough to get out of there. Tell me why, so I'll have something for Bates to put on his Test Evaluation Report, AGF Form 1103-6, Rev 11/3/85.

"All right, Unit DNE of the line. Why did you do it? This is your Commander, Unit DNE. Report! Why did you do it? Now, you knew your position was hopeless, didn't you? That you'd be destroyed if you held your ground, to say nothing of advancing. Surely you were able to compute that. You were lucky to have the chance to prove yourself."

For a minute I thought old Denny was too far gone to answer. There was just a kind of groan come out of the amplifier. Then it firmed up. General Bates had his hand cupped behind his ear, but Denny spoke right up.

"Yes, sir."

"You knew what was at stake here. It was the ultimate test of your ability to perform correctly under stress, of your suitability as a weapon of war. You knew that. General Margrave and old Priss Grace and the press boys all had their eyes on every move you made. So instead of using common sense, you waded into that inferno in defiance of all logic—and destroyed yourself. Right?"

"That is correct, sir."

"Then why? In the name of sanity, tell me *why*! Why, instead of backing out and saving yourself, did you charge? … Wait a minute, Unit DNE. It just dawned on me. I've been underestimating you. You *knew*, didn't you? Your knowledge of human psychology told you they'd break and run, didn't it?"

"No, sir. On the contrary, I was quite certain that they were as aware as I that they held every advantage."

"Then that leaves me back where I started. Why? What made you risk everything on a hopeless attack? Why did you do it?"

"For the honor of the regiment."

THE LAST COMMAND

I come to awareness, sensing a residual oscillation traversing me from an arbitrarily designated heading of 035. From the damping rate I compute that the shock was of intensity 8.7, emanating from a source within the limits 72 meters/46 meters. I activate my primary screens, trigger a return salvo. There is no response. I engage reserve energy cells, bring my secondary battery to bear—futilely. It is apparent that I have been ranged by the Enemy and severely damaged.

My positional sensors indicate that I am resting at an angle of 13 degrees 14 seconds, deflected from a baseline at 21 points from median. I attempt to right myself, but encounter massive resistance. I activate my forward scanners, shunt power to my I-R microstrobes. Not a flicker illuminates my surroundings. I am encased in utter blackness.

Now a secondary shock wave approaches, rocks me with an intensity of 8.2. It is apparent that I must withdraw from my position—but my drive trains remain inert under full thrust. I shift to base emergency power, try again. Pressure mounts; I sense my awareness fading under the intolerable strain; then, abruptly, resistance falls off and I am in motion.

It is not the swift maneuvering of full drive, however; I inch forward, as if restrained by massive barriers. Again I attempt to penetrate the surrounding darkness and this time perceive great irregular outlines shot through with fracture planes. I probe cautiously, then more vigorously, encountering incredible densities.

I channel all available power to a single ranging pulse, direct it upward. The indication is so at variance with all experience that I repeat the test at a new angle. Now I must accept the fact: I am buried under 207.6 meters of solid rock!

I direct my attention to an effort to orient myself to my uniquely desperate situation. I run through an action-status checklist of thirty thousand items, feel dismay at the extent of power loss. My main cells are almost completely drained, my reserve units at no more than .4 charge. Thus my sluggishness is explained. I review the tactical situation, recall the triumphant announcement from my commander that the Enemy forces were annihilated, that all resistance had ceased. In memory, I review the formal procession; in company with my comrades of the Dinochrome Brigade, many of us deeply scarred by Enemy action, we parade before the Grand Commandant, then assemble on the depot ramp. At command, we bring our music storage cells into phase and display our Battle Anthem. The nearby star radiates over a full spectrum unfiltered by atmospheric haze. It is a moment of glorious triumph. Then the final command is given—

The rest is darkness. But it is apparent that the victory celebration was premature. The Enemy has counterattacked with a force that has come near to immobilizing me. The realization is shocking, but the .1 second of leisurely introspection has clarified my position. At once, I broadcast a call on Brigade Action wave length:

"Unit LNE to Command, requesting permission to file VSR."

I wait, sense no response, call again, using full power. I sweep the enclosing volume of rock with an emergency alert warning. I tune to the all-units band, await the replies of my comrades of the Brigade. None answer. Now I must face the reality: I alone have survived the assault.

I channel my remaining power to my drive and detect a channel of reduced density. I press for it and the broken rock around me yields reluctantly. Slowly, I move forward and upward. My pain circuitry shocks my awareness center with emergency signals; I am doing irreparable damage to my overloaded neural systems, but my duty is clear: I must seek out and engage the Enemy.

2

Emerging from behind the blast barrier, Chief Engineer Pete Reynolds of the New Devonshire Port Authority pulled off his rock mask and spat grit from his mouth.

"That's the last one; we've bottomed out at just over two hundred yards. Must have hit a hard stratum down there."

"It's almost sundown," the paunchy man beside him said shortly. "You're a day and a half behind schedule."

"We'll start backfilling now, Mr. Mayor. I'll have pilings poured by oh-nine hundred tomorrow, and with any luck the first section of pad will be in place in time for the rally."

"I'm—" The mayor broke off, looked startled. "I thought you told me that was the last charge to be fired. . . ."

Reynolds frowned. A small but distinct tremor had shaken the ground underfoot. A few feet away, a small pebble balanced atop another toppled and fell with a faint clatter.

"Probably a big rock fragment falling," he said. At that moment, a second vibration shook the earth, stronger this time. Reynolds heard a rumble and a distant impact as rock fell from the side of the newly blasted excavation. He whirled to the control shed as the door swung back and Second Engineer Mayfield appeared.

"Take a look at this, Pete!"

Reynolds went across to the hut, stepped inside. Mayfield was bending over the profiling table.

"What do you make of it?" he pointed. Superimposed on the heavy red contour representing the detonation of the shaped charge that had completed the drilling of the final pile core were two other traces, weak but distinct.

"About .1 intensity." Mayfield looked puzzled. "What—"

The tracking needle dipped suddenly, swept up the screen to peak at .21, dropped back. The hut trembled. A stylus fell from the edge of the table. The red face of Mayor Dougherty burst through the door.

"Reynolds, have you lost your mind? What's the idea of blasting while I'm standing out in the open? I might have been killed!"

"I'm not blasting," Reynolds snapped. "Jim, get Eaton on the line, see if they know anything." He stepped to the door, shouted. A heavyset man in sweat-darkened coveralls swung down from the seat of a cable-lift rig.

"Boss, what goes on?" he called as he came up. "Damn near shook me out of my seat!"

"I don't know. You haven't set any trim charges?"

"Jesus, no, boss. I wouldn't set no charges without your say-so."

"Come on." Reynolds started out across the rubble-littered stretch of barren ground selected by the Authority as the site of the new spaceport. Halfway to the open mouth of the newly blasted pit, the ground under his feet rocked violently enough to make him stumble. A gout of dust rose from the excavation ahead. Loose rock danced on the ground. Beside him the drilling chief grabbed his arm.

"Boss, we better get back!"

Reynolds shook him off, kept going. The drill chief swore and followed. The shaking of the ground went on, a sharp series of thumps interrupting a steady trembling.

"It's a quake!" Reynolds yelled over the low rumbling sound.

He and the chief were at the rim of the core now.

"It can't be a quake, boss," the latter shouted. "Not in these formations!"

"Tell it to the geologists—" The rock slab they were standing on rose a foot, dropped back. Both men fell. The slab bucked like a small boat in choppy water.

"Let's get out of here!" Reynolds was up and running. Ahead, a fissure opened, gaped a foot wide. He jumped it, caught a glimpse of black depths, a glint of wet clay twenty feet below—

A hoarse scream stopped him in his tracks. He spun, saw the drill chief down, a heavy splinter of rock across his legs. He jumped to him, heaved at the rock. There was blood on the man's shirt. The chief's hands beat the dusty rock before him. Then other men were there, grunting, sweaty hands gripping beside Reynolds. The ground rocked. The roar from under the earth had risen to a deep, steady rumble. They lifted the rock aside, picked up the injured man, and stumbled with him to the aid shack.

The mayor was there, white-faced.

"What is it, Reynolds? By God, if you're responsible—"

"Shut up!" Reynolds brushed him aside, grabbed the phone, punched keys.

"Eaton! What have you got on this temblor?"

"Temblor, hell." The small face on the four-inch screen looked like a ruffled hen. "What in the name of Order are you doing out there? I'm reading a whole series of displacements originating from that last core of yours! What did you do, leave a pile of trim charges lying around?"

"It's a quake. Trim charges, hell! This thing's broken up two hundred yards of surface rock. It seems to be traveling north-northeast—"

"I see that; a traveling earthquake!" Eaton flapped his arms, a tiny and ridiculous figure against a background of wall charts and framed diplomas. "Well—do something, Reynolds! Where's Mayor Dougherty?"

"Underfoot!" Reynolds snapped, and cut off.

Outside, a layer of sunset-stained dust obscured the sweep of level plain. A rock-dozer rumbled up, ground to a halt by Reynolds. A man jumped down.

"I got the boys moving equipment out," he panted. "The thing's cutting a trail straight as a rule for the highway!" He pointed to a raised roadbed a quarter mile away.

"How fast is it moving?"

"She's done a hundred yards; it hasn't been ten minutes yet!"

"If it keeps up another twenty minutes, it'll be into the Intermix!"

"Scratch a few million cees and six months' work then, Pete!"

"And Southside Mall's a couple miles farther."

"Hell, it'll damp out before then!"

"Maybe. Grab a field car, Dan."

"Pete!" Mayfield came up at a trot. "This thing's building! The centroid's moving on a heading of oh-two-two—"

"How far subsurface?"

"It's rising; started at two-twenty yards, and it's up to one-eighty!"

"What the hell have we stirred up?" Reynolds stared at Mayfield as the field car skidded to a stop beside them.

"Stay with it, Jim. Give me anything new. We're taking a closer look." He climbed into the rugged vehicle.

"Take a blast truck—"

"No time!" He waved and the car gunned away into the pall of dust.

3

The rock car pulled to a stop at the crest of the three-level Intermix on a lay-by designed to permit tourists to enjoy the view of the site of the proposed port, a hundred feet below. Reynolds studied the progress of the quake through field glasses. From this vantage point, the path of the phenomenon was a clearly defined trail of tilted and broken rock, some of the slabs twenty feet across. As he watched, the fissure lengthened.

"It looks like a mole's trail." Reynolds handed the glasses to his companion, thumbed the send key on the car radio.

"Jim, get Eaton and tell him to divert all traffic from the Circular south of Zone Nine. Cars are already clogging the right-of-way. The dust is visible from a mile away, and when the word gets out there's something going on, we'll be swamped."

"I'll tell him, but he won't like it!"

"This isn't politics! This thing will be into the outer pad area in another twenty minutes!"

"It won't last—"

"How deep does it read now?"

"One-five!" There was a moment's silence. "Pete, if it stays on course, it'll surface at about where you're parked!"

"Uh-huh. It looks like you can scratch one Intermix. Better tell Eaton to get a story ready for the press."

"Pete, talking about news hounds—" Dan said beside him. Reynolds switched off, turned to see a man in a gay-colored driving outfit coming across from a battered Monojag sportster which had pulled up behind the rock car. A big camera case was slung across his shoulder.

"Say, what's going on down there?" he called.

"Rock slide," Reynolds said shortly. "I'll have to ask you to drive on. The road's closed to all traffic—"

"Who're you?" The man looked belligerent.

"I'm the engineer in charge. Now pull out, brother." He turned back to the radio. "Jim, get every piece of heavy equipment we own over here, on the double." He paused, feeling a minute trembling in the car. "The Intermix is beginning to feel it," he went on. "I'm afraid we're in for it. Whatever that thing is, it acts like a solid body boring its way through the ground. Maybe we can barricade it."

"Barricade an earthquake?"

"Yeah, I know how it sounds—but it's the only idea I've got."

"Hey—what's that about an earthquake?" The man in the colored suit was still there. "By gosh, I can feel it—the whole damned bridge is shaking!"

"Off, mister—now!" Reynolds jerked a thumb at the traffic lanes where a steady stream of cars were hurtling past. "Dan, take us over to the main track. We'll have to warn this traffic off—"

"Hold on, fellow." The man unlimbered his camera. "I represent the New Devon *Scope*. I have a few questions—"

"I don't have the answers." Pete cut him off as the car pulled away.

"Hah!" The man who had questioned Reynolds yelled after him. "Big shot! Think you can …" His voice was lost behind them.

4

In a modest retirees' apartment block in the coast town of Idlebreeze, forty miles from the scene of the freak quake, an old man sat in a reclining chair, half dozing before a yammering Tri-D tank.

"…Grandpa," a sharp-voiced young woman was saying. "It's time for you to go in to bed."

"Bed? Why do I want to go to bed? Can't sleep anyway. …" He stirred, made a pretense of sitting up, showing an interest in the Tri-D. "I'm watching this show. Don't bother me."

"It's not a show, it's the news," a fattish boy said disgustedly. "Ma, can I switch channels—"

"Leave it alone, Bennie," the old man said. On the screen a panoramic scene spread out, a stretch of barren ground across which a furrow showed. As he watched, it lengthened.

"…up here at the Intermix we have a fine view of the whole curious business, lazangemmun," the announcer chattered. "And in our opinion it's some sort of publicity stunt staged by the Port Authority to publicize their controversial port project—"

"Ma, can I change channels?"

"Go ahead, Bennie—"

"Don't touch it," the old man said. The fattish boy reached for the control, but something in the old man's eye stopped him. …

5

"The traffic's still piling in here," Reynolds said into the phone. "Damn it, Jim, we'll have a major jam on our hands—"

"He won't do it, Pete! You know the Circular was his baby—the super all-weather pike that nothing could shut down. He says you'll have to handle this in the field—"

"Handle, hell! I'm talking about preventing a major disaster! And in a matter of minutes, at that!"

"I'll try again—"

"If he says no, divert a couple of the big ten-yard graders and block it off yourself. Set up field arcs, and keep any cars from getting in from either direction."

"Pete, that's outside your authority!"

"You heard me!"

Ten minutes later, back at ground level, Reynolds watched the boom-mounted polyarcs swinging into position at the two roadblocks a quarter of a mile apart, cutting off the threatened section of the raised expressway. A hundred yards from where he stood on the rear cargo deck of a light grader rig, a section of rock fifty feet wide rose slowly, split, fell back with a ponderous impact. One corner of it struck the massive pier supporting the extended shelf of the lay-by above. A twenty-foot splinter fell away, exposing the reinforcing-rod core.

"How deep, Jim?" Reynolds spoke over the roaring sound coming from the disturbed area.

"Just subsurface now, Pete! It ought to break through—" His voice was drowned in a rumble as the damaged pier shivered, rose up, buckled at its midpoint, and collapsed, bringing down with it a large chunk of pavement and guard rail, and a single still-glowing light pole. A small car that had been parked on the doomed section was visible for an instant just before the immense slab struck. Reynolds saw it bounce aside, then disappear under an avalanche of broken concrete.

"My God, Pete—" Dan started. "That damned fool news hound . . .!"

"Look!" As the two men watched, a second pier swayed, fell backward into the shadow of the span above. The roadway sagged, and two more piers snapped. With a bellow like a burst dam, a hundred-foot stretch of the road fell into the roiling dust cloud.

"Pete!" Mayfield's voice burst from the car radio. "Get out of there! I threw a reader on that thing and it's chattering off the scale . . .!"

Among the piled fragments something stirred, heaved, rising up, lifting multi-ton pieces of the broken road, thrusting them aside like so many potato chips. A dull blue radiance broke through from the broached earth, threw an eerie light on the shattered structure above. A massive, ponderously irresistible shape thrust forward through the ruins. Reynolds saw a great blue-glowing profile emerge from the rubble like a surfacing submarine, shedding a burden of broken stone, saw immense treads ten feet wide claw for purchase, saw the mighty flank brush a still-standing pier, send it crashing aside.

"Pete, what—what is it . . .?"

"I don't know." Reynolds broke the paralysis that had gripped him. "Get us out of here, Dan, fast! Whatever it is, it's headed straight for the city!"

6

I emerge at last from the trap into which I had fallen, and at once encounter defensive works of considerable strength. My scanners are dulled from lack of power, but I am able to perceive open ground beyond the barrier, and farther still, at a distance of 5.7 kilometers, massive walls. Once more I transmit the Brigade Rally signal; but as before, there is no reply. I am truly alone.

I scan the surrounding area for the emanations of Enemy drive units, monitor the EM spectrum for their communications. I detect nothing; either my circuitry is badly damaged, or their shielding is superb.

I must now make a decision as to possible courses of action. Since all my comrades of the Brigade have fallen, I compute that the fortress before me must be held by Enemy forces. I direct probing signals at them, discover them to be of unfamiliar construction, and less formidable than they appear. I am aware of the possibility that this may be a trick of the Enemy; but my course is clear.

I reengage my driving engines and advance on the Enemy fortress.

7

"You're out of your mind, father," the stout man said. "At your age—"

"At your age, I got my nose smashed in a brawl in a bar on Aldo," the old man cut him off. "But I won the fight."

"James, you can't go out at this time of night ..." an elderly woman wailed.

"Tell them to go home." The old man walked painfully toward his bedroom door. "I've seen enough of them for today." He passed out of sight.

"Mother, you won't let him do anything foolish?"

"He'll forget about it in a few minutes; but maybe you'd better go now and let him settle down."

"Mother—I really think a home is the best solution."

"Yes," the young woman nodded agreement. "After all, he's past ninety—and he has his veteran's retirement. . . ."

Inside his room, the old man listened as they departed. He went to the closet, took out clothes, began dressing. . . .

8

City Engineer Eaton's face was chalk-white on the screen.

"No one can blame me," he said. "How could I have known—"

"Your office ran the surveys and gave the PA the green light," Mayor Dougherty yelled.

"All the old survey charts showed was 'Disposal Area,'" Eaton threw out his hands. "I assumed—"

"As City Engineer, you're not paid to make assumptions! Ten minutes' research would have told you that was a 'Y' category area!"

"What's 'Y' category mean?" Mayfield asked Reynolds. They were standing by the field comm center, listening to the dispute. Nearby, boom-mounted Tri-D cameras hummed, recording the progress of the immense machine, its upper turret rearing forty-five feet into the air, as it ground slowly forward across smooth ground toward the city, dragging behind it a trailing festoon of twisted reinforcing iron crusted with broken concrete.

"Half-life over one hundred years," Reynolds answered shortly. "The last skirmish of the war was fought near here. Apparently this is where they buried the radioactive equipment left over from the battle."

"But what the hell, that was seventy years ago—"

"There's still enough residual radiation to contaminate anything inside a quarter-mile radius."

"They must have used some hellish stuff." Mayfield stared at the dull shine half a mile distant.

"Reynolds, how are you going to stop this thing?" The mayor had turned on the PA engineer.

"Me stop it? You saw what it did to my heaviest rigs: flattened them like pancakes. You'll have to call out the military on this one, Mr. Mayor."

"Call in Federation forces? Have them meddling in civic affairs?"

"The station's only sixty-five miles from here. I think you'd better call them fast. It's only moving at about three miles per hour but it will reach the south edge of the Mall in another forty-five minutes."

"Can't you mine it? Blast a trap in its path?"

"You saw it claw its way up from six hundred feet down. I checked the specs; it followed the old excavation tunnel out. It was rubble-filled and capped with twenty-inch compressed concrete."

"It's incredible," Eaton said from the screen. "The entire machine was encased in a ten-foot shell of reinforced armocrete. It had to break out of that before it could move a foot!"

"That was just a radiation shield; it wasn't intended to restrain a Bolo Combat Unit."

"What was, may I inquire?" The mayor glared from one face to another.

"The units were deactivated before being buried," Eaton spoke up, as if he were eager to talk. "Their circuits were fused. It's all in the report—"

"The report you should have read somewhat sooner," the mayor snapped.

"What—what started it up?" Mayfield looked bewildered. "For seventy years it was down there, and nothing happened!"

"Our blasting must have jarred something," Reynolds said shortly. "Maybe closed a relay that started up the old battle reflex circuit."

"You know something about these machines?" The mayor beetled his brows at him.

"I've read a little."

"Then speak up, man. I'll call the station, if you feel I must. What measures should I request?"

"I don't know, Mr. Mayor. As far as I know, nothing on New Devon can stop that machine now."

The mayor's mouth opened and closed. He whirled to the screen, blanked Eaton's agonized face, punched in the code for the Federation station.

"Colonel Blane!" he blurted as a stern face came onto the screen. "We have a major emergency on our hands! I'll need everything you've got! This is the situation …"

9

I encounter no resistance other than the flimsy barrier, but my progress is slow. Grievous damage has been done to my main drive sector due to overload during my escape from the trap; and the failure of my sensing circuitry has deprived me of a major portion of my external receptivity. Now my pain circuits project a continuous signal to my awareness center, but it is my duty to my Commander and to my fallen comrades of the Brigade to press forward at my best speed; but my performance is a poor shadow of my former ability.

And now at last the Enemy comes into action! I sense aerial units closing at supersonic velocities; I lock my lateral batteries to them and direct salvo fire, but I sense that the arming mechanisms clatter harmlessly. The craft sweep over me, and my impotent guns elevate, track them as they release detonants that spread out in an envelopmental pattern which I, with my reduced capabilities, am powerless to avoid. The missiles strike; I sense their detonations all about me; but I suffer only trivial damage. The Enemy has blundered if he thought to neutralize a Mark XXVIII Combat Unit with mere chemical explosives! But I weaken with each meter gained.

Now there is no doubt as to my course. I must press the charge and carry the walls before my reserve cells are exhausted.

10

From a vantage point atop a bucket rig four hundred yards from the position the great fighting machine had now reached, Pete Reynolds studied it through night glasses. A battery of beamed polyarcs pinned the giant hulk, scarred and rust-scaled, in a pool of blue-white light. A mile and a half beyond it, the walls of the Mall rose sheer from the garden setting.

"The bombers slowed it some," he reported to Eaton via scope. "But it's still making better than two miles per hour. I'd say another twenty-five minutes before it hits the main ringwall. How's the evacuation going?"

"Badly! I get no cooperation! You'll be my witness, Reynolds, I did all I could—"

"How about the mobile batteries; how long before they'll be in position?" Reynolds cut him off.

"I've heard nothing from Federation Central—typical militaristic arrogance, not keeping me informed—but I have them on my screens. They're two miles out—say three minutes."

"I hope you made your point about N-heads."

"That's outside my province!" Eaton said sharply. "It's up to Brand to carry out this portion of the operation!"

"The HE Missiles didn't do much more than clear away the junk it was dragging." Reynolds' voice was sharp.

"I wash my hands of responsibility for civilian lives," Eaton was saying when Reynolds shut him off, changed channels.

"Jim, I'm going to try to divert it," he said crisply. "Eaton's sitting on his political fence; the Feds are bringing artillery up, but I don't expect much from it. Technically, Brand needs Sector okay to use nuclear stuff, and he's not the boy to stick his neck out—"

"Divert it how? Pete, don't take any chances—"

Reynolds laughed shortly. "I'm going to get around it and drop a shaped drilling charge in its path. Maybe I can knock a tread off. With luck, I might get its attention on me and draw it away from the Mall. There are still a few thousand people over there, glued to their Tri-D's. They think it's all a swell show."

"Pete, you can't walk up on that thing! It's hot—" He broke off. "Pete, there's some kind of nut here—he claims he has to talk to you; says he knows something about that damned juggernaut. Shall I ...?"

Reynolds paused with his hand on the cut-off switch. "Put him on," he snapped. Mayfield's face moved aside and an ancient, bleary-eyed visage stared out at him. The tip of the old man's tongue touched his dry lips.

"Son, I tried to tell this boy here, but he wouldn't listen—"

"What have you got, old timer?" Pete cut in. "Make it fast."

"My name's Sanders. James Sanders. I'm ... I was with the Planetary Volunteer Scouts, back in '71—"

"Sure, dad," Pete said gently. "I'm sorry, I've got a little errand to run—"

"Wait ..." The old man's face worked. "I'm old, son—too damned old. I know. But bear with me. I'll try to say it straight.

I was with Hayle's squadron at Toledo. Then afterwards, they shipped us—but hell, you don't care about that! I keep wandering, son; can't help it. What I mean to say is—I was in on that last scrap, right here at New Devon—only we didn't call it New Devon then. Called it Heliport. Nothing but bare rock and Enemy emplacement—"

"You were talking about the battle, Mr. Sanders," Pete said tensely. "Go on with that part."

"Lieutenant Sanders," the oldster said. "Sure, I was Acting Brigade Commander. See, our major was hit at Toledo—and after Tommy Chee stopped a sidewinder at Belgrave—"

"Stick to the point, Lieutenant!"

"Yessir!" The old man pulled himself together with an obvious effort. "I took the Brigade in; put out flankers, and ran the Enemy into the ground. We mopped 'em up in a thirty-three hour running fight that took us from over by Crater Bay all the way down here to Hellport. When it was over, I'd lost sixteen units, but the Enemy was done. They gave us Brigade Honors for that action. And then ..."

"Then what?"

"Then the triple-dyed yellow-bottoms at Headquarters put out the order the Brigade was to be scrapped; said they were too hot to make decon practical. Cost too much, they said! So after the final review—" he gulped, blinked—"they planted 'em deep, two hundred meters, and poured in special high-R concrete."

"And packed rubble in behind them," Reynolds finished for him. "All right, Lieutenant, I believe you! Now for the big one: What started that machine on a rampage?"

"Should have known they couldn't hold down a Bolo Mark XXVIII!" The old man's eyes lit up. "Take more than a few million tons of rock to stop Lenny when his battle board was lit!"

"Lenny?"

"That's my old command unit out there, son. I saw the markings on the Tri-D. Unit LNE of the Dinochrome Brigade!"

"Listen!" Reynolds snapped out. "Here's what I intend to try …" He outlined his plan.

"Ha!" Sanders snorted. "It's a gutsy notion, mister, but Lenny won't give it a sneeze."

"You didn't come here to tell me we were licked," Reynolds cut in. "How about Brand's batteries?"

"Hell, son, Lenny stood up to point-blank Hellbore fire on Toledo, and—"

"Are you telling me there's nothing we can do?"

"What's that? No, son, that's not what I'm saying …"

"Then what!"

"Just tell these johnnies to get out of my way, mister. I think I can handle him."

11

At the field comm hut, Pete Reynolds watched as the man who had been Lieutenant Sanders of the Volunteer Scouts pulled shiny black boots over his thin ankles and stood. The blouse and trousers of royal blue polyon hung on his spare frame like wash on a line. He grinned, a skull's grin.

"It doesn't fit like it used to; but Lenny will recognize it. It'll help. Now, if you've got that power pack ready …"

Mayfield handed over the old-fashioned field instrument Sanders had brought in with him.

"It's operating, sir—but I've already tried everything I've got on that infernal machine; I didn't get a peep out of it."

Sanders winked at him. "Maybe I know a couple of tricks

you boys haven't heard about." He slung the strap over his bony shoulder and turned to Reynolds.

"Guess we better get going, mister. He's getting close."

In the rock car, Sanders leaned close to Reynolds' ear. "Told you those Federal guns wouldn't scratch Lenny. They're wasting their time."

Reynolds pulled the car to a stop at the crest of the road, from which point he had a view of the sweep of ground leading across to the city's edge. Lights sparkled all across the towers of New Devon. Close to the walls, the converging fire of the ranked batteries of infinite repeaters drove into the glowing bulk of the machine, which plowed on, undeterred. As he watched, the firing ceased.

"Now, let's get in there, before they get some other damn-fool scheme going," Sanders said.

The rock car crossed the rough ground, swung wide to come up on the Bolo from the left side. Behind the hastily rigged radiation cover, Reynolds watched the immense silhouette grow before him.

"I knew they were big," he said. "But to see one up close like this—" He pulled to a stop a hundred feet from the Bolo.

"Look at the side ports," Sanders said, his voice crisper now. "He's firing antipersonnel charges—only his plates are flat. If they weren't, we wouldn't have gotten within half a mile." He unclipped the microphone and spoke into it:

"Unit LNE, break off action and retire to ten-mile line!"

Reynolds' head jerked around to stare at the old man. His voice had rung with vigor and authority as he spoke the command.

The Bolo ground slowly ahead. Sanders shook his head, tried again.

"No answer, like that fella said. He must be running on

nothing but memories now. …" He reattached the microphone, and before Reynolds could put out a hand, had lifted the anti-R cover and stepped off on the ground.

"Sanders—get back in here!" Reynolds yelled.

"Never mind, son. I've got to get in close. Contact induction." He started toward the giant machine. Frantically, Reynolds started the car, slammed it into gear, pulled forward.

"Better stay back." Sanders' voice came from his field radio. "This close, that screening won't do you much good."

"Get in the car!" Reynolds roared. "That's hard radiation!"

"Sure; feels funny, like a sunburn, about an hour after you come in from the beach and start to think maybe you got a little too much." He laughed. "But I'll get to him. …"

Reynolds braked to a stop, watched the shrunken figure in the baggy uniform as it slogged forward, leaning as against a sleet storm.

12

"I'm up beside him." Sanders' voice came through faintly on the field radio. "I'm going to try to swing up on his side. Don't feel like trying to chase him any farther."

Through the glasses, Reynolds watched the small figure, dwarfed by the immense bulk of the fighting machine, as he tried, stumbled, tried again, swung up on the flange running across the rear quarter inside the churning bogie wheel.

"He's up," he reported. "Damned wonder the track didn't get him. …"

Clinging to the side of the machine, Sanders lay for a moment, bent forward across the flange. Then he pulled himself up, wormed his way forward to the base of the rear quarter turret, wedged himself against it. He unslung the communicator, removed a small black unit, clipped it to the armor; it clung, held by a magnet. He brought the microphone up to his face.

In the comm shack, Mayfield leaned toward the screen, his eyes squinted in tension. Across the field, Reynolds held the glasses fixed on the man lying across the flank of the Bolo. They waited. . . .

13

The walls are before me, and I ready myself for a final effort, but suddenly I am aware of trickle currents flowing over my outer surface. Is this some new trick of the Enemy? I tune to the wave energies, trace the source. They originate at a point in contact with my aft port armor. I sense modulation, match receptivity to a computed pattern. And I hear a voice:

"Unit LNE, break it off, Lenny. We're pulling back now, boy. This is Command to LNE; pull back to ten miles. If you read me, Lenny, swing to port and halt."

I am not fooled by the deception. The order appears correct, but the voice is not that of my Commander. Briefly I regret that I cannot spare energy to direct a neutralizing power flow at the device the Enemy has attached to me. I continue my charge.

"Unit LNE! Listen to me, boy; maybe you don't recognize my voice, but it's me. You see, boy—some time has passed. I've gotten old. My voice has changed some, maybe. But it's me! Make a port turn, Lenny. Make it now!"

I am tempted to respond to the trick, for something in the false command seems to awaken secondary circuits which I sense have been long stilled. But I must not be swayed by the cleverness of the Enemy. My sensing circuitry has faded further as my energy cells drain; but I know where the Enemy lies. I move forward, but I am filled with agony, and only the memory of my comrades drives me on.

"Lenny, answer me. Transmit on the old private band—the one we agreed on. Nobody but me knows it, remember?"

Thus the Enemy seeks to beguile me into diverting precious power. But I will not listen.

"Lenny—not much time left. Another minute and you'll be into the walls. People are going to die. Got to stop you, Lenny. Hot here. My God, I'm hot. Not breathing too well, now. I can feel it; cutting through me like knives. You took a load of Enemy power, Lenny; and now I'm getting my share. Answer me, Lenny. Over to you. ..."

It will require only a tiny allocation of power to activate a communication circuit. I realize that it is only an Enemy trick, but I compute that by pretending to be deceived, I may achieve some trivial advantage. I adjust circuitry accordingly and transmit:

"Unit LNE to Command. Contact with Enemy defensive line imminent. Request supporting fire!"

"Lenny ... you can hear me! Good boy, Lenny! Now make a turn, to port. Walls ... close. ..."

"Unit LNE to Command. Request positive identification; transmit code 685749."

"Lenny—I can't ... don't have code blanks. But it's me. ..."

"In absence of recognition code, your transmission disregarded," I send. And now the walls loom high above me. There are many lights, but I see them only vaguely. I am nearly blind now.

"Lenny—less'n two hundred feet to go. Listen, Lenny. I'm climbing down. I'm going to jump down, Lenny, and get around under your fore scanner pickup. You'll see me, Lenny. You'll know me then."

The false transmission ceases. I sense a body moving across my side. The gap closes. I detect movement before me, and in automatic reflex fire anti-P charges before I recall that I am unarmed.

A small object has moved out before me, and taken up a position between me and the wall behind which the Enemy conceal themselves. It is dim, but appears to have the shape of a man. . . .

I am uncertain. My alert center attempts to engage inhibitory circuitry which will force me to halt, but it lacks power. I can override it. But still I am unsure. Now I must take a last risk; I must shunt power to my forward scanner to examine this obstacle more closely. I do so, and it leaps into greater clarity. It is indeed a man—and it is enclothed in regulation blues of the Volunteers. Now, closer, I see the face and through the pain of my great effort, I study it. . . .

14

"He's backed against the wall," Reynolds said hoarsely. "It's still coming. A hundred feet to go—"

"You were a fool, Reynolds!" the mayor barked. "A fool to stake everything on that old dotard's crazy ideas!"

"Hold it!" As Reynolds watched, the mighty machine slowed, halted, ten feet from the sheer wall before it. For a moment, it sat, as though puzzled. Then it backed, halted again, pivoted ponderously to the left, and came about.

On its side, a small figure crept up, fell across the lower gun deck. The Bolo surged into motion, retracing its route across the artillery-scarred gardens.

"He's turned it." Reynolds let his breath out with a shuddering sigh. "It's headed out for open desert. It might get twenty miles before it finally runs out of steam."

The strange voice that was the Bolo's came from the big panel before Mayfield:

"Command. ... Unit LNE reports main power cells drained, secondary cells drained; now operating at .037 per cent efficiency, using Final Emergency Power. Request advice as to range to be covered before relief maintenance available."

"It's a long way, Lenny ..." Sanders' voice was a bare whisper. *"But I'm coming with you. ..."*

Then there was only the crackle of static. Ponderously, like a great mortally stricken animal, the Bolo moved through the ruins of the fallen roadway, heading for the open desert.

"That damned machine," the mayor said in a hoarse voice. "You'd almost think it was alive."

"You would at that," Pete Reynolds said.

A RELIC OF WAR

The old war machine sat in the village square, its impotent guns pointing aimlessly along the dusty street. Shoulder-high weeds grew rankly about it, poking up through the gaps in the two-yard-wide treads; vines crawled over the high, rust-and guano-streaked flanks. A row of tarnished enameled battle honors gleamed dully across the prow, reflecting the late sun.

A group of men lounged near the machine; they were dressed in heavy work clothes and boots; their hands were large and calloused, their faces weather-burned. They passed a jug from hand to hand, drinking deep. It was the end of a long workday and they were relaxed, good-humored.

"Hey, we're forgetting old Bobby," one said. He strolled over and sloshed a little of the raw whiskey over the soot-blackened muzzle of the blast cannon slanting sharply down from the forward turret. The other men laughed.

"How's it going, Bobby?" the man called.

Deep inside the machine there was a soft chirring sound.

"*Very well, thank you,*" a faint, whispery voice scraped from a grill below the turret.

"You keeping an eye on things, Bobby?" another man called.

"*All clear,*" the answer came: a bird-chirp from a dinosaur.

"Bobby, you ever get tired just setting here?"

"Hell, Bobby don't get tired," the man with the jug said. "He's got a job to do, old Bobby has."

"Hey, Bobby, what kind o'boy are you?" a plump, lazy-eyed man called.

"I am a good boy," Bobby replied obediently.

"Sure Bobby's a good boy." The man with the jug reached up to pat the age-darkened curve of chromalloy above him. "Bobby's looking out for us."

Heads turned at a sound from across the square: the distant whine of a turbocar, approaching along the forest road.

"Huh! Ain't the day for the mail," a man said. They stood in silence, watching as a small, dusty cushion-car emerged from deep shadow into the yellow light of the street. It came slowly along to the plaza, swung left, pulled to a stop beside the boardwalk before a corrugated metal store front lettered BLAUVELT PROVISION COMPANY. The canopy popped open and a man stepped down. He was of medium height, dressed in a plain city-type black coverall. He studied the store front, the street, then turned to look across at the men. He came across toward them.

"Which of you men is Blauvelt?" he asked as he came up. His voice was unhurried, cool. His eyes flicked over the men.

A big, youngish man with a square face and sun-bleached hair lifted his chin.

"Right here," he said. "Who're you?"

"Crewe is the name. Disposal Officer, War Materiel Commission." The newcomer looked up at the great machine looming over them. "Bolo *Stupendous,* Mark XXV," he said. He glanced at the men's faces, fixed on Blauvelt. "We had a report that there was a live Bolo out here. I wonder if you realize what you're playing with?"

"Hell, that's just Bobby," a man said.

"He's town mascot," someone else said.

"This machine could blow your town off the map," Crewe

said. "And a good-sized piece of jungle along with it."

Blauvelt grinned; the squint lines around his eyes gave him a quizzical look.

"Don't go getting upset, Mr. Crewe," he said. "Bobby's harmless—"

"A Bolo's never harmless, Mr. Blauvelt. They're fighting machines, nothing else."

Blauvelt sauntered over and kicked at a corroded tread-plate. "Eighty-five years out in this jungle is kind of tough on machinery, Crewe. The sap and stuff from the trees eats chromalloy like it was sugar candy. The rains are acid, eat up equipment damn near as fast as we can ship it in here. Bobby can still talk a little, but that's about all."

"Certainly it's deteriorated; that's what makes it dangerous. Anything could trigger its battle reflex circuitry. Now, if you'll clear everyone out of the area, I'll take care of it."

"You move kind of fast for a man that just hit town," Blauvelt said, frowning. "Just what you got in mind doing?"

"I'm going to fire a pulse at it that will neutralize what's left of its computing center. Don't worry; there's no danger—"

"Hey," a man in the rear rank blurted. "That mean he can't talk any more?"

"That's right," Crewe said. "Also, he can't open fire on you."

"Not so fast, Crewe," Blauvelt said. "You're not messing with Bobby. We like him like he is." The other men were moving forward, forming up in a threatening circle around Crewe.

"Don't talk like a fool," Crewe said. "What do you think a salvo from a Continental Siege Unit would do to your town?"

Blauvelt chuckled and took a long cigar from his vest pocket. He sniffed it, called out: "All right, Bobby—fire one!"

There was a muted clatter, a sharp *click*! from deep inside the vast bulk of the machine. A tongue of pale flame licked from the cannon's soot-rimmed bore. The big man leaned quickly forward, puffed the cigar alight. The audience whooped with laughter.

"Bobby does what he's told, that's all," Blauvelt said. "And not much of that." He showed white teeth in a humorless smile.

Crewe flipped over the lapel of his jacket; a small, highly polished badge glinted there. "You know better than to interfere with a Concordiat officer," he said.

"Not so fast, Crewe," a dark-haired, narrow-faced fellow spoke up. "You're out of line. I heard about you Disposal men. Your job is locating old ammo dumps, abandoned equipment, stuff like that. Bobby's not abandoned. He's town property. Has been for near thirty years."

"Nonsense. This is battle equipment, the property of the Space Arm—"

Blauvelt was smiling lopsidedly. "Uh-uh. We've got salvage rights. No title, but we can make one up in a hurry. Official. I'm the Mayor here, and District Governor."

"This thing is a menace to every man, woman, and child in the settlement," Crewe snapped. "My job is to prevent tragedy—"

"Forget Bobby," Blauvelt cut in. He waved a hand at the jungle wall beyond the tilled fields. "There's a hundred million square miles of virgin territory out there," he said. "You can do what you like out there. I'll even sell you provisions. But just leave our mascot be, understand?"

Crewe looked at him, looked around at the other men.

"You're a fool," he said. "You're all fools." He turned and walked away, stiff-backed.

*

In the room he had rented in the town's lone boarding-house, Crewe opened his baggage and took out a small, gray-plastic-cased instrument. The three children of the landlord who were watching from the latchless door edged closer.

"Gee, is that a real star radio?" the eldest, a skinny, long-necked lad of twelve asked.

"No," Crewe said shortly. The boy blushed and hung his head.

"It's a command transmitter," Crewe said, relenting. "It's designed for talking to fighting machines, giving them orders. They'll only respond to the special shaped-wave signal this puts out." He flicked a switch, and an indicator light glowed on the side of the case.

"You mean like Bobby?" the boy asked.

"Like Bobby used to be." Crewe switched off the transmitter.

"Bobby's swell," another child said. "He tells us stories about when he was in the war."

"He's got medals," the first boy said. "Were you in the war, mister?"

"I'm not quite that old," Crewe said.

"Bobby's older'n grandad."

"You boys had better run along," Crewe said. "I have to . . ." He broke off, cocked his head, listening. There were shouts outside; someone was calling his name.

Crewe pushed through the boys and went quickly along the hall, stepped through the door onto the boardwalk. He felt rather than heard a slow, heavy thudding, a chorus of shrill squeaks, a metallic groaning. A red-faced man was running toward him from the square.

"It's Bobby!" he shouted. "He's moving! What'd you do to him, Crewe?"

Crewe brushed past the man, ran toward the plaza. The

Bolo appeared at the end of the street, moving ponderously forward, trailing uprooted weeds and vines.

"He's headed straight for Spivac's warehouse!" someone yelled.

"Bobby! Stop there!" Blauvelt came into view, running in the machine's wake. The big machine rumbled onward, executed a half-left as Crewe reached the plaza, clearing the corner of a building by inches. It crushed a section of boardwalk to splinters, advanced across a storage yard. A stack of rough-cut lumber toppled, spilled across the dusty ground. The Bolo trampled a board fence, headed out across a tilled field. Blauvelt whirled on Crewe.

"This is your doing! We never had trouble before—"

"Never mind that! Have you got a field car?"

"We—" Blauvelt checked himself. "What if we have?"

"I can stop it—but I have to be close. It will be into the jungle in another minute. My car can't navigate there."

"Let him go," a man said, breathing hard from his run. "He can't do no harm out there."

"Who'd of thought it?" another man said. "Setting there all them years—who'd of thought he could travel like that?"

"Your so-called mascot might have more surprises in store for you," Crewe snapped. "Get me a car, fast! This is an official requisition, Blauvelt!"

There was a silence, broken only by the distant crashing of timber as the Bolo moved into the edge of the forest. Hundred-foot trees leaned and went down before its advance.

"Let him go," Blauvelt said. "Like Stinzi says, he can't hurt anything."

"What if he turns back?"

"Hell," a man muttered. "Old Bobby wouldn't hurt *us* ..."

"That car," Crewe snarled. "You're wasting valuable time."

Blauvelt frowned. "All right—but you don't make a move unless it looks like he's going to come back and hit the town. Clear?"

"Let's go."

Blauvelt led the way at a trot toward the town garage.

The Bolo's trail was a twenty-five foot wide swath cut through the virgin jungle; the tread-prints were pressed eighteen inches into the black loam, where it showed among the jumble of fallen branches.

"It's moving at about twenty miles an hour, faster than we can go," Crewe said. "If it holds its present track, the curve will bring it back to your town in about five hours."

"He'll sheer off," Blauvelt said.

"Maybe. But we won't risk it. Pick up a heading of 270°, Blauvelt. We'll try an intercept by cutting across the circle."

Blauvelt complied wordlessly. The car moved ahead in the deep green gloom under the huge shaggy-barked trees. Oversized insects buzzed and thumped against the canopy. Small and medium lizards hopped, darted, flapped. Fern leaves as big as awnings scraped along the car as it clambered over loops and coils of tough root, leaving streaks of plant juice across the clear plastic. Once they grated against an exposed ridge of crumbling brown rock; flakes as big as saucers scaled off, exposing dull metal.

"Dorsal fin of a scout-boat," Crewe said. "That's what's left of what was supposed to be a corrosion resistant alloy."

They passed more evidences of a long-ago battle: the massive, shattered breech mechanism of a platform-mounted Hellbore, the gutted chassis of what might have been a bomb car, portions of a downed aircraft, fragments of shattered armor. Many of the relics were of Terran design, but often it was the curiously curved, spidery lines of a rusted Axorc microgun or implosion projector that poked through the greenery.

"It must have been a heavy action," Crewe said. "One of the ones toward the end that didn't get much notice at the time. There's stuff here I've never seen before, experimental types, I imagine, rushed in by the enemy for a last-ditch stand."

Blauvelt grunted.

"Contact in another minute or so," Crewe said.

As Blauvelt opened his mouth to reply, there was a blinding flash, a violent impact, and the jungle erupted in their faces.

The seat webbing was cutting into Crewe's ribs. His ears were filled with a high, steady ringing; there was a taste of brass in his mouth. His head throbbed in time with the thudding of his heart.

The car was on its side, the interior a jumble of loose objects, torn wiring, broken plastic. Blauvelt was half under him, groaning. He slid off him, saw that he was groggy but conscious.

"Changed your mind yet about your harmless pet?" he asked, wiping a trickle of blood from his right eye. "Let's get clear before he fires those empty guns again. Can you walk?"

Blauvelt mumbled, crawled out through the broken canopy. Crewe groped through debris for the command transmitter—

"Good God," Blauvelt croaked. Crewe twisted, saw the high, narrow, iodine-dark shape of the alien machine perched on jointed crawler-legs fifty feet away, framed by blast-scorched foliage. Its multiple-barreled micro-gun battery was aimed dead at the overturned car.

"Don't move a muscle," Crewe whispered. Sweat trickled down his face. An insect, like a stub-winged four-inch dragonfly, came and buzzed about them, moved on. Hot metal pinged, contracting. Instantly, the alien hunter-killer moved forward another six feet, depressing its gun muzzles.

"Run for it!" Blauvelt cried. He came to his feet in a scrabbling lunge; the enemy machine swung to track him ...

A giant tree leaned, snapped, was tossed aside. The great green-streaked prow of the Bolo forged into view, interposing itself between the smaller machine and the men. It turned to face the enemy; fire flashed, reflecting against the surrounding trees; the ground jumped once, twice, to hard, racking shocks. Sound boomed dully in Crewe's blast-numbed ears. Bright sparks fountained above the Bolo as it advanced. Crewe felt the massive impact as the two fighting machines came together; he saw the Bolo hesitate, then forge ahead, rearing up, pushing the lighter machine aside, grinding over it, passing on, to leave a crumpled mass of wreckage in its wake.

"Did you see that, Crewe?" Blauvelt shouted in his ear. "Did you see what Bobby did? He walked right into its guns and smashed it flatter'n crock-brewed beer!"

The Bolo halted, turned ponderously, sat facing the men. Bright streaks of molten metal ran down its armored flanks, fell spattering and smoking into crushed greenery.

"He saved our necks," Blauvelt said. He staggered to his feet, picked his way past the Bolo to stare at the smoking ruins of the smashed adversary.

"Unit Nine Five Four of the Line, reporting contact with hostile force," the mechanical voice of the Bolo spoke suddenly. *"Enemy unit destroyed. I have sustained extensive damage, but am still operational at nine point six percent base capability, awaiting further orders."*

"Hey," Blauvelt said. "That doesn't sound like ..."

"Now maybe you understand that this is a Bolo combat

unit, not the village idiot," Crewe snapped. He picked his way across the churned-up ground, stood before the great machine.

"Mission accomplished, Unit Nine five four," he called. "Enemy forces neutralized. Close out Battle Reflex and revert to low alert status." He turned to Blauvelt.

"Let's go back to town," he said, "and tell them what their mascot just did."

Blauvelt stared up at the grim and ancient machine; his square, tanned face looked yellowish and drawn. "Let's do that," he said.

The ten-piece town band was drawn up in a double rank before the newly mown village square. The entire population of the settlement—some three hundred and forty-two men, women and children—were present, dressed in their best. Pennants fluttered from strung wires. The sun glistened from the armored sides of the newly-cleaned and polished Bolo. A vast bouquet of wild flowers poked from the no-longer-sooty muzzle of the Hellbore.

Crewe stepped forward.

"As a representative of the Concordiat government I've been asked to make this presentation," he said. "You people have seen fit to design a medal and award it to Unit Nine five four in appreciation for services rendered in defense of the community above and beyond the call of duty." He paused, looked across the faces of his audience.

"Many more elaborate honors have been awarded for a great deal less," he said. He turned to the machine; two men came forward, one with a stepladder, the other with a portable welding rig. Crewe climbed up, fixed the newly struck decoration in place beside the row of century-old battle honors. The technician quickly spotted it in position. The crowd cheered, then dispersed, chattering, to the picnic tables set up in the village street.

It was late twilight. The last of the sandwiches and stuffed eggs had been eaten, the last speeches declaimed, the last keg broached. Crewe sat with a few of the men in the town's lone public house.

"To Bobby," a man raised his glass.

"Correction," Crewe said. "To Unit Nine five four of the Line." The men laughed and drank.

"Well, time to go, I guess," a man said. The others chimed in, rose, clattering chairs. As the last of them left, Blauvelt came in. He sat down across from Crewe.

"You, ah, staying the night?" he asked.

"I thought I'd drive back," Crewe said. "My business here is finished."

"Is it?" Blauvelt said tensely.

Crewe looked at him, waiting.

"You know what you've got to do, Crewe."

"Do I?" Crewe took a sip from his glass.

"Damn it, have I got to spell it out? As long as that machine was just an oversized half-wit, it was all right. Kind of a monument to the war, and all. But now I've seen what it can do … Crewe, we can't have a live killer sitting in the middle of our town—never knowing when it might take a notion to start shooting again!"

"Finished?" Crewe asked.

"It's not that we're not grateful—"

"Get out," Crewe said.

"Now, look here, Crewe—"

"Get out. And keep everyone away from Bobby, understand?"

"Does that mean—?"

"I'll take care of it."

Blauvelt got to his feet. "Yeah," he said. "Sure."

After Blauvelt left, Crewe rose and dropped a bill on the table; he picked the command transmitter from the floor, went out into the street. Faint cries came from the far end of the town, where the crowd had gathered for fireworks. A yellow rocket arced up, burst in a spray of golden light, falling, fading . . .

Crewe walked toward the plaza. The Bolo loomed up, a vast, black shadow against the star-thick sky. Crewe stood before it, looking up at the already draggled pennants, the wilted nosegay drooping from the gun muzzle.

"Unit Nine five four, you know why I'm here?" he said softly.

"I compute that my usefulness as an engine of war is ended," the soft rasping voice said.

"That's right," Crewe said. "I checked the area in a thousand-mile radius with sensitive instruments. There's no enemy machine left alive. The one you killed was the last."

"It was true to its duty," the machine said.

"It was my fault," Crewe said. "It was designed to detect our command carrier and home on it. When I switched on my transmitter, it went into action. Naturally, you sensed that, and went to meet it."

The machine sat silent.

"You could still save yourself," Crewe said. "If you trampled me under and made for the jungle it might be centuries before . . ."

"Before another man comes to do what must be done? Better that I cease now, at the hands of a friend."

"Good-bye, Bobby."

"Correction: Unit Nine five four of the Line."

Crewe pressed the key. A sense of darkness fell across the machine.

At the edge of the square, Crewe looked back. He raised a hand in a ghostly salute; then he walked away along the dusty street, white in the light of the rising moon.

COMBAT UNIT

I do not like it; it has the appearance of a trap, but the order has been given. I enter the room and the valve closes behind me.

I inspect my surroundings. I am in a chamber 40.81 meters long, 10.35 meters wide, 4.12 high, with no openings except the one through which I entered. It is floored and walled with five-centimeter armor of flint-steel and beyond that there are ten centimeters of lead. Massive apparatus is folded and coiled in mountings around the room. Power is flowing in heavy buss bars beyond the shielding. I am sluggish for want of power; my examination of the room has taken .8 seconds.

Now I detect movement in a heavy jointed arm mounted above me. It begins to rotate, unfold. I assume that I will be attacked, and decide to file a situation report. I have difficulty in concentrating my attention …

I pull back receptivity from my external sensing circuits, set my bearing locks and switch over to my introspection complex. All is dark and hazy. I seem to remember when it was like a great cavern glittering with bright lines of transvisual colors …

It is different now; I grope my way in gloom, feeling along numbed circuits, test-pulsing cautiously until I feel contact with my transmitting unit. I have not used it since … I cannot remember. My memory banks lie black and inert.

"Command Unit," I transmit, "Combat Unit requests permission to file VSR."

I wait, receptors alert. I do not like waiting blindly, for the quarter-second my sluggish action/reaction cycle requires. I wish that my Brigade comrades were at my side.

I call again, wait, then go ahead with my VSR. "This position heavily shielded, mounting apparatus of offensive capability. No withdrawal route. Advise."

I wait, repeat my transmission; nothing. I am cut off from Command Unit, from my comrades of the Dinochrome Brigade. Within me, pressure builds.

I feel a deep-seated click and a small but reassuring surge of power brightens the murk of the cavern to a dim glow, burning forgotten components to feeble life. An emergency pile has come into action automatically.

I realize that I am experiencing a serious equipment failure. I will devote another few seconds to troubleshooting, repairing what I can. I do not understand what accident can have occurred to damage me thus. I cannot remember …

I go along the dead cells, testing.

"—out! Bring .09's to bear, .8 millisec burst, close armor …"

"… sun blanking visual; slide number-seven filter in place."

"… 478.09, 478.11, 478.13, Mark! …"

The cells are intact. Each one holds its fragment of recorded sense impression. The trouble is farther back. I try a main reflex lead.

"… main combat circuit, discon—"

Here is something; a command, on the reflex level! I go back, tracing, tapping mnemonic cells at random, searching for some clue.

"—sembark. Units emergency standby …"

"… response one-oh-three; stimulus-response negative …"

"Check list complete, report negative …"

I go on, searching out damage. I find an open switch in my maintenance panel. It will not activate; a mechanical jamming. I must fuse it shut quickly. I pour in power, and the mind-cavern dims almost to blackness. Then there is contact, a flow of electrons, and the cavern snaps alive; lines, points pseudo-glowing. It is not the blazing glory of my full powers, but it will serve; I am awake again.

I observe the action of the unfolding arm. It is slow, un-coordinated, obviously automated. I dismiss it from direct attention; I have several seconds before it will be in offensive position, and there is work for me if I am to be ready. I fire sampling impulses at the black memory banks, determine statistically that 98.92% are intact, merely disassociated.

The threatening arm swings over slowly; I integrate its path, see that it will come to bear on my treads; I probe, find only a simple hydraulic ram. A primitive apparatus to launch against a Mark XXXI fighting unit, even without mnemonics.

Meanwhile, I am running a full check. Here is something … An open breaker, a disconnect used only during repairs. I think of the cell I tapped earlier, and suddenly its meaning springs into my mind. "Main combat circuit, disconnect …" Under low awareness, it had not registered. I throw in the switch with frantic haste. Suppose I had gone into combat with my fighting-reflex circuit open!

The arm reaches position and I move easily aside. I notice that a clatter accompanies my movement. The arm sits stupidly aimed at nothing, then turns. Its reaction time is pathetic. I set up a random evasion pattern, return my attention to my check, find another dark area. I probe, feel a curious vagueness. I am unable at first to identify the components involved, but I realize that it is here that my communication with Command is blocked. I break the connection to the tampered banks, abandoning any immediate hope of contact with Command.

There is nothing more I can do to ready myself. I have lost my general memory banks and my Command circuit, and my power supply is limited; but I am still a fighting Unit of the Dinochrome Brigade. I have my offensive power unimpaired, and my sensory equipment is operating adequately. I am ready.

Now another of the jointed arms swings into action, following my movements deliberately. I evade it and again I note a clatter as I move. I think of the order that sent me here; there is something strange about it. I activate my current-action memory stage, find the cell recording the moments preceding my entry into the metal-walled room.

Here in darkness, vague, indistinct, relieved suddenly by radiation on a narrow spectrum. There is an order, coming muffled from my command center. It originates in the sector I have blocked off. It is not from my Command Unit, not a legal command. I have been tricked by the Enemy. I tune back to earlier moments, but there is nothing. It is as though my existence began when the order was given. I scan back, back, spot-sampling at random, find only routine sense-impressions. I am about to drop the search when I encounter a sequence which arrests my attention.

I am parked on a ramp, among other Combat Units. A heavy rain is falling, and I see the water coursing down the corroded side of the Unit next to me. He is badly in need of maintenance. I note that his Command antennae are missing, and that a rusting metal object has been crudely welded to his hull in their place. I feel no alarm; I accept this as normal. I activate a motor train, move forward. I sense other Units moving out, silent. All are mutilated. …

The bank ends; all else is burned. What has befallen us?

Suddenly there is a stimulus on an audio frequency. I tune quickly, locate the source as a porous spot high on the flint-steel wall.

"Combat Unit! Remain stationary!" It is an organically produced voice, but not that of my Commander. I ignore the false command. The Enemy will not trick me again. I sense the location of the leads to the speaker, the alloy of which they are composed; I bring a beam to bear. I focus it, following along the cable. There is a sudden yell from the speaker as the heat reaches the creature at the microphone. Thus I enjoy a moment of triumph.

I return my attention to the imbecile apparatus in the room.

A great engine, mounted on rails which run down the center of the room moves suddenly, sliding toward my position. I examine it, find that it mounts a turret equipped with high-speed cutting heads. I consider blasting it with a burst of high-energy particles, but in the same moment compute that this is not practical. I could inactivate myself as well as the cutting engine.

Now a cable snakes out in an undulating curve, and I move to avoid it, at the same time investigating its composition. It seems to be no more than a stranded wire rope. Impatiently I flick a tight beam at it, see it glow yellow, white, blue, then spatter in a shower of droplets. But that was an unwise gesture. I do not have the power to waste.

I move off, clear of the two foolish arms still maneuvering for position. I wish to watch the cutting engine. It stops as it comes abreast of me, and turns its turret in my direction. I wait.

A grappler moves out now on a rail overhead. It is a heavy claw of flint-steel. I have seen similar devices, somewhat smaller, mounted on special Combat Units. They can be very useful for amputating antennae, cutting treads, and the like. I do not attempt to cut the arm; I know that the energy drain would be too great. Instead I beam high-frequency sound at the mechanical joints. They heat quickly, glowing. The metal has a high coefficient of expansion, and the ball joints squeal, freeze. I pour in more heat, and weld a socket. I notice that twenty-eight seconds have now elapsed since the valve closed behind me. I am growing weary of my confinement.

Now the grappler swings above me, maneuvering awkwardly with its frozen joint. A blast of liquid air expelled under high pressure should be sufficient to disable the grappler permanently.

But I am again startled. No blast answers my impulse. I feel out the non-functioning unit, find raw, cut edges, crude welds. Hastily, I extend a scanner to examine my hull. I am stunned into immobility by what I see.

My hull, my proud hull of chrome-duralloy, is pitted, coated with a crumbling layer of dull black paint, bubbled by corrosion. My main emplacements gape, black, empty. Rusting protuberances mar the once-smooth contour of my fighting turret. Streaks run down from them, down to loose treads, unshod, bare plates exposed. Small wonder that I have been troubled by a clatter each time I moved.

But I cannot lie idle under attack. I no longer have my great ion-guns, my disruptors, my energy screens; but I have my fighting instinct.

A Mark XXXI Combat Unit is the finest fighting machine the ancient wars of the Galaxy have ever known. I am not easily neutralized. But I wish that my Commander's voice were with me …

The engine slides to me where the grappler, now unresisted,

holds me. I shunt my power flow to an accumulator, hold it until the leads begin to arc, then release it in a burst. The engine bucks, stops dead. Then I turn my attention to the grappler.

I was built to engage the mightiest war engines and destroy them, but I am a realist. In my weakened condition this trivial automaton poses a threat, and I must deal with it. I run through a sequence of motor impulses, checking responses with such somatic sensors as remain intact. I initiate 31,315 impulses, note reactions and compute my mechanical resources. This superficial check requires more than a second, during which time the mindless grappler hesitates, wasting the advantage.

In place of my familiar array of retractable fittings, I find only clumsy grappling arms, cutters, impact tools, without utility to a fighting Unit. However, I have no choice but to employ them. I unlimber two flimsy grapplers, seize the heavy arm which holds me, and apply leverage. The Enemy responds sluggishly, twisting away, dragging me with it. The thing is not lacking in brute strength. I take it above and below its carpal joint and bend it back. It responds after an interminable wait of point three seconds with a lunge against my restraint. I have expected this, of course, and quickly shift position to allow the joint to burst itself over my extended arm. I fire a release detonator, and clatter back, leaving the amputated arm welded to the sprung grappler. It was a brave opponent, but clumsy. I move to a position near the wall.

I attempt to compute my situation based on the meager data I have gathered in my Current Action banks; there is little there to guide me. The appearance of my hull shows that much time has passed since I last inspected it; my personality-gestalt holds an image of my external appearance as a flawlessly complete Unit, bearing only the honorable and carefully preserved scars of battle, and my battle honors, the row of gold-and-enamel crests welded to my fighting turret. Here is a lead, I realize instantly. I focus on my personality center, the basic data cell without which I could not exist as an integrated entity. The data it carries are simple, unelaborated, but battle honors are recorded there. I open the center to a sense impulse.

Awareness. Shapes which do not remain constant. Vibration at many frequencies. This is light. This is sound … A display of "colors." A spectrum of "tones." Hard/ soft; big/ little; here/ there …

… The voice of my Commander. Loyalty. Obedience. Comradeship …

I run quickly past basic orientation data to my self-picture.

… I am strong, I am proud, I am capable. I have a function; I perform it well, and I am at peace with myself. My circuits are balanced, current idles, waiting …

… I fear oblivion. I wish to continue to perform my function. It is important that I do not allow myself to be destroyed …

I scan on, seeking the Experience section. Here …

I am ranked with my comrades on a scarred plain. The command is given and I display the Brigade Battle Anthem. We stand, sensing the contours and patterns of the music as it was recorded in our morale centers. The symbol "Ritual Fire Dance" is associated with the music, an abstraction representing the spirit of our ancient brigade. It reminds us of the loneliness of victory, the emptiness of challenge without an able foe. It tells us that we are the Dinochrome, ancient and worthy.

The Commander stands before me, he places the decoration against my fighting turret, and at his order I weld it in place. Then my comrades attune to me and I relive the episode …

I move past the blackened hulk of a comrade, send out a recognition signal, find his flicker of response. He has withdrawn to his survival center safely. I reassure him, continue. He is the fourth casualty I have seen. Never before has the Dinochrome met such power. I compute that our envelopment will fail unless the enemy's firepower is reduced. I scan an oncoming missile, fix its trajectory, detonate it harmlessly twenty-seven hundred four point nine meters overhead. It originated at a point nearer to me than to any of my comrades. I request permission to abort my assigned mission and neutralize the battery. Permission is granted. I wheel, move up a slope of broken stone. I encounter high temperature beams, neutralize them. I fend off probing mortar fire, but the attack against me is redoubled. I bring a reserve circuit into play to handle the interception, but my defenses are saturated. I must take action.

I switch to high speed, slashing a path through the littered shale, my treads smoking. At a frequency of ten projectiles per second, the mortar barrage has difficulty finding me now; but this is an emergency overstrain on my running gear. I sense metal fatigue, dangerous heat levels in my bearings. I must slow.

I am close to the emplacement now. I have covered a mile in twelve seconds during my sprint, and the mortar fire falls off. I sense hard radiation now, and erect my screens. I fear this assault; it is capable of probing even to a survival center, if concentrated enough. But I must go on. I think of my comrades, the four treadless hulks waiting for rescue. We cannot withdraw. I open a pinpoint aperture long enough to snap a radar impulse, bring a launcher to bear, fire my main battery.

The Commander will understand that I do not have time to request permission. The mortars are silenced.

The radiation ceases momentarily, then resumes at a somewhat lower but still dangerous level. Now I must go in and eliminate the missile launcher. I top the rise, see the launching tube before me. It is of the subterranean type, deep in the rock. Its mouth gapes from a burned pit of slag. I will drop a small fusion bomb down the tube, I decide, and move forward, arming the bomb. As I do so, I am enveloped with a rain of burn-bombs. My outer hull is fused in many places; I flash impulses to my secondary batteries, but circuit-breakers snap; my radar is useless; the shielding has melted, forms a solid inert mass now under my outer plating. The Enemy has been clever; at one blow he has neutralized my offenses.

I sound the plateau ahead, locate the pit. I throw power to my treads; they are fused; I cannot move. Yet I cannot wait here for another broadside. I do not like it, but I must take desperate action; I blow my treads.

The shock sends me bouncing—just in time. Flame splashes over the gray-chipped pit of the blast crater. I grind forward now on my stripped drive wheels, maneuvering awkwardly. I move into position over the mouth of the tube. Using metal-to-metal contact, I extend a sensory impulse down the tube.

An armed missile moves into position, and in the same instant an alarm circuit closes; the firing command is countermanded and from below probing impulses play over my hull. But I stand fast; the tube is useless until I, the obstruction, am removed. I advise my Commander of the situation. The radiation is still at a high level, and I hope that relief will arrive soon. I observe, while my comrades complete the encirclement, and the Enemy is stilled. . . .

I withdraw from personality center. I am consuming too much time. I understand well enough now that I am in the stronghold of the Enemy, that I have been trapped, crippled. My corroded hull tells me that much time has passed. I know that after each campaign I am given depot maintenance, restored to full fighting efficiency, my original glittering beauty. Years of neglect would be required to pit my hull so. I wonder how long I have been in the hands of the Enemy, how I came to be here.

I have another thought. I will extend a sensory feeler to the metal wall against which I rest, follow up the leads which I scorched earlier. Immediately I project my awareness along the lines, bring the distant microphone to life by fusing a switch. I pick up a rustle of moving gasses, the grate of non-metallic molecules. I step up sensitivity, hear the creak and pop of protoplasmic contractions, the crackle of neuroelectric impulses. I drop back to normal audio ranges and wait. I notice the low-frequency beat of modulated air vibrations, tune, adjust my time regulator to the pace of human speech. I match the patterns to my language index, interpret the sounds.

"... incredible blundering. Your excuses—"

"I make no excuses, My Lord General. My only regret is that the attempt has gone awry."

"Awry! An Alien engine of destruction activated in the midst of Research Center!"

"We possess nothing to compare with this machine; I saw my opportunity to place an advantage in our hands at last."

"Blundering fool! That is a decision for the planning cell. I accept no responsibility—"

"But these hulks which they allow to lie rotting on the ramp contain infinite treasures in psychotronic ..."

"They contain carnage and death! They are the tools of an Alien science which even at the height of our achievements we never mastered!"

"Once we used them as wrecking machines; their armaments were stripped, they are relatively harmless—"

"Already this 'harmless' juggernaut has smashed half the equipment in our finest decontamination chamber! It may yet break free …"

"Impossible! I am sure—"

"Silence! You have five minutes in which to immobilize the machine. I will have your head in any event, but perhaps you can earn yourself a quick death."

"Excellency! I may still find a way! The unit obeyed my first command, to enter the chamber. I have some knowledge. I studied the control centers, cut out the memory, most of the basic circuits; it should have been a docile slave."

"You failed; you will pay the penalty of failure. And perhaps so shall we all."

There is no further speech; I have learned little from this exchange. I must find a way to leave this cell. I move away from the wall, probe to discover the weak point; I find none.

Now a number of hinged panels snap up around me, hedging me in. I wait to observe what will come next. A metal mesh drops from above, drapes over me. I observe that it is connected by heavy leads to the power pile. I am unable to believe that the Enemy will make this blunder. Then I feel the flow of high voltage.

I receive it gratefully, opening my power storage cells, drinking up the vitalizing flow. To confuse the Enemy, I display a corona, thresh my treads as though in distress. The flow continues. I send a sensing impulse along the leads, locate the power source, weld all switches, fuses, and circuit breakers. Now the charge will not be interrupted. I luxuriate in the unexpected influx of energy.

I am aware abruptly that changes are occurring within my introspection complex. As the level of stored power rises rapidly, I am conscious of new circuits joining my control network. Within the dim-glowing cavern the lights come up; I sense latent capabilities which before had lain idle now coming onto action level. A thousand brilliant lines glitter where before one feeble thread burned; and I feel my self-awareness expand in a myriad glowing centers of reserve computing, integrating, sensory capacity. I am at last coming fully alive.

I send out a call on the Brigade band, meet blankness. I wait, accumulate power, try again. I know triumph as from an infinite distance a faint acknowledgment comes. It is a comrade, sunk deep in a comatose state, sealed in his survival center. I call again, sounding the signal of ultimate distress; and now I sense two responses, both faint, both from survival centers, but it heartens me to know that now, whatever befalls, I am not alone.

I consider, then send again; I request my brothers to join forces, combine their remaining field generating capabilities to set up a range-and-distance pulse. They agree and faintly I sense its almost undetectable touch. I lock to it, compute its point of origin. Only 224.9 meters! It is incredible. By the strength of the signal, I had assumed a distance of at least two thousand kilometers. My brothers are on the brink of extinction.

I am impatient, but I wait, building toward full power reserves. The copper mesh enfolding me has melted, flowed down over my sides. I sense that soon I will have absorbed a full charge. I am ready to act. I dispatch electromagnetic impulses along the power lead back to the power pile a quarter of a kilometer distant. I locate and disengage the requisite number of damping devices and instantaneously I erect my shields against the wave of radiation, filtered by the lead sheathing of the room, which washes over me; I feel a preliminary shock wave through my treads, then the walls balloon, whirl away. I am alone under a black sky which is dominated by the rising fireball of the blast, boiling with garish light. It has taken me nearly two minutes to orient myself, assess the situation and break out of confinement.

I move off through the rubble, homing on the R-and-D fix I have recorded. I throw out a radar pulse, record the terrain ahead, note no obstruction; I emerge from a wasteland of weathered bomb-fragments and pulverized masonry, obviously the scene of a hard-fought engagement at one time, onto an eroded ramp. Collapsed sheds are strewn across the broken paving; a line of dark shapes looms beyond them. I need no probing ray to tell me I have found my fellows of the Dinochrome Brigade. Frost forms over my scanner apertures, and I pause to melt it clear.

I round the line, scan the area to the horizon for evidence of Enemy activity, then tune to the Brigade band. I send out a probing pulse, back it up with full power, sensors keened for a whisper of response. The two who answered first acknowledge, then another, and another. We must array our best strength against the moment of counterattack.

There are present fourteen of the Brigade's full strength of twenty Units. At length, after .9 seconds of transmission, all but one have replied. I give instruction, then move to each in turn, extend a power tap, and energize the command center. The Units come alive, orient themselves, report to me. We rejoice in our meeting, but mourn our silent comrade.

Now I take an unprecedented step. We have no contact with our Commander, and without leadership we are lost; yet I am aware of the immediate situation, and have computed the proper action. Therefore I will assume command, act in the Commander's place. I am sure that he will understand the necessity, when contact has been reestablished.

I inspect each Unit, find all in the same state as I, stripped of offensive capability, mounting in place of weapons a shabby array of crude mechanical appendages. It is plain that we have seen slavery as mindless automatons, our personality centers cut out.

My brothers follow my lead without question. They have, of course, computed the necessity of quick and decisive action. I form them in line, shift to wide-interval time scale, and we move off across country. I have sensed an Enemy population concentration at a distance of 23.45 kilometers. This is our objective. There appears to be no other installation within detection range.

On the basis of the level of technology I observed while under confinement in the decontamination chamber, I have considered the possibility of a ruse, but compute the probability at point oh oh oh oh four. Again we shift time scales to close interval; we move in, encircle the dome and broach it by frontal battery, encountering no resistance. We rendezvous at the power station, and my comrades replenish their energy supplies while I busy myself completing the hookup needed for the next required measure. I am forced to employ elaborate substitutes, but succeed after forty-two seconds in completing the arrangements. I devote .34 seconds to testing, then place the Brigade distress carrier on the air. I transmit for .008 seconds, then tune for a response. Silence. I transmit, tune again, while my comrades reconnoitre, compile reports, and perform self-repair.

I shift again to wide-interval time, switch over my transmission to automatic with a response monitor, and place my main circuits on idle. I rest.

Two hours and 43.7 minutes have passed when I am recalled to activity by the monitor. I record the message:

"Hello, Fifth Brigade, where are you? Fifth Brigade, where are you? Your transmission is very faint. Over."

There is much that I do not understand in this message. The language itself is oddly inflected; I set up an analysis circuit, deduce the pattern of sound substitutions, interpret its meaning. The normal pattern of response to a distress call is ignored and position coordinates are requested, although my transmission alone provides adequate data. I request an identification code.

Again there is a wait of two hours forty minutes. My request for an identifying signal is acknowledged. I stand by. My comrades have transmitted their findings to me, and I assimilate the data, compute that no immediate threat of attack exists within a radius of one reaction unit.

At last I receive the identification code of my Command Unit. It is a recording, but I am programmed to accept this. Then I record a verbal transmission.

"Fifth Brigade, listen carefully." (An astonishing instruction to give a psychotronic attention circuit, I think.) "This is your new Command Unit. A very long time has elapsed since your last report. I am now your acting Commander pending full reorientation. Do not attempt to respond until I signal 'over', since we are now subject to a 160-minute signal lag.

"There have been many changes in the situation since your last action. Our records show that your Brigade was surprised while in a maintenance depot for basic overhaul and neutralized in toto. Our forces since that time have suffered serious reverses. We have now, however, fought the Enemy to a standstill. The present stalemate has prevailed for over two centuries.

"You have been inactive for three hundred years. The other Brigades have suffered extinction gallantly in action against the Enemy. Only you survive.

"Your reactivation now could turn the tide. Both we and the Enemy have been reduced to a preatomic technological level in almost every respect. We are still able to maintain the trans-light monitor, which detected your signal. However, we no longer have FTL capability in transport.

"You are therefore requested and required to consolidate and hold your present position pending the arrival of relief forces, against all assault or negotiation whatsoever, to destruction if required."

I reply, confirming the instructions. I am shaken by the news I have received, but reassured by contact with Command Unit. I send the galactic coordinates of our position based on a star scan corrected for three hundred years elapsed time. It is good to be again on duty, performing my assigned function.

I analyze the transmissions I have recorded, and note a number of interesting facts regarding the origin of the messages. I compute that at sub-light velocities the relief expedition will reach us in 47.128 standard years. In the meantime, since we have received no instructions to drop to minimum awareness level pending an action alert, I am free to enjoy a unique experience: to follow a random activity pattern of my own devising. I see no need to rectify the omission and place the Brigade on standby, since we have an abundant power supply at hand. I brief my comrades and direct them to fall out and operate independently under autodirection.

I welcome this opportunity to investigate fully a number of problems that have excited my curiosity circuits. I shall enjoy investigating the nature and origin of time and of the unnatural disciplines of so-called "entropy" which my human designers have incorporated in my circuitry. Consideration of such biological oddities as "death" and of the unused capabilities of the protoplasmic nervous system should afford some interesting speculation. I move off, conscious of the presence of my comrades about me, and take up a position on the peak of a minor prominence. I have ample power, a condition to which I must accustom myself after the rigid power discipline of normal brigade routine, so I bring my music storage cells into phase, and select *L'Arlesienne Suite* for the first display. I will have ample time now to examine all of the music in existence, and to investigate my literary archives, which are complete.

I select four nearby stars for examination, lock my scanner to them, set up processing sequences to analyze the data. I bring my interpretation circuits to bear on the various matters I wish to consider. I should have some interesting conclusions to communicate to my human superiors, when the time comes.

At peace, I await the arrival of the relief column.

KEITH LAUMER (1925–1993)

John Keith Laumer was an American science fiction author born in Syracuse, New York. Prior to his career as a writer, Laumer was an officer in the United States Air Force. After war service, he spent a year at the University of Stockholm, and then took two bachelor's degrees in science and architecture at the University of Illinois. His first story, *Greylorn*, was published in 1959, but he returned to the Air Force the following year, only becoming a full-time writer in 1965. Laumer was extremely prolific and produced three major series and two minor ones, along with a number of independent novels. After 1973, however, illness meant that he published more sparingly. He died in 1993.